The Price of Redemption

Richard D. Thielmann

Copyright © 2006 by Richard D. Thielmann

All rights reserved. No part of this book shall be reproduced or transmitted in any form or by any means, electronic, mechanical, magnetic, photographic including photocopying, recording or by any information storage and retrieval system, without prior written permission of the publisher. No patent liability is assumed with respect to the use of the information contained herein. Although every precaution has been taken in the preparation of this book, the publisher and author assume no responsibility for errors or omissions. Neither is any liability assumed for damages resulting from the use of the information contained herein.

This is a work of fiction. Names, characters, places, and incidents either are the product of the author's imagination or are used fictitiously. Any resemblance to actual events or locales or persons, living or dead, is entirely coincidental.

ISBN 0-7414-3215-3

Published by:

PUBLISHING.COM
1094 New DeHaven Street, Suite 100
West Conshohocken, PA 19428-2713
Info@buybooksontheweb.com
www.buybooksontheweb.com
Toll-free (877) BUY BOOK
Local Phone (610) 941-9999
Fax (610) 941-9959

Printed in the United States of America

Printed on Recycled Paper

Published July 2006

Other Works by Richard D. Thielmann

A Matter of Revenge

1.

I set My rainbow in the cloud, and it shall be for the sign of the covenant between Me and the earth. It shall be, when I bring a cloud over the earth, that the rainbow shall be seen in the cloud; and I will remember my covenant which is between Me and you and every living creature of all flesh; the waters shall never again become a flood to destroy all flesh.

-Genesis 9:13-15

The small color television on the counter proclaimed a stern warning:

"...a strong front is cutting across Indiana from the southwest, charging out of Missouri where it did considerable damage last night in counties around St Louis...continuing to build as it moves northeast. Right here on the map, this is where it's tracked at this hour."

The on-camera weather reporter pointed at a map by his side to an area near the border of the Hoosier state and Ohio:

"It's headed this way, folks, and gaining momentum all the time. You'll want to be on the lookout for this one, so be alert. This afternoon...mid afternoon...this front will cross over us. Strong winds, possible hail, and the chance of a tornado as well. Lots of rain. We're calling for at least an inch or more of rain. Possibly more. We'll get you additional details on this powerful storm later in our newscast. This is Roger Steinberg in the weather center...back to you Laurie..."

The weather report on the morning news was ominous and not to be taken lightly. But let it come, they needed rain. The television blared threats of high winds and, at the very least, heavy rain. Right then, warm, soft morning breezes that caressed the Howe farm belied the portent of it worsening. No earlier hint from the eastern sky. Surely, the old cliché couldn't be trusted if the weather service knew that they were correct. How did it go - Red sky at morning, sailors take warning? Cloudless, faded blue sky did not give any indication of devastating weather.

Betty Howe looked out the kitchen window for some obvious sign of the coming storm. She knew very well not to second guess the weatherman. She knew it best to heed the TV warning. Those folks at the weather bureau were quite accurate, although better with warnings of the bad than predictions of the good. But sometimes they over-reacted to the information they had. Horrendous weather that never appeared. We should be prepared, she thought. As she listened to the continuing television news, she attacked her chore of breakfast making with the gusto of a sumo wrestler and with the same subtlety of performance. Her intent was righteous, although her proficiency was limited by slight skill and hesitant desire. For Del it didn't matter, he loved her. He had not married her for her cooking prowess, but rather for her ability to make him laugh. Laughing was never easy for Del and he recognized that if she could make him laugh, she was special. For her part, Betty had never thought she would become a farm wife. He was a farmer, so what should she have expected? She had not figured that out in advance of marriage, so after all these years, it didn't matter. She could have run away years ago. That would have meant leaving the one man she truly cared about, and she knew full well that he cared about her in the same way. She stayed for the long haul and the rest of the farm stuff didn't really matter a whole lot. Besides, her faith gave her the strength to carry on, to fulfill her role. It had been ordained, she presumed, it was her lot in life.

"Roger Steinberg says we're going to get hit with heavy rain. You may want to wait until tomorrow."

She spoke in a lazy, contained way that would fool you if you didn't know her. She was reporting, not nagging. The difference was monumental for Del and, although he could not have articulated the difference, he understood its implications and responded positively to the underlying nuance of his wife's suggestion. She used the weather reporter's name to help support her contention that tomorrow might be a better day.

"Uuum," he sounded as he scratched his back through his shirt. "Got to get it done."

"Not tomorrow? Roger usually is right about these storms."

"No, I think we'll get 'er done today. Don't think the rain will come 'til later. Time ta finish."

There was no arguing, no sense in it. He had made up his mind and that was that. She knew the man well after thirty-eight years of marriage.

"Prudence is sometimes the better part of valor."

"Prudence never got anything done when it was s'posed ta git done."

She grimaced.

"Sometimes things can wait."

"This isn't one of those times," he said.

There was a finality in the tone of his voice that kept her from responding about it any further. She tended to the breakfast she had in progress on the stove and again looked out the window. It seemed like the coming of a beautiful day in spite of Roger Steinberg's dire predictions for foul weather. She knew that owning a farm meant dealing with several kinds of risks and one of those they could not control was the weather. They could fight weeds and insects and disease, but there wasn't much they could do about the weather.

Pancakes, sausage, fried eggs, and potatoes were on Betty's menu. Del liked a solid, hearty breakfast to start the day and she accommodated. He said it gave him the strength to do the work that needed to be done. God's work, as nature's assistant. Strength to pass up lunch, to keep going well past most folk's supper time until after the sunlight started to shorten. Strength to give the job his best effort. Stoke up the furnace early on so there was no need to pause or stop short of the day's goal.

Del took from the platter she put in front of him with noisy appreciation. Clattering of knife and fork, slurping of coffee, swishing and squashing of butter and jam that was slathered on freshly baked bread. In an almost hedonistic way he appreciated the meal before him, yet quite fundamental in his acceptance that it was a necessity.

"This is very good," he said between bites. "Very good."

"Same as yesterday," she said softly, muttering more to herself than in really answering Del.

He heard.

"Or the day before that...doesn't matter, it's still good. What I need."

He finished, wiped his face carefully with the napkin, pushed back from the empty plate, and rose. He stepped behind his chair and pushed it in to the table. Right then she sensed that he wanted to say something and was gathering his courage for whatever it was on his mind. She would wait. He might not get to it, but he probably would.

"You're a big help," he stumbled with the words. "Always been a big help." He paused for what seemed an eternity. "I think its time we think about getting out of here."

She turned to face him before she spoke and then didn't know what to say.

"Farmers work past their prime," Del said coldly, "and git all beat up. They die in the field or behind a barn or in some ditch, alone and quiet...no nine-one-one ta call. They usually don't die at a retirement place or on some warm beach in Florida. They die on their land. And nobody cares."

"God bless us, Del, you sound sad and crazy philosophical and dreary. Stop it. You aren't dying, so just stop it. But I like the idea of retiring. What are you thinking?"

"This is the last year. We sell out and we find a place to settle."

"Fine with me," she whooped, "I'll be ready to go."

"Good. Let's talk about it tonight. Gotta get this last field done. We'll talk more tonight. We'll plan your escape."

She frowned. She had not realized that he knew she was ready to go.

As Del walked out onto his front porch he saw Red Crier moving between the barn and the large shed that housed the tractor and other farm implements. There had to be a plan for Red also, he thought. What do we do with him? That's a tough one. Del frowned and then bunched his mouth to one side in reaction to his own consternation about Red. The farm, the animals, the equipment, we sell. Someone else takes over responsibility for everything else here, save for Red. Who becomes responsible for him?

Red Crier was what you would call a slow learner, a little dull. Not really retarded, just a bit slow. He worked hard, understood basic directions, and could be depended upon to get a job done. But, in truth, he could not fend for himself very long. He was more than a child in capability, a forty-eight year old, who was not quite an adult, caught in some never-land between those two distinctions. Never married, he had lived with his mama until she died. Then Betty and Del took him into their home. They believed it was the right thing to do. Red was a tall, lanky man without much physical coordination, but at least with a good sense of not overextending himself. He didn't know for sure he was limited, he only knew by some sort of instinct to work within those limitations. Del thanked Red's mama for giving him that sense of himself and only hoped he could provide Red a proper place to live. At the time, there had been nowhere else for Red to go.

Reverend Randy Stone had been a large part of the process that made it easy for Red to transition from his mama's to the

Howe's farm. Rev. Stone was sure of the change, that it was right. He was happy for Red, and recognized the reward for Betty and Del.

"I know," he had said, "it's like taking on a kid in some ways...bringing Red into your home. You've already got the empty nest with Dorothy and Don gone. Like starting over, I suppose, only easier. I...we, the congregation, appreciates what you are doing. It is God's will, it is God's work. You are blessed, you will be blessed.

Red had been no problem for them. Betty took him for a regular monthly interview with a county case worker who monitored Red's mental and physical states and the county paid for his health care. Red seemed quite contented on their farm. He only spoke of his mother once. To Betty. He never spoke of her again.

"Mama's gone," he had said not long after he had come to live.

"Yes," Betty sighed, "she's in a better place. She was sick...she felt bad...she was suffering...she needed peace. God took her home to his house where she could be comfortable and have peace."

"That's good," Red had nodded, "she needed peace...and a good place to rest." He seemed to be comforted with that understanding.

Betty came onto the porch and rubbed Del's back. She knew what he was thinking. It had been that way for a long time where their minds were in some kind of synchronization. What he thought, so had she and the reverse. Now, she knew what he was thinking about Red Crier. There needed to be a plan for him also.

"I don't need a penny for your thoughts."

"Probably not."

"We'll solve the problem of Red. It won't change what we do."

"I guess...I hope not."

Del was somewhat reassured by what she said even though deep down he had his doubts.

"It will all work out. One thing at a time. Isn't that what you always tell me?"

He was silent.

"Well, isn't it?"

He turned and looked at her. There was a longing in his face and she recognized it and he knew full well she saw the vulnerability in him. It was part of why she loved him so desperately. He smiled and welcomed her embrace. Her embrace was tight and strong, so primal in its spontaneity and intenseness. He liked how that felt.

"I'm sure it will," he said softly.

He walked off the porch, headed for the equipment shed where Red Crier was already getting things set for the day, then turned and faced her.

"You are one fine woman," Del proclaimed. "You better be ready for me to be done tonight. We have an appointment with..."

He halted, not sure of what he would say next, but he never took his eyes from her.

"...passion."

It was the word he settled on and he was satisfied with it.

Betty smiled. Those wonderful code words of love. Just say it straight out. Too bad men struggled with the words, she fretted somewhat to herself, things would be a lot easier if they just owned up to things. Especially about the relationship with their woman.

"Mornin', Red" Del smiled at the man. "Looks like you got things all ready for me."

"Sure do, Del. You said you was gonna fertilize today. Ya told me. I know what ya wanted."

"Very good...got the rig all hitched. Better gas up the Deere, though."

"Oh yeah, I forgot."

"No that's okay...something I'd rather do myself anyway."

Del felt a certain satisfaction handling the big green tractor, a feeling that came from all the positive things in his life that it represented. Any regrets he had, any pangs of doubt about the course of his life faded when he got control of this rig. Funny how such a simple thing as driving a tractor can release a man from the frustrations that might otherwise confront him. Oh sure, the thoughts that could bother him still flitted around in the back of his mind, but the chug of the engine and the rock and roll of charging cross the rough ground kept those thoughts away. And the demons that chased after him.

No doubt about the demons from the past. The agony of Vietnam cropped up when he least expected. Even during the day. For a long time the horrible visions came in his dreams and then they went away, only to resurface when he was awake. The devil playing peek-a-boo with him, awake, so he was sure of what they were, so he was sure they would never go away. The devil would never let them go away.

He had become able to battle the devil with determined control. A mind game. He thought of plowing, which was the steady, continuous process that opened and turned the earth. As he was opened to the misery of memory when the devil came calling. But his work was good and right, God's work, and the bad memories eventually faded away.

Del felt a certain satisfaction handling the big green tractor and time passed so quickly. Time went by faster than he could comprehend, faster than with anything else he knew. The devil could not keep up with time when he was doing this.

Methodically, Betty prepared lunch for herself and Red almost as soon as she had cleared the kitchen from breakfast. Her mind went to the far corners of the earth and settled on the Met in New York. She could see herself dressed so exquisitely, with tasteful, yet stylish pumps, a fur wrap flipped around her shoulders in casual elegance, her hair done by one of the best of the best hair dressers, knowing full well that she looked great and carried herself accordingly. Somehow, in this fantasy that suspended reality, Del, in a tux, accompanied her, walking a step behind so as not to intrude on her moment of triumph as she walked down the aisle to her seat near the front. It was her moment.

A sharp, nasty gust of wind blew away her entrance to the opera hall and the farm came back into view. She realized that the sun was gone and a dull, leaden sky hung low over the farm, a blatant warning of the weather that was to come. This was a double irritation: the opera was banished and the harshness of nature was on them before she had even realized it.

"Earth to the space commander, storm is coming. Come in for a landing and have something to drink. I have fresh iced tea."

Betty was on the porch to make sure she had better reception for the two-way radio she clutched against her cheek. She and Del had been using this technique for several years to stay in touch while he worked somewhere on the farm. This time she could see him, but he was too far and no way her voice could penetrate the chugging pulse of the tractor.

"Roger," came the voice of the space commander.

Del eased the rig to a halt near the fence that separated the field from the somewhat lawn that surrounded the house. He jumped down and called to Red who he didn't know was already in the kitchen.

"Didn't have breakfast with us this morning, Red." Del yanked the kitchen door with such force that it snapped open against the spring that was used to keep it from banging the house. He said the words kindly, but Red was a man never sure of himself. He functioned somewhat in a state of uneasiness and semi-fear. He was not able to discern if Del were angry or merely filled with energy.

Betty spoke for him.

"He had things to do, so he ate early."

And that was that.

"Who's doing the noon weather cast, that nitwit kid?"

"No, I think it's still Roger. He doesn't have good news. Anyway, come on Red, better eat. I've got the jug fixed for you, mister."

"Thanks," Del replied as she handed the container to him. "I guess I better get going if we want to beat the storm."

She grinned at him.

"I stand corrected. If *I* want to beat the storm."

Red had no idea what they were talking about and continued to eat.

"Good...tastes good," he said and nodded and looked at Betty.

"Thanks, Red."

Betty sat down to eat with Red and Del went back to the tractor. Red had eaten quickly, charged by the intensity he had seen in the other two. He took his plate and cup to the sink while murmuring more words of appreciation, and went on to his chores. In the background, the dull insistence of the television cast a spell on Betty.

"...and some damage around Ft. Wayne, including a mobile home park and several farm houses. There have been numerous injuries, but no deaths....which is good news. That front is headed our way and has the National Weather Service giving us advance notice of what we might expect this afternoon. Rain, of course, high winds, and the possibility of a tornado..."

Betty ran to the porch and out into the yard after Del.

"Roger is warning you to take the afternoon off," she called.

She caught up to him before he reached the rig.

"Roger doesn't have a farm to take care of."

She took his face in her hands, kissed him hard on the lips, held his head for a moment, then stepped back. He smiled and walked on to the field. She watched him climb on the big tractor, fire it up, and move out to continue his job. A wave of sadness swept over her and she did not know why. The gray sky did not help.

Part of farm life meant paying close attention to the weather, to appreciate its influence, and to understand its power. A fool ignored the weather, Del knew that, but some things just had to get done. It was not in him to wait around for a weather front. He could stop later if he had to do so.

Ominous black clouds began to build in the southwestern sky in a way not untypical for this June afternoon. They puffed up from the horizon as if Mother Nature were flexing her muscles for a fight. A stiff breeze surged from nowhere, the smell of freshness and moisture a party to its significance. Del took note of the impending weather as he sniffed at the air and inhaled the advance notice. He gripped the steering wheel of his tractor even tighter as if to commit himself more fully to getting his job done before he might be forced off the field.

He drove his huge rig back and forth, row after row, stalk after stalk slipping by, guiding the tractor with the accumulated skill he had gained after all these years. It was a monotonous, mind-numbing chore, but like all chores, it had to get done. He was determined, doggedly determined, jaw set, eyes squinting with purpose. For Del, there was no anxiety about the coming storm because, in truth, he liked what he saw. The farm needed the rain and rain was surely on its way.

Delwin Howe had spent his whole life on this farm save for the time he was away in the Army. All those years facing the elements told him that the rain would be on him in about two hours, maybe less. That would not be enough time to finish this field. He didn't care, he would do as much as he could, and tomorrow the rest of the chemicals would get put down. Not much about the weather fooled or surprised him, although today would provide a new experience.

He took pride in being a farmer. He was proud of being able to provide for his family. That meant a lot to him. He was proud of the crops he grew and of how self-sufficient they were. Oh sure, he realized that some people made fun of this business of farming. For some of the sophisticated city folks, it was uninteresting, dull work. However, it gave him a connection to the earth that made the endeavor have even more meaning for him. Then there was his sense that he was doing something for others that made his work worthwhile. Such thoughts were high-toned ideas for describing the simple task of farming, he figured, but it was how he felt. There was a glory in what he did, his part in God's scheme of things. It was one of the reasons why he went to church with Betty each Sunday. There were other reasons, also.

Memory of the days working by his papa's side never left him. Long, tedious days that ended with the young boy exhausted. Days filled with work and the lessons of tenacity that served him well as a soldier, that carried him through in tough times on his own as a farmer. Lessons that called for doing his best, all the time. They were lessons bolstered by the encouragement of his papa and his mama, both staunchly religious, and each devoted to God and farming in their own quiet assured way.

Papa talked mostly about what it took to be successful working the land. Although once in awhile, he would offer some piece of wisdom, part of what he called, "the main thing."

"The main thing," he would say, "is ta be honest. Other folks find out yer not honest, they'll never trust ya about nuthin'." Or he said, "The main thing is ta stand by yer word. Ya tell a man something, stick by it. Otherwise you'll not have character. Ya can't be respected without character. God prefers folks with character."

So they went, all "the main things" papa doled out that gave shape and meaning and significance in his life and the life he wanted for Del.

Mama talked about being polite, having manners, and speaking with a soft voice.

"A soft voice goes a long way in this world because folks like a soft voice," she cautioned. "Any fool can talk loud and usually does."

They were both gone, but Del could clearly see their faces, distinctly hear their voices as his tractor crawled along through the searing boredom that the seemingly endless task presented. He had comfort in their memory and he still missed them both.

The full heat of summer baked this rich farmland of northwestern Ohio as the parched ground waited for rain. Del ignored the heat. He merely continued to drive over the field as the fertilizing rig put in the correct chemical mixture. Chemicals were needed to increase yield and yet he wasn't happy about having to use them. However, if he wanted his work to be profitable, they were a necessary evil. It was a point of concern for him and more than a slight nudge of his conscience. He worried about all the chemicals he used and about how much water they pumped out for irrigation. He fretted about those issues, knowing full well they were necessary for the success of his farm. That they could be potentially problematical was a worry he kept to himself without sharing his frustration and conflict with Betty. He kept silent, but he was deeply troubled. Selling the farm would ease that burden, at least for him, but he knew it would not alter the underlying problem for the environment.

Even with such conflicting issues, if some pollster had come by and put it to him directly, he would surely have answered in the affirmative about his role as a farmer. Oh, yes, there had been thoughts about doing something else rather than take on farming, but he didn't give them a whole lot of consideration. He had gone to Viet Nam, survived, and thought it was a miracle to get back living with his family in the home where he was born. Providence had a hand in things, he assumed, to let him come home. He also accepted it as fact that providence directed him to farming. Farming was his life and he loved it.

Even when he wasn't driving his tractor or forking hay or tending to hogs and a few head of cattle, he was comforted with the notion that he was doing what he wanted to do. And it made him feel good.

Del's progress was monitored by Betty as she also kept track of the darkening sky. She clicked on the television with the remote, muted the soap opera, then selected the channel with the weather. An angry red crawl streamed across the bottom of the screen.

...SEVERE WEATHER ADVISORY FOR COUNTIES IN NW OHIO & SE MICHIGAN AS A STORM FRONT TRACKS NE AT 25 MILES PER HOUR...STRONG WINDS, ACCOMPANIED BY HEAVY RAIN AND OCCASIONAL HAIL CAN BE EXPECTED...WIND GUSTS CAN BE UP TO 60 MILES PER HOUR...FLOOD WARNINGS HAVE ALSO BEEN ISSUED FOR...

Betty went to the porch with her two-way radio and called Del.

"Hey, space commander, weather warning is big time on the TV. Take cover, Del, its coming fast. Look at that sky. Come on in here."

"Not yet," he squawked in return, "want to get some more done while I can. I'll be okay."

The storm came faster than Del had figured, based on what he had seen of the forming clouds. The onset didn't match up with his judgment of how much time he had before it hit. He was running west and slowed the rig to get a better look. The clouds were piled as clumps of clay, colored in dark grays with shadows of blue-black and purple. Jagged streaks of lightening pierced the piles randomly every few seconds. He counted. There was no sound. Too far away yet, but coming fast. Betty was right, not much time.

He resumed his march across the earth, now at higher speed, determined to make the spreader cover more ground by moving faster, working the rows from north to south. Periodically there was a quick glance, a fleeting look at the billowing dark sky, but all in all he did not want to look at the oncoming storm. There was this overriding compulsion to keep at it no matter what, a focused, almost demented obsession that would have the rig keep on running.

Then, turning a row and looking full bore at what was nearly upon him, concern pulled at him for the first time. This might be bad. Perhaps he had been wrong-headed about this, perhaps he should have listened to Betty, heeded Roger Steinberg's warning, believed what the television weather warning screamed at him. Perhaps it had been a mistake not to wait and this was an admission Del did not want to make. He had little time to consider it very much. The distinctive staccato of the engine reverberated over the wind that whipped around him. It was a sound of his work that usually gave him some satisfaction, but now was little consolation for his situation.

Overhead the gray sky had been replaced by a steely black cover. The sweet smell of rain overtook him and jogged his memory to other times, other storms when he had been caught out in the open, and swept with torrents of water drops blowing in at an angle almost like bullets. His rig had only a sun canopy, not an enclosed cab. He knew he would be soaked to the skin before he could get off the field and under shelter of the equipment shed. This was part of being a farmer, he consoled himself, of being part of the land, of nature, the role of the provider. He never thought about being hit by lightening.

The first drops of rain were big blobs of water that smacked randomly on the canopy, the tractor, the ground. Then came full blown sheets of water. Del was soaked to the skin in a matter of minutes and he knew darn well he should have headed for cover sooner. Lightening shot across the sky in a blinding slash of hot light. He counted. One, two, three, four...bang, five. Less than a mile away he calculated. He stepped the throttle a notch higher, pushing to get the rig off the field and into the shed as fast as possible.

The jagged brilliance of white he saw in front of him came from two distinct bolts stabbing the sky at once. One...two...bang came the noise of violent nature. Too close he thought, too close. A hundred yards from the edge of the field he stopped the rig, got off, and crawled underneath for cover. This action, motivated by respect for lightening, knowledge of its power, and fear for the consequences would save Del's life. He was face down in muddy earth that was running with water. He covered his head with his arms. The wind blew his Detroit Tigers ball cap away before he could hold it, so that it skipped down the row and across the field. It would never be found.

Lightning struck the top of the tractor with a noise and violence that he could never have imagined and that he had never experienced, even in Viet Nam. There was an intense brilliance from the power of the strike, the ground around him glowed from the energy that bounced off the rig. Every electrical wire on the tractor melted, the bulbs blew in the running lights, and the plastic steering wheel sagged misshapen around its steel core. The battery exploded in all directions, sending lead and hot acid flying. Others would remark in time to come that it was a miracle the gas tank did not let go. The tractor engine was, of course, now still, the big rig stopped in its tracks like a bison shot dead, still forming a massive silhouette against the darkened sky, no longer able to move.

The rain continued to pelt the tractor and the wind blew chunks of hail that fiercely clanged against the steel fenders and engine housing. Del was there under the tractor, face down in the sloppy mud. He was alive, but unconscious.

With no regard for himself, Red came running through the storm from the barn to see if Del were still alive. He was more frightened than he had ever been in his life, but his concern for Del pushed him beyond that fear. His worst thought was that Del was dead. Taken away from him like his mother. As he tore through the storm it would not have been possible to discern the tears that welled, but they were there.

"Del," he cried insistently, "Del, you okay?"

Del did not move.

The blinding flash that had confronted Betty ended with a blue glow that was an aura of terror for her. She had been standing on the porch clutching her apron, watching as Del had stopped. He wasn't that far away, but it seemed to her as if he were a lifetime away. She gasped from the shock and in doing so, filled and emptied her lungs to the extreme. She felt light-headed, but did not succumb to fainting. Jamming her fist to her teeth, still holding a corner of the apron, she looked skyward for help.

"God, please don't let him be dead."

It was only seconds from the time Red headed for the tractor that Betty ran across the field to get to her husband's side. Red had turned Del over on his back and Betty wiped the mud from his face with part of her apron. His face was the white of dried bone, drained of blood, the skin tightly drawn in agony from the trauma of all the electricity that had surged around and through him.

They tried to revive him, working on their hands and knees. But it was difficult because the space was limited by the dead tractor that hung over them. The rain was beginning to let up some, yet still coming down quite hard. Betty felt for his pulse and it was there strongly. She rubbed his cheeks, then his hands, then patted his cheeks rather firmly, trying all the while to bring him to consciousness.

"Pull his boots off, Red, and rub his feet. Please, hurry."

Red unlaced the boots and pulled Del's feet loose. He wasn't sure what to do.

"Here, like this." She took one foot and demonstrated. "Do that while I do his hands."

Both she and Red took turns for a few minutes alternately patting and massaging, but it was no use. They could not revive Del. She moved on her knees in the mud to get out from underneath the tractor, jumped up, and ran back to the house to call for help from the Jeffries farm up the road.

She charged into the front hall, paying no attention whatever to the mud and water she brought inside that spoiled her freshly cleaned floor. She grabbed the phone sitting on the small table there and punched in the number. After what seemed forever, Jack Jeffries answered the phone.

"Hello," he yelled, bellowing at her as if he were calling his response across an open field.

"Jack," Betty screamed, "Del's been hit by lightening. He's knocked out, lying in the mud. He's still out in the field. He's going to die."

There was a long pause, then Jack responded flatly, "Be right there."

As she hung up the phone, Red opened the front door and called to her.

"I've got him on the porch. He won't come in."

She ran out onto the front porch that provided some shelter from the weather, although swirls of rain flew onto it every so often. Del was there sitting in a chair, staring vacantly to the eastern sky and the receding storm, his arms hanging over the sides in a lifeless way, the finger tips almost touching the porch floor.

Betty went to him quickly, stood over him, and held the soft, tanned leather of his expressionless face between her hands. She kissed his brow first, then his cheeks, then his lips. He did not react. She brushed the water from his head, then ran her fingers through his hair as if to extract more water. She began the process of nursing him to consciousness. He seemed unconscious although, oddly enough, his eyes were open.

She grabbed his hands, dangling at his sides, and rubbed them vigorously to stimulate blood flow. They were cold and blue as if death were setting into his system.

"Red," she cried, "work on his feet again. Like I showed you. We've got to get his circulation going."

Red knelt down at Del's feet, coated with mud, and began rubbing the toes and arches.

"Oh dear," Betty said, "his feet are so dirty. I'm sorry, I should..."

"No. It's okay...it's okay. I don't mind. Got to help Del."

He started massaging the ankles.

Jack Jeffries' pickup careened up the drive at that point. He jumped out and ran onto the porch to see what needed to be done. He took one of Del's hands and began rubbing and talking to his friend and fellow farmer.

"Come on, Del," he exclaimed, "let's get the motor goin', let's fire up, come on, come on."

In a matter of minutes, Del's color came back to his hands and feet and he began to blink in regular turns. He moved his lips, but nothing in the way of sound emerged. Then his shoulders shook as he shuddered. The rest of his body didn't move and his arms and hands remained lifeless.

Betty put her face right up to his and asked him to speak. "Talk to us," she said in a trembling voice, "tell us you are okay. Tell us to relax. Tell us you won't die right now."

Del moved his lips as if speaking, but nothing could be heard. He continued, and finally they could hear what he was saying.

"Mrycon. Greeyon potobon gillen. Ducree filjon bocat moto."

His voice was quiet, without emotion, monotonous, and did not have expression or inflection. The pitch was just a fraction above his normal speaking voice and the spacing of the sounds gave no indication of meaning. Del was babbling in gibberish.

Betty, Red, and Jack looked at each other in disbelief.

"Toemon dorbu," Del intoned and continued in a continuous chant, "olo ta milsar debbas hankay parlot colef penge crill nis ogom basay."

He stared out over the rain-soaked field, not seeming to notice his wife and the two men by his side. His gaze was transfixed on some distant point, intent on its image, whatever it was.

Betty, who had been kneeling next to Del, stood slowly, then turned to Red.

"Call Doc Bennett, she directed firmly, "tell him Del's been hit by lightening and we need his help now. His number is on the card next to the phone."

Red sprang for the door to get to the phone inside. He yanked at the screen door and jumped to the phone in the hall.

"Red," Betty yelled after him, "after you get Doc, call Reverend Stone. I think we'll need him, too."

Del was now continuing with more sounds, voice projecting out over the fields, chanting a language of meaningless words, linking unknown phrases, imparting some indecipherable code to no one in particular. Del was talking to the wind, talking to the rain, speaking to the world around him with no attention given to anyone or anything. He was talking to the world at large, to those who would or could hear and understand. Del did not stop, but poured out a stream of sounds that floated out over the farm in a litany of discourse to the universe. He could not be stopped. He was a sound machine producing a flow of sounds as if they were words, but words that made no sense.

By the time Doc Bennett arrived, Del had discharged his reservoir of vocal energy and had slumped back into a chair with Red's help. Betty had washed his feet and Jack and Red had managed to lead him inside to the living room while they waited for Doc and Reverend Stone. He still seemed to have no recognition of what was going on around him. No one could make contact with him.

Doc Bennett stood with his arms folded, saying nothing as he stared at Del. To no one in particular he asked that Del's shirt be unbuttoned. He reached in his black bag and pulled out his stethoscope, carefully placing an ear piece in each ear, somewhat absently checking out a phantom spot on the wall across the room. Betty had responded to his request. Doc placed the scope on Del's bare chest, moving it about to hear what the body had to tell him. He didn't ask Del to take deep breaths, and in fact seemed to ignore the man's moans and the mouthings of strange sounds that started to get revved up again.

None of the onlookers had said a word for several minutes while Doc went about his business. As they watched intently, the sound of a car could be heard pulling up outside and in a few moments Reverend Stone was at the door. He rapped twice and let himself into the house. He nodded to Betty and without saying a word joined the audience.

Doc shined a pen light in each of Del's eyes, going from one to the other several times, and then clicked the light off with a flourish. He picked up Del's left wrist which was loosely draped over the arm of the chair where he was seated. Doc checked the pulse then placed the wrist back on the chair. He put the stethoscope back in his bag which he snapped shut.

"Body seems to be okay. Don't know what's happening inside his head. You best get him up to bed, needs some rest. Good night's sleep will help. He'll feel a lot better in the morning." Doc said all of that without looking at Betty, but it was meant for her. He headed for the door, then turned to speak. "Bring him into the clinic in the morning, we'll run some tests on him. Put him to bed, now."

He left the house without speaking to anyone directly or saying good-bye.

"That was a charming piece of medicine," Jack said. "if you ask me, I'd call Life Flight and get a chopper out here and take Del into the city where a good emergency room can take a look at him."

Del let go full blast with another torrent of incomprehensible words and this time his face got red. Beads of perspiration broke out on his forehead. He was delivering a message without meaning, but with intensity that bordered on rage.

"I don't think that's necessary," Reverend Stone responded calmly. "Del needs rest. You heard Doc, we need to get Del up to bed."

As he spoke, he patted Del on the shoulder.

"He is speaking to us in tongues," the Reverend stated emphatically. "He is blessed. Surely the Lord's word is coming to us through Del. It is a gift from the Lord. In that consideration, I believe I should take Del home with me. Betty, you would come too, of course."

"I don't think so, Reverend, no offense," Jack countered forcefully, "man's been hit by lightening, not by God. I'm gonna call nine-one-one."

Betty stepped forward at this point and motioned to Red.

"Red and I will take care of Del, Reverend, if you'll just say a prayer for us all in thanks for his being still alive."

The Reverend nodded, closed his eyes, and bowed his head. He spoke with a throaty, stentorian voice which was his custom for such weighty circumstances. There was an edge of nasal twang that he had tried to eliminate over the years, but still persisted.

"Heavenly father, we as your children ask that you point the way through our close friend Delwin Howe. We ask that you preserve his life, that you retain his mental capacities, that you make him strong and whole again, and that you renew his life as before with faith, and hope, and charity. We ask that any message that he brings to us in this strange and wondrous way we can interpret and appreciate and that it enriches and sustains us and works to make our meager lives more fulfilled and rewarded in concert with Gods wishes. Bless this family. Bless the friends and neighbors. Bless Delwin and his lovely wife Betty. And give us the comfort to withstand this unusual and wondrous occurrence in our lives. In Jesus name, we beseech thee oh Lord. Amen."

The storm had by now blown through and there was the nearly quiet aftermath of steamy calm that could almost smother the survivors. When the Reverend finished his short prayer, only the sound of water dripping from a variety of farm house overhangs punctuated the atmosphere, with pings and pongs of water drops bouncing through the down spouts, adding to the soft chorus of runoff. The gloominess that still prevailed outside was matched by the small group inside. They looked at each other without saying a word for several seconds. But then, in unison, they murmured, "Amen."

What to do now. Betty was temporarily at a loss. Reverend Stone wanted Del to go home with him, Doc wanted Del to go to the clinic for observation, and Del gave no indication as to what he wanted. In fact, it seemed he couldn't tell anyone what he wanted. Jack was already on the phone for emergency help.

"I think Del should be with me tonight, Betty, now that he is an instrument of the Lord I believe I should be with him."

Reverend Stone spoke solemnly, emphatically, with hands folded in front of him as a gesture of piety to reinforce his otherwise sanctimonious manner.

Betty was confused.

"Well, I..." Betty wasn't sure what to say.

"Chopper's on its way," Jack announced as he hung up the phone.

"How dare you make that decision?" Reverend Stone scolded. "Betty...Mrs. Howe had the right to decide what..."

"Del's my friend as well as my neighbor...he's been smacked by lightenin'...needs some good medical folks ta look him over...no offense ta Doc, but he's gotta be in an emergency room. Should be as quick as possible. Wastin' time here arguing where he's gonna be and who's gonna look after him doesn't make much sense ta me right now. They'll fly him ta the city...check him over...probably keep him awhile...then you folks can decide who's gonna do what."

"Perhaps you are right, Jack" the minister said slowly, backing off, regrouping for a new position. "Perhaps you are right. I'll accompany Betty and Del in the helicopter. I can give her the comfort and help she needs in dealing with this."

"I'm sure," Jack said. He was almost, but not quite sarcastic when he spoke. It was close.

They had heard the chopper coming well before it arrived and Jack and Red watched from the porch as it landed. The noisy, whirling machine jockeyed for a spot to come down, then settled in the open area half way to the field. The EMS team piled out before the rotor stopped spinning and trotted towards the house as Jack yelled and waved to them. They couldn't hear what he was saying, but they knew what he meant.

After checking Del's condition, a stretcher was brought into the living room. At first Del resisted lying down on it, then Betty coaxed him. He would not budge. Reverend Stone spoke to Del calmly, quietly, with the ponderous intonation he used for one of his prayers.

"Del, this is best for you right now. Betty and I will be close beside you. Trust in me and trust in the Lord. You will be all right."

With those words, Del got on the gurney.

"Thank you," Betty sighed.

She hugged Red and patted his back, released him, and patted his cheek. Then she took his hands and spoke directly to him, her face close to his.

"Now, Red, you know what to do with the animals, don't you?"

She spoke the words slowly, deliberately as if to make sure that they registered with him and she checked his eyes for confirmation.

He shook his head yes.

"Good. There's leftover meat loaf in the refrigerator that you can heat in the microwave for supper and some vegetables and the fixings for a salad. You can take care of that can't you?"

He shook his head yes.

"Good. I'll be back tomorrow. All right?"

The answer was in his eyes even before he spoke and she was relieved.

"Sure," he said, "sure can."

She smiled at him and squeezed his hands.

"Is Del gonna be okay?" Red asked. "I don't think he's doin' so good."

"Yes, he is Red, now don't you worry...he'll be just fine...just fine. I've got to go now."

He wasn't so sure that Del was okay and the look of acceptance he had given Betty for what she had said to him before faded from his eyes. He watched numbly as she walked to the helicopter, watched as it slowly rose and was soon gone.

"You gonna be okay, Red?" Jack asked.

"Yes, Mr. Jeffries, I can take care of things. I surely can."

"I thought so, but I'll check in on ya in the mornin' just in case ya need anythin'."

Red nodded silently and stared at Jack's truck as the man drove away. When the truck got out of sight his gaze turned toward the east, squinting, in the hope that he might still see the chopper. He felt something that bothered him, without knowing about being lonely. He only knew something was not right, something bad had happened, and now things were different. He was left with only the steel-gray of the clouds that formed a haunting background for a faded, less-than-perfect rainbow arcing gracelessly across the sky. He did not see the colors, segmented and sustained, nor would he have even understood the arc's intended meaning as a sign for something good.

2.

Yea, though I walk through the valley of the shadow of death, I will fear no evil; for You are with me; Your rod and Your staff, they comfort me.

-Psalm 23:4

The steady beat of the helicopter rotor blades where like an exaggerated echo of her own pounding heart. She could feel the tightness in her chest from the anxiety that had crept up on her. She had been calm until this point. Now, heightened by the fear she had for this ungainly machine, her sense of well-being was slipping away. Now, there were a few moments to reflect on what had happened to this ruggedly handsome man, to begin to worry about the worst kinds of things, to fret about what outcome might be in store for him - for them. Her immunity from the shock of the accident was beginning to wear off and the effect of the trauma was starting to roll over her like a giant boulder trying to crush her resiliency. She began to shake.

The emergency nurse recognized Betty's condition and wrapped a blanket around her, then poured coffee from a container into a styrofoam cup.

"Drink some of this...it will help. Your husband is quite stable, so I wouldn't worry, even though I know that's hard not to do."

The woman spoke with crisp professionalism, but there was kindness in her words.

Betty smiled in appreciation. Del was wrapped in some strange malady and someone beside herself cared. That was so nice.

"Thank you," she said, barely audible above the noise of the chopper.

Betty could not be inside his mind and it frustrated her. What was going on with this man? She looked intently at Del as he blankly stared straight up at nothing and she stifled her desire to weep. The reaction welled, but she did not let it get control. He could not see her cry, she determined. She wanted to make eye contact with him, although she could not get his attention. She spoke his name - nothing - no response. She waved her hand without extending her arm in a modest gesture that was quite like some dignitary giving passing homage to a crowd - still nothing. She stuck out her hand and wiggled her fingers. Del blinked a lot, otherwise he gave no indication he knew she was there.

"He's comfortable," the nurse consoled, "and it won't be long until we get to the hospital."

Betty smiled at her again. It was considerate of her to try to help, she thought, but not the same as if she were able to connect with Del.

She had never even flown on an airplane, so this perilous ride was a completely new experience. This was a bumpy, noisy ride, with a greater sense of movement, of disorientation, and of anxiety. She didn't like it one bit and was grateful when they finally arrived at the hospital. The trip from the farm had lasted only a matter of minutes, but had seemed a lot longer to Betty.

The chopper was on the ground still whirling and growling when they were met by hospital personnel who took Del immediately to the Emergency Room. Betty hurried along with them as Del was wheeled through a maze of corridors. Reverend Stone followed, lagging behind somewhat so that he could use his cell phone without Betty overhearing, yet close enough so that she would know he was with her. When they arrived in ER she began the formal process of admitting Del, while medical staff began their work.

Reverend Stone had realized it made little sense to argue with the neighbor Jack Jeffries. Take the line of least resistance and remain close to Del, close to what he saw as an opportunity of a lifetime. What he had quickly realized was that Del could be very helpful in pursuing God's work and would also be useful to furthering his ministry.

"...that's right, once you get the car," Stone spoke into his cell phone, "come on to Toledo Hospital...the emergency room. No, no, I think he's going to be all right...yes...yes...and we have our work cut out for us...yes, we've got a lot to do. That's right...get here as quickly as you can...but be safe...yes, yes...you, too."

Reverend Stone stood in a far corner of the ER away from the admitting desk where Betty was detailing pertinent information for the triage nurse. Satisfied that she was aware of his presence and still could not hear any of his conversation, he had another important call to make. He punched in three different telephone numbers before making the contact he wanted.

"Tom? Randy. Glad I finally got you. This is important...yes, of course I'm okay...this just...okay...how are you? Good...sorry I forgot my manners...I'm a little excited. This just happened this afternoon...during the storm...yes, yes...now listen. Del Howe got hit by lightening...I'm here at Toledo Hospital where they took him...helicopter, med flight...I came along with his wife. She called me to the farm to help...I think she thought he was going to die and she wanted me there. Anyway, he's not going to die, but, and here's the thing...he's talking in tongues...that's right, talking in tongues...no, I'm not kidding. For real. I'd like you to get here and help me. We need to figure out exactly how we are going to handle this. Yes, how we are going to handle this. I think Del Howe, in his present condition, is going to bring us God's blessing in some way...with a message of some sort...a revelation, I guess. I think this could benefit us...you and I. Sure, sure, but get here fast will you? Oh, and Tom...thanks."

Randy Stone frowned slightly, then looked to see if Betty were watching. She was still dealing with someone from the admitting office and paid no attention to him. He went to where she was seated and patted her shoulder.

"Betty, I'll be right over here when you are finished."

"All right," she nodded.

Stone went across the room to a group of chairs away from where anyone else was waiting. He wanted that separation so when Betty joined him there would be a bit of privacy for them. He turned his cell phone over and over in his hand, wishing he had shown enough presence of mind to grab his planner from his car before he climbed aboard the helicopter. Without his planner he felt disorganized, somewhat naked to the world, vulnerable to the unknown, and, perhaps, not fully able to function as well as he would have wanted. That planner is some kind of pacifier, he mused, aware of his obsessive dependency on it.

A man capable of thoughtful considerations about much in his life, Reverend Stone had a deep understanding of vulnerability. He knew what a strong grasp the feeling had on someone, and how the word of the Lord could comfort and clarify, could lessen the frustration and hopelessness that at times are part and parcel of feeling vulnerable. And he also knew how to subtly use the impact of that emotion to manipulate and control. Tom Fletcher had helped him hone that skill like the keen edge of a blade that could cut flesh and not be felt. Stone could rule a person's psyche without their realizing it was happening.

Tom had been a big help to him in so many ways. Stone was glad he had been able to reach him, glad he was on his way. With Tom he could formulate a plan. Something that would make sense, that would be fruitful for his ministry.

Randy Stone never intended to be a minister. He wanted to be a lawyer like his Uncle Ned from his Mama's side of the family. Everyone called him Uncle Ned, but remembering back, he wasn't sure the man was truly an uncle. Whatever Ned's real connection to the family might have been, he was surely an impressive man. Dressed so finely, shoes always polished, handsome ties and shirts, and he drove a big black Cadillac. Whenever he came to the house he gave Randy a quarter, always with advice on what should happen to it.

"Young man, save all the money you can for a good education," Uncle Ned would bellow.

Uncle Ned never talked, he always bellowed. Or so it seemed.

When Stone was older, he learned from Mama that Uncle Ned was a lawyer.

"Lawyers must make lots of money," he had said to his mother.

"They do if they're good," she remarked. "Uncle Ned is good at what he does."

"I think I'll be a lawyer someday," Stone had affirmed to his mother.

"Rather you be a preacher," she had sniffed, "y'all'd have some dignity...help folks..."

"I thought lawyers helped folks..."

"They do, sweetheart, but not like preachers."

Stone was caught between those two professions, but sure he did not want to follow his Daddy. His daddy was a barber and he was not going to be a barber.

The death of Granny Simpson changed everything for Randy. Her funeral brought folks from all over Tennessee and even from up North. Chicago and Detroit. Presiding was Pastor Jonathon Kyle Morgan, or as his Daddy would say, "Pastor J. K." Pastor Morgan loomed large in the eyes of an impressionable young man with his emotions wrapped up in the passing of this old woman he dearly loved. Pastor Morgan had as wonderful and commanding a voice as Uncle Ned, although he rarely spoke loudly unless he was castigating the devil. Pastor Morgan was the shepherd who gathered Granny Simpson into God's flock, called her one of

God's children going home to the Promised Land where she belonged. Pastor Morgan spoke and everyone in the congregation hung on every word and waited to hear what next he had to say. When Pastor Morgan recited the twenty-third Psalm, eyes closed, face towards heaven, chills caught Randy as if he had walked into an ice house. Pastor Morgan had the understanding of vulnerability and convinced Randy Stone of the decision he would make. Randy was no longer in doubt, he would heed the calling to the ministry of the Lord, apostle of God, future shepherd like Pastor Morgan. His Mama was elated.

There was high praise indeed, well beyond Mama, from others in the family, when news of Randy's choice became known. A confirming succession of phone calls to Mama gave full notice of how suited they thought the boy would be as a preacher. Have to hold down that temper a bit, but he'll be a fine one, a Christian demon from the pulpit, in the best sense of the word. The devil is in for it now, they said. He cannot fail in that honorable profession and we all will be proud of him. Mama was pleased.

There was another call Reverend Stone knew he should make and he had willfully avoided it. The neglect was not good, he decided. As much as he did not want to, he figured it better to get the call out of the way. Procrastination would not help. Besides, such behavior would not look good if someone found out that he had not made the call or that he even waited so long. He punched in the number on his cell phone almost without looking at it, vacantly, without much concentration as if he were preoccupied with something else. Which he was, of course. When he heard his wife answer, his voice took on a stern tone with deep, deep seriousness as if someone had died.

"Helen, glad I was finally able to call you...yes, yes, I'm okay. But I am here at Toledo Hospital with Del Howe and his wife. She asked me to come along. Del's been struck by lightening and the helicopter came out to their farm to pick him up. Yes, Betty had called me out to the farm. I was in the office...didn't have time to let you know before I headed out there...the call sounded frantic...Red Crier...yes, Red. Del's going to be all right, I believe, something...well, startling has developed...Del is speaking in tongues. Yes, isn't that amazing? Well, I assume all the electricity from the lightening caused...this condition. In any case, I think I need to stay close to him, dear, I think...I think this is a sign from God...God speaking to us through Del. Anyway, I'm going to stay here with Betty through the night...yes, I think they'll keep him here overnight...we'll see what tomorrow brings. I'll call you in the morning. No, no, that's not necessary...Miss Porter is getting someone to help her get my car and bring it here...you just get a good night's sleep. Fine, you too, dear."

Done and out of the way with that call. Not as bad as he thought it might be, with the quavering plaintive voice that could have been asking why he hadn't called sooner, asking when was he coming home. She might have expressed her dissatisfaction without saying it directly by slowly stretching her southern drawl even further and coating it with tinges of whining. No, he had been lucky this time. Maybe it was because the hand of God had entered the picture that made her reluctant to react in the usual way. No matter, he had escaped the whine.

As he nervously fingered his cell phone, he realized Betty was no longer at the admitting desk. Her disappearance made him sit upright stiffly, then stand to look around. He went to the desk.

"Mrs. Howe..." he started.

The woman ignored him as she thumbed through several file folders.

"Excuse me, where has Mrs. Howe gone?"

"In the hall, around the corner to the left...telephones."

The woman had not looked up at him.

Stone walked quickly to the hall. Sure enough, she was there using a telephone, in the middle of a conversation. He started to approach her, thought better of it, and stopped. She finally saw him and motioned to him to come closer.

"This is my daughter Dorothy...I'm letting her know what is going on. I'll just be a minute..."

"Take your time. I'm still sitting right over there."

He pointed towards the waiting room and she nodded.

"I've asked Tom Fletcher to meet us."

She nodded again, resumed her conversation, and he went back to sit down.

Betty did not come right away to where he was seated and he became impatient. He did not want to lose control and every minute he was not able to talk to her meant time that he was not able to influence Del's future. Calling her daughter. He hoped that did not mean Dorothy would be coming to the hospital; more than likely she would. And the son, he was another matter. The daughter could be handled, but the son might be trouble. She's probably calling him, he fretted. Patience, he said to himself, patience. Be patient like Mama said.

She had warned him many times as he was growing up and she warned him before he went away to school.

"Lack of patience can get you in a heap of trouble, son. No question it can. You use that energy...that fire you've got, to preach. Losing patience is not good, that's why they say patience is a virtue."

He said he would try hard to not lose that virtue.

Life at Jackson-Chase Bible College tested all of Randy Stone's patience and often threatened to loosen his clutch on this virtue. In turn, Randy Stone challenged the patience of the Jackson-Chase administration. His presence on campus was quickly recognized and he was a frustration until he graduated.

"Randy Stone is our newest project," Dean Watkins told several members of the staff. "His place in this world as a child of God seems to be set at tormenting us and begging us to contain him within Christendom's mantle. He will be a work in progress, but we will triumph and he will succeed with our help."

Arguing with instructors and fellow students was a constant behavior, much to their irritation and discomfort. He was searching for the truth, he said, that he must be sure what is right and that what is right made sense. Is God real, he asked? Is the wind real, they answered? Is God's power real, he wanted to know? As real as his handiwork in the world around us, they countered. Is God really profound or merely a myth, he probed? That you can think such thoughts, make such considerations gives evidence to his real omniscience, they explained. Eventually, their realities became his realities, but he was still full of questions.

Stone's inspiration to do God's work and fulfill his commitment to Granny Simpson's memory was contained in a recurring vision he had during his stay at Jackson-Chase. The vision would come to him in dreams and on several occasions when he was fully awake during quiet contemplation. Were these flights of prodigious imagination or pictures of fantastic reality from future vision? In any case, he had described the vision to his mother. "I could see that I spoke to Jesus and he was with me when I preached to thousands in a huge crowd before me. The Lord was at my right hand and I gloried in his presence." Over time, he had many visions of how successful he would be as a preacher of God's Word. They were visions that sustained him and reassured him of his success. The Christian realities he adopted at Jackson-Chase he molded into his own picture of faith and beliefs that guided his ministry.

Trying to make sense of this situation with Del Howe needed Tom's able hand, Stone thought, as he watched Betty approach.

"Don will be here soon," she said, her relief at that prospect sounding in her words. "I just talked to him. He's very concerned."

What he feared, the dreaded Don would have to be dealt with before anything else.

"That's good, Betty, now come on...sit down and try to relax. Let me say a quick prayer."

She folded her hands and closed her eyes.

"Dear Lord," and his solemn tone was upon her, "we pray for peace of mind for this caring wife, a sense of calm for her concerns at this time, Dear God...You are merciful in understanding our needs, gracious in comprehending for us what is best that we may be more at ease in our life. Thank you, oh Lord, for hearing our prayer. Amen."

Betty softly said, "Amen."

Tom Fletcher breezed into the Emergency waiting room with all the confidence and slight touch of arrogance as any aging movie star would have. Self-assured in his mission, the tall, athletic, and good-looking man almost fifty years old knew his place in the world, knew full well that every eye was on him. There was that essence of the famous, the star quality that makes folks run for the autograph. In this case, it was Toledo, and no one, but no one, knew him or cared. After the initial flash of curiosity, most in the waiting room looked away and went back to whatever it was they were doing before he pushed through the swinging doors. Tom was a dedicated, hard-working insurance agent in Swanton, Ohio, where his flamboyance and philanthropy mattered. Here, he was away from home and anonymous. To Reverend Stone, on the other hand, he might well be that star or something akin to it.

"Mrs. Howe, I came as soon as I got the news from Randy. How is Del...? And you, how are you doing? Don't worry about a thing. We'll give you all the support and help you need. This congregation...your congregation, is always at the ready for one of its own."

He shook Reverend Stone's hand as he was speaking, then extended his hand to her.

"Thank you, Tom, I'm grateful, but I think we'll be all right as long as Del is okay."

"And he will be, I'm sure. What does the doc say?"

"No word yet. My kids are on their way, though, so I'll have their support. I'm fine."

"You are a strong woman, Betty, I know that."

"Farm life does that for you," she said firmly, a slight smile crossing her face. "I hope you can excuse me for a moment, but I do need to...to...to freshen up some..."

"Certainly," Stone said with all the graciousness he could muster.

"Yes, yes, of course," Fletcher said.

The two men looked at each other, a knowing cast of their eyes as if to say, "what a break," and sat down side by side on the couch that Betty had just vacated.

"Well?" Fletcher pulled at his right ear lobe as if that would help him think better. It was one of a series of nervous tics he exhibited, one that was called upon at serious moments.

Randy described in detail how he had been called to the farm, how he had seen Del speak in tongues, how he had escorted Betty to the hospital, and how he had sought to keep control of the situation.

"Been better if he had stayed at the farm," Fletcher groused. "Whose idea was it to get him here?" His scowl and the nod of his head meant he was displeased.

"Neighbor...called in a medical emergency that brought the hospital med flight. She would have gone along with me, I think, but he just went ahead and called. Next thing you know, the chopper was there in front of the house."

"Hmmm." Fletcher pulled the ear lobe again.

"I figure once we get him out of here I can take over. Although there might be a problem with the son. I hate to admit it, but I think it's a real possibility."

"How so?"

"He is very strong-willed...a wretched ambassador of Satan...an atheist know-it-all who might try to keep me from...from bringing God's word through Del to our congregation. Del is speaking to us from the Lord, I am sure of it, and I will make sense of whatever message he brings to us, make no mistake about that. I will interpret the word so that our flock understands. This is a wonderful opportunity for me...for us. I had heard about people speaking in tongues when I was in the seminary, read about cases where the word of God came forth from those who seemed incoherent, but where the word was translated by blessed pastors who were there. This is my chance to reveal a glorious message directly from God."

"We must get him in front of the congregation...after we get you in charge of his divine gift...and soon...by next Sunday," Fletcher said, wide-eyed with excitement. "Plus, we need to let the parishioners know what is in store for them. I'll take care of that."

"One good thing is that the daughter, Dorothy, will side with me. She is extremely..."

"Do you have room at your house for him?" Fletcher asked, disregarding the comment about the daughter. "You have to keep watch on him, take notes, and after he babbles, create and transcribe whatever message he has into material that makes a great sermon. Then get him to babble in front of the congregation."

"It would be difficult. We'd have to do some shuffling around of the kids to make it work. I think maybe it's not as good an idea as I had thought. A better plan would be to stay there at the farm with him. There's a certain kind of tranquility out there on that farm, a peace that will allow God's message to be revealed to me."

"You didn't hear me...I used the word "create." There will be no revelation for you, dear minister of mine, there will only be your ability to make sense of something that does not make sense."

"You don't believe he is speaking in tongues?"

"Of course not. He was hit by lightening and his brain has been short-circuited or something like that...a lousy neurological problem. But that doesn't mean we have to tell anyone else that. As far as anyone else is concerned, you know he is speaking in tongues and you are going to be the instrument by which the word gets out. And in no small measure helps your cause immensely."

"And furthers God's ministry?"

"Certainly...furthering God's ministry and furthering your ministry. After all, his ministry *is* you. It is in you. It is about you. You are the instrument, you are God's weapon against Satan, you are God's voice to his flock. Amen. And don't forget that, dear minister. It is and shall be your mantra for achieving big things...big things at the hand of God, as the will of God. Amen again from all of us in your care."

As he spoke, Fletcher played with a lock of his curly hair, a somewhat unruly portion just above the right ear. Another of his tics. Probably unruly because it had been pulled at so often.

"I can see us there...Del and I...before the congregation...he is speaking in tongues with all the intensity he can muster and I by his side am receiving the message. We are both sweating fiercely, the strain of the moment evident on both our faces. Somehow I am able to translate what Del speaks, am able to bring to understanding his incomprehensible sounds. It is a magic time and the congregation is enraptured and we bask in the Glory of God's Word. I can see that, Tom, and you can make it come true, I know you can."

"Indeed I can…and I will."

"I believe that…"

"I know you do. Here she comes."

Fletcher and Stone rose as Betty returned.

"Oh please stay seated…"

"No, no, I have to get going…lots to do. Glad things are under control here…very pleased Reverend Stone can be with you right now…mighty important, I think. Anyway, I'll check in with you all tomorrow."

"Thanks, Tom," Betty said.

"I'll talk to you tomorrow," Stone almost whispered, "thanks."

Fletcher was gone and no one else noticed.

For Randy Stone, Tom Fletcher's appearance had been a settling influence, although his take on Del's speech was slightly disquieting. Ever since Randy had arrived in Swanton two years ago, Tom had guided him as a friend and mentor.

"Reverend, I know you have the degree from the Seminary," Tom had told him, "but I know how to run this congregation."

Surely true. Fletcher had led the search for a new minister, deftly manipulating the committee that interviewed and hired Randy. He was the minister Tom wanted: young, dedicated, energetic, and manageable. Tom Fletcher was also a man well-versed in all aspects of vulnerability.

Tom had been the business manager of the Calvary Fundamentalist Christian Church for more than ten years, a job he got by default, inherited from Dean Chalmers, who died suddenly. Oh sure, he had carefully, deliberately positioned himself for the assignment so that it was a foregone conclusion by the trustees as to what decision they would make. Tom was their man, all agreed. Tom was well-liked, honest, a strong Christian in his beliefs, and definitely knew about business. He also was named to the board. Slowly, he got control of the board and for the last three years has been president of the trustees. He was the master puppeteer and took delight in how his puppets danced at his will. His motives could be described as uncertain by some outside observer, but the results he wanted, the results he achieved were not. The church membership had grown substantially and the congregation prospered significantly under his guiding hand. His effort was coupled with the often startling, consistently mesmerizing results of Randy Stone's dynamic prowess in the pulpit and the powerful, week-to-week program they presented to the congregation. The program was contemporary faith-based, intensified with music-driven segments, bible indoctrinated, and modulated with Randy Stone's personality. It was a formula that worked. Tom knew it would.

Their relationship advanced in a strange sort of way. Tom was unmarried, never been married, yet considered attractive and desirable by the unattached women in his life. He became Uncle Tom to Helen and Randy's children and he was quite comfortable with this. There was an edge to that circumstance as far as Randy was concerned; a sense that something was not quite right about it, but Helen was pleased and happy to have Uncle Tom around on any occasion.

Mentor, friend, it didn't matter. Randy understood that Tom was in charge. And yes, Randy still knew that he was the leader of the flock, the minister, the Reverend with respect, but it was Tom that controlled things. Controlled the money, controlled the musicians, and the other performers and participants on Sunday. After all, it was a pageant. Tom had emphasized this when he helped Randy construct the service. It was pageantry that required the utmost attention to detail. Pageantry that relied on the importance of competency, skill, and talent. Tom made sure that everyone in "the show" as he called it, was the best they could bring together as part of their service. He made sure they delivered. He would have made a great promoter of a rock group or an NBA team.

Tom knew about Keri. He made little comment, although once he had told Randy to "be careful."

"We wouldn't want *this* to spoil things for you...for us."

"This," the pointed, in fact, heavily stressed word in Tom's comment was Randy's relationship with Keri. Tom really didn't care if Randy cheated on his wife, he didn't want it to be found out, didn't want it to change things. The situation at Calvary was working too well to have it spoiled now.

Tom Fletcher managed to use his advantage at every opportunity, every circumstance, every meeting, every relationship that came about within the church congregation and with his position as business manager and trustee. He parlayed all of these connections and conditions into furthering his insurance business. He was the beneficiary of the good will he generated, as he made all of those lives he touched to feel as if they benefited.

It was true that he had never married and as such was the case there was a constant, almost incessant need by numerous women in the congregation to match him with some female in want of a husband. His ability to remain out of the clutches of this parade of prospects without offending anyone was a marvel of tact, diplomacy, and charm. Yet no one suggested that he was other than a confirmed and dedicated bachelor. No hint or whisper that he might not be quite "normal." His reputation stayed unsullied. Such was the power of his personality, no less his enthusiasm for the Lord.

Keri Porter was obviously out of breath as she approached Stone and Betty. She carried Stone's planner with both hands as she battled with the difficulty of keeping the strap of her purse on her shoulder.

"I got here as soon as I could," she exhaled as she handed Randy the planner. "Is Mr. Howe all right.?"

"Yes, Keri, I think he is. We still haven't talked to the doctor, but..."

"Mom," the shrill voice interrupted, "Mom..."

"Dorothy, I'm so glad you could get here..."

"What's the word?"

"I don't know..."

"Have you talked to the doctor?" Dorothy suddenly realized Randy was there. "Reverend Stone, I'm really glad you could be here with mom...thank you."

"Yes, of course, we wanted..."

Using the editorial "we," he was about to pontificate on the importance of the role of the minister in being with parishioners in time of need. He never got a chance to finish because Don Howe was on top of them demanding answers. At nearly six feet six inches, he did tower over them all.

"Ah, Reverend Stone, tell me, since you are the immediate representative of God. Is the God you represent the one who allowed my father to be hit by lightening or the one who is going to save him?"

"There is no...," Stone began.

"Never mind, you don't have an answer." He turned to his mother, gave her a gentle kiss on the cheek and squeeze of the arm. "I suppose they don't know anything. Or do they?"

"No, dear." Betty smiled at him and held his hand.

"Well, let's rattle their cage a little bit and see what is going on."

With that, he quickly walked to the reception desk.

"I think you folks have had enough time to find out what's wrong with Mr. Howe. So..."

"Who are you?" The woman behind the desk cut him off with a snarl.

"I'm his son and I want to know..."

"Our responsibility is to Mrs. Howe," she stated curtly. "I know you are concerned, but we will deal with her, thank you."

By now, Betty, Dorothy, Stone, and Keri had gotten to the desk behind Don.

"It has been a long time," Betty said, an anguished tone in her voice, a tone that influenced the woman. "Could you find out?"

"I'll check with the doctor," the woman said and disappeared.

"Bunch of nonsense," Don muttered.

"Son you haven't even been here..."

"Yeah, yeah, I know, but I also know about how much time has elapsed since he got struck. We should have..."

"Mrs. Howe, I'm Dr. Monroe."

The man was out through the doors to the emergency room care center even before the woman could get back to her station behind the desk.

"Doctor, yes...," Betty seemed very relieved.

"Your husband is stable, vital signs good, seems to be no physiological damage we can determine..."

"How about his brain?" Don snapped. "He's got scrambled speech."

"Yes, I know and we'd like to keep him overnight for observation and testing."

Reverend Stone stood by helpless. Helpless to control or maneuver, helpless to change the situation. What would this mean to his plans?

Reverend Stone knew that it would not be easy with Don, but had to admit the young man accomplished something in the few minutes since he had arrived. He could not counter the doctor's request for an overnight stay - that was the way it would be. His next step would be tomorrow, when Del was released.

"I've already been on the phone with some people in Columbus," Don announced to his mother. "Some professionals…they know how to deal with this kind of thing. They're coming day after tomorrow…"

"Well, Don, we don't even know anything yet." The pleading in Betty's voice was apparent.

"Yes, mom we do know something. We know that dad was hit by lightening and we know that he is talking crazy…"

"Don, no, he's…" Betty started to protest.

"We believe," Reverend Stone stepped in, "that your father is speaking in tongues…most definitely not talking "crazy.". He's now an emissary of the Lord God bringing us a message of revelation, an important message that I will interpret. Out of your father's misfortune comes something for all of us."

"Hey, listen, Reverend, most respectfully, that's bullshit."

"We all know that God works in mysterious ways. Out of the power of that thunderstorm that swept over your father, out of that power which came from the hand of God came this opportunity for all of us to get the word of God directly. Such a chance does not come often and should not be considered lightly."

"Well, look…," Don was about to take the position of the non-believer.

"No, I think you need to look at what has happened to your father in the context of your mother's faith and mine…and I would assume that of your sister, also." Reverend Stone knew that he could not stand by while Don spoiled things; he had to go on the ministerial offensive. "We believe, most sincerely, that he is speaking in tongues and that he has become, by accident, an instrument of God. We are all blessed as a result. That is not to say that your father should not be tested and checked out by the doctors, we know that is important for his health, but his destiny is in the hands of God. That we know."

Dr. Malone had stood by, patiently waiting, as this interchange took place. Now, he wanted to proceed with what he thought was necessary.

"I'd like to get Mr. Howe admitted so he can get settled," Dr Malone pressed.

"Can I stay with him?" Betty asked. "We haven't been separated for a long time."

"I don't see why not," Dr. Malone smiled.

"I'd like to see my father," Don said. His manner was more restrained than when he had first arrived, the soft calm in his tone a far cry from his initial forcefulness.

"I do too," Dorothy said.

"I think it's good of both of you to be with your mother and comfort your father." Reverend Stone soothed. "Will you be staying with her all night?"

"I can't," Don said, "I've got to run as soon as I see dad."

"I can't either, mom, I'm sorry." Dorothy frowned when she spoke. "I've got to get home…"

"I know, dear, you run along after you see dad…I know how busy you are with the kids and Jerry. I'll be fine."

At that moment, Reverend Stone was caught with the frustration of what to do. Up until then, it had been his plan to leave and come back the next day, but this chance was too good to let slip away. What to do about Keri? He was torn, but decided that he would leave with her and return tomorrow early. He hated to pass up what was in store with her. He said goodbye, explaining that he would be here in the morning, Keri smiled her leave, and the two them went to the parking lot.

Don followed his mother and sister almost to the door that entered into the emergency treatment area, stopped, and went back through the doors to the hallway by the exit to the parking lot. He watched through the window next to the exit door as Reverend Stone and Keri walked toward his car. She had linked her arm in his and leaned her head against his shoulder as they made their way.

"What was that all about?" Dorothy asked when he caught up with them.

"Just checking on something," he muttered.

Reverend Stone and Keri did not speak until they reached his Ford sedan.

"Are you coming to my place?" she asked. She was not subtle with the seductiveness of her voice.

He unlocked the car without answering, opened the door for her, then got in the driver's seat, and sat contemplating what he might say. He wanted to be enthusiastic, but realized now that he wasn't. Back in the hospital, the thought of being with her again, close, and naked, and making love was what he desired. Here at this moment, his ambivalence nearly crippled him from speaking. He did know –ah, yes, how well he did know - that in dealing with a young woman in this kind of situation was like…like playing with lightening. Dangerous. You could be struck with a bolt if something went wrong, something not to her liking. He was caught in the vise of an affair and he could not retreat. Not yet, anyway. His answer – what he said and how he said it – was oh so important.

"I couldn't wait to get out of there," he lied. "Once you showed up I had a hard time keeping my mind on the Howes."

She giggled and leaned into him to receive a kiss. He obliged with the appropriate passion.

"But I need to keep my eye on the ball…and the ball is Del. He is going to help our ministry big time and right away. I need your help...seriously...seriously need your help. I need your understanding and support for how the next days and weeks play out. Things won't be the same, but over time...you'll see...over time it will work for us. Be patient, be understanding and all will be well. I know you are up to the challenge."

"Of course I am...you know I am."

They kissed again, his signature on this emotional document. The kiss of modulated passion was his way of stabilizing any apprehension she might have about what he proposed. He knew her vulnerabilities, he knew what she wanted.

He clutched his planner against his side and relaxed somewhat with the knowledge that he was in control again. The important book was in his grasp. Keri thought his whole demeanor was a sense of intimacy for her and she nuzzled herself into him as he was pacified by the leather binding.

Del was awake and staring at the ceiling when Betty, Don, and Dorothy pushed aside the curtain surrounding his gurney. He had been readied to be moved upstairs and waited in what seemed to be a relaxed manner.

"Hi, Pop," Don greeted.

Hi, daddy," Dorothy said, fighting back tears, "you look so good."

Del looked at them and smiled.

"Gemish bezeer," he voiced. Then he turned to Betty, the smile broadening. "Gibooh taymath. Bloss." His face was beginning to turn red and the first small beads of perspiration broke out on his forehead.

"Easy, Pop, relax. Don't try to talk." Don put his hand on his father's shoulder.

A grinning, heavy-set nurse appeared through the curtains and took charge.

"We'll move him up to his room now…you can follow along if you want."

Behind her was a burly man of swarthy complexion who would do the actual work of pushing the gurney. He never said a word. The big nurse was in charge.

Don and Dorothy said their good-byes and left, and Betty and the big nurse and the burly man got Del to his room on the eighth floor where he shared space with an automobile accident victim who had just had brain surgery that afternoon.

It was quiet in the room, except for the occasional whir and electrical clicking of the monitoring machines. The television sets were silent. Betty could hear various staff bantering in the hall and away at the nurses' station. Del was watching her and he smiled and she smiled back at him. She tried not to show any fear.

"Desho, callie," he vocalized quietly, his eyes showing he was just a bit frantic, it seemed to her.

"Relax, dear, everything is going to be all right. We'll go home tomorrow."

He smiled, closed his eyes, and was gone into the land of sleep, breathing deeply, separated now from the reality that still clung to her.

She settled into a chair next to the bed in order to relax and suffer the wait until morning. She was neither hungry nor thirsty, merely eager for time to pass and Del to be told he could go home. She was ready to hold out against the night. She thought of many things, yet focused on the twenty-third Psalm for comfort. She repeated it over and over in her mind and eventually went to sleep in her chair.

3.

The Lord looks from heaven; He sees all the sons of men. From the place of his dwelling He looks on all the inhabitants of the earth; He fashions their hearts individually; He considers all of their works.

-Psalm 33:13-15

There were few interruptions during the night to disturb Betty's sleep. Twice a nurse came to the room to check on the man in the next bed and at some point - Betty knew from her watch that it was about two thirty - there was a mild commotion in the hall. It was some confrontation between a doctor and nurse, and Betty could not make out much of what was said, but knew that the doctor was upset about something. Otherwise she slept fairly well for most of the night. A small cot had been brought in near Del's bed and she flopped down with exhaustion; not taking off her clothes, pulling a light blanket over herself.

She awoke periodically as the nighttime mysteries of the hospital created an ebb and flow of activity. Secrets abound, secret things go on at night, secrets the staff retains and protects, secrets they talk about at parties and small social gatherings where work stories are related. At those times, the life at night in the hospital is talked about with a certain openness and calm that could never be stated outside of the inner sanctum of the working professionals that care for life and are confronted by death.

Betty could hear the whisperings, could sense the call of death, and could imagine the serious conditions that came and went. She could know that here there was a protected, defined universe within a universe where her husband abided with his life suspended and where others cared about how he was and how he would be. In one fleeting moment, caught between being awake and being asleep, Betty reckoned that this was somewhat like being on the farm where she awoke at night and wondered about their stock, wondered about the crops, and wondered about the man who slept quietly by her side. It had always worked out on the farm, surely it would work here in this place of caring and comfort, and surely everything would be all right when the sun came again, just as it was on the farm.

Towards morning she began the fitful, light sleep that told her the day was soon on its way. She thought of the farm again, knew there were so many things to do with the animals and wondered if Red would be able to handle his mission without her and Del. She pulled the blanket to her chin and kept her eyes tightly closed. There was nothing she could do for Red right now, he was on his own. It will all be okay she determined and slid gradually back to a deeper sleep.

Betty was awakened by the day nurse who came to check on Del. It was six thirty. The woman checked his pulse, otherwise made sure he was alive, and went about her rounds. Betty went to the bedside and held Del's hands. She massaged his wrists and rubbed his hands, then brushed his hair back from his brow. He was awake, but impassive, calmly, quietly relenting to her tending. He looked at her without smiling, then stared at the ceiling. He closed his eyes and breathed deeply, but she knew he was not asleep. It did not matter. She held her hand on his brow, touched the back of her hand to his cheek, and sat down.

Breakfast came in due course as the organization of the hospital began to methodically grind out its daily routine with all of the consistency and impersonal repetitive monotony of a manufacturing plant. Del refused to eat and Betty only picked at the food a bit before deciding it really was not to her liking. For all of its emphasis on cleanliness, sterility, and the rapid disposal of waste, the hospital still had a smell of some sort that permeated the atmosphere and was unpleasant for Betty. She longed for the fresh air of the farm and wished they both were there.

Farm life was all she had ever known. It was a life simple and straightforward in its demands, a life of frustration and reward, and a life of constant reminder how fragile was the existence of all living things. She knew she was blessed by having Del as her husband, knew the light of the Lord had shone upon her with his presence in her daily existence. After he returned from Vietnam they had never been separated for more than a few hours. Now he was still physically nearby, but there seemed to be some huge chasm of separation that had torn them apart. The lightening had done more than just give Del a strange way of speaking, it had split them into separate beings when for years they had been one, inseparable, resolute in dealing with all manner of frustrations and joys, heartaches and bounties, and so powerful in unison as they sustained each other.

The farm was truly a symbol of their life together, a metaphor for how they viewed the world and what they wanted for themselves, it was their place in their reality, and was so solid and dependable. She was very young when she knew for sure that he was the man she wanted. Del was still a boy, but she could see what he would be some day, in a way that he himself could not envision.

"Mama," Betty said firmly to her mother, "he's the one…"

"Who's that, honey…"

"Del, Mama, Del."

Her mother laughed and thought little more about the subject. After all, Betty was only twelve. But Betty's Mama had scant understanding of the determination in her young child's soul. There was within Betty a source of strength in her commitment to this boy. A boy she foresaw as a man and with all of the characteristics that she believed he carried within him. Her wish was to become a bond of life, a joint-venture, a fulfillment of what she wanted. Theirs became a life of shared strong values and religious convictions and beliefs fundamentally captured by the Holy Scripture of the Bible.

The road of relationship with Del from age twelve to age twenty-two was bumpier than she could ever have imagined. Nowhere in her picture of their future life was there a segment called Vietnam, nor was there a scenario of Del being wounded, arriving home dour and bitter and sullen. Nowhere had she seen the image of Del recuperating by rejecting her and his family and so much that had been a part of his existence before he went away to that strange faraway country. What had happened to have him be that way? He would not say. Or could not say. At least he did not talk about his time there. Instead, he hid away, silent, wanting little contact and when he was with her or others in the family he was moody. Time, she figured would take care of things, and she did not press him for any explanation. She waited, patiently, alone in many respects, although her mother consoled her and Del's mother also was some comfort. Her Papa wasn't so understanding and told her to move on with her life.

"He's just messed up that's all," her Papa told her, "forget about him and go on with your life. He's just another casualty of war...combat...they see things, experience stuff...we saw a lot of that after WW two. Nothing you can do. You can't change anything, so forget it. Get used to the idea he's a lost cause."

But she could not and did not. She waited. She knew he was still her man.

Betty could even yet smell the distinctive aroma of wet grass, newly mowed, the water dripping from the leaves of the grape arbor not far from the back porch of her parents' home. A brief rain shower had come and gone and there was still a glimmer of daylight in the western sky of a late August evening. She had handed Del a cold lemonade and waited for him to say something. He had driven into the side drive just a few minutes before, knocked at the kitchen door, and stood there quite forlornly.

"Just came by," he said simply, noting the obvious.

"I'm glad." She kissed his cheek.

"Let me get you a lemonade, Mama just made some."

He did not come in from the porch and when she brought the glass to him he turned and walked away to the grape arbor. He took a long drink and stared off at the fading light. She came to stand by him and was silent, waiting for him to speak.

Finally, after several minutes, he cleared his throat and she was poised for what was to come.

"There's a lot to say," he whispered huskily, "I'll get to it sometime."

He handed her the glass, walked quickly to his car, and was gone.

It was the next spring before Del seemed like himself. It had been a brooding winter for him and tough on those around him, but friends, relatives, and Betty let him resolve whatever it was festering inside him. Christmas time was especially somber. Dinner at Betty's home on Christmas Eve was a combination of restrained conversation and muted eagerness opening presents by the Collins family. They respected Del's "condition," as Betty's mother termed how Del was behaving, and believed it was only polite to subdue their usual festive gaiety this year considering how Del was. Besides, they liked Del. Christmas Day the same sort of restraint prevailed with the Howe household. Betty was glad when the New Year arrived. The struggle through the Holidays had left her weary, but unflagging in her belief that Del would work out of his funk.

When the weather broke and the first blooms appeared, Del seemed to follow suit. Not that he had fully blossomed yet, however the positive signs were beginning to show.

By early May there was a new tone, a significant change of demeanor when Del spoke and he smiled once in awhile. Betty discovered that she could gently tease him. Then, one day in late May, he was a new person, surely still as she had known him, yet a new person tempered by experience. She could see it even before he spoke. He had driven into their drive and bounced out of the car lively as a cat as soon as the car stopped. There was a spring in his walk that had been missing and she could see brightness and life in his eyes. She went to the porch to greet him. He was smiling as he neared and she knew everything would be okay.

"Like some lemonade?"

"Betty, we need to…ah, ah…yeah, sure that would be great and then we…we can talk."

She poured the lemonade and he stood beside her fidgeting, standing on one foot then the other, barely able to contain himself, straining to unleash what was on his mind. Betty noticed and she thought she knew why.

"Let's go outside," she said softly.

They sat on the porch swing, Del paying no attention to the glass of lemonade she had given him, Betty patiently at his side.

"I know it's been hard on you since I got home," he started, "I mean with me. I guess it has for everybody around me. I guess I just had to…to…" He faltered and looked off somewhere.

"Maybe that's in the past, now," she whispered.

"Yeah, yeah, I think so…I know so. I had a talk with my dad a few days ago and he said something very profound to me."

"Oh?" she murmured.

"Yeah, he said, 'Son, knock off this moping stuff and hanging your head. Get over it…whatever happened, it's all in the past. You can have a nice future if you want it. And then there's that Betty.' How's that for advice?"

They both laughed and he kissed her. It was one of those spontaneous kisses that happen at the right moment, a kiss meaningful for lots of reasons, a kiss that quickly was filled with passion and heat, the kiss of lovers.

"There's that Betty," he repeated. "It's what he said, 'That Betty.' Isn't that something?"

"And then there's that Betty. I am that Betty," she said firmly, almost seriously, but with an impish grin.

"Will you marry me?" he asked. He said the words quickly to make sure that it came out right. And before he lost his courage.

"Of course," she laughed, "I've been waiting for you to ask for a long time."

"How do you mean?"

"Never mind, it doesn't matter."

She kissed him and this time they put their arms around each other and kissed again.

It took only six weeks to get everything arranged and on a hot, muggy Saturday in July, Betty Jane Collins became Mrs. Delwin Howe. The ceremony was held in the non air-conditioned Swanton First Baptist Church, where a horde of sweltering family and friends were delighted by the short service and the release to the relative relief of the reception in the Howe side yard.

Reverend David McCall's words were punctuated by the sound of a dog barking that intruded through the open window. Del was very calm and recited his part in the proceedings flawlessly and could be heard in the back row. Betty remembered being proud of him for that.

After the service, everyone went out to the Howe farm. Tables and chairs had been set up in the shade of several trees where numerous couples sat politely; others were on the screened porch and in the kitchen and living room, while some of the men gathered in the open barn. The barn crowd had the booze. Since Del's father didn't like liquor around, they felt it best to keep it there for their celebrating. Del had one drink with them which he thought appropriate.

Betty could smell the booze on his breath and she frowned.

"Just had one with the boys," Del said, "just one. Might never have another."

And he didn't as far as she remembered.

As the reception in the yard pulsed with gossip and talk of farm problems and periodic laughter, men pulled off ties and unbuttoned shirts while ladies made fans flutter like giant insects. Most of the fans were bamboo, but a few made of cardboard could be seen with the name Swanton Funeral Home printed on one side, the Lord's Prayer on the other. It was surely hot, but folks didn't seem to mind.

The bride and groom went off to a northern Michigan honeymoon, the reception crowd dwindled, and by late evening of that July Saturday it was quiet at the Howe farm. Betty still savored the pleasure of looking at the pictures from that day.

These events happened so long ago, yet were still so pure in her memory as she watched Del's rhythmic breathing, the subtle rising and falling of his chest.

"Good morning," Dr. Monroe said pleasantly as he came into the room and reached for Del's chart.

He looked at the notations and numbers for a minute or so, pursed his lips, then went alongside the bed next to Del.

"How are you feeling there, Mr. Howe?"

Del smiled at him and did not answer.

"Well, you seem to be functioning well..." He turned to Betty. "Should have some more tests I think...get a neurological specialist involved, but that's up to you."

"My son has someone coming to check on his father," she said. "I'd really like to take him home."

"I see. That's good. If your son knows someone competent that he trusts then that's the thing to do. Your husband seems fine other than his speech so there's not much we can do besides a series of tests. Keeping him overnight let us make sure he didn't have any other problems. Okay then, I'll sign the discharge sheet and you can take him home. The nurses will get that arranged for you."

"Thank you, Dr. Monroe."

"You're welcome, Mrs. Howe. Good luck."

Betty could see Reverend Stone and Tom Fletcher standing by the doorway as Dr. Monroe turned to leave. She was relieved without knowing why, some nagging intuition about her circumstances. Her mind had not even shifted to how she would get Del home since she was without a car.

As Dr. Monroe exited without acknowledging them, the two men entered, smiling, ready to be the Samaritans she certainly needed. Whether they were good or not was debatable, but they would help her at this difficult juncture.

"Morning, Betty," Stone spoke first, "we're here to get you back on your farm."

"I'm so glad," she sighed, "I want to get Del out of here. What a night...lots of dreaming, lots of reminiscing."

"Could you sleep any?"

"Oh my yes. You can see they brought in a cot for me. I slept all right, but not like home...in my...in our own bed."

"That was the doctor just leaving," Tom observed. "Was he going to discharge Del?"

"Yes, Tom, we can go as soon as the nurse says so."

"Yeah, I suppose they want to take him out in a wheelchair," Tom groused, "so darned scared of being sued. The word damn came into his head first, but he had learned a long time ago to curb that kind of talk if he wanted to have his position in the church. The word damn and words much stronger came naturally to Tom. He had put them away somewhere in his brain, but his inclination to use them continued. He managed to refrain.

It was true, the nurse and an orderly got Del in a wheelchair and the orderly took him downstairs to the patient exit. Tom went on ahead for the car and Reverend Stone took Betty's arm as they followed along.

"Thank you, Reverend, you've been a great help. Everyone has…Dr. Monroe, the nurses, Don, Dorothy, Tom…I'm grateful…very grateful."

"It's everyone's job, Betty, but it's their job because they want to help people. It's my life's work and I'm going to be close at hand as we get Del through this. Of course, there's the side benefit that Del is a messenger of God, let's not forget that fact. And I'll need your help as I interpret the Word."

"I do want to be at home. Please don't try to change my mind about that because…"

"No, no, no…don't worry. I think it is best for him to be in his own home with the surroundings that he knows so that he is most comfortable. I can…I'll work with him there."

"Oh, I'm so glad you see it that way. I would have a hard time if Del were away. Perhaps…perhaps you could stay with us…at our farm…while you listen to Del. You could use one of the extra bedrooms. Is that possible?"

"Yes…my yes, very possible and, in fact, I think that is the way we should proceed."

Del managed to get himself into Tom's Lincoln Town Car, ignoring the orderly who wanted to assist. There was not much agility left in this middle-aged farmer whose body had been savaged by grueling years of difficult physical labor; however he wanted his independence in making the move out of the wheelchair. Betty watched his effort with a degree of sadness. She could see how he struggled and understood for the first time that her man was an older man than she had realized. Until this moment she had retained a picture of him in her mind of that strong, vital man she had married. It pained her at this point, probably more than it bothered him. He was too involved in securing his independence to have insight into his diminished ability. That concept would come later to him.

As Del was getting into the car, Stone was able to speak to Tom quietly, away from the others, so he could not be overheard.

"It's going to work out fine…she's invited me to stay in the house to be with Del so I can interpret the Word."

"Great…I've already made some phone calls to get things ready for Sunday. I'll have the rest of the arrangements pretty well set today. You start working on a special sermon…showcasing Del…"

"Thank you very much for your help," Stone called after the orderly, cutting off Tom in mid-direction. Turning back to Tom, he said, "Let's get going…Betty is already in with Del."

What had been a short jump in the emergency helicopter was now a drive of more than an hour to reach the Howe farm. In that time Tom did most of the talking. He was hardly able to hold back his enthusiasm for the potential of Del's contribution to the church, which privately he calculated in financial terms, but expressed to Betty as "a blessing from the Lord."

Early on in his life, a blessing from the Lord was all Tom Fletcher had needed for getting started in pursuit of his dreams for success. The blessing was wealthy Marcia Dowling, a young woman almost attractive, trusting, and not very bright, but above all, wealthy. Nearly from the moment they met, Marcia was caught up in Fletcher charm which he realized and which he used to his fullest advantage. Plus, she wanted to have sex with him all the time. She was rich and oversexed. It was a combination most men would have wanted, but Tom didn't quite know how to deal with the sex stuff. Tom could not resist being with her even if Marcia were not the best looking girl he could have dated and even though he was not physically attracted to her. She was energetic and he did like that about her. And he liked the idea she had lots of money and liked to spend it on him.

Although her father was fairly well off, Marcia had substantial money of her own thanks to her grandmother. Grandma Whitney had inherited quite a fortune. She was the widow of Dr. Lawrence Whitney, a frugal man who had parlayed income from his veterinarian practice into a multi-million dollar investment portfolio and real estate holdings. Papa Dowling, her father, had managed to squander some of that before he got his own business going, but a good-sized chunk still passed on to Marcia, the only grandchild. There came all that money tumbling through the generations to fall into her lap without much fanfare. In one of the nicest, easiest ways to gain riches – the inheritance – Marcia found herself with more money than she had imagined and more than she knew what to do with or even cared. It was, however, clear enough in her mind that she wanted a man. Then, of all things, her Mama died suddenly and the money Mama got from Grandma Whitney also came to her. Mama had kept that money from Papa and the Last Will and Testament of Evelyn Whitney said very clearly that it now was hers. She became a very popular girl in Florence, Alabama. A number of eligible young men called for dates and she tried them all out before she met Tom.

She always thought they met by accident. Tom only made it seem that was the case. He heard about Marcia, did some investigating, and learned where she went to socialize with her friends. It was a small, nondescript cinder-block nightclub just over the border in Tennessee where they could sell booze and had a jazz band of black musicians that played until two in the morning. He asked her to dance, she accepted without paying much attention to him, and while dancing made his first assessment of this young woman. It was something subtle she said or the way she smelled or the feel of her body against his, but whatever it was he knew she was in heat. The slow, rhythmic throbbing of the beat enhanced the mood, gave a sense of passion, and brought raw sexuality to the surface.

"I can feel your spirit," he whispered in her ear as he drew her close to him.

"I bet you'd like to feel more than that," she whispered back.

"Maybe," he said with a chuckle, "but I think it's your heart beating or something...sort of like a cat purring...the energy from being alive. You're alive, I know that."

She laughed, not quite out loud, more a guttural voicing of her appreciation for what he said, a sound blurred somewhat by shots of bourbon, and not a whole lot of sleep in the past couple of days.

"Then again, maybe it's the smell...your smell..."

"My perfume?"

"Naw, its you...something besides the perfume...that's good, too...but its the smell of...of your soul...hot, spicy like a good bowl of jambalaya...or some other kind of Cajun food that makes your tongue take notice, can water your eyes, make your nose run..."

"So I'm some kind of food?"

"Yeah, could be. Could be some that I'd like to taste...see if it's as good as it smells."

The song ended, but he didn't take her off the dance floor.

"You want to keep dancing?" She stood close to him, hands on her hips.

"Yeah, can you stand it? I'm only going to give you more compliments. Maybe feel your body some more."

"You didn't do much of that..."

"Wait 'til the music starts again."

Almost on cue the band slid into another soft, bluesy melody that evoked passion from those so programmed. Tom took Marcia in his arms and moved her with him in unison, body melted against body, cheek pressed to cheek, and the free-flowing movement of intimate foreplay dealt to an audience seated at the bar and tables that understood what they were watching.

When the song ended, she clung to him for several moments, then slowly pulled back slightly, and for the first time looked at him. She could tell he was handsome even through foggy eyes. She liked that and she liked the way he seemed to have her and the whole situation under control.

"You're good looking," she said almost as an accusation, "bet you already know that. Bet you already know how to handle a woman."

He smiled at her.

"Yeah…you know."

"Why don't we get out of here and get better acquainted someplace else," he proposed.

She could not and did not respond to that offer quickly, but rather stared at him as if his proposition were being viewed in a television commercial, distant, abstract, impersonal, and independent of her life. She thought she was ambivalent to those kinds of pitches, but he looked good, sounded good, and she knew the answer he wanted.

"Okay," she said slowly, almost as if she were contemplating death.

Tom led her from the dance floor, through the bar area, out the door, and into the black night of sultry summer air infused with the smell of wild flowers and pine trees. The parking lot was lighted by one dirty yellow bulb from a tall pole near the building with shadows quickly receding to ever-increasing darkness. Once outside he kissed her and she responded in a way he knew she would.

"Let's go to my place," she gasped as she came away from the kiss. "Drive my car...I don't think I can...do it...not drive."

She showed him where her car was parked off to the side of the building. He got her in the front passenger seat and drove to her home. Her directions were erratic, but he made it. She ran the window down for fresh air even though the air conditioner was on and she leaned her head out the window. This was not a good situation, he realized, but it was a start for what he wanted. She did not pass out in the car, but he knew she would as soon as he got her home.

He could feel her pushing the key into his side as he helped her to the door. He took the keys from her as she hung on his arm with one hand and the other hand pulled at his shoulder. Once inside, she unceremoniously threw up on the slate tile of the foyer with an animal-like retching and gurgling, and fell sideways, twisting as she went. He thought he was lucky that she didn't fall into her own vomit - one more small blessing.

"Damn, that's awful," she gasped as she rolled over on the floor away from the mess and into a fetal position. "Can you help me...I should...I need to...to get to bed. God, I'm tired."

Tom got her to her bedroom which he readily located up the stairs in what was a master suite. He pulled off her clothes and stood for awhile looking at her naked body, white, almost lifeless, not athletic, and with lines and curvatures he realized were not particularly pleasing to him. She had large breasts that he had felt press against him when they were dancing closely and he fondled those nipples as she lay on her back on the purple sheet. He was not aroused.

He stood there looking at her wondering what it would be like to have sex with this inert creature, to actually have an erection and enter this motionless, expressionless form. Slowly, he took off his clothes.

Now, somewhat interested, somewhat enlarged, he spread her legs and climbed on top of her. He rubbed his penis across her pubis, but he did not get more excited, did not get more erect. His breath came quickly as he lay against her, crushing his full weight down on her. He could smell the foul odor of her breath as he rose on his elbows, and in spite of this, kissed her cheeks gently several times before rolling over on his back next to her. He took his member in his hands, but it didn't matter, it remained flaccid. He was lost in some world of desire he could not reach, could not accept, could not attain, and could not reject. He stared at the ceiling and wondered what this all meant. What he knew for sure was that he had Marcia Dowling under control.

In the following weeks, the whole deal with Marcia developed almost the way he wanted. She adored him and she wanted him to make love to her every day. She was a woman who did not have to work, wealthy enough to indulge her whims, and she could focus on herself and having sex every day. If she had her way it would be more than once a day. The challenge for Tom was to tactfully avoid this duty as much as he could without causing her to suspect something was wrong. There was something wrong, but he didn't know what it was; something wrong with him, some disconnect he had with actual sex. Thinking about sex was exciting, doing it was not.

Marcia's insatiable lust must have kept her from figuring out something was amiss, because she didn't get turned off by his lackluster, perfunctory love making. Once she was in the throes of passion all evaluation of the lover was not important. Besides, she was infatuated with him even if she hadn't been bedding him. She was crazy about him and this was the edge he needed to gain her confidence, to convince her that he could be a sharp businessman, and to make her think his plan was her idea. Plain old charm, lots of compliments, the sex she wanted, and his polite manners made the richest girl in Florence, Alabama, turn from prey to victim.

His request was innocent enough: twenty thousand dollars to get him started. The money was so he could get his own construction company underway. Her answer to that was to give him a hundred thousand without asking any questions or asking for any guarantees. She told him she just knew he would make it a success. No promissory note, no paperwork of any kind, just her hand-written check with all those zeroes. After she handed him the check and watched his surprised look, she unzipped his fly.

Marcia was naked on her side, knees pulled toward her breasts, rocking her body a bit, with her right hand between her legs, fingering herself, and softly moaning. The sun streamed in through the windows and highlighted her as if a spotlight had been turned on for her performance. It warmed her. She could feel the heat on her skin and she was content to be naked. Tom Fletcher could not believe his good fortune. He sat on a chair nearby looking at the check he had dropped on the coffee table. He was naked, but sat away from the sunlight and a slight chill ran over him producing gooseflesh on his legs. He wanted to grab the check and run, but he was patient and accommodating and went back to her body.

As a salesman for Highsmith Mobile Homes, Tom had always been their biggest producer. He wanted more than that, however, more than the modest wage and minimal commission he received, more than the pats on the back and reluctant compliments Frank Highsmith gave him periodically. He wanted to build actual homes, he wanted to make money doing it, and he wanted to be a big deal in Florence. He stood in the kitchen of the plush apartment Marcia had moved him into, stared silently at the check lying on the counter, and picked it up to again examine it. He shook his head slowly, almost in disbelief, and stuffed it into his shirt pocket.

Neal Locket looked at him almost wide-eyed, although he tried to restrain himself, tried to be professional. Neal was the assistant manager of the Florence National Bank.

"You want to cash this…you want all in cash?"

"Naw, I guess not. That would be pretty dumb wouldn't it?"

Neal nodded his head in agreement.

"Well then, let's see…how about fifty grand in cash and fifty grand in a…a…what do you call it…"

"A bank draft?"

"Yeah, that's it. What do you think about that Neal? Good way to go?"

"Well, if that's what you want…"

"No problem is there? One of your checks…Miss Dowling has the money, I assume…"

"Oh, yes, yes…"

"Well, good, let's get this taken care of right away."

"Yes, sir, right away."

After Tom left the bank, Neal called Marcia and asked if she had indeed given a check for one hundred thousand dollars to Tom Fletcher. Yes, she told him, she had and what about it. He told her it was just a formality, just making sure for her protection. She asked Neal if the bank had the money to cover the check and he assured her they did. When he told her Tom had cashed the check the line was very quiet.

Marcia called Tom's apartment and no one answered. She called Highsmith Mobile Homes and was told Tom had not come into work yet. After two days she knew what had happened. She stayed drunk for about ten days trying to get over Tom, alternately crying and raging with top-notch profanity, then settled in to hard drinking. Within the month she bumped into the husband of a friend of hers at one of her favorite restaurants and they spent the afternoon in bed. For the time being she forgot about Tom, but that would not last.

He thought about Marcia once in a while and wondered if he should have stuck around, maybe married her. Each time it came across his mind he considered the possibilities and figured he was way better off having left.

"Light changed," Stone said quietly without turning toward Tom.

"Yeah, right," Tom answered as if he had been paying attention and pulled at his ear lobe.

4.

The Lord will strengthen him on his bed of illness; You will sustain him on his sickbed. I said "Lord, be merciful to me; heal my soul, for I have sinned against You."

-Psalm 41:3-4

Heading back to the farm was exhilarating for Betty even though she had only been gone overnight. One night was enough. This was her home, where she was most comfortable, her place and her role well defined. She thought getting back here would pick up Del's spirits, too, but he seemed not to react when they pulled into the drive and headed for the house. The impact of full sunlight fell on them as they got out of the car, almost blinding, bleaching the real color out of everything. There was heavy humid heat, the kind that made sweaty clothes stick to your skin. A somewhat breeze of hot air didn't help.

Red stood by the front porch, hands at his sides, looking sheepish in his position as greeter. Jack Jeffries sat on the steps behind him. Jack had come over earlier just as a precaution to make sure Red was making out all right. Red had acted sort of surly and Jack figured Red was insulted by being checked up on, but Jack ignored him and complimented him on the good job he had done taking care of things. Red had stayed in a sour mood until the call came from Tom on his cell phone that they were on their way.

Betty went to Red as Tom and Reverend Stone helped Del out of the car.

"Thanks, Red, for seeing to everything. I...we really appreciate it."

Red smiled and blushed just a bit.

"Morning, Jack," she said, pointing her finger at him "you, sir, are a good neighbor...a great neighbor...with a great heart."

Tom leaned against the Town Car as Betty and Stone continued to help Del into the house. Del went straight away to the kitchen, sat down, and stared out the window, waiting for something. Betty followed along and began the preparations for iced tea. Stone patted Del's shoulders then leaned against the counter. This was the beginning, he thought, this was where I have to take over, make sure I can get his cooperation.

"How you feeling now, Del, now that you're home?"

Del nodded somewhat. He was seated with his arms on the table, hands together, one on top the other, limply, like a pair of cloth gloves tossed down. Two days before, these were the strong, active hands that worked this farm. Today, they had little life or energy about them. Del slowly drew his fingers into fists, not quite clenched, and smiled at Stone.

"I need to get my briefcase," Stone said, "I'll be right back."

"Stay right there, Reverend," Tom said from the doorway, "you continue your important work with Del...I'll fetch your stuff."

Tom had followed the three of them into the house and he had been trailed by neighbor Jack and finally Red. All of them had waited in the hall, an audience of wide-ranging expectations, as Del had slumped onto the chair. Tom turned quickly and was out the front door. By the time he returned to the kitchen, Del was a torrent of incomprehensible sounds, voicing nonstop with cockeyed intonation, inflection, and emphasis that made no sense.

Stone took a spiral notebook from his briefcase and began writing in his own shorthand. He used true words and phrases, but almost as a code to what he was hearing, sort of like taking notes in college when the instructor talks very fast. This interpretation would be strictly intuitive, but oddly enough, he was starting to get some sense from what Del was babbling, some feeling for the essence of what Del was communicating. Real or imagined, he was gaining some structure from the sounds like getting harmonic meaning from some piece of atonal music. It was instinctive, but Biblical passages began to readily come to him.

Betty served the tea, patted Del's shoulder, and stepped back to watch. Tom marveled at how his protégé became totally enmeshed in what Del was vocalizing, became a receiver for the message, a conduit from God. A conduit from God. Is that what was happening? Was God speaking through this man? Right now it seemed that way. Oh my, Randy, you are on a roll. You have got this thing going. Tom was delighted.

"Let us go on outside," Tom instructed, "we need to let Reverend Stone proceed with his work without any distractions."

The three of them went to the front porch.

"You think that's what's goin' on," Jack asked, "gettin' words from God on high? Don't seem hardly possible."

"That is precisely what is happening, Jack, and Sunday, in front of the whole congregation, the Word of God through Delwin Howe will be revealed. It will be a life altering experience for all of us, an exciting and important time for all of us. Reverend Stone is right now gaining access to what it is Del has to deliver from the Lord. We are very fortunate indeed to have this opportunity given to us. Make sure you tell everyone you know to be in church on Sunday…it will be a landmark time for all of us. We will all benefit immensely. Tell everyone…they need to be there."

Red stared at Tom almost dumbstruck by what he had said.

"Del's talkin' fer God?"

"Very good, Red, yes. Del is talking for God in a way. God is using Del to get his word to us. God is speaking through Del; that's why it is so hard to understand what God is saying.

That's why Reverend Stone needs to listen, hear what God has to say, then let us know what the message is."

"Wow."

"Wow is right. It's a big job for Reverend Stone."

"Well," Jack said slowly, "I think I'll head on…everything seems okay here. Call if you need anything."

"Thanks, Jack, we will."

With that, Jack got in his truck and drove away.

"I better get on to the chores," Red mumbled and was off toward the barn.

Tom walked back inside, sat down on a bench in the hallway, and listened to Del mouth meaningless syllables in a non-stop barrage. Then he stopped and they, the witnesses, were stunned, like when an alarm stops after ringing incessantly. There is shock. Is this over? Will there be more? But there was no more right now; Del had concluded this session. Stone was relieved and he sat back in his chair, perspiration running down each side of his face. Betty mopped his brow and cheeks with a cool cloth and it was the first time he realized that she was there with them. It was as if he had been in a trance, transported away from the kitchen someplace else, as if he had become part of Del. Betty sensed that something wonderful had taken place and she was sure God was right there with them.

"You are inspired," she whispered to Reverend Stone, "you have received the Word."

"Yes," he said and slumped back in his chair.

She rinsed the cloth, wrung it out carefully, and worked on his brow and the sides of his face again. Del sat there stoically, not really watching her, not moving, not perspiring, and not seeming to be in touch with what had transpired. She went to him and kissed him gently on the cheek and brow and hugged him to her. It was silent now save for the whirr of the refrigerator. Windows were closed for the air conditioning so they could not hear the birds raucous in the side yard, nor the steady drone of the power mower Red was using, nor the wind pulling half-heartedly at the trees. This quiet moment was ended when Don pushed his way through the front door.

"Nice to let someone know what is going on," he yelled, ignoring Tom. "Good thing I called the hospital…would have made a needless trip otherwise. Dad had already been checked out."

"Hello, son," Betty called.

"Hi, mom," he returned as he blustered into the kitchen. "Well, I see the main cast of characters is here…probably into their mumbo-jumbo about God and Dad's speech by now."

Reverend Stone hardly looked up at first, still so enraptured from listening to Del. Don ignored him as he had Tom.

"Don this is so important, I wish you wouldn't be so critical."

"It is important, Mom, that's why I am critical. Dad's got a problem that has to be taken care of."

"Let's try to be a little calm about this. I think Reverend Stone is doing the right thing. You'll see…this will all work out fine and your father will have made a huge contribution for our church. You don't believe in anything, Don, but we do and we believe in this…what the Reverend is doing."

"Yeah, I believe in something, Mom, I believe in science and in good medicine based on science. I don't believe in myths…"

"Please, let's not argue…

"Okay, okay, you're right," he said, holding up his hands in mock surrender, "we shouldn't argue. But keep in mind that I have hired two professionals from Ohio State to exam Dad and they will be here tomorrow morning. I insist on that."

Don put his hands on his father's slumped shoulders.

"You'll let me insist on that, won't you?"

She smiled at him. "Yes, of course."

He sat down at the table next to his father.

"Dad, I know you can't talk like you used to, but we're going to get you fixed up. Tomorrow, there will be two people coming up from Columbus…a man and a woman…they are going to check you over…maybe give you some tests. They are going to help you get this speech thing corrected. Everything will be just fine…you're going to be fine."

Del turned to look at his son, smiled, and nodded his head in a funny sort of way in agreement.

"Are you hungry?"

Del moved his head from side to side slowly and frowned.

"He got breakfast at the hospital, but I don't think he liked it."

"You'll get back on track here with Mom's cooking. A few days…bingo, good as new."

Del smiled and sipped the iced tea Betty had made for him.

"Drozo, veegit," he said, again nodding affirmatively.

"Tell me, Preacher," Don snarled at Reverend Stone, "what did he say? Now that you're the official interpreter of dad's gibberish that simple expression he just gave us should be easy for you."

"He concurs with the effects of your mother's cooking," Stone said without hesitation. "He knows he will get better, although after this morning I think he already feels recovered."

"How so?"

"He gave a powerful delivery to me of the Word of God…an emotional dispatch, full of energy that reached me, touched my Soul...came through to me clearly. I'm still stunned by the magnificence of it."

"What was it about?" Don demanded sarcastically.

"It was about redemption, Don, God's redemption. Almost immediately I knew your father was talking about adversity and God's will and God's granting of redemption...redemption for all of us should we as sinners take the right action. Come to church on Sunday, listen to how your father's message is manifested through me...with my sermon, a sermon titled, Adversity."

Don stared at Reverend Stone.

"I'll take your word for it, Rev, so don't look for me Sunday."

He patted Del's arm and stood.

"We'll be here tomorrow about ten, Mom, please have the mumbo-jumbo boys out of the way. I don't want unnecessary introductions and distractions from these professionals when they examine Dad."

He was out of the kitchen and gone before Betty could answer.

"Betty, I'm going to get some clothes and toiletries for Reverend Stone," Tom explained, "and I'll be back with those and I'll make arrangements for his car to be brought here. But I won't be here tomorrow to get in the way. I have enough to get done besides aggravating your son."

"He is forceful," Betty sighed. "Thank you for your help...your support. This is difficult."

"I'll walk you to your car," Stone said. "I need to tell you what things I need. Helen can get them together for you."

Once outside, they spoke only when they reached the car.

"What do you think?" Stone asked.

"I agree with Don…everything is going to be fine. You were fantastic in there. Just keep up the good work and I'll have it all set for Sunday. Here comes your man…I'll see you later."

Stone turned to see Del coming down the porch steps, looking the best he had since the lightening got him, walking briskly to the barn. Betty had come outside behind him, sort of trying to hold him back, but she remained on the porch shaking her head as if to say – "What about this man?"

It appeared that Del wanted to survey his farm, to walk the fields, to touch the soil, to check the crops and animals, and to stay in the fresh air. He spent several hours doing this, ignoring Betty's pleas to come inside for lunch and to get cool.

Stone used the time to work with his notes and begin to prepare his sermon, and to figure out just how he would present Del and Del's message in real time on Sunday.

Later that afternoon when Tom returned with a packed suitcase for him, Reverend Stone was walking back to the house with Betty. They had looked in on Del, who was now camped on a hay bale in the barn contemplating something they could not determine. He acknowledged them with a nod and continued staring at something out the big door, off somewhere, studying something, or maybe nothing, maybe just letting his brain rest in idle. In any case, he was still not the old Del.

"I'll go on in and get some iced tea," Betty said.

She greeted Tom and went on to the house. Keri pulled into the drive right then and Betty waved to her from the porch and went inside.

"Thanks, Tom," Stone said as he took his suitcase.

"She's not happy, Tom, better give her a call."

"Helen?"

"Helen."

"Why, what did she say?"

"Not what she said, Randy; was how she acted…unhappy…tense. I could tell, I didn't need words to let me know."

"I'll call her."

"Do that."

"It's just that I got busy here…"

"Reverend, hello." It was Keri. She had parked his car near the garage. "Is that all right," she asked, pointing to the car.

"I think so, yes, thank you."

This was not the time or place for anything other than a cursory greeting, yet she wanted to reach out to him, touch him, and put her arms around him. She controlled herself and waited for Tom's cue to leave.

"I assume," Tom said, "that you've made more progress."

"Yes, I have my sermon nicely sorted out. I'll get it written this evening and perhaps tomorrow."

"That's good, real good."

Betty appeared on the porch carrying a tray with glasses and a pitcher of iced tea.

"Come on and have some iced tea with us before you run off."

"Guess we should" Tom said to Keri, "this is a situation where we need to be sociable."

"It's not so bad here in the shade on the porch. Breeze is nice. We can go inside if you're too hot."

"No this is just fine, Betty," Tom said as he came onto the porch, "and certainly hospitable of you. Iced tea is perfect on a day like this."

He looked at the iced tea she handed him and he thought of a wonderfully good glass of Kentucky bourbon.

Streaks of daylight danced on the wall across from Stone's bed. The previous evening had been uneventful, although at one point Del tried to tell Betty something. Unsuccessful in getting her to understand him, he turned to Stone and repeated the unintelligible phrases. Stone could not help, but saved himself in the situation by turning to prayer and leading Betty and Del in thanks to the Lord for the good life they had been blessed with over the years. The manifestation of the Holy Spirit was not evident last evening and there was no communion with Del for him, no revelations.

He could hear Betty in the kitchen talking to someone he figured was Red. The other voice was so soft that he could not discern what was said or who was saying it, just the muffled sounds of speech. Not Del, he thought, got to be Red. He rose, went to the window, and looked out at the farm glowing in first light, radiating with color, awash in the dawn aura that revealed rustling leaves and fluttering flower blossoms. There was peace here, he decided, that is why the Holy Spirit can touch us.

Breakfast was a feast he was unaccustomed to in his own home.

"I'm letting Del sleep," Betty explained, "I think it's good for him. All those mornings of early rising, staying in bed is a treat, I think."

No sooner had the words gotten out of her mouth than Del came into the kitchen. He was fully dressed in his overalls and blue work shirt and appeared to be alert. Face had been washed, hair combed. Gray flannel socks covered his feet. He never wore his farming boots in the house. Stone caught his breath, tense, wondering whether Del could now speak coherently. It would certainly change things if that were the case. But his tension was quickly eased when Del tried to speak. Out came the same kinds of sounds of the past two days, quietly at first, then quickly increasing in tempo and volume. A startled look came to Del's face as he realized his normal speech had not returned. Frustration brought redness to his face; anger intensified it and gave a desperate look to his eyes.

What was going on inside that brain, Stone wondered? Unable to communicate with speech, he must feel crazed.

"Maybe he could write us a note," Red said softly, wanting to be helpful in some way.

Stone and Betty stared at him.

"I just thought…"

Oh, Red, of course," Betty yelled. "Why didn't I think of that?"

She jumped to a counter drawer, pulled out a pad of paper and a pen, and laid it on the table.

"Come on, Del, sit here and write down what you want to say…come on, sit here."

Del sat, took the pen from her, pulled the pad in front of him, and began to write. Betty, Red, and Reverend Stone stared at the pad in anticipation, hardly daring to breathe, frozen as if a spell had been cast upon them. Del pushed the pen to the paper and began moving his hand. A line drawn down, then a line out from that: an "L." They were at rapt attention to his every move. Then the pen meandered in a squiggly slant upward from the "L," continued into two loops side-by-side, squiggled sort of straight away from the loops, did several more loops, before ending with a squiggle line at the edge of the pad. This was as nonsensical as his speech. Del looked at Betty with pleading eyes, eyes near tears, a look that said everything about his disappointment and frustration. Del pushed the pen and paper away from him and slumped onto the table with his forearms. Stone sat back and relaxed.

"We'll get through this," Betty said, patting his shoulder. "Have something to eat…you need to get your strength back."

Betty served up breakfast and Red slipped quietly out the door.

"When Don comes with the two people from Ohio State, I'll go up to the bedroom and work on my sermon."

Stone could see that Del was looking at him quizzically.

"Del, two professionals are coming this morning to make some observations of you…perhaps do some testing, I don't know exactly what they will do, but Don hired them to see if they can't help get your speech back. I think it's a good idea. We need all the help we can get right now. Isn't that right, Betty?"

"Yes…it is."

"This afternoon I'd like you and I to have another chance to…to…to communicate…like we did yesterday. It's important for me to get a complete message from the Holy Spirit. If you can tolerate it."

Del shook his head in confirmation.

When he heard Don's car pull up out front, Stone went upstairs before Don could get inside.

The front door opened as if a blast of wind had shoved it wide with Don charging through like a fullback breeching a defensive line.

"Does that car out there belong to one of the hocus-pocus guys?"

"Yes, but…"

"Mom, I didn't want them around when…"

"You must be the people from Columbus that Don said were coming," Betty said, ignoring his rebuke.

"Yeah, Mom, this is Doctor Sarah White and Doctor Sid Fisher…they're on the faculty at Ohio State."

"Hello," White greeted. "Nice to meet you Mrs. Howe."

Fisher followed White into the house.

"Good to meet both of you...and this is my husband Del," she said, as Del came up beside her.

Each of the professionals shook hands with Del.

"Hi, Dad, they're going to try to make some sense out of all this."

"Where would you like to...ah...to talk to Del?" Betty asked. "The kitchen is a mess, maybe..."

"I think right here in the living room, Mrs. Howe, would be fine."

Fisher looked at White for confirmation when he said it and she nodded okay to him. So they all sat down as Del took his favorite chair. Fisher and White took seats on the sofa near him and Betty and Don went to chairs across the room.

"Let me start," Fisher opened, "by telling you that I am a PhD clinical psychologist at Ohio State University. I am on the faculty as a professor and I also have a private practice in Columbus. I have more than thirty years experience in the profession."

"And I" White continued, "am a PhD speech pathologist at Ohio State, also on the faculty, and I also consult for the Central Ohio Speech and Audiology Clinic. I have been in the profession for fifteen years."

For the next hour White and Fisher worked with Del and interviewed Betty. Betty served them coffee as they got the story of what happened to Del and they were able to observe his attempts at speech. Del gave short bursts of gibberish, punctuated with hand gestures and facial contortions as he tried unsuccessfully to make himself understood. Both took notes in the binders that each of them carried. Almost on the minute of the time an hour had passed, Fisher looked at his watch, stood up, and closed his binder. He smiled at Del, then nodded and smiled to Betty. He had concluded. White sat for a moment, closed her binder, and stood up, looking at the floor as she came to parade rest, hands behind her back, holding the binder. She waited for Fisher to speak.

I think that about does it for us. We'd like to give you" he nodded to Don, then to Betty, "some feedback. I…ah…well, ah…"

"Anything you have to say," Don interjected, "can and should be said in front of Dad."

"Yes, well…ahem," Fisher cleared his throat as he paused. "I'd like to confer with Dr. White first for a moment if you don't mind…privately. Then we can give you an assessment."

Reverend Stone, in stocking feet, had crept from the bedroom to the staircase until he was almost half-way down, listening on the stairs as a child might do to catch adult business. He now moved back up to lurk in the hallway shadows. He desperately wanted to hear what transpired.

"Why don't we go in the kitchen," Betty offered, "let these two confer…we'll have some more coffee."

After five minutes or so had passed, White and Fisher came into the kitchen where the others were seated at the table.

"Would either of you like another cup of coffee?" Betty asked.

Each declined.

"Sit down," Don requested. "Give us the word."

"It is our feeling, based on this brief observation of Mr. Howe, in a non-clinical setting of course, and without any other medical evidence or report…that Mr. Howe should return to the hospital for a CAT scan and an MRI examination." Dr White chose her words carefully. "A full cerebral and complete physiological workup is advised. This would be the best way to get a complete understanding of Mr. Howe's true condition."

"I'm not surprised," Don sputtered, "why, hell, I knew he needed some more testing...more, damn it, he didn't get any that I know of."

"That's all we can do, today," Fisher said. "Good luck, Mrs. Howe...Mr. Howe."

"I'll talk to you later Mom; I've got to take them back to the airport. We'll make arrangements for the testing."

Stone glided along the wall to the front window. He could see Don standing with the two consultants by his car. He realized they were telling him more than what they had revealed in the kitchen. Somehow he had to convince Betty to hold off on the testing, at least until after Sunday. He thought he could manage that.

"What else?" Don demanded as they approached his car.

"First of all," Fisher answered, "it's a negative to your question about speaking in tongues. Your father does not fit the characterizations of classic cases of glossolalia...not the right profile of symptoms seen in anecdotal evidence."

"Second," White went on, "we think he clearly has neurological damage at the least and perhaps other physiological damage to organs, internal tissue, and so forth. More than likely the lightning created one or more small lesions in his brain that cause the speech dysfunction."

"Recovery? Don grimaced. "What do you think about him getting better...getting his speech back?"

"Don't know at this point," Fisher shrugged, "it's hard to say. Tests will tell more, that's for sure. At this point I...well, I can't be very encouraging based on what I observed today..."

"Nor I," White concurred.

"It's very possible your father will never speak normally again." Fisher frowned as he said the words. "Let's wait and see what the tests show. A better prognosis can be made then."

Reverend Stone watched them get in the car and drive away. He had heard almost everything that had been said inside, but it was what they said out there that he wanted to know. He pushed his feet back into his shoes, grabbed his work sheets and notebook, and went back downstairs to the kitchen. Gloom hung over Betty and Del like a low-hanging cloud that was saturated and poised for rain, and was ominous, menacing, and uncontrollable. Each of them had a sense for the critical aspect of Del's condition, some innate sense that there was more to all of this than the doctors stated, more than those two professionals wanted to share, and in some measure, so awful that it could not be spoken about with either Del or Betty. But Del could not tell Betty how he felt or what he thought and she could not possibly share her terrible fears with Del. He was trapped in his condition, she caught in the self-imposed decision of protecting him. Within this tableau of emotions and desperation, Reverend Stone was a rock of salvation and strength, a light unto the world of reconciliation and contribution, a channel for understanding the purpose of life and the meaning of trusting the Lord's word. For the Lord would carry Del forward, would comfort Betty, and would give peace and eternal life to both of them. Amen.

Stone sat down again at the kitchen table across from Del. Betty also sat down. Stone spoke softly, calmly as he began his blessing of Del. Slowly, as he spoke, he picked up the pace, increased his intensity, and laid the power of God almost as a soft blanket on Del's shoulders. He avoided addressing the appearance of Don and the other two, ignored they had ever been there, which was a denial by omission of their intrusion on the Lord's work.

Del reacted almost immediately to Stone's words with sweat breaking out on his forehead and the clenching, unclenching of his fists. His eyes rolled back in his head, came back to a straight forward stare, and he unloaded a burst of sound. Those babbling, incomprehensible vocalizations came first in a high-pitched whiny tone that gradually reverted to his own baritone pattern. He picked up steam and for the next half hour raged about something no one could comprehend. A witness to this explosion could only imagine what articulation Del wanted for this outburst, what meaning he gave, what understanding he wanted. This did not matter to Reverend Stone for he, in fact, did know what Del was saying and he could not make notes fast enough to keep up with the rapid rambling and steady stream of sound that was the Word from the Holy Spirit.

When Del suddenly stopped, Stone was perspiration-soaked, reeling mentally, and barely able to continue holding his pen. He leaned back in his chair, took deep breaths to stabilize himself, and dearly wished for strength from the Lord, because he thought he might pass out from the effort.

"I believe it's clear that Del is a conduit from the Holy Spirit, Betty. I think his role is crucial for all of us. The message I am getting through Del has immense importance for our congregation, perhaps for others...for other churches, for other peoples."

"Oh, he is blessed, Reverend Stone, truly blessed..."

"Yes, he is and I'm relieved that you recognize it...glad you understand what Del's contribution might be...for all of us."

"I do...he's God's choice..."

"God' choice, yes...yes he is God's choice. And in that role we cannot take any chances with other so-called professionals poking and probing. Del needs quiet, comfortable and compassionate surroundings, and your love and caring, Betty."

"Those two that were here wanted to get Del back in the hospital for tests...MRI...CAT scan..."

"Del doesn't want that. Do you Del?"

Del shook his head "no."

Í think we should hold off on any tests, Betty. You can have Del tested in a couple of weeks if he doesn't regain normal speech, but for right now, I think we should stay right here. We have a big day ahead of us on Sunday…we need to be prepared…have Del ready to give his message to the congregation. This is a monumental time for all of us. I know the Holy Spirit is counting on us…on you and me."

After supper, Reverend Stone, Del, and Red took a walk around the farm while Betty loaded the dishwasher. During the meal, Red had talked about the destroyed John Deere sitting in the shed next to the barn, described how God-awful it looked, and how thankful he was that the lightning didn't kill Del. He went on about how he had helped Jack get the machine out of the field and into the shed, how hard it was to steer as Jack towed it with his truck, and how worried he was that they didn't tear up the field too much.

Betty finally cut him off by changing the subject to dessert and by an accentuated frown she gave him after getting his attention by giving him a light under-the-table kick. He wasn't sure what she wanted, but he did stop talking and concentrated on the wedge of berry pie Betty slid in front of him.

Red led the way for the walk, carrying on a constant one-man dialog that required no one to listen to or answer. After circling Betty's garden, marching along the long grape arbor, and winding through the orchard, Red headed for the shed with quickened pace. He was determined to show Del the tractor.

"Whaddaya think?" Red asked as he slid open the shed door. "Kind of a mess, huh?"

Del looked at the scorched green paint, ran his hands on one of the big tires, but said nothing. His eyes glazed over and he stepped back from the Deere with hands on hips. He was silent. Then he turned away and slowly walked back to the house.

"A mess, huh, Reverend?" Red wanted to get confirmed.

"It is, Red. Del's lucky."

"Yeah, Del's lucky." Red slid the door closed. "Del's lucky."

Red followed Del without noticing or caring that Stone did not come with him. Instead, Stone walked back by the grape arbor and rested on a wooden bench nearby. This was a perfect location to take in the fading light as the sun moved low to the northwest. The random sounds of grasshoppers, birds, bawling cows, snorting pigs, clucking chickens, and of a dog barking somewhere off in the distance created a familiar ambiance for him.

It was so easy to relate to this lifestyle on the farm, Stone thought. Growing up in rural Tennessee gave him the understanding for a simple life that valued basic pleasures. It was pure, fundamental, and closer to God than city folk understood. The simplicity made it possible for a clear understanding of the universe to be realized, even though no one from his home town ever talked in those terms or ever thought about their relationship to the universe. Those folks had a connection to the universe that was a given, an accepted principle that was not discussed because it was not contested or debated. Life was one with the Holy Spirit; life was a direct result of God, and the everlasting nature of things solid in their minds. They believed they were from Eternity, within Eternity, and on to Eternity. No one disputed such a gift of the Lord. Mama and Granny said it: life fulfillment does not come to us in life; it comes to us long term, in the hereafter, in the presence of God when he has chosen us to come home.

Could that be true, Stone wondered?

Like an apparition Betty was standing next to him. So deeply was he caught in his thoughts, he had not heard her approach. She handed him a cup of tea as she sat down on the bench. She did not look at him, but rather stared out at the setting sun, the long shadows that spread across the farm.

"Del is not going to get better," she said flatly, almost devoid of emotion.

"Yes, I think he will, and quickly, too. But there is a litany of revelation that must take place first. God's will must be done and God's direction through the Holy Spirit must be fulfilled. We are so privileged to be a part of this, you and I. But Satan lurks. We must beware of Satan who would stand in the way of our mission. There are those who would discount what Del will bring us, there are those who would say that we are fools, and there are those who would challenge and suggest that only science can determine things when we know that what is happening is the work of the Lord. The minions of Satan will always be nipping at our heels. We must cast them aside, hold steady to our beliefs, and bring Del to the congregation and possibly to the World.

"I'll help you," she said solemnly.

"Thank you, Betty. I felt in my heart that I could count on you. This will be my last night here. Tomorrow is Friday. I need to finalize my sermon and make preparations for Sunday. I know that I can count on you to protect Del, to nurture him, to keep him calm, to have your own peace of mind, and to get Del to the church Sunday morning.

"I will," she said with tears in her eyes, "of course I will."

5.

Your prophets have seen for you false and deceptive visions; they have not uncovered your iniquity, to bring back your captives, but have envisioned for you false prophecies and delusions.

-Lamentations 2:14

Defining the architectural features of Calvary Fundamentalist Christian Church means something quite different from the description of a classical cathedral or even a typical protestant church building. There is no apse, no nave, no traditional altar, no majestic center aisle, merely a large, open assembly area that has been designed for the presentation of speakers and well-choreographed musical productions. Basic building materials had been used, nothing fancy or austere like granite or marble or slate, just cinder block and concrete and steel. The interior finish had accents of hardwood, but it, too, had been kept simple. Banners, woven wall hangings, and a carpeted floor of soothing dark blue nylon helped give fairly decent acoustics to what was a large, yet seemingly intimate, auditorium.

There is a sound system with rock concert quality, complete with cordless microphones, stereo speakers, and a control board in the rear of what might be likened to a concert venue. Strategically positioned video cameras that feed to a master control booth which was elevated at the rear wall are also not a usual part of traditional religious ambiance.

All of these electronic marvels are features that Tom insisted were necessary for a contemporary presentation to the congregation. He said that indeed it was contemporary positioning that brought young people to their flock. A 65-member choir backs up six performing singers who are accompanied by an eight-piece instrumental ensemble. Tom described these performers as the "religious glue" that held the service together and heightened the emotional experience their parishioners had with the Holy Spirit.

The choir, singers, and musicians sat at attention, in concentrated anticipation as Tom Fletcher spoke to them about the importance of the upcoming service. Most would have preferred to have been somewhere else on this gorgeous sun-drenched Saturday, but no one was willing to forego this rehearsal for selfish pleasures or their own ego-driven pursuits. Tom had made sure that all participants in Sunday's service understood the importance of the occasion. Not a typical Sunday, not a usual service, not a time for casual approach to what was needed to accompany the revelation of a parishioner who would be speaking in tongues. This day was truly special and needed a special performance from everyone.

"People, I know that each of you has a sheet that we handed out when you came in, but I want to review it. Any questions need to be cleared up today. Remember, tape will be rolling, we will need perfection. I know, I know…we can edit, but the less editing we have to do will give greater overall strength to the presentation we want to capture. This day will be monumental for all of us. The Holy Spirit comes to life and our effort defines our congregation and offers us the opportunity to give the word of God to others. We need to be on television and you and I know that is true. It is a magnificent and worthy goal and one that we can achieve. You know that you are gifted, that you are more than good enough to be seen on a regular basis to bring the word of God to a larger audience, an audience that, in large measure, is not able or is not inclined to attend our wonderful worship services. This day…tomorrow I'm talking about people…this day is a day that will bring blessings to us and certainly bring changes for all of us. Now, let's review: first, we open at ten o'clock sharp with the choir. They set the tone for us, full, lush, and with the depth of a single voice that puts everyone in mind of why we are here. We are here to count our blessings, to bask in the light of the Lord, and to speak to God of our full commitment to him. Your voices must do that, people. Then you fade behind the voice of Mrs. Kent as she sings God's praises with the musicians' support, and all fade to Reverend Stone's appearance on stage with Delwin Howe. We move into the service, Reverend Stone offers Mr. Howe to God's notice, Reverend Stone interprets and gives his sermon, and we close with Judy and the choir. Now, people, I want the Gittle brothers to underscore Mr. Howe…and we have discussed that technique. Please read and understand the program…please memorize…memorize, memorize, because I don't want to see anyone consulting the sheets on camera. Have small cheat sheets if you need them, but please no reading so that the congregation or the viewing television audience is distracted. Does anyone have any questions?"

No one acknowledged his request. Of course there were questions, several of them, but none of the performers wanted to be recognized in that way. All wanted Tom to believe they were right with him. He knew better.

"People, there are nearly a hundred of us here practicing to have a wonderful flawless exposition tomorrow. Statistically, it is impossible for no one to have a question, which means, of course, that someone, some few, are holding back. Fess up, please."

Smatterings of laughter bounced around the hall. Davie Young spoke.

"Tom, I think we all get it…that is, your script for what should happen…and I am very sure that everyone is going to know the order of things down pat. None of this is new to us. The apprehension I have and, I don't know if I'm speaking for others, but the big unknown is Mr. Howe…what will happen, how can we spontaneously react and interact with whatever happens with him. We want that to be right, but we have no idea what to expect."

"Good point, Davie, good point. I think that Reverend Stone will ask Mr. Howe some important questions about adversity and God's will and we will hear Mr. Howe speak in tongues…we will not be able to understand what he says as he passes the Word of the Holy Spirit to us. Reverend Stone will then tell us what Mr. Howe has said and at that time you, the musicians, and the choir must be prepared to provide a backdrop that is counterpoint to this message and then its anthem. It's a little bit of improv, people, so we need to be on our toes. Take over Davie and go on with the rehearsal."

Tom Fletcher was a showman at heart. There is some gene, yet undiscovered, that differentiates men like Tom, who want to orchestrate the talents, actions, motivations, and performance of others. No realm of exhibitionism for them, no sir, they want some other kind of satisfaction. They achieve some secret, contained satisfaction that comes from knowing that they brought a presentation forward to an audience that gave its approval. And the approval is really theirs. The applause, the credit, the accolades can be privately relished in a way that is outside of anyone else's enjoyment or contribution. They are strictly alone in the venture, it is theirs and it is part of the essence of who they are. They are master controllers in a world where everyone strives for control.

Tom sat down next to Keri, who was making notes for him.

"How's he doing?"

Keri was startled by Tom's question, since he had never asked her something like that before. In fact, he rarely spoke to her. Most often, he communicated to her through hand written notes and typed memos he dictated to his secretary at his office. Other directives, suggestions, and requests came from Stone, but she knew they originated with Tom.

"Tired…exhausted is more like it. He had several sessions with Del Howe that were very demanding. And he…he had a session with Helen. She feels left out…wants more of his time…wants him to be with the kids more. If this thing works out she's going to be crushed…she'll never see him then.

"Works out?" Tom raised his eyebrows when he spoke.

"Sure. Other congregations are going to want to hear Del Howe and Rand...Reverend Stone. That means traveling to other churches, more preaching, maybe even a tour as guest minister. That means a lot of time-consuming preparations, arrangements, travel, and sermon writing. The message has to change, it can't stay the same. I'd say all of that would be a problem for Helen."

"Sounds like you've got it all scoped out. And here I thought all along that I was the business manager for the congregation. Low and behold, it's really you with all the big ideas."

Oh no, Mr. Fletcher, I didn't mean anything by..."

"No, that's all right, little darlin', I know full well you have only the best of intentions with your ideas. You only want the best for Reverend Stone. You're looking out for him, I know it."

"Yes, yes, of course, and I..."

"Tell me, is that the scenario our minister has for himself or is that your idea of what might happen?"

He did not wait for her answer.

"Davie," Tom yelled to the music director, interrupting the song the musicians were rehearsing. "Do you think you need more brass...be a little more triumphant? Or would that be overkill for what we want to accomplish?"

Davie Young walked back to where Tom and Keri were seated before he responded.

"Tom, I think we have the right blend. I don't think we want to overwhelm Mr. Howe or crowd out Reverend Stone's sermon. If I understand you, those two will be quite dramatic and I think we should let the drama carry itself. I think we're a supporting cast rather than a pump-up situation."

"Okay, it was just a thought. You know best."

Young went back to the musicians and they resumed their playing.

"It's what I thought might happen," she said. "This is going to be big and I…"

"Okay, good."

He cut her off and she did not pursue it. She looked at him, only turning her head slightly. He was not paying any attention to her, but was intent on the performers at work in front of him. He was smiling, she noted, bobbing his head in time with the reverberation that came from the talent. He was in his own world with this, she figured, his own ego trip as master puppeteer of this mass of people. He was tenacious, contentedly tenacious with his grip on these performers, and he enjoyed his power just by watching and listening to them. She was impressed as she had not been before of this man's talent for directing the success of this congregation. He was a master of detail, he was involved with all aspects of what went on, and he made judgments on all that transpired. She would not soon forget this moment. It was when she realized she finally understood his command of her world. What would he do about Randy and her? Did he even care? Could he, would he, put an end to her relationship with Reverend Stone? She would be on guard for the first signs of that happening to her. She would be prepared.

Helen Stone had been crying quietly for almost a half hour. She was seated on the edge of their bed and had not yet gotten dressed. She wiped her eyes on the sleeve of her nightgown.

"Why are you crying?" Stone asked softly.

"I don't know."

"Then why cry?"

"I feel sad."

"About what?"

"About…"

"Yes...about. And?"

"About...about...about. You know I feel like you are badgering me...grilling me and its...it's...its angering me. Why should I have to tell you...why should I have to explain myself. I'm crying because I...I feel lousy. That's why I'm crying."

Stone sat down in the chair across the room and waited. There was no consoling her; he had tried that now for going on forty minutes. He wondered what she was thinking, what had prompted this breakdown of crying. Certainly there had been more reasons in the past for this kind of tear shedding, so he could not imagine what the reason was this morning. And why would it be this morning? She knew where he was, what he was doing with Del. Of course he had to be there with the man. Couldn't she understand that?

"Can I help...or should I go away? I have a lot to do to get ready for tomorrow...I'm pretty well set for it so I can stay with you for awhile if you like, but I don't see any sense in it if you are just going to keep crying or you want me to leave. Where are we on this? Please let me know."

"You can't help. I'll be fine...fine as I ever am. Do you know what that means?"

"Well, I think..."

"You think...hah...you think about you. I am raising three children in case you forgot. Shelby...she's eight...she has a birthday soon. Remember her? Madison...she's five and Brent is two and hardly knows who you are. Yes, I'm fine...slowly losing my mind. I want a husband back...and your children need a father. That's what it means."

"When we get this whole situation with Del Howe taken care of...under control...things will get back to normal...I promise."

He came to the bed and touched her shoulder. It wasn't a loving touch, but rather a point of contact to make a point that would some how absolve him for the real and perceived wrongs he had made her suffer.

"Please…please just go do what you have to do. Please, at some point, come back here and uphold your responsibility."

He withdrew his hand.

"I will. Don't worry…there's nothing to worry about. I'll be back later."

The main worship center for Calvary Fundamentalist Christian Church was designed much like a covered, enclosed amphitheater. The structure spread round in a semi-circle and rose in a steady incline from where a central mahogany dais stood; a magnificent piece of carpentry, beautifully stained and polished. A matching wooden cross twelve feet tall was suspended from the ceiling above the dais. More than six hundred worshipers could be comfortably seated in cushioned theater seats. A tiered circular section directly behind the dais was where the sixty-five voice choir was stationed. The eight instrumental musicians were positioned to the left of the dais in a prominent location clearly visible to the entire congregation. Near them sat the six vocalists who would perform. To the right of the dais was seating for Reverend Stone and any guests such as Del Howe. The combination of good acoustics and strategically placed speakers meant that everyone in the church could readily hear what transpired.

The ten o'clock service was full almost an hour before it was to start. The excited buzz of conversation about Del droned heavily from the parishioner's anticipation. Just before ten, Helen entered from the side and took her seat in the front row. A hush gradually came to the crowd. They were ready; they were waiting for the service in heightened attention. Then, on cue, Betty, Red, daughter Dorothy and husband Jerry, and Jack Jeffries came into the center and sat next to Helen.

The choir began its opening moment, softly singing "Christ, Revealed in Me," gradually building to the point where Judy Darby Kent took over as soloist and in the background they hummed the melody. Judy was a gorgeous and glorious soprano who was known in religious circles throughout northwestern Ohio. Her voice was carried through Tom's electronic amplification to the far corners of the center, but she would have achieved this without being miked. Hear me, Oh Lord.

> Christ/revealed/in/me
>
> Can/I/answer/his/call?
>
> What/lesson/should/I/see?
>
> How/can/I/stand/tall?
>
> Christ/is/my/Lord
>
> He/points/the/way
>
> I/know/his/word
>
> I/know/what/he'd/say.

She sang exquisitely with the restrained power she was capable of displaying. As she sang the third and fourth verses, Reverend Stone and Del entered from the right side of the dais and sat down. Reverend Stone was in his usual place and Del next to him. Judy finished, the choir humming gradually diminished to nothing, and Stone let the entire scenario fall to silence, except for a cough or two and the buzz of the electronics. He rose, walked to the center of the dais with his Bible in his left hand, raised both arms, and after a short pause, spoke.

"Lord…Lord…Amen."

"Amen," all said.

"Christ is revealed in all of us. Amen."

"Amen," all said.

"Christ is my Lord."

"Amen," all said.

"We have an obligation to deal with life as it is presented to us."

"Amen," all said.

"We have an obligation to take advantage of every opportunity the Lord presents to us."

"Amen," all said.

"We have an obligation to listen when he speaks to us no matter what kind of voice, no matter how the message is sent to us, and no matter how difficult it may seem that his voice is heard. There are mysterious ways for his message to come to us. There are strange and unfathomable channels to bring the Word of God to all of us. But sinners know that God has not forsaken them, that he constantly gives direction for our lives, direction to help us achieve eternal life...a message of redemption, a message of joy, and a clear voice that we have been claimed for him, that we may reach eternal salvation through him."

"Amen," the congregation rejoiced.

"This is truly a great day for all of us, for we shall be witness to the unfathomable, the misunderstood, and the often misrepresented voice of God that is a gift. From the eternal universe that is God's pavilion to the earthly monuments of man, nothing prevails like the word of God. It is written in First Corinthians, Fourteen, Verse Six: "But now brethren, if I come to you speaking with tongues, what shall I profit you unless I speak to you either by revelation, by knowledge, by prophesying, or by teaching?"

Scattered "Amens" wafted forward from the assembled, a murmur of suspended apprehension for what they thought was awaiting them. Reverend Stone closed his eyes and held his Bible to his throat. He continued.

"This is also a special day for Del Howe...a man who has been a member of this congregation for as far back as any of you can remember. He is here for a purpose…my guest before you on this platform…God's witness to life, for he has been spared death, he has been allowed by God to live through terrible circumstances, and to be the embodiment of life for all of us. Proof of faith, proof of belief in God, and proof in God's overriding protection in time of great stress. That is not to say that Del was totally able to withstand powerful forces. He was not. But with God's help he eluded death and he became, therefore, an instrument of the Holy Spirit."

Reverend Stone turned toward Del and motioned to him to rise and come to the center of the dais. Del complied, and to Betty's way of thinking as she watched, and Tom's also from the rear of the worship center, with an alacrity and positive manner not seen in him since the accident. He was motivated. His stride was almost a bounce as he moved to Stone's side. Even Reverend Stone was somewhat shocked by this display.

Del stood poised at attention, ready to come forth with his sounds. In his gray suit, modest striped tie, and starched white shirt, he made a good impression on everyone. A far cry from the dust covered farmer in denim overalls. Betty was pleased with the way he looked next to Reverend Stone. She had made sure he was dressed the way Tom had instructed when he phoned her on Saturday. Tom left little to chance.

"Praise the Lord, Delwin Howe…praise God."

"Praise God," a few echoed.

Del stared into space above the heads of the congregation gathering himself for his response.

"Meesure," he began, "bazee."

"Praise the Lord," Reverend Stone exclaimed, "God's message is begun."

The sounds of gibberish flowed from Del for the next fifteen minutes with little prompting from Reverend Stone. Intonation went up and down, volume increased and decreased, then increased as Del seemed to race to a conclusion with a flourish. His face was ruddy, the sweat on his head and face shined in the bright lights that accentuated his presence. It was a stunning performance, an exhibition so powerful that the congregation was dumbstruck for several moments after he finished. Finally, a woman in the fourth row to the right of Del stood and cried out.

"Praise the Lord…praise you Del Howe. I give thanks for the Word."

"Praise the Lord" and "Hallelujah" came from a sprinkling of others who also stood. Soon everyone was standing.

Davie Young knew that this was the time to improvise and gave the cue to the musicians who started playing, "What A Friend We Have In Jesus," with the four Gittle brothers singing the words. By the third line the choir had joined.

Reverend Stone, with quick thinking, stepped off the dais and came to Betty. He took her hand, escorted her to where Del was still standing in a stupor, linked her arm with his, and ushered them to seats at the side of the dais. When the hymn finished, he motioned the parishioners to be seated. Many were in tears, others continued to quietly say the words "Praise the Lord" out loud.

Reverend Stone spent the next thirty minutes or so revealing the message that Del had brought to them this day. It was a message of hope, temptation, sacrifice, admonition, and redemption. He then based his sermon, which he always called his "lesson for living," on adversity as being part of God's plan, how the challenge of adversity can and must be met with the help of the Holy Spirit, how sacrifices in God's name were so vital, how resisting temptation was crucial, and how adhering to God's plan was the way to God's promise of eternal life.

Tom thought Reverend Stone had been brilliant. The interpretation held the congregation mesmerized and building the homily on the interpretation was a stroke of genius. And, he noted for himself, it had all been captured on video.

The rest of the service was anti-climactic. Songs were song by the choir, the Gittle brothers, and Davie Young; verses read from the Bible, a prayer was read by Deacon Albert Connors, and the benediction given by Reverend Stone in a way that again made some folks weep. Everyone was thrilled, uplifted, and exhausted. Few wanted to leave the worship center and milled about in animated conversation about how wonderful the Reverend was today. Most stayed because they wanted to talk to Reverend Stone, others wanted to meet and talk to Del, although they had already learned through the whisper circuit that he could not really talk to anyone. Too embarrassing to try to deal with Del, they figured, and they didn't want to make Betty feel badly.

By the time the last of the lingering crowd had finally exited, Tom, Craig Stevens his video man, and Bo Anders his sound man, were already at work in the post production studio in the basement. Craig had used three cameras with his two assistants to capture the entire service on tape. Anders had recorded all the sound of the event in stereo from numerous microphones, each having its own recording track. This was a sophisticated and dedicated operation that Tom had created. It was meant for a moment just like today and they had been ready.

Carefully, Tom and the other two built the production through painstaking editing. Tom had the heart of a producer and the mind of an artistic director. He knew what he wanted, he was incisive in decisions of what camera angle he wanted to use and which shot he thought best blended or cut to the next, yet worked with the other two men in a loose, give-and-take manner without being authoritarian. He knew full well how talented each of them was. Craig and Bo had their own ideas about what to use, so the bantering, debate, and discussions of reasons why filled the room.

"Look at her," Craig almost yelled, as they watched the main editing monitor, "Larry got that shot...see the tears welling up...there...there, right there, she busts out in full tears. Man, that is great stuff."

"We're real lucky...real lucky," Tom offered. "Having that third camera to catch the crowd was important for us, boys."

"Stoke of genius for you, Tom," Bo said. "It'll give this thing a real look of quality."

"That's what we want, boys...that's what we need. Got to have a broadcast look and feel. I think we're getting there."

"What do you think about a split screen with Del going full tilt in the largest section and then showing the Reverend in deep concentration...above and to the right? We've got terrific cover shots of him with the Bible to his head, eyes closed, absorbing what Del is trying to tell him."

"Not a bad idea," Tom decided.

It took a little over four hours to put all of the pieces together in a way that met with their mutual satisfaction. The final edited version resulted in a running time of one hour. Using all of the digital technology at their command they created an inspiring visual opening for the video with highly charged music to create greater emotional stimulation. The video ended with scenes of those in the congregation weeping as the inspiring sound of the choir and the Gittle brothers could be heard, and made a slow dissolve to Reverend Stone, eyes closed, face turned to heaven, having just given the benediction. It was a masterpiece as far as Tom was concerned.

"This is real nice, Tom," Bo said as he slid the finished video in a case, "but what are we going to do with it? We've been shooting the Reverend for weeks now and never put in an effort like today. 'Course we never had Del Howe before."

"Right you are, Mr. Anders, everything before this was just dress rehearsal for today. Today was the show."

Tom didn't go any father. Bo and Craig looked at him, waiting for an answer.

"You guys will find out soon enough, but…here's the deal…this tape is going to further our ministry and place Reverend Stone where he belongs…in front of a larger audience."

"Get the Reverend on TV?" Craig blurted.

"Let's just say we ought to make the effort…and that's all I'm going to say right now…"

"Wow," Bo said.

"Let's just keep this quiet until I can accomplish a few things…okay?"

"You bet," Craig agreed.

"Yeah," Bo concurred, "you can count on us to keep it quiet until you announce something."

"Thanks, boys."

Tom had a clear purpose for producing such a video tape, one he had not yet shared with anyone else, not even Stone, until he gave the hint to the two men. This was his little secret, part of his agenda for advancing Stone's career, and, of course, his own. This was an audition tape and tomorrow it would be in the mail to Christian Gospel Broadcasting. This tape was their ticket for bigger things. Thank you, Lord, for Del. He is the frosting.

Reverend Stone drove Betty, Del, and Red out to the Howe farm. Del sat in the passenger seat next to Stone, Betty and Red in the rear seat. They had hardly gotten out of the church parking lot when Del let his head fall back against the head rest and he went sound asleep. Betty patted his shoulder.

"I am so proud of Del," she said, her voice quivering with feelings of reverence and respect. "He was able to bring the Word of the Lord to everyone there…it was wonderful."

"Betty, you have so much to be proud of…and there may be more…there may be other chances for Del to get the word out."

"What do you mean?"

"Del has so much to give…it…it…I think his contribution did not end today. He has more to give for us."

Betty fell silent trying to figure out what that would mean for her and for Del. She assessed that it would not be good for the two of them. They had the farm, they were responsible for Red, and besides there was a whole world of need that had to be addressed. She wondered if she had the strength to deal with all of the things she conjured up in her mind in regard to this whole issue not ending today. She was woefully inept in being prepared for what was to occur, what was to be the circumstance of their life as Del was featured as part of a divine revelation. She was to be merely an enabler for what was to transpire and she didn't know that yet.

"He had quite a workout, Reverend."

"Yes, he did, Betty, and he was marvelous. We were all thrilled. It was a privilege for me to have been able to bring the Word of the Holy Spirit to life through Del…and you should be proud of him."

"I am…truly I am."

As Reverend Stone's car approached the Howe farm house, they could see someone standing on the porch. It was Don. He was pacing like a caged animal, but only Betty and Stone understood they had to brace themselves for his onslaught. Del and Red were unaware there would be a confrontation.

"I suppose he's a big religious star about now," Don scoffed loudly, "I'm sure you used him in your service today. I bet he was spectacular with his nonsensical babbling. I bet you used his gibberish to your benefit…oh, oh, wait a minute…to the benefit of the Lord. Yes, the Lord will take credit…you are merely the instrument of the Lord…ready to make sense from what doesn't make sense."

"Don, this means a great deal to…" Betty started to offer.

"I know…I know…but it means something to me as well, Mom. This is my father…I have more than a passing interest in his condition, how he is treated medically, and how he recovers from the lightning strike. No, of course, it is not a religious thing to me…it is a medical issue. You and the Reverend want to keep it a religious thing…it is not…it is medical. His condition must be evaluated medically, not by the church…your church. We've got to get him in for an MRI and CAT scan tomorrow."

This contentious conversation took place as they had walked from Stone's car, where Don took after his mother, to the front porch of the house. Red was embarrassed by the words and ideas he did not understand and headed for the barn. He could escape; he could get away from Don's accusations and recriminations. Betty and Del, on the other hand, stood there accepting the verbal pummeling Don administered. The look on Del's face almost seemed to indicate that he understood what Don was ranting. Reverend Stone would have none of it.

"You have done nothing since you came to the hospital until right now but criticize, complain, disregard, denigrate, and mock our religious beliefs, our convictions, and our pursuit of the Holy Word. That shall not stand with us…your mockery is a vestige of the Devil, a manifestation of how evil preys on the unsuspecting, and how the non-believer can attempt to make Believers feel they have done something wrong. Well, we have not done wrong…you have done wrong by indicting us…by trying to diminish the nobility of our purpose, and by slandering the Holy Spirit, the Word of God, and God himself. Truly the work of Satan, truly the work of a Devil who wants to take away hope, charity, and the good works provided in real lives. You, Don, are a true apparition of Evil and you can not, you will not hold us back from our mission with your father. The Lord has spoken through him today…you will not reverse that. You will not stop our cause. A cause that we have in the name of Jesus Christ."

"I want my father…" Don started, but was cut off by Betty.

"Your father is my husband and my responsibility. I will decide what happens and I want my husband to help Reverend Stone in every way possible in bringing the Word of the Holy Spirit to our people. You will not stop that. I know all about these medical things…tests, procedures, time in the hospital while people poke and probe and treat your father as if he were a side of beef that we were having butchered for us. He is not a side of beef…he is a man…a man who is now giving his life to God. God spared his life…there is a payback; there is a way to return that blessing. It is our sacrifice to our God and I will make that sacrifice with him. And you, son, will not interfere."

Reverend Stone was certainly gratified by Betty's renouncing Don's attempts at directing Del back to the hospital. This meant that plans could be made to have Del visit other churches, to let others hear his message. It meant he was fully in control of Del and Betty.

Without another word, Don stomped off to his car, muttering, and shaking his head, and drove quickly away from the farm.

Betty had steeled herself for that confrontation. Her chin jutted out in silent defiance as she watched Don leave. She wheeled around, went into the house, and started lunch preparation. Stone and Del settled on the front porch.

"Betty knows what's best," Stone said as they got comfortable in the cushioned chairs.

Del nodded, but Stone didn't see him, he was watching Don's car as it disappeared down the road.

She served iced tea, called Red in from somewhere, and they had lunch that was as filling as a dinner. Fried chicken, mashed potatoes, green beans, lettuce and tomato salad, fresh bread, and chocolate cake baked the previous day. It was as delicious as it was bountiful. Red went off again to do something that would get him away from the tension he felt in the other three, Betty made sure Del rested in their bed, and she and Stone went back on the front porch.

"I know there is more to do," she said.

"Yes, there is."

"I'll help as best I can."

"Yes, I know you will. I respect and appreciate that. I know that you realize that the Word of the Holy Spirit is too important to let fade away to nothing."

As the warm afternoon took Reverend Stone into a stupor, Betty went back inside to clean the kitchen, and bake a pie she had intended. She felt released from Don, yet felt guilty about it at the same time. How could this be? She was confused. Perhaps when Reverend Stone woke up they could discuss this matter.

She had worked in her kitchen and waited as Stone dozed and then, suddenly, Tom's big car rolled up in front of the house. She watched as he came toward the porch, saw that he recognized Reverend Stone napping, wondered what he would do.

Tom said nothing, eased into another chair, and waited. She came to the front door and spoke to him softly.

"Iced tea?"

"That would be nice, Betty."

6.

Let another man praise you, and not your own mouth; a stranger, and not your own lips.

-Proverbs 27:2

The next day, Monday, the phone was a persistent intrusion on Keri's usual routine in the church office. In fact, it was ringing when she unlocked the office door shortly after nine. Her scribbled phone messages were piling up when Reverend Stone appeared just before ten. She was talking to the Pastor of Stony Ridge Baptist Church in Lima when he entered. She had seen him out of the corner of her eye, but almost immediately he was gone. The next she knew, he was behind her, nuzzling her neck, nibbling her ear. He kissed her cheek and ran his hand over her arm to her breast and gently felt for the nipple. It was nearly unbearable for her to retain her composure as she took the Pastor's message. He too wanted Reverend Stone to call, he too had heard of the parishioner who spoke in tongues, and he too wanted that man and the Reverend to visit his congregation. It seemed forever until the phone call could get completed.

She could feel the warmth of his kiss, the sensations from her breast, and she desperately wanted more. He had not come to her apartment last night as she had wanted and he had not called. Her loneliness and yearning had fueled anger and resentment when he didn't show and didn't call. She felt resentment that she knew she had no right to feel, loneliness she knew was of her own making, but both justified within the reality she wanted for herself. She was the "other woman," on the outside looking in, excluded except for special occasions when they could sneak time together. It was an open-ended deal, because she had no idea when the situation might change. He was what she wanted, she thought, he was worth the wait. The excitement with him was real and the pleasure exquisite, and he made her feel like a person, someone worthwhile. Worthwhile, how? How could it be, cheating with a man of God, a minister? It was a contradiction she could not resolve and did not even want to consider.

"Yes, I'll certainly let him know you called, Pastor…I've written it down, I'll give it to him as soon as he arrives. Thank you…good-by."

As she hung up, he moved away, to the other side of her desk.

"I thought I heard someone," he lied.

She turned her head somewhat in a move to check the possibility. There was no sound; there was no one else but the two of them in the complex. Maintenance man Ned Schuster had not arrived.

"You didn't show up…you didn't call," she said flatly, trying to stay composed, knowing full well he understood what she meant.

"I stayed late at Howe's…I had to…"

"I know, I know…you always have a good reason."

"I'm glad you didn't use the word "excuse," that would make me feel badly."

"Oh, my, fancy that."

She tried to grin at him, but it came off as more of a smirk.

"Would it count for something if I told you I missed you?"

"It would count for something if you came back here and continued what you were doing."

He walked around the desk, bent down, took her face in his hands, and kissed her full on the mouth. She cradled his head with one hand and reached for his crotch with the other. He could sense her movement and retreated just as her finger tips touched him.

"When?" she asked.

"Soon," he answered in his best, most soothing manner, conveying in one word enough sensuality and caring so that she could be content with the anticipation.

The number of calls that had come in overwhelmed Stone as he sifted through the notes Keri gave him. Fourteen phone messages, all congratulatory, several requesting a chance to schedule Del and him in their church. Tom had accurately predicted that news of Del would spread quickly, although most likely he would not have guessed how quickly. For many in the congregation, seeing the Word of the Holy Spirit passed from Del to Reverend Stone was a miracle and they had to tell others what they had witnessed.

Most interesting of the messages, perhaps, was the one from a Bob Saunders, who told Keri he was a reporter for the Swanton Times, and wanted to interview Reverend Stone. Stone vaguely remembered Saunders as the young man who interviewed him when he first took over his assignment with the church. Publicity was certainly important, part of Tom's domain. Tom would also want to know about the personal appearance requests. Stone got him on his cell phone.

"You won't believe what is happening," Stone teased.

"Try me, Reverend."

"Fourteen calls about Del, congratulations from all of them, some ministers, some lay people…and…get this: four requests to bring Del to their church. They want to share in the miracle."

"I'm in my car right now…I'll be there in two minutes."

True to his word, it seemed only moments before Tom charged into the church office. The phone was ringing again.

"Let's have a look," Tom said eagerly.

"Look at this one first."

Stone handed Tom the note about Bob Saunders. He read it with raised eyebrows and whistled approval.

"This will help."

"I'll get him in here right away…"

"Yeah, but let me check my planner. I want to be part of the interview. Let's see here…yes…yes, tomorrow is good around ten thirty."

Stone walked from his office with the Saunders note to Keri's office across the hall.

"Keri, would you get hold of this Saunders guy…see if he can meet with us tomorrow? Ten thirty would be good."

Tom was in Stone's chair behind his desk when Stone returned to his office, so he sat nearby in one of the upholstered guest chairs arranged around the room. Tom propped one leg on the desk and proceeded to go through the rest of the messages.

"This is good…very good. We'll have to get a tour arranged, get the word out…this Bob guy can help. It all works in our favor. Supports the other endeavor I believe we will be embarking upon in due course, Reverend Stone, something that will bring your ministry to national attention…"

"We need to talk to Betty first," Stone advised, not picking up on the real implications of Tom's remark.

"No, we set the tour first, then we get to her and explain…you will explain…how important this mission is for delivering the Word of the Holy Spirit to those who need and want to hear Del…and you, of course."

"I think she'll agree, she believes in what is happening. And I'd like to get daughter Dorothy involved somehow."

Oh, I think she'll agree, all right…she trusts you, Reverend…and that's probably a good idea about the daughter. Anyway, I have to run…I'll get with you later…something else I want to share with you…this is all good stuff...we're on a roll. Thank you, Lord, and praise God. Have Keri get you scheduled in these churches...mid week...make them special services...save Sunday for us...compress the four appearances into less than two weeks. And remind the dear Pastors that we have expenses to cover."

Keri could hear his directions for her and grimaced. She did not like getting assignments from Tom.

"We probably will have other fish to fry," Tom called as he left, "tell you about it later."

The whirlwind insurance executive was gone as quickly as he had blown into their morning.

Keri had little trouble scheduling what Tom wanted although it took her most of the rest of the day: the four church appearances she arranged within the next ten days and Bob Saunders at Tuesday morning ten thirty. Early that afternoon, Stone reached Dorothy Price, the Howe's daughter, and had little difficulty enlisting her assistance. He wasn't sure what Tom had in mind, so he was somewhat nebulous in describing to her what she would be doing. Without knowing what else to do, he asked her to meet with him and Tom for a planning meeting the next afternoon, to which she agreed.

This was all moving very quickly, Stone thought, quicker than I might have realized. Perhaps Tom is not correct about contacting Betty. Dorothy will surely call her. It would be better, he decided, if he were to talk to Betty right away. He called the Howe farm and talked to Betty at length, describing what the outside reaction had been, the invitations, the plans for the tour, and the help Dorothy would give. She needed to give her permission and support for Del who would be the centerpiece for the arrangements.

"Would Dorothy be with him, too?" she asked.

"That would be our wish," Reverend Stone said solemnly. "She would provide emotional support to him; make it easier for him to handle the travel and the new people we will be meeting. Several of our staff will be with us, of course, but it would be best to have one of his own by his side...and I know, Betty, that you feel a responsibility to the farm...to Red. And Del will be home every night...with you, safe and secure. Certainly, we would like you to be with us if Red can handle things on the days we're gone, but if not, we understand your decision."

"Well, yes, I do have to watch over the farm...and poor Red...we hate to put him in a position where he feels the stress of responsibility...one overnight was almost too much for him. But he should be able to handle this...its not forever and I do want to be with Del. I think Red can cope...besides Jack can watch over him."

After some deliberation within herself, she agreed, telling Stone how important she knew this was for everyone and how much she wanted to be by Del's side and to have Dorothy with them. God's work, she explained to him, was of the highest priority. All of life needed to be prioritized, she contended, this was the only way things got accomplished. When people complained that they could not get things done, she knew it was because they did not set priorities. God should be at the top of the list, staying in touch with the Holy Spirit a major effort in everyone's lives.

Reverend Stone waited patiently while Betty spoke at length of her connection to God and God's promise of eternal life. She spoke almost as if she had forgotten that she was in a telephone conversation with him, but rather engaged in a monologue presenting her beliefs to the world at large. He heard many of the words and phrases coming back to him that he had used in sermons. Even so, she was indeed quite eloquent and he found himself suddenly taking notes as if she were an instructor in the seminary. She provided him with some excellent material for the sermon he would use in one of his "lessons" on the upcoming tour.

Keri brought lunch in for them so they could keep working, keep responding to the continuing phone calls, and by the end of the day things were well in place for the round of appearances. The interview with Bob would be the next hurdle. In the meantime, there was Keri to consider. He called Helen to tell her he would be late. She whimpered somewhat in saying it was okay, but pled for him to be home as soon as he could. He said good night to Keri, left the church, drove to Keri's apartment and let himself in with his key, and waited. He passed the time watching the TV news just to see if yesterday's service was reported. It was not.

Standing in the living room of the apartment, rocking on the balls of his feet, nervously waiting, edgy, Stone suddenly caught his reflection in the large round mirror on the side wall. It took him off guard, almost as if someone else had entered the room, some stranger he did not recognize. Who is that man standing there, he thought, what does he want? Can it be? Do I look like that, a man wondering what it all means? Mirror, mirror on the wall, who is the best Christian of them all? Certainly not I. Oh, my no, but I am not bad…not evil…not sinful. The Commandments are sacred words from the Old Testament adhered to by me save one. I hold the Lord, thy God as one God without false witness to any other God or to any worldly image. I take not the name of the Lord in vain, my life is the essence of Sabbath sanctity, I have revered my parents, and I am against all killing, killing of any kind even in the name of the law. I have never stolen or told lies about any one. I covet nothing, am jealous of no one, and I am not perfect. I am a man…a mere mortal trying his best. But I cannot escape the title of adulterer. That Commandment I have broken. It has been the one I could not live up to, my failure. It is not an excuse, but I am a man. In other cultures, with other religions, men have more than one woman. It is accepted, it is expected. How can that be within the bounds of virtue for them and yet wrong for me? What is my crime, oh Lord, what is my sin? Have I failed you?

Reverend Stone was stalked by the continuing dread of not being perfect as a man of God, while knowing full well that man is not perfect, and he was haunted by the clear understanding of which Commandment he has desecrated. He was trapped in the conflict of ministering the Faith with conviction for his work, realizing his failing, and not quite being able to accept his condition. His denial was his undoing for peace within himself for his work, work which should have given him great satisfaction. As good as he was at what he did, there was a hollowness for him to the attendant reward. Was God with him? He reconciled himself with the belief that the Lord on high was a good and gracious God who would understand his position and accept his condition. He knew full well such reconciliation would not play well with most Christians.

The sound of Keri's key being slid into the front door lock startled him. He saw himself in the glass again, showing the wide eyes, desperate looking as a criminal caught red-handed, shocked at being discovered, and knowing precisely that he had revealed himself to himself.

Her closeness, her smell, her sweet physical beauty, washed away all thoughts of his conflict with God. His debate with himself for his conduct within the Lord's realm was quickly dismissed, and she became tantamount to the false image he knew not to worship. So now it was two commandments, although he only believed it was one that he disobeyed.

She came for him almost savagely, intent on his body, insistent on a physically passionate sexual connection to him. He was overmatched in desire and intensity, overwhelmed by her unabashed primal heat. God was a concept of goodness, she was the reality of great passion. Her lips pulled at his as she began to undress him. Patient at this juncture, she did not rip off buttons or tear cloth, but rather systematically got his clothes off of him. She was still fully dressed.

Stone slipped away from her grasp onto the sofa, sprawled somewhat, on his back. He was not pulling away from her, on the contrary, he was allowing himself to be stripped of his clothes, but she lost her grip on his naked waist and she could not counter his weight.

Soon he was on top of her and his full weight pressed her hips to her bed. It was if they were in some wrestling match and he had made a reverse move to be on top, point scored. A reversal she wanted, a point she was willing to concede. Technically, she was losing at wrestling, practically she was winning at sex. His penetration, their connection was born of mutual lust, mutual longing for some unattainable satisfaction that neither could describe nor direct to the other. Mutual, temporary satisfaction was all they had; it would have to do for them.

His full weight now pressed her entire body to the bed. She had been pinned to the mat, accepted the defeat as she understood victory and relished the feeling of his body against hers. Her breasts smashed flat, his head buried in the pillow next to hers, his hips against hers, his legs hot and sweaty, tight to her legs; this was an element of oneness that she wanted. That he was married meant nothing to her, that he was at the right hand of God meant a lot to her. She overlooked his marriage as he overlooked or disregarded adultery. Her reasoning explained to her the importance of committing intimacy with this man who stood close to the Lord, understood the voice of the Holy Spirit, evoked goodness, and challenged the Devil that would have been in the minds of his parishioners were they aware of this transgression. To her, he was a perfect man, a man she wanted, who towered over other men, and a man who understood her needs and made a place for her in the world. She was content with their relationship at this point, believing full well that it would change sooner rather than later, and that he and she would, at some not-to-distant future, be united in life circumstance. She had no doubts about this.

Reverend Stone slipped gingerly into the steaming hot water of Keri's bathtub. He let himself slide down so that the water covered him almost to his neck. He was being cooked like a lobster, his skin turning ruddy. She came into the bathroom and stood over him naked, voluptuous, desirable, somehow looking vulnerable when he knew she wasn't. As she made the move to climb into the tub with him he held up his hand as if in benediction, but meant to stop her progress, and she understood. She smiled, unoffended, and backed away to put on her robe. He needed to be in that water alone, to wash away the smell of passion, remove the odor of her that might otherwise cling to him, to feel clean again as if this bath could baptize him so that he were reclaimed from sin, a renewed apostle, and cleanse his mind and soul as much as his body.

Keri waited for him in the bedroom and she watched intently as he dressed. She was consumed with this man, but she was able to temper that intensity with carefully controlled discipline. There was the control she had over herself, she realized, when there was no control over the situation. To complain was a mistake, to make demands would be a disaster. There was so much that she wanted to say, to ask, to get him to reveal, but she waited for him to speak.

"You are a mischief in my life," he spoke wistfully as he noticed her looking at him. "But one who comes more and more to front and center…a mischief who is not an irritation, but rather a solace and a comfort…a mischief who pleases me."

She still did not say anything, but smiled the smile of appreciation at him. In time, this would all work out for her.

"We'll make arrangements tomorrow with Tom about who is going with us on this tour. I'll need you to be with me to help. This will…will give us some time…together. What do you think?"

"I think Tom will decide if I go. If I do…"

"What?"

"That would be good. I think you could use my…my…"

He waited.

"My closeness."

"The smell of you would give me encouragement to do well."

She laughed, they kissed good night, and he was gone.

When Stone arrived home he could see that Tom's car was parked in front. The sight made him tense, on guard, and he could not fathom why. He trusted Tom, but there was something dangerous about this, some strange thing happening he didn't understand, something that would be revealed to him without warning. Or had there been a warning? Was it something Tom had said earlier in the day that he had made note of, but glossed over in the confusion and hustle-bustle of dealing with the many phone calls and monitoring the appointment making? Tom had given him notice of something. But what was it?

Tom would not make this difficult for him, he knew it. He knew that Tom would have told Helen something plausible once he realized Stone was not at home. It was not that late, but it still would be touchy.

"Hi, you two, sorry I'm late…"

"No, no, you're not late…I just got here a few minutes ago…" Tom seemed a little backed off of his usual high energy.

"We were waiting dinner for you, dear; Tom said you'd be right along. Hungry?"

Stone did not know quite how to read her. She was the perfect hostess, gracious, charming, and accommodating. She did not seem upset even though it was almost eight o'clock. He knew Tom would not let him down.

"Starved. It's been some day, hasn't it, Tom?"

"Monumental for all of us. That's why I wanted to talk to the two of you together."

Stone stared at Tom wondered what in heaven's name could be coming.

"That's right...monumental."

"How, Tom?" Helen asked softly.

"We have been video taping Randy's sermons for several months...perfecting the technique, checking out what we can do with the equipment, that sort of thing...with the idea that we wanted to be in the position of offering the broadcast of our services to a television station. Randy knew this and I'm sure you did, too, Helen..."

"Yes, but what..."

Hear me out, Helen. It came to me that maybe there was a better idea than using one of the local TV stations...maybe there was a bigger, better opportunity for us."

She stared at him not fully comprehending what she was hearing. She was a minister's wife, they had a flock, there was a religion, a church to be responsible for...what they did was not some...some entertainment program, some sporting event, something that could be cheapened or diminished by television. She was appalled, she had to take a deep breath, and she had to change the subject.

"Let me get the food on the table."

She went to the kitchen.

"Better I do this than you," Tom said.

"What are you saying?"

"Bo and Davie and I made a sensational video presentation of Sunday's service. Del was stunning, you were terrific, and the whole piece worthy of a national audience. Today, I sent a copy of that video to Reverend Harland Dewayne Kenny, the power behind Christian Gospel Broadcasting. He's in Columbia, South Carolina...has the most watched program in Christian broadcasting. He doesn't own CGB, but he's their biggest audience getter."

"Kenny? He's …he's probably the most…"

"That's right…he reaches across the country with his "Faith For Your Future" program…what's more important, he's got pull with CGB…he and his wife, that is."

"To accomplish what, exactly?"

"To get you on the "Faith For Your Future" program, to make you nationally known, to give you the stature that is commensurate with your ability and talent, my dear Reverend, and to make your special lessons available to more folks who have faith in the Lord."

"And for you…where are you in all of this…what do you want?"

Before Tom could answer, he and Stone were called to the dining room for dinner. The three Stone children had been rounded up to join the adults, but not to eat since they had been fed hours before. No, they were called to say hello to Mr. Fletcher and their Dad and to stand quietly while prayer was given.

"Holy Spirit bless this food and those who are about to partake; Let our hearts rejoice in the bounty that comes from you, oh Lord, and let us not forget those less fortunate in our prayers; Keep us always mindful of you in all that we do, our caring God; We ask Your forgiveness and blessing in the name of Jesus Christ, our Savior. Amen."

All said Amen.

The children said their good nights and were off upstairs leaving three silent adults to be seated and begin eating the dinner of pot roast that Helen had served. After a few moments of robust chewing, mainly with his mouth open, Tom continued his explanation for what he had done.

"Helen, you didn't get a chance to hear what I did."

"No, I was in the kitchen."

"We all know, of course, what a strong support you've been for Randy...most important in how well he's done since you folks came to Calvary...most important. Your critical role, Helen, is recognized by everyone. But the biggest challenge lies ahead of us...all of us...and we need your help again and with strength from the Lord and your continued effort, what we have coming for us will be most worthwhile."

She looked at him, dazed, hardly knowing what to make of what he was saying. Whatever it was it probably would not be good for her, she surmised. She had no way of knowing what she was being set up for, but she just knew she was. Tom was so smooth, but he always had an angle. His angles weren't always good for her. She was the silent, strong, supportive wife, usually off to the side someplace, not to be a part of anything, but to be seen so that others realized the Reverend had a lovely wife and three delightful children. It could be depressing if she dwelled on it.

"What *do* we have coming?" she asked.

He laid it all out for her: the appearances starting Wednesday that would take them away to four other towns, the tape of Randy's marvelous Sunday service sent to Reverend Kenny, and the possibility that there might be an extended stay in Columbia, South Carolina, if all went well. He called on her for understanding and for the understanding of the children. He talked of the compassion she would have to have for all who would give up what they were doing to make the sacrifice of temporarily moving to Columbia, and he evoked a sense of guilt for anyone who would not work to make their sacrifice possible. He was a master of making it nearly impossible for her to do anything but confirm that she would support and facilitate her husband's gallant effort in the name of the Holy Spirit.

He might as well have hit her with a brick and he knew it by the look on her face. He also knew that after the shock, the utter disbelief in what he said, and the consummate sadness that gripped her, she would recover from the blow and be the dutiful wife. Cornered in a position she could not control would produce an anger within her, he assumed, but he also smugly believed quite correctly that she would curtail any outward manifestation of that anger.

When Tom walked into Reverend Stone's office the next morning, he quietly closed the door. He did not want the assistant across the hall to hear what they were about to discuss. He certainly understood that anything said to Stone could be known by Keri in short order, but he wanted to give Stone the option of whether or not he would tell her.

The two men looked at each other for a long time without speaking. Neither had said good morning.

"How was it after I left?"

"She cried for awhile without saying much, but then seemed to get control of herself and began a diatribe that was incoherent…sort of like Del, except you could understand some of the words."

He chuckled when he said it and few of his parishioners would have liked hearing him make that unseemly comment about his wife. Tom laughed heartily, caught himself, not wanting Keri to overhear his guffaw even with the door closed.

"She ended by saying she would do anything to make sure what I did was a success…"

"I knew it…I knew we could count on her."

"We'll see."

There was a sharp rap on the door that startled the two men and Keri stuck her head in to say that Bob Saunders had arrived.

Saunders was in his late forties, portly, with a big, round head, and eyes set too far apart as if someone had carved a pumpkin incorrectly. Short in stature and carrying far more weight than he should or wanted, he rolled himself into a guest chair near Stone's desk after shaking hands with both men. He had difficulty getting comfortable, squirming around somewhat as he pulled a pen and reporter's notepad from an inside pocket of his wrinkled blue blazer. He wore a flowered sport shirt, no tie, and the collar of a tee-shirt was evident at the neck. Dimples were apparent in his cheeks even when he didn't smile and he smiled a lot so that it seemed as if he were always in a good mood. His tan chinos had two stains; one, just below the right front pocket that appeared to be from some kind of grease, and the other one was at the left knee. The one on the knee was a grass stain. He wore heavily scuffed loafers without socks, an uncommon sight in Swanton, and Tom and the Reverend took due notice.

"Thanks for giving me an interview, Reverend…like to get stories from interviews I do in person…could get it over the phone, but this is better."

When Saunders spoke, his voice was pitched higher than should have come out of this large man. He didn't sound exactly like a young woman, but it was close.

"We're glad you could get in here today, Bob," Tom came back, "because tomorrow we leave town and the Reverend would be tough to track down. Yessir, Reverend Stone and Del Howe have received invitations to be part of worship services in four other churches in this part of the country…and there may be other big things in the works we can't talk about yet."

Saunders looked at Tom as if to say, "Why are you talking and not the Reverend?" and then furrowed his brow. There was almost a scowl.

"Go ahead, Bob, ask your questions."

"Thank you." Bob smiled again and the dimples were deep.

Saunders took forty minutes to ask about Del, what it was like for Reverend Stone, and what was going to happen in the future. He carefully noted names and their spellings, diligently asked for quotations to be repeated so he could write them accurately, and got all of the background information he needed.

"Sorry I missed it, yesterday," Saunders sighed, "it would have been wonderful."

"Well, its not over...like the we said, we're going to be at four churches on this tour...matter of fact you should come with us...see first hand how Del speaks for the Holy Spirit, see how well Reverend Stone interprets the word of God. It's a sight. Its worthy of your attention...you need to see it and write about it."

"I just might do that, Tom...let me check my schedule...let me check...it just might work."

Bob Saunders wasn't able to get his story written before he headed out on the tour. He would be making notes and writing on his laptop evenings and the big story would come later. Tom made sure that Bob did not have to pay for anything, knowing full well the impact that perk would have on the slant of the story. Tom wanted a favorable article about all of this and was willing to pay for one. A small price, he contended, for what he wanted from Bob.

The "grand tour of northwestern Ohio," as Tom liked to call it, was a resounding success in several ways. It was a success, as he liked to describe, "on my terms in conjunction with the Lord." First of all, almost three thousand worshipers were inspired by the word of God and many of those were moved to do good works in their family, in their neighborhood, and in their community at large. Second, a greater awareness outside of the church was achieved for fundamental Christianity so that a substantial gain in new members was made at each of the churches. And third, the four services pulled in big money that gave huge contributions to each of the four congregations, covered all of the expenses of the Calvary folks, and put a nice increase in the pot of investments that Tom hovered over for Calvary.

These tangible results were exciting and exhilarating for everyone concerned, but only Betty made an evaluation of how the tour affected Del. After all, by the end of the tour, Del had become a showcase persona. He was almost like a piece of artwork being hauled around from museum to museum. She sensed he was suffering somewhat, but no one else was aware of his condition, even though they asked after him with such questions about "how is he holding up" and "is this too much for him" being the main queries.

Del was like a performing seal or someone's pet dog doing fantastic tricks that made you wonder how they could accomplish that. The link to the Holy Spirit gave the "act" an even greater connection to the congregations he appeared before and brought them in tune with what was occurring. Simply letting Del babble before just any audience would probably not have worked; he needed an understanding, fundamentalist Christian crowd to fulfill his promise of revelation. The most significant aspect for Tom was that Del's appearances before strangers turned out to be even more emotional than those in front of his own fellow parishioners whom he knew and knew him.

Another huge factor for Tom, who commented about it often, as did Reverend Stone privately, the marvel about Del was how he was ready for every service and how powerful was the consistency of the outpouring of sounds that he gave. For Stone, it was as if when he spoke to Del he triggered something, as if he turned on a faucet that let forth a creation of some kind of simulated language that is said by the experts not to be a language. Del was a reliable performer and that was a wonderful relief for Tom.

Although the Calvary group of Del, Reverend Stone, Betty, Dorothy, Keri, Bo, and Davie did not go from city to city as a tour truly would, they spent several nights away from home. Stone and Keri were very discrete. There were no furtive looks, no hand holding, no loving glances, and no displays of emotion between them. There was only the professional interaction of boss and assistant; cool, calm, and orderly efficient. However, it is nearly impossible to hide the electrochemical something that exudes from lovers to each other. Whatever that something is - an energy charge, a vibration, or a sensation wave – it most often is detected by whoever is around. In this case, Tom knew, but Betty and Dorothy were so involved with Del they didn't pick up on the vibes, and as far as Bo and Davie were concerned, they knew it didn't matter what they suspected or thought.

It was easy for Reverend Stone and Keri to accomplish spending the night together in the motels where they stayed. The two of them discovered that being able to spend the night together made it bearable to get through the next day without obviously giving themselves away. With that being the case, their behavior still made Tom very nervous. Their masks of professionalism kept them discrete, kept them from clinging to each other in public, kept them from being a teenage kind of nuisance that would have made Tom crazy and necessitated yanking them back into his reality. Propriety was Tom's guideline for morality. Don't make it obvious and it was okay. As far as he was concerned, the Lord knew we were imperfect, but we should not show the rest of the world our imperfections. Let us be judged later by God for what we do, was his motto, let's not give those as imperfect and less Godly as we are the chance to prejudge us. When the role is called, when the balance sheet of life is tallied, when our Maker takes stock of our life – that is when it counts. Otherwise, what we do is no one else's business. Amen.

At Stony Ridge Baptist Church in Lima they had the largest attendance of the tour, with over nine hundred attentive, reverential worshipers hanging on every word Reverend Stone used to translate Del's message. The most money also hit the collection plates there. Keri and Reverend Stone spent twelve hours in bed at one stretch. Everyone was upbeat and Del smiled a great deal as Betty and Dorothy patted his hands. Bob Saunders found a restaurant he liked that offered barbequed ribs and draft beer. There was a silly country-western band that came in at nine, with dancing until midnight. Bob enjoyed watching the girls while he soaked up the draft beer.

Van Wert Christian Church had numerous parishioners who would faint dead away, overcome with what they observed. Del held up well as he gave even more than his usual enthusiasm and Reverend Stone held the congregation transfixed. Keri and Reverend Stone got in ten hours of bed time and everyone was excited with the tour. Bob Saunders spent time at a bar with gigantic burgers and hung out there until some bikers came in and scared him away.

After the two appearances, the group returned to Swanton for Sunday services and the second of Del's presentations before the home crowd. Much like the first, this time was just as sensational. Reverend Stone, in a calculated move to keep things smooth with Helen, spent all of his free time at home which wasn't all that much. Helen didn't complain about anything, but made little effort to get close to her husband. It was easier to focus on the children and it was also less depressing. Bob Saunders did not show up for the Sunday service and Tom was surprised and disappointed he was not in attendance. Tom felt Bob would have been duly impressed.

God bless Bob Saunders. Del's exaltations of gibberish and the wailing and fainting of the devoted had finally gotten to him. It took some will power on his part to resist continuing with the all-expenses-paid tour, but he had enough. He would write his story without the other two stops. Bob was cynical about what he had observed, a doubter, without conviction for what was termed as "revealed," but he would not write his story that way. He would keep his opinion to himself and report what he saw and heard in a way that he knew Tom would approve.

Bob had written almost fifteen thousand words about Del and Reverend Stone, far more than the usual story length his paper would run in their Religion section and way more than would any of the other papers he submitted his articles to on religious topics. The Toledo Blade, on the other hand, highlighted his story, including two of the digital photos he included and, as a big plus in Tom's way of thinking, sent their story to the wire services with Bob's byline.

This account of half the Calvary tour would pave the way for national attention in Christian Fundamentalist circles and have a tremendous affect on the success of Tom's pitch to Reverend Kenny. Bob Saunders had created a stir and he would find himself enmeshed with Tom Fletcher, Reverend Stone, and Delwin Howe way more than he could ever have imagined. Celebrity status was not something he aspired to or wanted. However, he could and would accept the role.

The following week, they were on to Sydney, Ohio, at God's Mission Church. The gross weeping of the congregation was overwhelming, but they didn't match up in contributions. They did, however, present each of the Calvary team with several expensive gifts that included clothes, food, and jewelry. Keri and Stone spent two brief sessions of love making, but they could not maneuver a sustained effort. Tom was in constant contact with Pam Dover back at the church, checking on a message from Reverend Kenny. Pam, handling the phone answering duty for Keri, was patient in telling him there had been no calls from a Reverend Kenny. It was frustrating for Tom, even though he knew these things take time. In his heart he believed Kenny would call. How could he not?

The final stop, after nine days of concentrated effort, was at First Christian Church of Archbold. This congregation reacted as strongly and as positively as the others, and Reverend Stone was at his absolute best. He held them spellbound and yes, there was fainting and weeping and wailing and screaming of all kinds for all manner of reasons, and afterward they surged forward to touch Del and Reverend Stone. It was scintillating and Tom could not believe what he observed. Del and Reverend Stone were a combination that Reverend Kenny had to have on his program, there was no doubt about it.

Then out of the blue, something happened that Tom had not expected, had not planned for, and had not even thought might occur. It was that Don Howe would show up in Archbold as if he were the police making a raid on a gambling den. Self-righteous Don made the moments after the service very unpleasant. He accosted Reverend Stone first as the most visible target, fuming with a barrage of words of accusation that were almost as incomprehensible as those of his father. Then he saw his mother and Dorothy in the front row and took off at them. Masses of parishioners pushed him aside to get to Del and Reverend Stone and he was swallowed up by the crowd for the time being. Once the congratulations and accolades to Del and Stone died down and the throng dispersed, Don again became an enraged accuser forcing the confrontation that now included the entire Calvary group.

Before he could gain momentum, Dorothy took him on with her own anger, her own righteousness.

"You've got a lot of nerve coming out here to cause trouble. Where were you for Dad before he got hit by lightning…off in your own world, disregarding us, whining and sniveling about your divorce, taking it out on your second wife like you took it out on the first. What gives you the right to come after us? You can't dump on us like you did on them. This…with all of us, is all about the word of God and you are all about Godlessness…without God…without the Holy Spirit to give you guidance. You chastise us…give me a break."

"This man…your husband…," Don hesitated, seething, not in the least stiff-armed by her criticism and accusations, "needs medical help. He needs testing…he should have been back in the hospital a week ago getting checked over properly. He's not right. You…all of you…you think he's speaking…"

"Excuse me," Tom interrupted, drawing Don up short, "this is not appropriate talk here in the sanctuary…could we move outside and discuss this privately…and calmly. Perhaps we can work with Don on this so he is not so upset."

Tom ushered Del and Reverend Stone out the side door and to a grassy area at the side of the church. The others followed with Don bringing up the rear. They assembled in somewhat of a circle.

"We want only the best for your father…" Tom started.

"Well, if you do you will see to it that he gets back to the hospital right away." Don was livid.

"It does absolutely no good to rant and rave here in public, in front of your father, making your mother distraught, upsetting your sister, and causing a scene. We're heading back to Swanton in a few minutes, we'll confer about all of this, and decide what is best for Del in light of what your mother wants to do."

Don backed away from the circle before he spoke, pointing his finger at Tom as he moved.

"I hold you responsible for this man's life," he snarled.

"I am not God," Tom snapped, "only God is responsible for his life and for all of our lives. The Holy Spirit lives in your father, the Lord will help the decision, and your mother will follow the Lord."

Don had no answer for that rebuttal and stomped off to his car.

7.

Seek the Lord while he may be found, call upon him while he is near.
-Isaiah 55:6

The eleven by sixteen Persian rug that spread before the massive mahogany desk of Harland Dewayne Kenny cost the New World Gospel Church purchasing department slightly more than twenty three thousand dollars, not including shipping. It was an illegal Persian, but came from a reliable source. The rest of the art and artifacts in his large office were of similar quality and related cost. Reverend Kenny liked to be surrounded with beautiful things. The beauty in the world was God's gift to us, His reassurance of His presence, and the manifestation of His great Works. Harland believed that aesthetic appreciation was a true sign of recognition for what God has delivered to us, and meant a higher level of understanding of God's creation for all of us. Qualified - certainly expensive - wonderful art helped his thought processes, he explained to his staff, helped his concentration on the Lord, and provided the right atmosphere for reverence of God's wishes. He felt these things provided an environment for postulating a clear message of the Holy Spirit to those who needed, desired, and yes, clamored for the Word of God to move them to Salvation.

Sam Turco, a Columbia, South Carolina, art dealer, had shown Harland a picture of the rug knowing full well his customer would want it. He was not disappointed. The purchase was made soon after that with no quibble on the price. Sam was one of those rare individuals who could be termed a "character." Almost flamboyant, yet something else, mysterious perhaps, always speaking in hushed tones as if he were afraid of being overheard, guarding his words, but still seeming to reveal some great secret. The secret, of course, was the special item, the special deal, the elegant and perhaps suspicious history of whatever it was that he wanted to sell. He was letting the prospective buyer in on something so monumental, so extraordinary in value that it would be impossible to resist the purchase. He was the consummate insider who brought the prospect inside with him to share in the delight of whatever it was he wanted to sell.

Networking, connecting, and linking were terms Sam would not have used because they were not in his vocabulary, but they were the mainstays of how he operated. He was a miniature, one man, old-fashioned form unto himself of how the Internet worked, and although he knew what the Internet was he liked doing business the way he had for many years. The telephone and face-to-face communication were best, he believed. He fully understood what he could do, what he could accomplish. He could be a frenzy of activity or he could quietly calculate his next move, but in either mode Sam was a model of efficiency and purpose. There was one goal for him: make money. In a city, in a state that held Christian morality with prime importance, Sam could link up with, connect to, and network with every aspect and element outside of Christian morality. Immorality to Sam was an avenue for making extra money, easy money. This side of Sam was, of course, beyond his fundamental job in the art world and it was not known by Harland.

Sam had spent the last hour presenting photographs of several new pieces that "he was convinced" New World needed. These were massive bronze statues that would be considered in the realm of Rodin or at least quite like those of the master sculptor. He contended they should grace the grounds of the New World campus. Harland had been polite, listened, looked, but gave no indication of commitment. Sam left the office disappointed, curiously frustrated with his inability to make a sale, and doggedly determined he would be back for another go at it.

Harland was too preoccupied with something else to consider art purchases right now. Earlier, he had seen parts of Tom's tape and was antsy to view the entire video. What he had seen caught his attention. It triggered his uncanny ability to validate his take on Christian value when he saw it, and his ability to envision what he saw on that tape as something his Faith For Your Future program could use. Harland knew that the same-old same-old got stale and that something new and exciting was required. Like Del speaking in tongues. Here was something he knew could work well in his program format and be a highlight on Christian Gospel Broadcasting.

As soon as Sam had exited, Harland triggered the tape to play from the beginning. He relaxed in the very expensive leather executive chair that was the throne of his command at New World. He watched with excited attention fully appreciating the effort Tom had made in producing this video. He was impressed with everything about it.

"The guy who did this for Stone knows what he is doing. Fletcher...Tom Fletcher. It was his cover letter that came with the tape. He has sent me an E-mail, left me a couple of voice mails, and has done his job on follow-up. I like what I see...I like how Fletcher handles the whole thing. What do you folks think?"

No one from the inner circle of confidants and subordinates said anything at first. This was a select group, the round table of knights who carried through with the management of New World's considerable operation and gave counsel to Harland when asked for it. His style seemed like consensus management on casual observation, but, in reality, his was an authoritarian regime. Harland was nicer than most ego-driven, somewhat maniacal, power possessed CEOs, dictators, or tyrants. He was quite easy to work for and carefully fostered that impression. He had the last word, they knew it, and knew also that he would not heavy-hand his discretion. Still, they were reluctant to jump ahead of him and wanted to wait to be sure of his opinion, more sure than his remarks about the video might indicate.

"What matters, darlin,' is what *you* think about it." Katherine Louise Kenny smiled at her husband when she spoke.

She was a petite, blonde woman with salon coiffed hair style that was short, in vogue, and only slightly tinted. Her look showed impeccable makeup application and precisely manicured nails. She wore a skirted business suit with the skirt perhaps a tad short for the business they were in, but she had great legs and did not want them to be overlooked. No man would. She spoke with a lilt of the Southern belle, but not overblown or syrupy. At a little over five feet tall, her large bust might have given her the Dolly Parton look if it were not for the other toned-down aspects of her features and dress. She never showed cleavage, she was not a flirt, and rarely tried to draw attention to herself. Although she was an individual and an independent woman, she also recognized that she was a minister's wife. This meant she had to know her place and she did. Her background and upbringing made her leery of strangers and not quick to make friends even though she gave the impression of being everyone's friend. Gregarious, yet cautious, open-faced, yet closed to revealing herself; with her, what you saw was not necessarily what you got.

Katherine Louise Townes met Harland when she worked the circuit for the Harvard Brothers Fun Rides and Carnival and he was a summer job construction worker. It was Asheville, North Carolina, July, 1973, a cool evening, a restless, impatient crowd that elbowed their way through the attractions. She saw him coming along the midway and focused on him and it surprised her. Every night she saw a lot of good-looking guys, but they were just faces that came and went, meaning nothing beyond the joy of looking. Harland was different, he caught her attention and she could not let go. It was like magic, she would later reflect, a special moment in her life. For some reason she knew God had come to her. That was a stretch because at this point in her life she was a long way from Godliness. She could hardly have guessed that Harland was a fourth-year Bible college student. This image, this boy, this transcendent creature was caught freeze-frame in her mind. She wanted the connection. This was a new emotion for her and she liked the way it felt.

When she finally caught his eye the connection was made. For Harland, there was nothing mystical or God-centered about it, it was pure and simple lust. She was the most beautiful woman he had ever seen. Tousled blonde hair piled on her head, low-cut blouse that exhibited, yea emphasized, her huge bosom, tight-fitting slacks, the inviting lips with the cherry red lipstick, and the wanton eyes of seduction, sensuality, and sin that blazed like a neon sign: Pleasure begins here.

Katherine Louise last heard about God when her mother screamed at her about her naughty, unseemly behavior. She had fooled around for awhile after high school graduation, then accepted Ron Harvard's offer and left her mother and God behind. His offer of good money for working the concessions, steady employment most of the year, and winter in Florida was too good to deny. At seventeen, her prospects were slim. She could clean houses with her mother, burger flip, cashier at the Arrow Motor Mart, or help Dad Phillips try to survive the new K-Mart. Or work at the new K-Mart for even less. She didn't even know about turning tricks, but that would not have been an option; not then, at least. She liked partying with a crowd her mother thought best in jail, occasionally did drugs, and drank beer most nights with her friends. She was nowhere and she knew it and she wanted to be somewhere. The carnival was a move up, up, and away; it was somewhere. It was somewhere else other than Cressy, South Carolina.

The next nine years were her baccalaureate and masters degrees on life. The Harvard Brothers were her professors, mentors, and on and off lovers. Her education was raw and ragged, a series of experiences that shed her of her youth, yanked her toward adulthood, and gave her a case-hardened, cynical outlook on the world. Katherine Louise could be a sweet, gentle lover when it was the right time and a ferocious demon when it suited her. The rest of the time she suffered from the nagging uneasiness of wanting something more in life, although she wasn't sure what that might be. She figured there had to be a better way to live than with the carnie. She hardly understood what her longing meant; she just knew that life had to be easier, smoother, some other way. She had just finished high school when Ron Harvard spotted her in a Greenville shopping center, so there was a lot of catching up to get done before she could discover what it was she wanted.

She was on the road to that discovery when she saw Harland. As soon as she knew he was looking at her she started to speak to him, but choked, the words strangled somehow. She swallowed hard to clear her dry throat and tried again.

"Hi, darlin,' y'all enjoyin' yerself this fine night?"

His broad smile and the blushing cheeks made him even more attractive to her.

"Yes, ma'am, having a fine time…enjoying your carnival."

"I wish it were mine…I'd be sittin' in the office if it was."

I didn't mean yours, I meant…"

"Yeah, I know what ya meant…I was just teasin' ya."

Her job that night was to hustle folks into the Weird Man side show, but she forgot about the hustle right now. She was intent on Harland, sizing him up, trying to figure out just who he was, how to proceed with him, and how she might get him in bed without being too obvious or too eager. As she looked him over she noticed that he smelled clean as if he had just showered or bathed. It was a smell that touched a trigger within her, a trigger of desire, a trigger that multiplied her curiosity about him, and made her want to reach out to touch him. She resisted the impulse.

He laughed and his cheeks got even redder. She looked around to see if one of the Harvards or Ed Martin her midway boss were watching her. None of them were around, but she knew she didn't have a lot of time.

"My name is Kate...I get done at eleven...after the show closes...maybe we could get a cup of coffee or something..."

"Harland...Harland Kenny." He started to stick out his hand, thought better of it, and brought his hand up to his left arm in an awkward pose. "My pleasure. Where will I meet up with you?"

"At the main entrance...little after eleven."

It was a strange beginning for two seemingly unlikely personalities to get together. He had no idea she was a woman with a loose background who was aroused just by the sight of him and on the other hand, she could not have dreamed his greatest desire was to be a powerful minister of God. Their discoveries of each other were monumental, their acceptance of those discoveries was a severe challenge to overcome, and their balancing of life choices within those revelations quite remarkable. It was ardent, passionate love from the start with little intellectual linking involved, but that would change over time as Katherine Louise began to play catch up with the minister-to-be.

She was away from the midway before Ron Harvard or Martin knew she was gone and there he was, that boy Harland, waiting just outside the main gate.

"Harland Kenny, that's such a nice name...and so nice of y'all ta meet me. Y'all got a car?"

He did and they spent several hours together. It was a long time ago.

Harland looked out over the green campus that sprawled eastward from the administration building. Pine, sweet gum, magnolia, dogwood, and Bradbury pear trees dotted the landscape. The azaleas, long bloomed out, still flourished, the pansies sparkled, and the trimmed lawn gave a sense of unity and formality to the setting. He had worked hard for this and it pleased him to reflect on how this was accomplished, it pleased him to view the reward. He savored the view in a visceral way. He knew that the carnie girl had helped get him to where he was in achievement and he liked that memory. He was not alone in gaining his accomplishments and he knew that, too. He fully recognized that God championed his cause, and that Katherine Louise gave the cause meaning and definition, and had intensified the purpose that Harland had ultimately fulfilled. It was that carnie spirit and background that made her drive Harland and be able to manage him so well. He knew it was true and he liked it.

"He's got something here…something we can use, if you ask me. This is the kind of thing that takes us to the next level…to leapfrog over the other missionaries. Speaking in tongues is an event true Christians can appreciate…even if it is second hand experience. Look at how that congregation reacted to that man. We need him to be on our broadcasts. That's what I think. But let's go round the room here and get everyone's take on this. Larry…what do you think?"

"A winner. They couldn't fake that thing…this guy is in the zone…we could use him."

"That's what I thought. Fred, what do you think?"

Fred Wallace was like a pernicious cloud hanging over the office, but certainly a balance to the consummate optimism of the others. He was a clever accountant, master planner, dedicated to the New World cause, and brutally honest about how they all should conduct themselves in the context of religious communication.

"I think this man…this speaker…and his minister could be a good thing for us. We could do a contract for a three program trial…see how it works. Feedback will let us know soon enough."

Everyone in the room nodded as Fred spoke. He was the confirmation that made them all feel comfortable with what they already believed. It was his blessing that made it easy for their decision.

"Yes, yes," Harland nodded vigorously, "we've got to get him on the program. Next Sunday, if possible. Let's get the ball in play. Larry figure out how we handle this...get a script ready, get everyone clued in about this man...Fred, you get hold of this Thatcher guy and find out what they can do, what they want. We need to move on this."

Harland Dewayne Kenny was the host of Faith For Your Future as part of the Christian Gospel Broadcasting programming. They could not get carried on many of the cable companies, but their influence was growing and viewership was on a steady rise. They now reached about two million viewers nationwide, a considerable audience for cable. Faith For Your Future was considered one of the premier Christian programs available. But it was true they needed something to distance and fully differentiate themselves from the other religious programs in the competition for audience. Del Howe could do that, Harland reasoned.

"Let's get going on this," Harland said tersely, "let's get it done...today."

The room cleared. The next steps needed to be executed, the assignments needed to get done.

"You are magnificent, darlin',' simply magnificent."

"Don't you think he can be a big help with the production?'

"Of course he can...you made the right decision...Fred gave you his blessing. That's all you need..."

No...not so, I need your blessing...I need..."

"What..."

"I need you to help me make this...a...a wonderful success."

"Not to worry, darlin,' this will be a bonus for us."

She walked over to him as he stood by the window and gave him a light peck on the cheek, took his hand in hers, and wrapped the other arm around his waist. There they were, the king and queen of Christian broadcasting, looking out over a sumptuous domain of their making, still impressed by it, still worried it might evaporate before their eyes. It was a small community of low-profile buildings that were almost prairie style architecture, except for the church. The buildings included the sprawling structure where they were standing, a very large educational facility for grades K through twelve, a recreation center with a pool nearly Olympic size, a maintenance garage that housed all of the necessary equipment and the fleet of church vehicles, and, of course, the New World Gospel Church. At the rear of the church stood three large satellite transmission dishes used for broadcasting. The church was inauspicious in design on the outside, but nonetheless imposing in relation to the other structures. Inside it was a bold, colossal expression of devotion to God and a paragon of dedication to broadcasting. Cost was not spared in any aspect of its construction from the large stage to the comfortable seating. It could accommodate nearly two thousand worshipers at each of the Saturday night and Sunday morning services.

In the woods not quite half a mile from the other buildings, amid a mixed stand of pines, magnolias, and sycamores, sprawled the palatial residence of king Harland and queen Katherine Louise. The home was a luxury and an extravagance, and certainly way larger than necessary for a couple without children. It had been built as a modern day replica of a classic southern plantation manor house, just as Katherine Louise requested – Tara revisited.

"I hope you don't think I'm foolish, darlin', but it would be nice if it looked like Scarlett's house…you know, in "Gone With the Wind."

There was a master bedroom suite, plus seven more bedrooms, each with a private bathroom; an immense kitchen with adjoining bedroom and bathroom for the live-in cook; a formal dining room that could comfortably seat sixteen; the living room; and an entertainment room with its own half-bathroom. A four-car garage was also incorporated into the design. French doors in the master suite opened onto a screened-in deck at the rear of the house that looked out over a wonderfully planted and landscaped garden, and the woods beyond. The constant interplay of numerous bird varieties could be seen from the deck and in the spring the smell of Jasmine was almost overpowering.

Katherine Louise loved walking around the house just to look at the luxury. She would stop for several minutes, standing in one spot to absorb that view, exhilarated, knowing she was living in this rich environment.

Not bad for a carnie girl, she thought, such a shady past I've got it's a true miracle I'm living here. Please, God, let the miracle continue for a while longer. Amen.

Fred Wallace had found this rolling piece of land that was slightly more than ten acres of trees and open fields. It was land repossessed from a retired Columbia fireman who wasn't exactly sure what he would do with it, but thought maybe he could develop a gun club. The fireman bought it from the family who inherited it from their uncle who had lived in the property's rundown house until he died. The fireman's lost cause of keeping up with the payments brought the property back to the bank. Fred knew a good deal when he found it and this was a good deal. Perfect for what Harland Kenny's mission had in mind for their ultimate location. The idea for a campus-like setting was Katherine Louise's, but she let Fred and Harland take the credit. After all, she got what she wanted without worrying who claimed it to be their vision. The old cottage was torn down, land was cleared, and the Faith For Your Future complex was built. The carefully budgeted and planned building program evolved in orderly fashion over the next five years.

Winding sidewalks connected the buildings as did a matching system of streets and driveways. A bevy of golf carts shuttled back and forth as staff moved from building to building to conduct the work of the mission, although those walking and the users of bicycles were also a common sight when it wasn't raining. Harland's gospel ministry supported nearly seventy-five workers, not including the volunteers who showed up to stuff envelopes, process mail, and perform other chores that were part of the outreach program. There were requests to be fulfilled for copies of sermons, copies of broadcast videos, for literature and pamphlets the church produced, and other related materials that Harland talked about on television. All of the mail had to be opened and sorted and the donation money counted, recorded, and deposited. This was a great deal of work that took many hands, but the most important of the tasks centered on the donations. Contributions that were sent in provided the life blood of the church's work, well beyond the contributions of parishioners and other attendees to the broadcast services. On average, about one hundred thousand dollars a week dropped onto the counting tables in the administration building - more than five million dollars a year. Close attention was given to incoming mail as a result. Orders for all the items being sold amounted to twenty or more thousand dollars a week. They were carefully detailed for fulfillment and the names added to a database list for solicitation mailings. Contributions at the Saturday and Sunday services usually totaled around twenty-five thousand dollars a week. The money flowed and added up to substantial numbers. The king and queen had a very successful operation. Harland believed Del Howe could help make the revenue stream even better.

The contract with Christian Gospel Broadcasting made the money pot even bigger. Fifteen thousand dollars a week was what New World received to provide the network with a fifty-five minute program. CGB reserved five minutes to promote their programming and leave time for advertising. This was enough money to cover the production costs with some left over for the ministry. What a deal. The program was sent to CGB broadcast headquarters in Charlotte via satellite uplink in real time. CGB recorded the feed and had the option of broadcasting live or delayed depending on their schedule, and could use the program at least three times in a week to serve various markets across the country. In this way, CGB provided Harland with a national audience. It was an opportunity beyond what he had hoped for when he began the New World ministry. Harland knew that CGB would be thrilled with Del Howe. Del would be a promotional bonanza for the entire network.

Harland Dewayne Kenny was riding the crest of success in the most glorious terms of the American dream. Far more than he had envisioned, far more than he had planned. He was comfortable with his success and little changed with the immense wealth that could be his. He was, he knew full well, an instrument of the Lord. The Holy Spirit made it all possible and the Holy Spirit could take it all away in a flash if that were God's will. He prayed silently and also openly with Katherine Louise and others of his management council in thanks for the bountiful works of the Lord in generously supporting his mission and his ministry.

He had known for a long time that he was working as an implementation for the Holy Spirit. For him there was no illusion of being some kind of new messiah, but rather being a manifestation of the Word. He was blessed in many ways and that realization he had understood for a long time. He walked hand-in-hand with God every day, and so it was inevitable that he could graciously accept worldly success without wondering about it or having doubts of his worthiness. So it was, too, that at the same time he could feel righteous in his motives and methods. Harland was true to his committed goal of making God's Word his Calling and executing Christ's command to proselytize to those not yet Saved.

Harland was impatient. He had assigned contact with Tom Fletcher, but he wanted to be part of that conversation and he wanted to nail down something as soon as possible. He buzzed Fred Wallace to summon him back to his office.

"Fred, come on in here and let's get this Fletcher guy on the squawk box…I'd like to hear what he's got to say."

In a few moments Fred was back and Tom's number had been dialed.

"Insurance...Mr. Fletcher's office."

The woman's voice was somewhat shrill on the speaker.

"Tom in?" Harland asked casually.

"May I tell him who is calling?"

"Yes, tell him Reverend Harland Kenny is on the phone."

"Thank you, Reverend Kenny."

There was a click, a buzz, then silence, a long pause, and another loud click.

"Reverend Kenny, good morning, Tom Fletcher here...thanks for calling." His voice boomed from the speaker. "Really appreciate your quick response to our tape."

Harland noted the editorial "our" instead of "my" in describing the video. He thought that was a good sign.

"Yes, of course. We found your video most interesting...the staff watched it...very impressed with your preacher and his work with Del Howe...most enlightening and uplifting. Your production by the way is excellent..."

"Thanks, we take pride in that..."

"I have Fred Wallace our business manager here in the office with me..."

"Good morning, Fred," Tom offered.

"Good morning," Fred replied. "Can we call you Tom?"

"Sure can..."

Fred nodded at Harland.

"Tell us about Del if you would, Tom..."

"Well, the video shows how he does with the language...its just gibberish to most folks, but Randy...Reverend Stone...he believes Del is speaking in tongues...that the

Holy Spirit is bringing us the Word of God through Del and that the Word is about Redemption, among other things. You can see for yourself how effective, how really powerful a message is given."

"Yes, we did see that, Tom. But what I mean is…ah…his condition. Tell me, is this man stable? I mean he's not crazy is he?"

"Gosh no…a solid farmer citizen, war veteran, patriot…not crazy, far from crazy, and a faithful Christian in the best sense. Got hit by lightening…darnedest thing…that's what has affected his speech. A sign from God we think…intervening on our behalf for our benefit. He's been checked by doctors and he's okay. I believe they think eventually he'll recover his ability to talk clearly again."

Harland listened to Tom speak and he knew that this was their man. He would rationalize Del's condition until the cows come home, caught with the fervor that was Reverend Stone's. Harland liked that, liked their zeal. It was important if they were to present Del to a national audience.

"That's good, Tom, I really, really like your candor. We need to be open about this…it could mean a lot to all of us."

Fred held up a contract and nodded insistently to Harland. He had written the words "three weeks" on it.

"Tom, hear me clearly on this…we are all about the work of the Lord, but things being the way they are from a legal point of view we need a contract signed by the responsible party for your church…maybe that's you, maybe Reverend Stone, but in any case…"

"It would be me. I'm the business manager for Calvary and president of the trustees. I have been given the authority. What are you proposing?"

"We'd like to offer you a three week contract…that is to say, a contract for three services where Reverend Stone and Del appear on our program. That's not close ended, of course, we could extend if you and we thought an extension was appropriate. If it goes well, three programs would certainly not be sufficient."

Tom did not answer at first. He sat bolt upright in his chair, silently sucked in his breath, and let his eyes drift to the ceiling as he silently mouthed a prayer. Thank you, Lord, for your divine intervention on our behalf. Tom had only hoped for one shot at the Faith For Your Future program, so to get two additional programs was a bonus beyond his expectation. He stayed calm and answered accordingly.

"That is a consideration for us, but we would have expenses and the congregation would have some expectation that…"

"We can handle that," Fred responded. "We would cover all of your expenses, plus make sure a proper donation was made to you congregation so that it would compensate them for the temporary loss of their pastor."

"We do have an entourage that would have to make the trip to Columbia…"

"Whoever is necessary…it doesn't matter, we'll cover the expenses."

Harland silently mouthed "how many" to Fred.

"How many would be in your group, Tom?"

"Let's see now…" he paused to figure the number. "I think we would have…five…yes, I think five. Reverend Stone, Del and his wife…"

Harland nodded and gestured to Fred, pointing at the house in the distance.

"No that's fine…five, six, we can handle that. We'd have you stay with Reverend Kenny and his wife in their house…you would be most comfortable there. It's on the grounds here and very convenient…I think Reverend Stone would like that."

"Tom, plan on being our guests," Harland said, "we would be delighted and you and your group will like the serenity and the comfort. We insist."

"Tom, we have your fax number so we'll get a contract sent to you in the next few minutes. Sign it and fax it back and we'll go from there." Fred rubbed his hands together as he spoke.

"Tom…something else." There was a sense of urgency in Harland's voice. "We need you folks here at New World by this weekend. We want to go on with Reverend Stone and Del on Sunday. Is that doable?"

Tom's brain began to whirl. This meant they were wanted badly and it also meant a logistical, psychological nightmare for him. He and Stone had to convince Betty, he had to deal with his business affairs, and Stone would have to deal with Helen. When he gave Fred a number, he included Keri as an automatic and deleted Helen. He hoped it worked that way, figured it probably would.

"No problem," Tom said, his heart beating wildly, his chest tight with tension, "we'll be there Saturday."

"Very good," Fred said, "we look forward to meeting all of you folks."

"Excellent," Harland cried out. "Now remember you'll all be our guests. Do you need directions?"

"It would help," Tom said trying to stay calm.

"We will fax that sheet with the contract. Call us if you have any questions."

Tom sat back in his chair as he breathed deeply to maintain his composure. They were moving on to the big time and he could hardly wait to tell Randy.

8.

Hear a just cause, O Lord, attend to my cry; give ear to my prayer which is not from deceitful lips. Let my vindication come from Your presence; let Your eyes look on the things that are upright.

-Psalm 17:1-2

Reverend Stone stared out the bedroom window at the sullen gray sky. A steady rain dampened his spirit and even the sounds of children playing downstairs could not hearten him. Usually the sounds of their play were a tonic for him, he took joy from the cries and yelps and the words of pretending that create make-believe worlds. It was not noise, but rather a kind of music, a lyrical expression that let him feel in touch with them when, in truth, he was far removed. He wished that he could pretend and it would be thus, the creation of a new reality. His reality was the summer rain that had crept in overnight, the dreariness of the morning, and the prospect of telling Helen about going to South Carolina.

His vision for doing well at New World tempered his somber reality as he could see himself before their huge congregation. He would be masterful as he gave Del's sounds meaning and brought forth the message of God. They would be as enthralled as the others had been who were witness to his skill and the ensuing rapture from what took place would make him nationally known. He would be famous; surely he would have great fame. He just knew it. He could see it happening.

He was unsure what Helen's reaction might be and that prospect bothered him. He should not be uncertain of that, he should know how she would react, have the expectation that she would be happy and excited for him and the opportunity to have his preaching be on nationwide television. Being unsure also made him feel guilty for some reason. Why should he feel guilty? His motives were in tune with his ministry, but it was as if there were failure on his part for not knowing. As if he should have known, as if he were the reason for this blank. He could easily blame Helen for the inconsistency of her reactions over the years, the negativity when he expected support and the support that was unexpected. Then there were the times of no reaction whatsoever. The nagging suspicion within him, however, was that the fault was his. This made it even more difficult to approach her. It had been easier to avoid, sidestep, or flee from dealing with things. It all made the excuse of his relationship with Keri easy to justify.

"Meditating?" Helen's sad voice startled him.

"No...I...well, sort of," he said as he turned to face her, "...just trying to figure out some things..."

"Like what?"

There it was: the opening, the point at which he would have made the dodge to avoid a straight answer, the place where he emotionally removed himself from direct communication with her. That had to change, he thought, or the guilt will never go away, being unsure will linger, and nothing would ever get better. Now is the time to make a change.

"About all of the things required of me to handle a rare opportunity for me...for the church...for my ministry..."

That was still sort of a dodge, he thought, the nasty little issue here is being gone for a month. That's the sort of thing she hates, he did know that much.

"What would that be?"

"Tom has managed to get me on the Faith For Your Future program for three services...Harland Kenny's program on Christian Gospel Broadcasting...with Del."

"Wow," Helen exclaimed with what seemed real enthusiasm, "that's wonderful."

She moved quickly to where he stood, opening her arms to give him a hug as she got to him. He was surprised by her reaction, but they had not gotten to the out-of-town part yet. He accepted and returned her embrace before he continued.

"Yeah, it is exciting…means that we will have to go to Columbia…be gone for awhile…"

"We…?"

She continued to hold on to him.

"Del and I…Tom sent Harland a video of our service with Del…he was very impressed…wants both of us to come down there to be on their program…three Sundays…"

"How long?" Her question nearly strangled him.

"At least three weeks…if they want us more it might be longer…"

"You have a congregation here, Randy, that need you…"

"Yes, I know, but this is short term and they will benefit, too…"

"You have someone to cover services for you?"

"Yes, Tom arranged for…"

"Tom arranges everything doesn't he?"

She let go of him and sat on their bed.

"Tom? Yes, Tom does a lot…he's been very good for us…"

"Perhaps…"

"He has and he cares about us…our future and the future of my ministry…"

"I think Tom cares about Tom," she said caustically.

"He is a businessman…he knows how to take care of himself…and he does care about us."

"I suppose this is all arranged and you leave right away."

"No, not exactly...Tom and I have to talk to Betty and Del yet to get their agreement...at least get Betty's okay...Del would have no problem with it. We're going to talk to them this afternoon."

Helen rose and went to him by the window. She looked out at the steady drizzle that continued to drench everything. Then she reached for his cheek and rubbed her hand gently across his skin several times.

"If this is what you want to do...that's the way it will be. Good luck with Del...good luck with Harland. I understand he is very powerful and they live in a different world than we do...that's what I hear...and read."

He was not prepared for her response. The touch, the caresses, the softness of her response were far removed from her histrionics of the past when she was not included or when she received news that was not to her liking. He was not sure how to react, unsure of what his normal reaction would or should be. So often his reactions were contrived for the occasion as he thought they should be. What was his honest answer to her? A pity he had to question himself, a pity he did not know himself better.

"Thanks, I...I appreciate getting your support."

He thought about kissing her, but she had turned away and again sat on the edge of their bed. She smiled at him.

"I better get going...I've got to meet Tom...at the church."

She did not say more and stayed seated on the bed as he left, staring out the window at the dripping trees and the soggy lawn. She was still there as his car backed down the drive and was gone.

As he rode with Tom to the Howe farm, he thought about his confusion about how Helen reacted and how he truly did not know how to automatically communicate back to her truthfully. Where had that honesty and directness gone that they once had with each other? How did it get lost? Where was the turning point when he shaded an answer? How long ago? Like the erosion from constantly running water, the honesty gap that he fell prey to had insidiously grown wider and wider until he had lost track of what the honesty should be. How simple it should be to react truthfully, but the lies and avoidance and hiding had become a routine. A routine to protect, defend, and fortify himself against any critical onslaught she might muster. A routine that provided a wall around him, shielded him as he snuck about with Keri, and gave Keri more time than he gave her.

"Something's gnawing at you, Reverend."

Tom knew his man very well, his moods, his demeanor, and how he thought about things. This pensiveness was a new turn for Stone, but Tom recognized it immediately.

"Umm, yes…yes, it is."

"Care to share? Or is it too dark for sharing? At least with me."

"I…I need…we need to accomplish our mission today with Betty…and with Del…then maybe we can talk about it…maybe."

"Fair enough, Reverend."

Tom's acceptance helped him relax a bit, but he continued to be tense, and quietly thoughtful. He would give up on his reserved demeanor when they got to the farm.

Del sat in his rocker on the front porch as he did most days since he got home from the hospital, at least the days he had not been on tour. Betty had lunch waiting. Tom had called her, told her they needed to talk about an important matter. She had agreed. He had noted the slight reluctance in her voice, but he knew she did not want to disappoint Reverend Stone. He knew that with some nudging she would agree to take Del to Columbia.

After Reverend Stone's short prayer, they sat around the kitchen table eating the ham sandwiches and potato salad

Betty had served, as he explained the opportunity with Harland Kenny and the Faith For Your Future television program.

"He is quite compelling," Betty said when Stone had finished. "I watch his program every now and then...sometimes when we've missed your service, Reverend."

She blushed a little when she made the admission.

"He certainly is a worthy substitute, Betty," Stone chuckled. "This is terrific potato salad, Betty; it was awfully thoughtful of you to have lunch for us. It's a joy."

"We would need to leave Friday morning, Betty." Tom said softly, speaking for the first time since their arrival greetings had been exchanged.

Tom didn't want to be pushy, but there was a lot to do yet and he didn't want to dally over lunch. He knew all too well that Stone had his own pace, his own way of doing things, but he was caught in the dilemma of being driven by the unchecked items on his own To-Do list.

"Do you really think we should make this trip...accept Reverend Kenny's invitation?" Betty asked.

She was confused about a decision because she was so concerned about Del. The tug of war between Dorothy and her with Don had sown seeds of doubt about proceeding with the religious efforts instead of pursuing further medical tests immediately. Reverend Stone carefully consoled her and accepted the burden of responsibility as an emissary of the Holy Spirit. She could hardly resist.

Tom smiled and patted her hand. His faith in Reverend Stone had been fulfilled.

"Betty, we'd like to make this commitment because we think it's the right thing to do. It's a great honor to be chosen for their program. Reverend Kenny believes a broader audience of Christians should be able to see and hear Del. His program can make that possible. I want to give you my assurance that when we finish the three services with Reverend Kenny, it will be the last time Del will be part of a service…until he has further medical testing."

"Yes…yes, I believe you are right."

It was arranged that Del and Betty would be picked up early Friday morning. As Tom drove Stone back to the church in Swanton, he was whistling. He was so pleased with himself he could hardly be contained.

"You knew she would agree, didn't you? You were sure of it…"

"Yes, I was, Reverend…I love a plan that unfolds the way I want it to…thanks to you."

"Am I an instrument of the Holy Spirit…or a pawn of Tom Fletcher…sometimes I wonder?"

"You are the consummate visionary of your flock's needs and the ultimate messenger of God's word. I am merely…your able assistant for the Works of the Lord."

"Let us pray this trip works out the way we want…"

"Amen for that, to the Lord we pray…and Amen again," Tom agreed, and he was dead serious.

Tom had rented a van and drove around to pick up Stone, the Howes, and finally Keri. He got Keri last because he certainly did not want Helen to see that she was included in the trip. He turned the driving over to Keri at the first rest stop once they were eastbound on the Ohio Turnpike.

"Well, folks, we're on our way to one of the most important religious broadcasting cities of the world. We are going to become part of their history…we will become legendary…at least Reverend Stone and Del will."

Tom was in high spirits and his eagerness for reaching their destination readily showed. He wanted the others to be at ease and comfortable, especially Betty and Del. There were numerous snacks, a cooler with cold drinks, a container of hot coffee, and blankets and pillows. He was most concerned about Del. How would Del hold up for the two-day jaunt, cooped up in a van for hours, and away from the farm he loved so much? Through all of his consummate arranging was the underlying feeling that perhaps, in Del, he was transporting a circus act. There was a slight air of that in all that had transpired, he suspected, or at least could be viewed as such by an outsider. This trepidation caused some uneasiness within him that he refused to show or dare share with Stone. And how long would Del continue to sound this way? What if all of a sudden at Kenny's service Del spoke normally? Secretly, he hoped Del would keep speaking in gibberish, at least until they got back to Ohio.

"Let me know when you have to make a pit stop," Tom laughed, "we can stop any time you want."

"In awhile," Betty offered.

"No problem…and Keri, you hang in with the driving until we get to Marietta…then I'll take over…get us through the mountains."

Green mile after green mile floated by with the five travelers each caught up in their own thoughts. At least four of them seemed to be pondering something; there was no telling what Del might be thinking, if indeed he were thinking at all. Del slept much of the time so it was not easy to determine his mental state. Eventually, each of them but Keri had dozed off with slack jaw and bobbing head.

They were well south of Akron when Reverend Stone pled for relief. Keri responded in short order and took them off the highway into a State rest stop. Tom and Reverend Stone parted ways from the women as they escorted Del to the Men's room. Stone emerged first from the building and stretched his legs in the shade of a nearby tree. Outside of the air conditioned van the humid heat was oppressive, but the chance to move around could not be resisted. Keri joined him as Tom ushered Betty and Del to a picnic table not far away.

"We're staying in the Kenny mansion," Stone almost whispered, "might present a problem for us…"

"I know…Tom told me. He…he warned me, rather…said I had to be very careful or this whole trip would go up in smoke…"

"He said…"

"Yes…the whole thing would go up in smoke…it was up to me to keep things cool. Our relationship could ruin everything if someone there found out about us…he didn't say that exactly, but that's what he meant."

"It will all work out…you'll see."

"Better get back on the road, folks," Tom suggested, moving to the van as he spoke.

The others dutifully followed him and boarded the van. With nap taking behind them the next order of business was snacking and drinking. They were perked up by the rest and the rest stop. It became time for the free flow of conversation. It started with Betty.

"Del likes being a part of services with you, Reverend Stone, they seem to energize him. He's very quiet until he knows he is going to be with you. This trip to Reverend Kenny's church will be a big experience for us. I've only been out of Ohio a few times and then only over the line to Indiana or up to Michigan. I've never been in the South. I think Reverend Kenny has blessed us with his invitation."

"We are blessed in many ways," Stone sighed, "so blessed. First of all, Del was not killed right off the bat…the Good Lord spared his life and for that we are most grateful. And Del was not seriously hurt, another reason to be thankful…of course, we can also be thankful that he has maintained his strength and is able to continue with me in our ministry…and, yes, the invitation is a blessing for our congregation."

Del became excited and tried to speak, his head bouncing up and down with small jerking motions as if he were keeping time to rock music. Hard to tell if his reaction was of agreement or some other agitation. He uttered his staccato gibberish for a dozen meaningless phrases, stopped, cocked his head to the left as if listening, and followed-up with another flurry of pulsed sounds that mimicked a fast-talking auctioneer.

Reverend Stone closed his eyes as he looked at Betty. He bowed his head for a moment, then turned his face skyward, and clasped his hands. He meditated for a few seconds before he spoke.

"Thank you, dear God, for your good and gracious hand that is guiding our journey...through our Lord Jesus Christ we can understand your closeness, your partnership in our new venture...know you are with us every step of the way."

"Amen to that, Reverend Stone," Tom followed, "Del is surely a miracle come into our lives. Our time in Columbia can't help but be successful."

The next afternoon, the group arrived in Columbia after an overnight motel stay in Statesville, North Carolina. They were talked out and tired. Keri was driving again and Tom easily directed her to the New World Gospel Church. They could hardly believe what they saw as they came up the main drive from the street. Flowers and flowering shrubs were everywhere. Dozens of trees had been spared when the buildings were built so there was not the picture of naked land that usually characterizes a development like this one. The map Fred Wallace had faxed to Tom showed exactly how to get to the administration building and where to park. Parking was simple because their slot was right in front of the building by the sign that read CALVARY FUNDAMENTALIST CHRISTIAN CHURCH in bold blue lettering.

"Now there's a nice touch," Tom said quietly.

"Guess they're expecting us," Keri laughed.

Like bumpkin tourists they all gawked at the surroundings as they traipsed to the door. Inside, they found themselves in a small wood-paneled reception area that was thickly carpeted. Several brightly colored watercolor paintings were displayed, obviously produced by an amateur. They were scenes of the shore with birds and water and boats, and a glimpse of the same beach house in each. In the bottom right corner of each were the initials *KLK* in one-inch high script. On the wall straight in from the entrance was a four by six feet framed aerial photograph of the campus. It clearly showed how stunning the complex really was. The room was furnished with two large uninviting leather couches with a coffee table in front of each and matching leather chairs. On each coffee table was an array of New World Gospel Church literature. There was no receptionist. Instead, a modest library table, with the look of an antique, stood underneath the aerial photo. In the center of the table was a white telephone with a label that read: DIAL GOD. The numerals 463 on the touch-pad were in bright blue, leaving no doubt as to which buttons to push. Flanking the phone stood photographs of Harland and Katherine Louise. Harland was on the right. Toward the left corner of the room was the solid door that lead to the rest of the building.

"My, my," Stone murmured, "this is not quite what I expected.

"Low key," Tom said, "very low key. Doesn't match up with what you see outside…"

Betty and Del sat on one of the couches, with Del's head fallen back as if he were passed out.

"He's just tired," Betty explained, as the others' attention focused on Del.

Keri picked up the phone and punched in 463.

"Yes…hello, we're here from Ohio…Calvary Fundamentalist…yes…thank you."

She hung up the phone and turned to Tom.

"Someone is coming to get us."

Tom quickly stepped to the door and tried the handle. It turned. He pulled the door slightly ajar, then let it slip shut.

"Just wondered," he said with a smile.

As they waited, Betty and Del dropped into their own world with a one-sided conversation about one of the trees that could be seen through the glass wall where they had entered. The tree was in full bloom with pink flowers. Del pointed and mumbled something incoherent to Betty, and she, in turn, commented to him about how pretty it was, how she did not recognize what it was, and how nice it would be to have one by their farm house.

"Welcome to New World Gospel Church," the man said, "I'm Fred Wallace...I assist Reverend Kenny. Won't y'all please come in?"

He had opened the door wide without warning. A tall, thin stalk of a man, seemingly without muscles, he gave them a smile almost impish in quality, implying something that only he knew and they would never know. He held the door for the group as they filed in, with Tom last.

"Tom Fletcher...we spoke on the phone."

"Yes, Tom, so glad to have you here."

"This is Reverend Stone," Tom introduced, "Keri Porter our church secretary...Betty and Del Howe."

They each shook Fred's hand.

"Well, Mr. Howe, we're delighted this has worked out. We saw your wonderful work with Reverend Stone..."

He saw the blank look Del gave him.

"...we saw the video of the service in your church..."

Del smiled.

"He understands, Mr. Wallace," Betty interceded, "but he won't respond. He only responds to Reverend Stone...and sometimes to me if he gets excited."

"I see...well, okay. Why don't y'all follow me and we'll meet Reverend Kenny and some of our staff."

As they walked to Kenny's office, Tom spoke.

"Grounds are very impressive..."

"Thank you, we're mighty proud of our landscaping. Reverend Kenny feels the proper surroundings...he means those that are beautiful and are well cared for...have an importance in our lives. He feels they are beneficial to provide a Godly atmosphere for everyone who works here and most especially for our parishioners who come to visit with the Holy Spirit. Makes folks feel good and see God's blessings."

"Didn't realize you have all the buildings we saw...

"Yes, we do," Fred said crisply, "I'll show you around after we meet with Reverend Kenny."

Harland Kenny's office was a marvel. More art gallery than office, its beautiful things were impressive, but the room lacked the warmth that might otherwise be expected. Kenny himself, however, was counterpoint to that deficiency. His personality radiated positively even before he spoke. With arms thrown open wide, flashing a broad smile of familiarity that said: "I don't know you yet, but I will and I already love you," he greeted Tom and the others as if they were five conquering heroes.

"This is so wonderful of you to come be with us. We are immensely grateful. All of us...and I do mean all of us...are thrilled you could get here so quickly. I feel especially privileged to have Reverend Stone and Mr. Howe become part of our services, even if it is for a brief time. Please, please, won't you have a seat? Can we get you something? Refreshments...iced tea, soda? Anyone hungry?"

"I could use a restroom," Betty sighed.

"Probably all of us could," Tom added. "We came right here from the Interstate."

"Why, of course," Harland wailed, "how inhospitable of us. Larry, why don't you show these folks where the facilities are? In the meantime, we'll get some food and drink prepared."

As the group followed Larry, Katherine Louise and Doris Miller, the church secretary, went into action. There was a small kitchenette adjacent to Harland's office and there they prepared a tray of chicken salad sandwiches and potato chips they had ready. That tray, a pitcher of iced tea, and another tray of soda and a bowl of ice cubes were carried back into the office and arranged on the small conference table to the left of Harland's imposing desk.

"I believe this will do fine until dinner," Katherine Louise purred. "These nice people can really enjoy that good ol' Southern cookin', good ol' Southern hospitality…"

Harland nodded to her. He was on the phone. He seemed to be on the phone a great deal of the time.

She grimaced at him, making sure neither Doris nor Fred could see her expression. It was if she were saying: "Better get off the phone, they'll be back soon." She was sure he saw her, but he did not react. So she stepped closer to his desk to get his attention. He nodded again, this time giving her a thumb's up sign.

Larry and the group came back into Harland's office.

"Now we can have some refreshments," Harland said as he hung up the phone, his voice commanding, never far from the presentation-quality timbre, tone, and inflection he used on the church dais.

Katherine Louise introduced herself and Doris, acted the hostess, and made sure everyone got something to eat and drink, and find a comfortable place to sit. She was most attentive to Betty and Del. She figured Reverend Stone could take care of himself all right and Tom and Keri didn't matter much. She wondered why this young girl was even with the group. She did not like what she imagined the reason might be.

"Just a little tide-me-over for you folks…we'll have a real nice dinner up at the house later." Harland was under way. "Let's see, we've got a lot of ground to cover before tomorrow's service. Do wish we could have done tonight's, but that's okay. Doris, pass out the program packets to our guests if you would please. Now then…"

Harland went into a long explanation of what the packets contained, detailing their outlined agenda, and answering Tom and Stone's questions. Keri's eyes glazed over, partly from the long drive they had just finished and partly because she was overwhelmed with the details. Harland droned on about it with great elaboration. Her eyelids flickered, but she fought the urge to let them slam shut. She worked at distracting the urge by making notes, looking intently at Harland without blinking, concentrating on the pattern of the large Persian rug, and by digging her nails into her thighs from time to time. Through this ritual of staying awake she noticed Larry Stovall and she realized that he was watching her very carefully. In fact, she well understood that he was scrutinizing her with that appreciative relish that appears on a man's face when he is mentally salivating over an attractive woman. He was so obvious, she thought, but no one else was paying attention to him as no one else was paying attention to her. She checked her skirt. Had it pulled up too far? No cleavage. She did have nice legs, but sitting down…? What was it? It didn't matter, he had focused on her. She would have to talk to him and find out what it was. This trip might just be more interesting than she had thought it could be.

Larry was just about as good-looking as a Georgia farm boy could ever be. He could have been the highlight of the room if it were not for Harland. He was the New World television production manager, single, thirty years old, and, in the eyes of most women, including Keri, he was gorgeous. Wavy blonde hair, the trim, muscular body of an athlete, and a flashing, grinning, infectious kind of movie-star smile. He had been fixed on Keri since she had come into the office. Then there was that thing that took place, the thing where their eyes finally meet and whammo, instant heat. He looked to see if there were a ring on her left hand, relieved there was not.

Harland became animated with excitement when he got to the explanation of how the service would go the next day. Everything was well planned, much the same way Tom orchestrated the services at Calvary. Only this was a much more elaborate scripting of events; not in the generalities Tom used, but with precise instructions and directions for everyone involved. When he was satisfied that Reverend Stone and Del and Betty understood exactly what they were to do and when, he finished with a flourish.

"This will be a stunning service Reverend Stone...Del...Betty..."

"Are you sure you want me up there with you?" Betty asked timidly.

"Of course, Mrs. Howe, of course. Our parishioners and the viewers on national television will want to see Del's partner also. Yes, indeed, you are a part of our service."

"All right," she said quietly.

She, too, was tired from the drive and running out of energy. Harland realized it.

"I think its time for a quick tour, Fred, then up to the house to get some rest before dinner. What do you say folks? Why don't you go with Fred?"

They all nodded and voiced agreement and Fred took them through a maze of hallways until they reached the rear entrance where several golf carts were parked. One of the carts was larger than the others and able to carry all of them.

Tom sat next to Fred, Betty and Del right behind them, and Stone and Keri on the rear seats, facing backward. As Fred started away from the building, Tom decided to shortstop the tour.

"Fred, since we came here right after a long drive we're pretty tired...and since we're going to be here for several weeks maybe we shouldn't try to do a tour right now. Why don't you just show us the church?"

"We can do that," Fred agreed, "y'all can see what we've got around here later. Good idea to see where we're going to be tomorrow, though."

The building that housed the church was immense. Four of Calvary Fundamentalist could have fit inside the main auditorium. There was nothing elaborate about it, a clear message that function not frills was the watchword in its construction and furnishings. The expansive dais was contained at the front of a tiered section that held the choir. A speaker's podium was positioned just left of center with seating available at either side for speakers and participants in the service. There was no visible cross, which caused both Tom and Stone to wonder about as they gawked at the setting. For Tom, it was reminiscent of the Grand Old Opry hall in Nashville.

"I don't see a cross..." Stone said, almost as if he were thinking aloud rather than asking a question.

"No, you won't see one right away...we have them...they're here all right, you can find them in the woodwork in strategic places. Then for services, we project a large cross on that back wall over the choir. We have a special projector in the rear at the lighting station next to the television control booth. We can change the size, color, or configuration on the fly as the service is progressing...makes for an excellent effect and shows up well on camera. Larry runs everything from up there."

New World Gospel Church was impressive, but for Tom, except for its size, not much different than Calvary, or, in fact, several of the churches on their Ohio tour. This meant for familiar and comfortable surroundings for Del, he figured, and no problem in working with Harland's script.

They did not spend much time in the church. Fatigue gripped all of them and was very apparent to Fred. He got them back in the golf cart and headed to the house. The drive took several minutes, time for the group to enjoy the lush groupings of shrubs and colorful bed after bed of flowers.

"Is that it?" Reverend Stone asked as the mansion came into sight.

"Sure 'nough," Fred nodded. "This is the humble abode of Reverend and Mrs. Kenny…your hosts for the next three weeks."

Tom and Stone thought perhaps Fred was being a bit sarcastic about the place since it was light years from being "humble." But he was serious and the look on his face confirmed it to them as they each took note of his reaction after making the proclamation.

"Looks like something out of a movie to me," Tom offered.

"Like every postcard of the old South I've seen," Betty added.

"It's very nice…y'all are going to enjoy your stay, I'm sure." Fred was being gracious, but somehow still sounded sarcastic.

As they paraded up the steps to the porch, Tom got Fred's attention and slowed him to lag behind the others.

"We need to confer a bit," Tom said awkwardly. "…about our expenses?"

"Folks, go on inside, Tom and I will be right with you."

They stopped and Fred handed Tom two envelopes.

"This one has a thousand dollars in cash for expenses. That should cover things for a few days...and we'll get you more as you need. That one has a check for five thousand. That's not firm. Let's see how we do with contributions after tomorrow and we'll go from there."

"Thanks," Tom said as he pocketed the envelopes.

The door to the mansion was opened by a short, thin black man with a light gray mat of marcelled hair, in his mid-fifties, with few facial lines, and erect posture. He bowed his head just slightly before he spoke.

"Welcome to the Kenny home. Y'all please come in."

"Thanks, Carlton," Fred said. "Folks, this is Carlton Moore...man who helps the Kennys with the house along with Jessie Reed who does the cooking. Y'all will find they can take good care of you. Isn't that right, Carlton?"

"Yessuh, it certainly is."

Not only was the house monumental in size, it was as luxuriously detailed and furnished as Harland's office, if that were possible, and stunning to behold. Furniture had been shipped from Europe, pristine Southern antiques were there plus a few well-done knock-offs, and art of all kinds and tastes was in abundance. Art in abundance meant that it was overdone. Too many paintings, too much statuary, and too many nick-knacks stuck on tables and various shelves. It was as if there were enough money to buy these things, so why not? The odd thing about this collection, and its saving grace, was that nothing clashed in terms of patterns, designs, and color schemes. They all seemed to go together, disparate though they were, even with as much chance as there was to be a décor disaster.

"Welcome, welcome, welcome," Katherine Louise cried as she came down the hall toward them. "Time to relax and undo and freshen up for dinner. Come on in and I'll show you where y'all be staying."

She took over as hostess and Fred sort of oozed himself out of the picture without another word. He simply vanished as the power and the to-do of her flamboyance took over, relieved of any more responsibility to the group right then. She never acknowledged him and he exited without being noticed. She was proud of her home which she called "our nest" and regaled everyone with descriptions and explanations of items they passed as she showed them to the second floor and their rooms. A tour guide in her own house, she had full command of information about all of the things on display and in use. Good things, even precious things need to be used, she lectured, and restated that proposition several times as she went from room to room getting them situated. Beautiful things are part of the reverence for God, she exclaimed, and this she emphasized with the phrase: "Beauty is God…God in our life every day."

Whether for reasons of propriety or just plain circumstance, Tom's room was between Stone's and Keri's. In either case, it kept their rooms apart and not quite as easy for nighttime movement between the rooms. Stone and Keri had separate rooms on the Ohio tour, but that did not keep them apart at night. Although at this point she could not yet understand why, Keri was glad she was not right next to Stone. She would eventually come to know the meaning of her relief.

Katherine Louise left them alone to do whatever they needed to do for rest and recovery from the long day filled with travel, introduction to their new surroundings, and the pressures of facing tomorrow's service. She made sure everything was progressing in the kitchen the way she had instructed, reminded Carlton to call the guests at seven sharp, checked herself in the full length mirror in the back hall, and left for the evening service. The conflict could not be avoided; she had to be with Harland at the church. There was no way she could be hostess for dinner. The prospect made her uneasy and the conflict gave her a dull throbbing sensation at the back of her neck.

Tom rapped on Stone's door.

"Come in…"

Tom opened the door to find Reverend Stone lying on the bed in his boxer shorts and tee-shirt. A vague look of disappointment flitted across Stone's face. It had been very brief, but Tom was sure he had seen it.

"Expecting someone else?"

"Ah, no…"

"A word of advice, Reverend…be very careful while we're here."

"Discretion is my guideline…not to worry."

"Quite the deal, isn't it?"

Tom sat in the ornately upholstered chair near the solid walnut dresser.

"It's something else. What do you make of it so far?"

Tom clasped his hands behind his head before he spoke and drew in a deep breath through his nose and exhaled, also through his nose. It made a slight whistling sound and he pinched his nose in response. He pulled at his ear before he spoke.

"Our man Fred passed money to me outside. I put it in my briefcase. A thousand cash…five thousand in a check. He said there's more expense money as we need it and…"

"Yeah?"

"And more money based on what comes in after tomorrow."

"My oh my…the bounty of the Lord."

"Amen," Tom said with his eyes closed.

Carlton served dinner after every one of the group was seated. He was very precise, very deliberate in his manner of bringing each course to the table on a rolling cart made from solid cherry, dating to the mid 1920s. It was a piece in excellent condition that Katherine Louise had successfully bid for at an estate auction in Greenwood. She outbid several dealers from Charleston who didn't have her nerve or her money. The cart was a thing of pride for Carlton, almost a status symbol for his esteemed position in the Kenny mansion. He was, after all, a polished servant of note and merit. He had chosen to work for Katherine Louise and could have been employed by any number of wealthy Columbians who wished dearly that he would have been in their household.

None of the five had ever before been served a meal with quite the pomp, efficiency, attentiveness, and flair that Carlton bestowed on them. He assisted Betty and Keri with their linen napkins the way any professional waiter would do in a fine restaurant, he made sure their crystal water goblets were filled, secured coffee and iced tea to their liking, and determined that each of them was pleased with their meal.

"The only thing missing," Stone commented, "is a great wine."

On hearing this, Carlton stiffened, stopped what he was doing.

'No alcohol is served in this house, Reverend."

"Oh, of course not, Carlton, just an observation based on the spread you've put out for us. None of us use alcohol anyway."

"I had forgotten about the Saturday night service," Tom said, changing the subject, "too bad the Kennys aren't here for dinner."

"They always eat late on Saturdays," Carlton explained, "we'll take good care of them later."

"I'm sure."

No one spoke again until Carlton pushed his cart back to the kitchen.

"How is your room, Betty?" Reverend Stone asked.

"Lovely, Reverend, Del and I will be very comfortable. There's a nice bathroom, you know."

Del nodded agreement and continued eating.

"It's important for both of you to be comfortable while you are here. This will be a lot of work for Del...and you."

"We'll be fine, I think."

"What do you think so far, Tom?" Keri asked the question tentatively as she dabbed at her salad.

Before Tom answered, he looked over at the closed door where Carlton had exited.

"Harland and KL certainly know how to do it up big time..."

"KL?" Stone voiced.

"Sure, it was on the paintings in the lobby over at their office building. KL was on all of them. Katherine Louise. Anyway they've got quite a thing going here...a real enterprise...and a cook and a...a...let's see, Carlton is a what? A butler, a waiter, a what? Man in waiting?"

"Butler, probably," Keri ventured. "Very good at what he does."

"Yes he is," Tom agreed.

They continued eating silently for a few minutes. Fatigue had overtaken them and it became easier to not talk. Then Tom broke the silence.

"Let me answer Keri's question..."

"Which?" Stone asked.

"She asked what I thought so far..."

"Oh...yes."

"Here's what I think. I think we have stumbled into one of the nicest situations I could have imagined for us...for Calvary...for Reverend Stone. I knew that Harland was maybe one or two in the country with his mission here...with the broadcasts and everything, but just look at the surroundings. Look at what we've seen today. They are a success and they provide us...me, Reverend Stone, and our board...with a model that we can pattern ourselves after. We need to learn as much about their operation as possible. Now, Keri, I want you to get next to that church secretary...what's her name...oh, you know...the one we met..."

"Doris," Keri interjected, "I think her last name is Miller."

"Yes, Doris...Mrs. Miller...that's her. I want you to get close to her and find out about the mechanics of things...soliciting donations, handling the money...scheduling, programming, arrangements, everything you can. Make notes, get it written up. Like a report...so we have something tangible to take to our board of trustees. We are going to get more out of this trip then I ever dreamed of."

"I will, Tom."

"Starting tomorrow, if she is around...and if it's doable." He was excited and tugged at his ear.

"Okay."

"I also think," Tom went on, "that we have connected to someone in Harland who knows the spirit of the Lord and communicates the Holy Spirit, and as a result the Lord has blessed Harland. Faith, my fellow Christians, by Faith shall ye lead and by Faith shall the flock follow. What say you Reverend Stone?"

"You know, in my prayer tonight before dinner, I spoke of what we are receiving from God as we get involved with Harland and his church. We can never forget how God has given us this chance to fulfill our mission with our own flock with the benefits we are receiving here. Again, God has spoken through Del and given us the light to lead our way on this path to bringing His message to Believers nationwide. I also think this is a fabulous setting to do our work. We receive and we shall give in return...give praise to Almighty God and give by spreading his word to those who need to know about His salvation. Perhaps Katherine Louise is right...beauty beside us is the power of the Lord visibly with us. We can certainly enjoy his bounty here at New World."

"That's very true, Reverend Stone," Keri said absently, wrapped in her own thoughts, her own emotions reflecting her experiences of the day.

"So true," Betty echoed.

Del smiled and nodded and went on eating.

"What do you think of Harland and Katherine Louise?"

Tom directed his question to Reverend Stone, but Keri and Betty were ready to answer.

"He's very engaging and she's charming...good team I would guess. I agree with you that they can guide us...we can learn a lot from them."

"They mean to make it easy for us to be here," Betty said.

"Yes...yes, they do."

Tom said the words as if he agreed with her. Inside, he wondered who the Kennys really were. His own dubious past cast a shadow on his thinking because he assumed the possibility for anyone to have something in their history they would rather not have anyone else know.

Carlton cleared the dishes and then served cherry pie with each piece topped by a generous dollop of vanilla ice cream. He waited until they left the dining room and had gone upstairs to their rooms before he rolled out from the kitchen with his cart to pick up the dessert dishes. He had enough of them for one day and wished no more interchange with these Yankees.

Keri and Reverend Stone lay naked beneath the covers of her bed, caught in the after-sex purgatory of semi-consciousness. The sounds of the Kennys returning home from the evening service jarred their senses, brought a tension that gripped both of them. They could not hear exactly what was being said, but the excited voices and laughter probably meant the service went well. They could hear Carlton talking and then quieter conversation replaced the loud talking.

"They must be eating…"

"Yes…" Keri agreed.

"I better get back to my room…"

"Uh-huh."

He pulled on his robe, picked up his pajamas, and left her room without kissing her. It was a poignant oversight, one that shocked her, but did not disappoint. She realized she was glad he had not kissed her again. She was not sure why and she tossed and turned for some time trying to sort out what the reason might be. She finally decided it did not matter and dropped away into sleep.

It had been a long day for all of them.

9.

Out of the depths I have cried to You, O Lord; Lord, hear my voice! Let Your ears be attentive to the voice of my supplications.

-Psalm 130:1-2

The smell of freshly cut wet grass was a tonic for Betty and Del as they took their Sunday morning walk. Because the years of memories were so strong and because they were reminded of the farm they missed, the smell was fairly intoxicating. They often took walks together, but Sunday morning walks had always been special. Sunday had always been the day of rest and reflection, a time reserved for church going and praise to the Almighty in thanks for what they had, and a time when family could come together for council, support, encouragement, and the interchange of ideas. Del had frequently stressed the importance of expressing opinions and talking about the news and new ways of looking at things. Sunday had been a special day in their lives.

Betty remarked how heavy the dew was without knowing a sophisticated, computer-controlled sprinkling system had saturated the green expanse. The lawn glistened as it mirrored the morning sun, an early warning reminder of the oppressively hot and humid day ahead. Right now the slowly increasing heat did not matter to them. It was so quiet, with only the songs of the many birds breaking through. Far from a street or road, there was no sound of traffic. A narrow stream burbled across the campus wending its way to the Saluda River, but the shallow trickle of running water hardly made a sound. The walkway Del and Betty were following crossed the stream on a wooden footbridge where they stopped to stare at their own reflection in the clear water. The image was an amusing picture of them that was periodically distorted by water bugs or minnows. The result was a fun-house kind of twisting and misshaping as if their heads were made of taffy that was being pulled.

Betty still carried the cup that Carlton had given her as they began their walk. He had made sure it was full of hot decaffeinated coffee with just the right amount of cream as she liked it. She had finished the coffee, but there were still a few drops left and she tilted the cup so they dropped to the stream. The image changed again as ripples formed, spreading rings of bouncing faces, fracturing their heads into pieces, a crazy-quilt that slowly came back to taffy-pulling focus. Betty wondered to herself if that were some kind of omen. Could the beautiful picture she had of her life with Del be shattered by all of this effort with Reverend Stone? All of the travel, the intense worship services, and being away from home? She hoped not and said a silent prayer to God that it would not be so. Please, God, I don't want Del to be a sacrifice. She believed, she knew, that it did not work that way with God. What is, is. You cannot pray for rain, or for your hockey team to win, or for your husband not to die. Such prayers were an insult to God, she figured, because God did not intercede in life on a moment-to-moment basis. Real prayer was different, real prayer was for goodness, salvation, and redemption. Real prayer was for the basic feelings held within the heart and soul. Real prayer was for a peaceful world and help for the poor and an end to mankind's sufferings.

The morning walk in this beautiful setting seemed to energize Del's spirit. He strode with enthusiasm and purpose, stopping to smell flowers, constantly looking and pointing, and periodically murmuring some sort of commentary about what they were experiencing. The full measure of enjoyment for Betty was sapped by not being able to understand Del and by not being able to have the banter and talk that at one time would have characterized these moments together. She made the best of the situation however, fully believing that one day they would have those times back again.

The enormity of the Kenny mansion was very apparent from where they stood, the structure framed between two huge pine trees, its bulk a monument of wild proportions. Betty could see the others gathering on the veranda for breakfast, could see Carlton bustling about making sure all were being properly served. She was content in her decision to get up early with Del, suspecting Carlton would take care of them. Based on what she had seen the previous night at dinner, he would take very good care of them for breakfast, and indeed he did.

The side table of food that Carlton had delivered on his cart for the buffet breakfast was a feast to start the day. A pot of strong decaffeinated coffee, bags and hot water for tea, several selections of sweet rolls, grits, scrambled eggs, sausage, bacon, ham slices, fried potatoes, and three kinds of toast with four varieties of jams were set out for all to savor. Carlton was most proud of the table. He had placed a tall vase of freshly cut flowers from the garden at the table center to be surrounded by the food, a fitting touch to his handiwork. He stood by handing out warm plates as each person came to the buffet table.

"Wonderful spread, Carlton," Harland bellowed, "and give our congratulations to Jessie. She always does a fine breakfast. On second thought, I'll tell her myself before we leave...she needs to hear it from me...she deserves it, in fact."

As the others, including Katherine Louise, arrived he urged them to eat substantially.

"Fuel up, everyone...we need our strength this morning. Is everyone here? No...we're missing Del and Betty, of course..."

"They's walkin' on the grounds," Carlton reported dutifully. "Says they needs their Sunday morning walk. I made sure they were well fed before they went off. Back soon, they told me."

"Well, that's just fine. So we can proceed without them right now, but let's offer words of prayer to our Lord and Savior Jesus Christ on this momentous day. Lord God Almighty, please accept our praise and gratitude for this glorious day filled with sunshine to light and brighten our day and enlighten our hearts and minds...it is your countenance on our lives. We give thanks for the blessing of this food and the company of these outstanding, hard-working, and diligent Christians from Ohio who are on a mission with us to bring forth your word in a new way, in a new spirit, and with profound meaning. Provide us with the strength and ability to do your work well. In Christ's name...Amen."

"Amen," all said except Carlton, who stood silently, motionless, with eyes closed. He had said a prayer of his own to himself.

Harland ate ravenously as if he had not eaten in days, talking all the while about his excitement in anticipation of the program they would have that morning. They were seated in cushioned directors' chairs around a large circular wrought-iron table that Carlton had furnished with flowered linen place mats. He periodically talked with food in his mouth and when he did, Katherine Louise tapped him gently on the arm. She understood his exuberance, but her studied sense of refinement was not curtailed because it was Harland. Appearances were important to her, even for these farmers from Ohio.

As Reverend Stone fed a hearty appetite, Tom was more careful, more reserved in what he ate, conscious of watching his weight. Keri had taken little of what was offered on the buffet and she picked at that. She poked her fork into and around the dab of scrambled eggs and grits, nibbled slightly on a piece of toast, and only sipped a few times from her coffee cup. She was in a funk, but no one else paid attention to her, so wrapped up as they were in what Harland was saying. She had not heard a word he had said.

Harland was finished eating well before the others, excused himself from the table, and went inside to the kitchen to thank Jessie. After several minutes he returned to the table, standing behind Katherine Louise with his hand on her shoulder. "Now, you folks just take your time and enjoy your breakfast. I'm going on over to the church to make sure things are ready for today. Come on over quarter to nine or so with Del and Betty and we'll sort of walk through how we want things to go. Okay? See y'all later." Brief case in hand, he was off to the church in a custom-made golf cart emblazoned with the New World Gospel Church logo and his and Katherine Louise's names. There were still two hours until the church service. As Harland drove off, Katherine Louise excused herself and went inside.

"When we get back," Tom determined, "we're going to get an artist to make us a design for Calvary. Did you see that on the golf cart? Very nice. We need something like that."

Keri looked on as she twirled her hair and wished she were someplace else.

Harland had not been gone long when Del and Betty wandered back to the mansion and out onto the veranda. The day's heat was cranking up and Del showed its effects with the beads of perspiration that stood out on his forehead. They sat down with the others.

"More coffee ma'am?" Carlton offered.

"Ice water would be nice," Betty came back to him.

"You, sir?" Carlton knew Del could not answer him, but he extended the courtesy nonetheless.

"Ice water for Del, too, Carlton, if you would."

"How was your walk?" Reverend Stone asked.

"Very pleasant," Betty said, "but Del is very agitated…sort of restless. I think he is keyed up about this morning. I know he understands how important this service is…he wants it to go well…"

"It can't not go well, Betty," Reverend Stone stated seriously, "there is no bad or poor situation about it..."

Del grinned and shook his head affirmatively, and spilled coffee as he bumped the table in excitement.

"Del is ready and raring to go," Tom agreed, "and so are all of us."

Carlton was relieved when these guests left the veranda and pleased when they were out of the mansion headed for the church. He wondered how he would cope during the next three weeks with these Yankee farmers. He would manage, he figured, because his God was with him, his patience blessed by his Lord.

The Calvary folks dutifully got to the church at eight forty-five, with Del, Betty, and Reverend Stone moving down to the large stage, and Tom and Keri taking seats in the control room. Larry was already full steam ahead with his staff making final preparations for the service, which they called the "action."

Any metaphor such as "heart" or "brain" or "nerve center," used to describe the control room in New World Gospel Church would be appropriate. Here, Larry Stovall commanded the television production that was uplinked to a satellite that carried the program to Christian Gospel Broadcasting. Faith For Your Future was a firmly entrenched staple in CGB's programming lineup and Harland Kenny had established his stature as that program's weekly pastor. His message was always upbeat, emphasizing the positive in his viewers, examining the possible for all who wanted the possible to occur.

From this eight by twenty feet sound-proof room, Larry controlled four dolly-mounted cameras and two hand-held cameras. To his left, was a technician who handled the lights and the sound using a large panel of switches and meters. Three other technicians were responsible for the technical direction of the video picture from the service; on-screen word generation that gave subtitles, names, and other information; and the feed to the satellite uplink that went to the network. Doris Miller stood by as Larry's assistant during the entire production.

Fred Wallace strode into the room soon after Tom and Keri arrived. He was there to say "God Bless all of you hard working production people," before he took his place with the choir which was in the process of assembling across the back of the stage.

"Let's make this a memorable show today, everyone" Fred evoked, "and keep your fingers crossed that this guy Del turns out to be what we think he is. No offense, Tom, but the Lord's mission needs to be achieved. The Lord's mission today is a live television program broadcast nationwide. We have a commitment to CGB...they expect us to fulfill that commitment and provide a wonderful hour of Christian broadcasting."

Tom said that he understood, but the truth was he did not really understand...yet.

Fred smiled openly, easily, and left the control room.

"One hour to action," Tom heard one of the engineering crew announce at nine.

"Doors open," Doris announced.

"How did she know?" Tom whispered to Keri.

"She has a thing in her ear," Keri whispered back.

"So I see...she's in contact with other people around the building..."

"I think so," Keri said softly. "She must have some way of talking..."

"Make a note of that."

Less than twenty minutes after the doors of the church were unlocked, the first arrivals entered and sat in a scattered pattern throughout the large auditorium. In the next fifteen minutes more and more came in and were seated so that almost half of the seats were occupied thirty minutes before the time of the service. Curiosity on this day was part of the reason, but even on ordinary Sundays a large contingent was on hand when the choir began at nine-thirty.

The sweep and magnitude of vocal sound from this body musical, roughly one hundred-fifty strong, was produced with breathtaking effect that was a majestic backdrop to the New World services. They sang as one voice, effortlessly it seemed, a blend quite astounding in its union. Their contribution to the power of a service at New World could not be overstated. Their contribution was in providing an emotionally charged backdrop that held everything together that got presented from Sunday to Sunday. They offered one musical voice to heighten the feelings that emanated from rational words, and that gave tangible offering to the covenant of faith.

"Now there's a choir," Tom observed critically, "there's a choir that has been drilled like an Army unit…precision, precision, precision…and with passion. They have passion. We need to find out who their director is and talk to him…or her."

"I made a note," Keri answered.

In the area directly in front of the stage was a supporting musical ensemble that included a lead guitar and piano as well as an additional assemblage of guitars, saxes, and horns. Standing by them was a young black girl singer who was specially miked for her performances. Each of them had carefully been noted in the script that was established by Larry and given to everyone who would have a part in today's service; the very script that had been given to Reverend Stone.

As the choir was singing their fourth number, Katherine Louise came onto the stage from the right. She was dressed in a floor length summer dress that was well-designed, modest, yet very attractive, and sedately colored. Her bearing, her manner, commanded attention. She walked slowly to the center of the stage as the choir muted its song. She was now the star of New World until Harland appeared, the star that she had created and desperately wanted to be. Not far removed from the carnie midway, but a whole lot more respectable.

"Hear my cry, oh Lord, for I am the lamb of God...have mercy on us all..."

She was carefully miked so that she could be distinctly heard anywhere in the auditorium. The sound of the choir came up behind her as she paused, fully attuned to her speech pattern and intonation. Her pause for dramatic affect was deliberately extended then released with the expertise of true showmanship and timing that would make any actor proud and their director congratulate himself.

"...for we are sinners, here today so that You can wash away our sins...so that you can bless our lives and lead us from temptation to the paths of righteousness...that is our goal, oh Lord. Let the Holy Spirit free us from worry and doubt and longing and fear so that we may revel in Christ's name with the understanding that we can be saved in his name. Amen, Lord, Amen. Amen, Amen."

She sang rather than spoke the last two amens and the choir reinforced her plea.

"Let us rejoice in the name of the Lord, so that we as sinners may achieve the peace we so desire in this life...for in his name do we find a New World of calm and satisfaction in our life...He is the way."

Now, many steps removed and a whole world apart from the carnie, she still retained her skill at reaching individuals in an audience. As that adroit ability came into play, the connection she made with them was so palpable Tom stood up in reaction. It was an involuntary, utterly reflexive move on his part as if she had physically touched him. The choir reinforced the impact.

"We're so glad you're here with us today…I know some are from close by, but others make the effort to drive long distances to get here…"

She went on for several minutes with her personal outreach as more and more people found their way into the auditorium. The manner in which she did it, each of them thought that she was talking specifically to them. Her body language, eye contact, the way she tilted her head and moved her arms and hands, all went together in communication symmetry. She made them feel a part of New World.

It was now two minutes until broadcast time. Katherine Louise continued her connection with the congregation as the television cameramen took positions that Larry directed from the control center. Everyone in the control room was tense, ready for the program to start, hoping there were no hitches in the live broadcast. Larry's support team was ready and waiting, marveling at Katherine Louise, when Reverend Harland Kenny, Reverend Stone, Betty, and Del began their procession to the stage. With one minute to air time Katherine Louise concluded her audience warm-up and sat down on the left side of the stage. The choir filled the church with song and the band picked up underneath them. As their music swelled, Carol Robinson became a lone voice carrying the music to full amplification with a complex series of vocal gymnastics that would make both Aretha Franklin and Whitney Houston envious and proud. Carol was a marvel. Statuesque at just over six feet tall, slim, with perfect facial features, and with the exotic looks and quality of a Nubian princess, she commanded attention from the audience and from viewers at home. She was quite an introduction to the New World service.

"Camera three, get a wide shot of the choir for the opening," Larry droned into the microphone in front of him, "camera one pick up Reverend Kenny and the others and be ready. Floater one, keep on Carol. Camera two get set on KL…ready camera two…cut to camera two…camera four get a wide shot of Reverend Kenny and the others…that's it…fade to two…now cut back to one. Camera three pick up the audience, see if you can get some good facials, smiles right now, we'll get more emotional later. Sonny, get around low to the side of the stage and pick them up as they come up on stage…"

The program was underway ten seconds before Harland Kenny reached the stage. It was dramatic just as Larry wanted, but Del's forlorn look diminished the impact. That would soon be overcome, however, when Harland spoke to the audience. He was a gifted speaker and his voice resonated throughout the auditorium, fixing attention on him, instantly capturing the spirits of the audience, and at the same time, making them feel at ease with being in this place on this Sunday. Harland was not fire and brimstone, he was touchy-feely, and he made his audience and his viewers hunger for the Word of God that he preached.

Harland was poised, center stage, with Carol holding lilting notes, holding the attention, maintaining a quality of showmanship that went beyond a juggling act or a trapeze artist. She was shining, like a glorious star, with only Chuck Simpson on guitar and Ted Blauvet on piano to hold her to earth. She was a helium balloon on their tether, dancing in the wind of her own making. It was her moment and she gave it all she had. Then she let the notes slide away and Harland took over with his first word spoken just as her last note died. Harland was now ready to be king. He was ready to tend to his flock.

"God Almighty is ever present for us," Harland bellowed, his voice carrying to the back of the church without a microphone, "but we do not, no, we do not always see his works. Today, yes, this very day…right now, we have a chance, a rare opportunity to be blessed with the manifestation of his presence…the reality of God is with us…the breath of the Holy Spirit will fall upon us. Yes, yes…a miracle of God awaits us in the body of Delwin Howe. He has come to us from Ohio…stricken, one might say, yet blessed in the assessment of others. He is blessed with the word of God, given to us in the manner of the Biblical speakers in tongues. Interpreted and ordained by Reverend Stone. Reverend Stone gives us the message God wants us to hear. To hear and to learn…to foster better lives in Christ's name…"

The choir murmured a plaintive background of support.

"In Corinthians, Paul makes note of speaking in tongues, the altered state of a man when God talks through him. The Greek scholars knew about this and they named it Glossolalia, based on the Greek roots for tongue or language and to speak in such. The production of this speech historically has had religious significance because we know that it is filled with the Holy Spirit…a bountiful gift of the Holy Spirit."

"This guy does his homework," Tom snapped at Keri, "get the spelling of that word…glossa something and look it up."

She dutifully made a note.

Chester Ridenour stepped forward from the tenor section of the choir and began a simple solo of righteousness in God's name, a song of words fraught with the pain of man's temptation and salvation, words that conveyed man's struggle with the world around him, and his desire to be saved, to have his life synchronized with God as the Bible taught the Way. Chester had a luscious voice that moved easily between baritone and tenor, but rested comfortably most often in the tenor range. He did not seem to breathe, his effortless delivery a vocal stroke of beauty the way a perfect sunset sets calmly within those who view its magnificence. His last gilded note carrying through until Harland had brought Reverend Stone and Del to center stage. Betty stayed seated nearby, next to Katherine Louise. The audience was transfixed.

Harland nodded to Stone, his cue for beginning with Del.

"Let us pray," Stone asked, "please rise and pray with me."

All rose as if one body, anticipating and receptive for what was to come. Most heads were bowed. No one seemed to notice the six camera men duly intent on the action before them.

"Oh Lord our God, we come again to have you speak to us through this man Delwin Howe. We have been most grateful for what you have revealed to us in the past and now await your word through him again. He is the vessel to receive your gift to us. He is the way of truth and the mode of contact with your voice...your spirit...your determination for our lives. Thank you Lord, for Del, thank you Lord for this gift, thank you Lord for allowing me to help bring your Word to this wonderful congregation, this body of living Disciples of Christ..."

Reverend Stone raised his left hand to the audience in a clever way that asked for, almost demanded a response, and they gave back to him.

"Amen," all said.

"Amen," Stone echoed. "The Amen of acceptance and reception, the Amen that says Lord speak to me. Tell me Lord what you want me to hear. Use Delwin Howe to bring your word to me. Yes, Amen, Lord, Amen and thank you for this wonderful blessing."

Stone touched Del on the shoulder before he spoke again using the index finger on his right hand as if he were part of the apparition on the ceiling of the Sistine Chapel. This touch was a trigger, a signal that transformed Del from a defeated, embattled Christian into a defiant warrior of God. Del stood taller, his eyes suddenly shone brighter, and he flexed his muscles like a boxer waiting for the bell.

For the next several minutes Del babbled in the usual incomprehensible gibberish that Tom had seen come from him. But then it changed in intensity. His voice rose in volume, his eyes rolled back so that only the whites showed, he began twitching with spasms, his face was flushed, spittle flew from his mouth as he uttered the strange sounds, and his body moved in rhythmic patterns as mucous slid out of his nose across his mouth and dripped from his chin. Betty came to his side and held his arm. Her body seemed to twitch and jump in concert with his movements and she was afraid for him. This outpouring went on for nearly twenty minutes with Betty hanging on for dear life, Stone directing the finger of God to him, and the audience mesmerized with the specter as they were caught between abject fascination and the fear of total Damnation. Finally, Del suddenly stopped vocalizing and nearly collapsed. He was totally exhausted and could barely walk as Betty lead him to the chairs by Katherine Louise to the left of center stage.

"That's a first," Tom said, "looks like he's ready to drop dead. I'm not sure he can do that sort of thing two more times."

"That sort of thing?" Keri scoffed.

"Shut up," Tom came back, "you know what I mean."

Larry was frantic with directions to his camera men, a maniac of commands and counter-manned commands. He was intent on getting the best shots for the television audience and he got them.

"Thank you Betty for your tremendous support of Del. Let's have Del sit down and rest. He has given us a roadmap of God's choosing that will be a beacon for our lives..."

Betty helped Del to his seat as quickly as she could. He was so exhausted that he could barely walk. Twice his knees buckled slightly before he could get to the chair. He slumped down, a jumble of rumpled suit coat and wrinkled pants, a pitiful wretch with chin down on his chest. His tie that Betty had neatly tied for him was askew, his white shirt showing the stains of perspiration, and his hair messed as if he had never combed it. She patted his arm, whispered consoling words to him, and kissed him sweetly on the cheek. He was as disoriented and bedraggled as a drowned cat much like that day right after the lightening had struck. Betty wondered how he could possibly go through this sort of thing on two more Sundays.

Reverend Stone smiled at them, acknowledging her comforting, and then embarked on a presentation that was the revelation of Del's words. It was brilliant in content, connecting with the problems and perils of everyday life. He spoke softly at first, but soon launched into a powerful story of redemption, righteousness, and reward that was tightly based in Biblical verse and deftly referenced by him. He talked directly to the television cameras as if they were individuals and Larry salivated in appreciation for his poise and demeanor as the pictures processed through the control center. Reverend Stone made love to the television camera as well as any Hollywood star, perhaps better, probably with more conviction. His word was Del's word which was God's word, which was the voice and the message that was wanted. Del's performance was a smashing success. Stone knew it. Larry knew it, and Katherine Louise knew it.

Harland sniffed and no one saw his fleeting sign of derision. It didn't matter because there were two more shows to get finished and his true reactions were best kept to himself. He was poised to take over as soon as Stone finished, but the Ohio Reverend was on a roll and continued to let it rip in God's name.

"We are all sinners and God knows that about us…he knows, believe me he knows and he doesn't care…as long as we come to him in Christ's name…come to him with our prayer for forgiveness…our prayer to be saved in Christ's name…our prayer to be born again in the light of the Holy Spirit and stand before God as his faithful servant." Reverend Stone was finishing. "Let this be the understanding that we received from Del today. Lord hear our prayer…Lord we cry out to you to hear our prayer. And we know that you will, for your Son said it would be so. Amen, Lord God, Amen."

"Amen," all said loudly and amen continued to be heard randomly across the congregation for several minutes as Chester Ridenour's beautiful voice carried forth. He was backed by the choir and all the instrumentalists, and joined by Carol Robinson. Eventually, those in the congregation who knew the words added their voices to the singing. This was Harland's cue to come forward again and regain center stage.

Harland delivered a short homily that centered on the importance of being aware and attuned for, listening to and hearing, and, at last, receptive to the Word of God. It was a cleverly presented follow-up to Stone's interpretation of Del, and devised without making notes as he had listened to the other minister's remarks. The facileness in the way he accomplished this more than likely went unnoticed to most parishioners, but did not get by Tom. Tom fully appreciated what Harland was able to do.

Harland finished with a prayer that thanked God for bringing Del, Reverend Stone, and Betty to their house of worship and be seen by the loyal viewing faithful.

"Amen," all said loudly and the choir echoed Amen.

Chester and Carol broke into song giving Glory to God and with band and choir support. The congregation gave full participation by clapping their hands enthusiastically. Their music continued through the fifty-fifth minute as the credits, phone number, and e-mail address rolled and the satellite up-link ended. The show was over.

"Nice job, everyone," Larry spoke into his mike, "I believe Reverend Kenny and CGB will be very pleased with what we got here today…very pleased. You all did a great job…thanks."

"Wow," Tom exclaimed, "all I can say is wow."

This was the most powerful service Tom had ever seen or heard and his realization that it had been televised and broadcast, and the fact it had been sent nationwide made it take on a grandeur and monumental aspect he found almost impossible to comprehend. He knew the details of how the program was put together, watched the behind-the-scenes goings on, he understood what had taken place, but still he was overcome with how magnificent the presentation had been.

"We have a lot to learn from this Keri," he said as he stared out of the control booth window as the crowd dwindled, vanishing through the several sets of doors.

But she was not listening and he did not notice. She had spent the entire time of the broadcast exchanging glances and hard looks with Larry. Now, she had moved closer to him as he wrapped up with the tech personnel, ignoring Tom, totally intent on this bundle of energy who had directed the telecast. She did not even hear Tom's comments. Tom's cell phone rang and she turned to see him answer it and then turned back to Larry. In a few moments they were out of the control room. Tom was not aware they had exited, so involved was he in the call that had just come to him.

"Burton," Tom yelled the man's name into the phone, "was that sensational or what? Our Reverend Stone was terrific wasn't he? Yes…Del…yes…oh boy, I know it. You folks could see and hear everything? Good…good…"

Burton Strong was on the board of trustees for Calvary and Tom's main man in seeing to the details of how the congregation was able to share in the day's service. Tom had arranged for a satellite hook-up directly to the church with several large-screen televisions brought in for viewing. Stone's congregation had been duly impressed with their minister and with fellow parishioner Del Howe. Burton's report was glowing. The sacrifice they made in giving up Reverend Stone to New World Gospel Church and Reverend Kenny's Faith For You Future program was well worth it, Burton emphasized. The whole country watched, it was their gift to Fundamentalist Christians everywhere, and they understood what it meant.

"We miss you folks," Burton said with unabashed admiration for what had transpired. "But how is Del holding up?"

""Doing well, doing well," Tom nodded in affirmation almost as much to convince himself as to assure Burton. "We're on target for next Sunday."

"That's good, real good. We'll all be watching."

Burton was a distant voice of assurance and confidence and support that Tom wished really meant something.

Tom clicked off from the call not realizing he was alone in the control room. The last of the crowd was filing out and the silence around him was startling, the monitors and instrumentation dead. A peaceful calm had settled on the room. He was the lone sentinel of the day's proceedings, a now somber, possessed demon created by the outcome of the service. It was a winner, he knew it, and it would mean something for Stone and Calvary. It would mean more money, he knew it would.

He went out of the control room and slowly walked through the auditorium onto the stage where he stood for a moment and surveyed what amounted to him as a playing field. It had been like a sports event with all of the gusto, emotional impact, and adulation for the participants. The audience came, they witnessed, and they rejoiced. He noticed the unmanned television cameras stood right where their operators had left them, he saw the empty choir chairs, eyed the musicians' stands by the stage, and looked back at the glass window of the control room. Yes, this had been something wonderful and they – he and Stone - would reap the reward.

Tom found a golf cart outside and drove back to the Kenny mansion. The others must already be there by now, he thought, as he brought the cart to a halt near the bridge over the creek. Once again he made a survey of the surroundings. Better than the kings of England, he observed, the kind of setting one could get used to very quickly. So wrapped up was he in his thoughts and reactions to the service that he had forgotten about Keri and was not even aware that she was not with him.

Back at the house, he discovered a crush of parishioners gathered around the front porch eager to speak with Reverend Kenny and Reverend Stone. The two men were working their way through the crowd like veteran politicians, shaking hands, excepting compliments, and smiling so broadly their faces might break. From within, he could hear the din of voices coming from key staff personnel and the main performers in the service. Carol Robinson and Chester Ridenour were there, the band had set up in the huge living room almost ready to play, and Fred Wallace was talking loudly on a cell phone. This was when he realized that Keri was no longer with him.

A rush of anger gripped Tom, he stiffened, checked to make sure no one else paid attention to him, and got off the golf cart and stood waiting in the front yard. He watched as Kenny and Stone glad-handed their way around the porch. Why wasn't she with him? Where did she go? She was the note keeper, she should be with him to record his thoughts. Why wasn't she? As congregation members drifted away and the crowd thinned, Tom worked his way through the dwindling throng to the porch and on into the house. He looked around for Keri, thinking perhaps she had gotten here ahead of him. She was nowhere to be seen. Scanning those present, he realized Larry was not there, either, and the answer to the whys clicked into place. He felt his neck redden as the realization caught him. He was more upset with her neglect of him than with the possibility she would take up with Larry. He did not really care if she were bedding Larry or Stone or both of them, but he resented not having her assistance.

Katherine Louise approached him, gushing with excitement. She too had a smile that almost exploded and she animatedly grabbed his hand.

"Tom, that was wonderful…we're so excited. Fred is on the phone now with the executive vice president of Christian Gospel Broadcasting…they are overwhelmed…already phone calls are flooding their switchboard and our call center over in the administration building is having trouble handling the volume. This is monumental, Tom, totally monumental. And y'all are the reason."

"That's…ah…sensational," Tom beamed as he tried to shake off his anger at Keri and focus on the good news.

"We're so proud of the job your Reverend Stone did…just amazing…"

"How is Del?" Tom asked.

"Betty has him lying down now…upstairs…in bed, I think."

"Y'all have gotta know we hit a home run today, Tom," Fred almost yelled, trying to be heard over the sounds of Chester and Carol vocalizing with the band behind, and the buzz of conversation still storming throughout the living room and vestibule. "We made high marks the network says. The response is fabulous for them and for us."

Then Fred leaned toward Tom so that he could speak directly into Tom's right ear. It was the move of uninvited confidentiality, closing the gap of communications to one of intimacy and mutual understanding, a gesture that is meant to ingratiate and to command a kind of you-know-what-I-mean bonding that Tom did not want although he understood it quite well. He recognized the gesture and he did not like it. He held his pose nonetheless, knowing his responsibilities, expecting bad breath, and fully ready to give the appropriate answer.

"This means more for all of us." Fred whispered, "y'all know what I mean?"

Tom nodded showing the required smile, affecting the necessary body language of assent, and, within his own mind, patted himself on the back for a job well done.

"We'll talk about it some more tomorrow." Fred used his soft voice of confidentiality, gave Tom another knowing look, and went off to the dining room to find food.

Carlton had set up a glorious buffet for brunch on the dining room table. Jessie had prepared a fine spread of food ranging from fried chicken and boiled shrimp to apple pie and fudge brownies. In short order, the crowded living room moved to Jessie's feast.

Tom walked back to the front porch where Kenny and Stone were still engaged with the last few well-wishers. Kenny had perched his rump on the front railing with Stone next to him, leaning slightly, balancing against the railing. This remaining group was special; three of the largest contributors and their wives. They did not seem to want to leave, so Kenny invited them inside for brunch and, of course, more conversation. For Kenny they were worth the time and, besides, he adored the adulation. As they all started to go inside, Tom touched Stone's arm.

"Reverend Stone, can I speak to you for a minute?" Tom smiled at Kenny when he spoke. He did not want the man to think there was something wrong, which there was sort of, depending on who's perspective was being considered.

Stone stopped and the others went ahead.

"What's wrong?"

"I wanted you to be aware that Keri is not here…she did not come back with me. I was so caught up in the service and the reaction of the congregation that afterwards…well, I didn't even see her leave the control room. Bang, just gone…I assume with Larry."

"Oh, really?"

"Yeah…my guess is that it's over between you two. Which, from my standpoint, is just as well."

Stone looked at Tom without speaking, turned, and walked toward the front door.

"There's good news…you're a hit…with Del you…"

But Stone ignore him and went inside. The rest of the day was a struggle for him. He would have wanted it to work another way, a way that was easier on his ego, a way where he ended the relationship, not the other way around. He felt one-upped, although he well knew that was not Keri's intent, knew this was not planned. He speculated that this would have happened at some point anyway, what with the age difference. Some young buck her age would come along, make a move for her, and she would be gone. For the first time he felt old, older than he knew he really was. It was the old of defeat, it was the old of losing his touch, and it was the old that could break a man's spirit.

He would not wallow in his feelings and mustered the strength to be heard above the clamor in the dining room to ask for heads to be bowed for a word of prayer.

"Thank you, dear God, for your mercy this day. Bless us all as we bask in your radiant light in the joy of celebration for the revelation we have received. Your light to guide us and to keep us whole. Bless this food and the wonder of our communion with You. In the name of our Lord and Savior, Jesus Christ, we humbly pray. Amen.

"Amen," all said.

He managed his composure throughout the rest of the day. There was plenty to be positive about, much to revel in, accolades to accept, and the sure knowledge he had done well with the service. Certainly, he had surpassed his vision for the glory that would be his on this day. However, he kept waiting for Keri to appear, but she did not before he had finally gone to his room and was in bed unable to sleep. He tossed and turned, agitated with thoughts that it was more than age that separated Keri from him. As he reviewed the differences, a balance sheet that ultimately didn't make sense for her, he accepted the clincher. There was no getting around his being married. Unless he got rid of Helen, there was never a chance for them together. He did not want to get rid of Helen, he just wanted Keri, too. The ultimate conflict was the ultimate undoing. When an opportunity came along for her to move along, she jumped for it and that was that.

He got up and stared out the window at the garden still aglow from accent lights. Odd shadows and muted colors stared back at him. He vowed never to speak of it to her. It would be as if their affair had never happened, as if the ache within him had never occurred, and as though nothing, but nothing was wrong. Ah, what a strong man, a martyr, a paragon of understanding, a quiet-suffering reject without a hint of accusation or recrimination. He got back in bed and closed his eyes with the wish, a painful longing that it had never happened, that they had never begun their intimate time together.

The end of their relationship came so quickly, he thought, it was almost as if surgically she had been cut away from him. Now, guilt stalked him and he tried to deny its presence. He had no right to feel bitter or hurt or angry, all the plagues of a man, a lover scorned. He was married, he had no right. He was on the verge of an appeal to his Lord for forgiveness, but he hesitated, unsure of what to say. He gave no voice of supplication and the blackness of sleep took him before the dark arms of guilt could enfold him.

10.

No one has power over the spirit to retain the spirit, and no one has power in the day of death. There is no release from that war and wickedness will not deliver those who are given to it.

-Ecclesiastes 8:8

Monday morning had the usual hot beginning at the New World Gospel Church campus, the air heavy with humidity, the spacious lawns wet from sprinklers that sprayed before dawn. The gathering heat would be oppressive and gardeners were already at work two hours before the administration office would come alive. The sound of mowers or other power equipment had been banned by Fred until eight o'clock, but weeding and other chores began at six. Moses Campbell walked from the maintenance barn toward a large flower bed on the other side of the road that ran behind the administration building and up to the mansion. He didn't care that he could not ride in one of the small tractors the maintenance staff used. It didn't make that much noise; but those were also a no-no before eight. He liked the walk through the wet grass, the sound of the birds chirping up a storm before the greater heat of the day made them seek refuge in the cooler stands of trees, and there was the fresh smell of everything in bloom.

The pansies needed edging and the weeds pulled from around the bloomed-out azaleas that formed a backdrop for the bed. He started to one side and worked toward the first azalea, on his knees, carefully pulling and clipping, being sure to deposit the weeds and clippings in the basket he had brought with him. He was almost next to the azalea when he saw a shoe sticking out from behind the shrub. He stood up. There was the body of a man with a bullet hole in his forehead. Moses knew a bullet hole when he saw it and he knew the man was dead.

Sam Turco was indeed dead, several hours dead, and several gun shots dead. Sam was dressed in a suit and tie, on his back, his suit coat buttoned. His shoes were well polished, his socks pulled up in place, and an appropriately scarlet handkerchief flopped out of the breast pocket. It was as if he had dressed for his own funeral.

Moses wanted to yell, but he did not make a sound because he respected the morning quiet that Mr. Wallace wanted. Part of our reverence for God, Mr. Wallace had said. He turned and ran as fast as his sore knees would allow. At the maintenance barn he found manager Jimmy Phillips reading the morning paper. Moses' chest ached and he could hardly talk. He bent over and leaned against the door jamb.

"What's a matter witchew, old man, don't you know a seventy-five year old ought not ta run like that? Yeah, I seen ya runnin' over here. What's wrong, man?"

Moses still had not gotten his breath and he struggled to get out the words he wanted. They did not come right away. He looked at Jimmy without revealing the contempt he felt. Here was another black man, a kid at that, who bossed him around and didn't know squat about landscaping or gardening or nothin' much. But he had a nice way about him to some folks that was for sure and he could talk real nice to the white man, Mr. Wallace, and he could do a prayer almost as good as Reverend Harland or miz Katherine Louise. White folks thought Jimmy was a fine black man; respectful, well-spoken, and always got a smile. Shit, if they jist knew what kinda trash Jimmy really was it would be a different story.

"Man's dead...been shot...," Moses gasped for air after he spoke.

"What man? Down by the bed you was workin' at?" Jimmy closed the newspaper and rolled it tightly into his left hand.

"Bullet hole in de head...he been around this place before, I seen 'im." Moses was breathing better now.

"Jesus loves us, that's all we need right now. Sit down over there while I get Mr. Wallace."

Jimmy pulled out his cell phone and punched hard at one of the numbers. He waited for the connection, tapping the rolled up newspaper on his thigh, and scowling at Moses.

"Mr. Wallace…sorry to call you so early…yes sir…yes sir. No sir, everything's not okay. Well, it's kinda bad…man's dead here on the grounds. Moses found him just awhile ago. Yes sir, by the big pansy bed right behind the main building…been shot…Moses says he seen a hole in the man's head. Yes sir, Moses would know a gun shot hole. Yes sir. Moses says it's somebody he's seen before…yes sir, here at New World. Yes sir, yes sir, I will" Jimmy punched the phone off and put it back in the holder on his belt.

"What's he say?" Moses asked, now fully recovered from his running, still scornful of Jimmy.

He's comin' right away. Gonna call the police from his car. Wants me to go meet the cops…you wait here…relax."

Moses settled in on the old sofa the gardeners used when they were on break, let his head fall back, and went sound asleep.

The news of tragedy reached the mansion parsonage in short order. Carlton answered Fred's phone call.

"Reverend Kenny is in the shower, Mr. Wallace. May I take a message?"

Carlton was impassive as he listened to the message. No witness to his end of the conversation would have guessed the truth of its content.

"I will, sir," he said quietly after a few moments and placed the phone in its place on the kitchen wall.

"Bad?" Jessie asked as she continued breakfast preparations.

"Very," Carlton answered, "Moses found a dead man this morning behind the administration building. Means police will come, there will be an investigation, reporters will snoop and pry and distort and make things up, and we will have notoriety that New World does not need. Bad publicity never helps. Could well spoil yesterday for everyone, Jessie, but I will not say that out loud to anyone else."

Carlton left the kitchen and went upstairs to tell Reverend Kenny.

Katherine Louise had come out onto the screened-in veranda, not expecting to see Reverend Stone seated there. She was surprised, yet pleased because she had wanted to speak to him without others around to stifle answers to the pointed question she wished to ask. This was her chance. She smiled when she realized he was not aware she was near. He was the unsuspecting fly in the web. Was she a spider? She was certainly not deadly, merely curious.

"Good morning."

He was not startled, so perhaps he was not as unaware of her presence as she surmised.

"Good morning…a beautiful morning…going to be hot, though." Stone seemed to be in a good mood.

"Yes, this time of year…well, it gets hot. May I join y'all?"

"Of course, of course…good grief, this is your house, you certainly don't have to ask my permission."

"Oh I know, but I am breaking into your…your thoughts…your quiet time."

"No, no, just sort of reviewing yesterday…how it went…"

"It went wonderfully well and you were fabulous. We'll get more feedback today, but I'd say you and Del caused quite a stir. It's a terrific thing for the work of the Lord."

"It is and the blessings are manifold…"

"Amen to that, Reverend…but it's too bad your wife isn't here to share in the glory of God's work with you. Why is that? Why isn't she here?"

Stone looked carefully at Katherine Louise and saw a well-tempered steel pry bar that was about to attempt a look into his soul. He had wondered if and when and how there would be questions; so now, the inquisition was at hand. He had gotten this far without the subject of the absent wife being broached. He had to face up to her questions while caught in the tension of guilt and remorse on one hand and self-pity on the other. There was no way of escaping, no method he understood that would save him from the smiling pry bar. He could see that she was going to be relentless and the embarrassment of the questions she might pose he surely understood. He could feel the blood rushing toward his face, the tiny beads of perspiration form at the rear of his neck just below the hairline, and the clamminess already marshalling in his arm pits. The day seemed just a bit less bright than it had a few moments before her question.

"She has the three children…" he began lamely.

"Does *she* have a name?"

Katherine Louise asked the question sharply, obviously annoyed. It was a pet peeve of hers when men referred to a special female in their life without using her name. She did not let them get away with it.

"Helen…Helen didn't want to bring them here for a month…she's never traveled a lot…doesn't like to travel, so was more comfortable staying home with…Shelby…eight, Madison…five, and baby Brent…just two…"

"So you brought the young girl…Keri."

"Yes, she's my…"

"I know what she is, Reverend. Tell me about Helen."

"Helen is…I met Helen at school. We were…we hit it off right away…"

"Is she attractive?"

"Yes, yes she is…"

"Let's see a picture of her. You must have a picture. Don't you?"

Stone fumbled for his wallet and brought out a photograph of all of them. He held Brent, Helen and the girls were posed around him. He handed the photo to her.

"She's very beautiful."

"Indeed, she is."

"Go on…"

Stone proceeded to describe Helen physically and emotionally, emphasizing every good point, every positive aspect of her personality as wife and mother, and her importance to his work. It was a rhapsody of compliments.

"She sounds wonderful…"

"She is…"

"Then why in heaven's name are you screwing this young girl you brought along."

Wary as he was for what might come from her he was not prepared for that question.

"I…ah…I…I don't know. It just happened…"

"It usually does," she snapped.

"But it's over…definitely over…and I know I have sinned, but I will…"

"Don't start with some kind of forgiveness thing, we've all sinned…we're all sinners, Reverend, we're all sinners working our way down the road to Heaven. Did you end it?"

"No. No, it seems she's found Larry Stovall more to her liking…she's done with me, I guess…well, more than a guess. I would have ended it while we were here. I had come to the realization…"

"Oh please, spare me."

"It's true...I knew it had to be over. I couldn't keep going on..."

"My, my, our Larry. Isn't that something?"

"I'm relieved," Stone lied.

"God's work is accomplished in mysterious ways," Katherine Louise sighed, "that's why y'all are here. Just keep on doing the Lord's work and everything will be fine. It's His message that's important...for all of us."

They both heard the phone ring and she turned to go find out who was calling at this early hour.

"We can talk some more if you like," she trilled, "maybe later."

Stone was soaken wet beneath his clothes, but only a few traces had begun to show. He would have to change his clothes and the day had hardly started.

Breakfast was all but forgotten with the commotion that stirred the household once Reverend Kenny finished with Fred's phone call. This was turmoil no one wanted and as Carlton had told Jessie, it was trouble they did not need. Kenny came downstairs quickly, voice raised with fear as he announced what had happened, what could be expected.

"...police are on their way...they'll come here...ask a lot of questions. It's a mess. Naturally, reporters will be all over us. Lord, have mercy on us."

As Kenny gave the details of his phone conversation to Katherine Louise and Stone, Betty stood listening from the top of the stairs. Del was still sleeping. Keri heard the commotion, slipped quietly out of her room, and softly made her way down the rear stairs. When she reached the first floor she was startled to see Carlton standing in the doorway nearby. She reacted swiftly, placing her finger to her lips in her plea for silence. He complied. She eased out the back door and walked around to the side of the house where the golf carts were parked.

"Good morning," Tom said.

She jumped with surprise, fell back against a cart, and slithered along its side until her rump smacked against the ground. She sat with her back against the cart and glowered at Tom.

"You…you scared me…"

"I know. Where are you going?"

"I…I…I have to…"

"Never mind."

He bent down, took her arm, and pulled her to her feet. She tried to move away, but he held her in a firm grasp.

"Let go of me…"

"After we have an understanding."

"Fine. What understanding?"

"That you say or do nothing that undermines Reverend Stone or our mission here. If you've ended your fling with him…great. Don't get into any discussions or debates with him. Keep it to yourself no matter what."

"Why? What will you do…what can you do?"

"You should know me by now, Keri, I'm very resourceful. Any scene, any problem that you cause…you'll regret it."

She stared at him for a few seconds, knew full well that he meant what he said, and looked away.

"Okay," she said, without looking at him.

"Now go back inside, get involved, and do your job. You can get with lover boy Larry some other time."

She hesitated, whirled around, and went back inside through the rear. Neither of them knew that Carlton had been witness to their encounter.

Keri and Tom joined the others as Reverend Kenny and Katherine Louise were leaving for the administration building. Kenny would be interviewed by the police and he wanted that to take place in his office, not here at the mansion. Stone had decided to go with them.

"Go ahead," Tom said, "Keri and I will grab another one of the carts. Betty you stay here with Del...make sure he rests and recovers. He had a tough day yesterday."

The excitement running through the administration building was electric when they walked in, even though most of the staff had not arrived. They could hear phones ringing and the voices of loud, excited conversations that came in rapid bursts from some of the offices and the coffee-break room. Rebecca Howland, the office manager, ran out from one office and scurried down the hall into another office without noticing their presence.

"Rebecca...Miss Howland," Kenny yelled, "what's going on?"

Rebecca's head popped out of the office she had just entered. Panic was etched into her face, the look of fear that something awful had happened or was about to happen, or both. As she realized who was coming toward her in the hall her eyes widened as if she were witness to impending doom.

"What...what's happening?"

Tom already knew. Murder has a way of making turmoil, he figured, and reporters calling asking questions about a dead body have a way of creating havoc. After all, she was the one charged with the responsibility of getting things done for New World; she and Doris, Kenny's secretary, who had not yet gotten to work. She had it all on her shoulders. Besides there might just be some good news mixed in to cause her consternation. Reaction to yesterday had to be powerful, he was sure of it.

"Oh, Reverend Kenny, I'm so glad you're here...the police came in looking for you or Mr. Wallace and the reporters are driving us crazy…about our service yesterday and about…the police say there is a dead man out back. It's so awful. I just called your house…"

"Relax, relax…we'll have this under control soon. This police matter is simply a strange set of circumstances…someone put a body on our property to get rid of it…"

"Or to make us look bad," Fred Wallace boomed as he came up behind them. "Miss Howland please direct any reporters' calls to me if they pertain to the police business…calls from religion writers get to Tom. I assume that's all right with you, Tom? Help in an emergency?"

"Absolutely, just show me someplace where I can work."

"Fine, use my office. Miss Howland get Tom to my office, I'll work with Reverend Kenny in his office. Get Doris into us as soon as she gets here. But first give me an update on feedback from yesterday."

"The fax machine is out of paper from so many messages, the phone won't stop ringing, our website manager says we had thousands of hits, and…and it's a mess."

She handed him a stack of messages.

"A good mess, Miss Howland, a very good mess," he said as he scanned the yellow sheets of paper. "Let's get going with these phones."

With that he headed to Kenny's office with the Reverend in step. Tom followed Rebecca's direction to Fred's office as she flew away leaving Katherine Louise, Stone, and Keri standing there with no assignment.

"Keri, dear, go with Rebecca," Katherine Louise directed, "and help as best you can. All right? Thank you."

She waited and watched as Keri grudgingly went after Rebecca before she spoke to Stone.

"Reverend, why don't you join me in my office?"

It was nearly thirty minutes after they had gone about the church business before two detectives entered the building looking for Reverend Kenny. Detective Lionel Mitchell, the lead investigator for the Columbia police department, and his assistant Dean Ross were shown into Kenny's office. There were introductions, the two detectives showed their credentials, and they sat down. Both men tried to focus on Kenny, but were so impressed with the office size and its furnishings that their heads swiveled for several moments.

Kenny and Fred watched the two detectives, looked at each other with raised eyebrows, and wondered how this might go. Would the obvious opulence cause them to back off with intimidation or would they bore in beyond what was necessary out of jealousy or envy? They would soon find out which way it would go. Kenny thought the former, Fred the latter.

When Mitchell folded his hands and placed them on his crossed knees, both Fred and Kenny noticed their immense size. A tall heavy-set black man, he could easily palm a basketball and twenty-five years before had been a star for the Clemson basketball team. He seemed bored with what he was doing because he moved languidly and spoke with a tired voice. Those mannerisms belied his true demeanor and the clever, highly analytical ability he possessed. Ross, on the other hand, looked like a hick and a redneck, complete with a tuft of wild hair that would not lie down no matter how hard he combed it. He, too, could not be accurately judged by outward appearance. Ross did the note taking for the pair.

"Reverend Kenny," Detective Mitchell began, "we're sorry to interrupt your work here, but under the circumstances it can't be avoided. You know, of course, that a body...a dead body was found by one of your workers?"

"Yes," Kenny nodded.

"Well, we...Detective Ross and I need to ask you a few questions. Do y'all mind?"

"No we don't...go right ahead."

"Well, good...ah...I...I wonder if we could do this with just you. Could Mr. Wallace be excused, please?"

"Mr. Wallace is my assistant," Kenny explained, "and he's also my attorney. I believe he has a right to be present during any questioning. My best interests would be served that way, I think."

"Any reason for you to need an attorney?" Mitchell asked, almost casually.

"Not in the least, but from a legal standpoint there's no reason he can't be here."

"Sure 'nuff," Mitchell said.

"Thank you, detective, this is very trying for all of us...yesterday was a monumental day for us in God's work and to have this...this dead person found here...well, it puts a pall on things. I'm sure you can understand."

"Indeed I do, Reverend."

"The dead man's identification found on him," Detective Ross said as he moved into the questioning, "shows him to be Sam Turco, a local businessman. Is he someone you might know...a member of your congregation or maybe done business with?"

Fred and Kenny were stunned at the revelation. Stunned was putting it mildly, struck dumb is more like it. They could not look at each other, each trying to stay calm, each not wanting to show the fear they felt. Their fear was rooted in the fact they knew Sam, had done substantial business with him, and that even the slightest connection could bring suspicion. They assumed nothing good could come from this.

Fred gained his composure first and walked to the center of the room. He stood on the large Oriental rug.

"Sam was a man we purchased art items from," he said pointing to the floor, "this rug is one he sold us...and there are other things here in this office. In fact, he was here recently trying to sell us some statues for the grounds. We've been buying art from Sam for several years. That's about it."

"Y'all know anything about the man himself," Ross continued, "personal stuff...like if y'all socialized with him or anything?"

"No," Fred answered, "he was not a man we would be socializing with...he was a supplier, a vendor...like a supplier of office material or computers or janitorial supplies. As you might imagine, Detective, our socializing is done with our parishioners almost exclusively."

"Yessir, I can 'preciate that fact. What day was he last here?"

"Last Monday, I think," Kenny said.

"It was," Fred concurred.

"Did he seem okay? Jumpy...afraid...something not normal?"

"I don't remember anything unusual," Fred said, "he seemed his regular insistent salesman self. Frustrated we didn't buy something right then, but that was about right for him."

"We're not going to take any more of your time," Mitchell said suddenly and rose. "You gentlemen are not suspects, but we might need to speak with you again as the investigation continues. We've already interviewed some of your workers and no one here is a suspect. Crime lab people say the body was placed here on your grounds, he was not murdered here..."

"He was murdered?" Kenny asked.

"We believe so. Wounds indicate away from suicide or accident...no, he pretty definitely was shot...three times. Have any idea why someone would put him here on church property? A theory?"

Kenny and Fred looked at each other and shook their heads.

"No...no theory," Fred said.

"Think about it…if you get any ideas or any other information comes to mind you think might be helpful give me a call."

He handed Fred his card and headed for the door followed by Ross.

"We'll find our way out," he tossed over his shoulder and they exited.

Fred picked up the phone and buzzed Doris.

"Please get everyone in Reverend Kenny's office."

All assembled around Reverend Kenny's massive desk; Katherine Louise in a chair to his left, Stone and Tom in chairs in front, and Doris, Rebecca, and Keri standing behind them. Fred stood by a corner window with his back to them.

There was a strange kind of tension that gripped the room, a nervous continuation of a day that started with tension. Only Stone and Tom were at ease, content in the knowledge that they had nothing to do with the dead man. Yesterday had been terrific, and nothing, not even a murder, was going to spoil their success. They had not had a chance to speak privately since the day before, but there was a communion of unspoken understanding between them that allowed them to sense they had a comfort zone not found by the others. Stone had quickly become well on his way to getting over Keri thanks to Katherine Louise, even though Keri herself was still as tense as a tight piano wire. Tom rarely got uptight no matter what happened and these were surely not circumstances to make him tense.

"Where are we with everything?" Kenny demanded. "Rebecca, why don't you give us an update…?"

"Well…I…ah…ah, I hate to be insensitive, Reverend Kenny…I'm really sorry, but things couldn't be better for us. I mean…I understand the difficulty about the dead man…I surely do, but this is the largest day of commitments for donations that we have ever had…a little more than one hundred twenty three thousand dollars…and this is only Monday. The phones continue…"

"How much?" Fred turned to face them when he spoke.

She repeated the number.

Tom looked at Stone and smiled. This was the kind of result he had dreamed about, secretly prayed for, but beyond what he had thought could get accomplished. Stone smiled slightly and looked away to catch a glimpse of Keri. Her eyes were closed and she and the other two women stood at uncomfortable attention as they waited to be released from the seemingly interminable reporting.

"Still coming in?" Kenny asked.

"Yes, Reverend, the phones don't stop ringing and faxes continue to come in about five or six an hour. The whole crew is working as hard as they can to take care of everything. We're on top of it, but it's a chore…a glorious blessing, though it is hard work."

"Great, great…that's outstanding. You get back with your staff and tell them that we're all very proud of them for the excellent work they're doing…and…and we will have a special reward for all of them."

Tom turned again on that remark, but said nothing. Rebecca scooted out the door, glad to get away, relieved to get back to her work.

"Doris, what do you and Keri have for us?"

"We can't avoid the interviews…"

"I know, I know…" Kenny muttered.

"There's good and bad, of course," Doris offered, "just like this whole day, but I think it will all work in our favor…"

"How so?"

"Cal Dobson from *The State* is coming this morning at ten thirty. He's their crime reporter. On the other hand, Sara Bird, their religion reporter is coming at about eleven…"

"She's new, isn't she? She hasn't been here before. I don't think…"

"No, she is new…wants to meet everyone…wants to have a big spread for Saturday's paper. She saw the service and is…is…well, almost ecstatic about what she witnessed and also about her prospects for meeting with everyone. We need to get Del and Betty over here for that…"

"Anyone else?"

Yes…oh, my yes…all the television news departments are sending someone and several of the radio stations want to talk to someone…preferably Reverend Kenny. Fact is, some of them have arrived."

"We don't want to deal with them right now…bad enough we have to deal with Cal today. Let them interview the police…that's who they should be after, anyway. We're going to stay away from them as long as we can. Just tell them we are saddened by Mr. Turco's death, share the burden his family now suffers, etcetera, blah blah blah…you know how it all goes.

"I will," Doris said plaintively. "And I almost hate to tell you, but Ben Simmons is coming tomorrow from the *Charlotte Observer*…"

"Ol' Ben…how about that…driving all the way down here from Charlotte. How long's it been since we saw him…three, maybe four years…?"

"Almost five…"

"Well, well…this gives him another chance to harass us, but we'll be ready for him. How did he hear about the service, did he say?"

"He said there were dozens of phone calls this morning to his office. Folks were asking him if he knew about Del. Of course, he had no idea what they were talking about, so he called Christian Gospel Broadcasting there in Charlotte and they referred him to New World. Hallelujah, Reverend Kenny, we are blessed by the Lord."

"Yes, Doris we are and Amen to that."

"Anything more, Reverend? Otherwise, Keri and I will help Rebecca and the others…"

"Yes, if you would…call Carlton and tell him to have Jessie get a real nice lunch ready. Now, I know you're too busy to get away, so we'll have someone bring you and Rebecca and Keri some of the fixin's. "Preciate your help, really do…God Bless."

Doris the proud and fulfilled assistant smiled and felt exhilarated. Keri the dejected assistant was trapped in all of this when she wanted to be somewhere else with Larry.

"Well, how about that. Come on, Fred, we have some time to get ready for our first reporter, Mr. Dobson. He's no brain trust so I think we'll do okay, but let's be prepared.

Fifteen minutes later than the scheduled interview, Cal Dobson arrived. He was young, but already jaded from his contact with crime in Columbia. There were few murders where the police didn't know who did it, so a real murder investigation that was like the sleuthing on television stimulated his interest. This was one of those crimes where evidence had to be gathered and detective work would be necessary to determine who the killer was. Clues, leads, forensics, all the stuff that formed a real murder investigation would come into play. Nothing could be better than this, he figured.

"Sorry about being late, Reverend. Got into a real hot and heavy discussion with one of my best sources. Drug stuff…I follow that pretty closely."

"It was not inconvenient," Kenny said with just a bit of haughtiness.

Kenny did not know Cal, but he disliked reporters generally and had little regard for the news media that he believed was devoutly secular and biased against religious groups He viewed Cal as an adversary in the best of circumstances.

Cal was shy of thirty-three, a graduate of the University of South Carolina with a major in beer drinking and a minor in horse play. He knew about journalism and political science and had been a bit-part actor for the university theater. Gregarious, verbose, and full of himself made him seem larger than life at times. In reality, he was physically slight, stretching one hundred fifty-five pounds over a six feet one frame. His dark complexion made him perpetually appear to have just come back from Florida beaches. He coughed a great deal from twenty years of smoking, but suffered the withdrawal and continued to make the effort to not smoke. The cough was residual and he wondered if he would ever be free from such convulsions. He had compared notes with Sara Bird, his co-worker who handled the week's religious news, so he already had background knowledge of New World and Reverend Kenny. His initial questions were about Stone and Del.

"You folks had this guy that spoke in tongues yesterday, I guess? Crazy kind of talk. Quite a service…right?"

"It was a wonderful service where the Word of God was given to us in a miraculous way…there was nothing crazy about it." Kenny was incensed.

"Probably help your church out a lot…right?"

"It was a bountiful addition to our successful and well-attended services, yes," Kenny said tersely.

Cal quickly sensed he was not doing well with Kenny and decided to move on about Turco.

"Reverend Kenny you have succeeded in building a very successful church here…as you said. Certainly worthy of anyone's praise. Why would a dead man be dumped here on church property?"

"To the best of my knowledge…"

"Did you know the dead man?"

"As we told the police…surely you know all this, Cal."

"Yeah, I do, but I wanted to get your story. No one knows much about Turco, so I thought you might be able to give me some stuff about him…any background…where he came from…"

"You probably know more about him than we do," Fred said. "He was simply a person who sold us things. Art works."

"When did you start buying from him," Cal asked, as if he did not hear Fred or if he had, he ignored.

"About six years ago," Fred said, "maybe a little more…"

"How did you get together? I mean did you see his ad…did he send you a letter…what was it that got him here?"

"We heard from one of our parishioners that he was selling fabulous Oriental rugs. It was suggested that we look into this and perhaps get one for the parsonage."

"Your mansion…"

"Our house," Kenny said quickly, "our home."

"Yeah, so what happened?"

"We contacted Mr. Turco and eventually purchased the rug that is spread out underneath your chair. We subsequently got other items."

"All straight deals…nothing special or unusual?"

"That's right," Fred answered, a testiness coming through in his voice. "What are you getting at?"

"Oh, I don't know…some special deal, some special price…maybe some goods that were so low priced maybe they were…ah…ah, well stolen or illegal in some way. Is this thing from Iran, for instance?"

"It is from Iran, but perfectly legal that's for sure."

Fred frowned when he emphasized the words, but he wasn't truly sure. Perhaps Sam had sold them something that was not legal, despite his claims that the rugs he sold and, in fact, all of the art was legally his or on legal consignment to him. Perhaps he lied, even though he gave them papers of authenticity and legality. Perhaps this was why Sam was dead.

"We have the papers," Fred insisted.

"Can I see them?" Cal asked.

"No, of course not. It has nothing to do with this murder…it only has to do with your curiosity. Use your curiosity, Cal, to go after who might have done this. Don't spend a lot of time here where you will get nowhere. The answers you want are someplace else. Believe me, you need to move on."

Cal looked at Fred, took a deep breath, closed his reporter's notebook and slapped it against his chest, then leaned back in his chair. He eyed Fred intently, squinting, lips pursed, his neck red.

"Yeah, well, probably you're right. Y'all wouldn't be involved. Y'all will have a better time with Sara."

With that, he got up and left. As he moved out through the door he took one long, last look at Fred. Something about the man pricked his curiosity and he knew there was more with him that needed to be looked into before this story was set.

Sara Bird had been waiting for her turn in the outer office. She had given pleasantries to Cal as he left and was thrilled to be shown into Reverend Kenny's office. She had never interviewed him, but held him in high esteem. Casual observation would credit her with being mousy, but she was far from it, belying her outward appearance, which in polite terms seemed to be a rejection of convention. She had flat, gray-streaked brown hair that would display unkempt no matter how she cared for it. Her eyes were dull as if she had not slept in days when in reality she was acutely alert and well-rested. The contradictory outward appearance could be both a disservice and an advantage. She was aware of the contradiction and used it accordingly in her work as a reporter.

No matter what her motive might be and no matter how the story might evolve, she respected Reverend Kenny and thought him to be among the best modern preachers that could be heard. She felt he had surpassed Billy Graham and others and was among the two or three top ministers to deliverer God's message. His sermons were the best that could be experienced today. She had witnessed yesterday's service on television and had been enthralled. She also had been very impressed with Reverend Stone.

Kenny greeted her as if she were an old friend and considering how she felt about him and New World, she was very flattered. He introduced her to Stone and Tom, who came into the office behind her. He made sure she met Fred and then, Katherine Louise, who also came in with Stone and Tom.

"As you might understand," Reverend Kenny explained, "Del has been resting at our house. His wife is to bring him up here for your interview and that will take a few minutes. Did anyone offer you some tea?"

"Yes, Doris said she would get me some. I do so appreciate y'all taking the time for me…what with all that's going on. Dreadful about Mr. Turco…Cal told me. So sorry about it. Yesterday was so wonderful and now this…this puts a cloud over y'all when you least need it. Reverend Stone, I'm so delighted to be able to tell you in person how wonderful you were with Mr., ah…Mr., ah…"

"Howe," Stone answered for her, "Del Howe…wife is Betty…"

"Yes, yes…all the way from Ohio, I understand."

"We are, Miss Bird…"

"Oh go on, y'all can call me Sara. Wonderful Biblical name, I think."

She laughed and it was a kind of cackle, almost as if something were caught in her throat. She then settled back in her chair next to Stone, right in front of Kenny's desk. She was comfortable there and knew this was going to be a wonderful interview.

After a few minutes of preliminary banter and the usual clarifying of name spellings, Del and Betty were shown into the office and introduced.

Sara asked a lot of questions, curious with Del's inability to answer her questions coherently, and the time pushed at the noon hour. Kenny decided they should go up to the house for lunch, including Sara, and she was thrilled with the invitation.

"This is just such a wonderful home," Sara gushed several times during lunch.

She managed to slip in her questioning as conversation and praise, even as she demonstrated a hearty appetite. Katherine Louise was pleased that Sara chewed her food with her mouth closed and did not talk when she was eating; beyond that, the lunch seemed to last forever.

Fred knew this was the kind of effort with a reporter that would pay huge dividends. Tomorrow, Ben Simmons would be another matter.

Sure enough, just before noon the next morning, someone on the New World office staff eyed a man walking around the grounds. He had a note book in hand, stopped to scribble every so often, and then continued his tour. New World did not have a formal security team, but several of the maintenance crew were prepared and ready if the need arose. A call was made to Jimmy Phillips to find out who this stranger was and what he wanted. A report was also made to Fred.

"Can I hep ya?"

Jimmy asked it politely, but there was an edge to his voice that indicated he meant business and this was no casual question.

"Yeah, you can…good morning…just looking around. Got here earlier than I thought. Name's Ben Simmons…Charlotte Observer. Got an appointment here with Reverend Kenny…Reverend Stone…this guy with Stone…ah, Reverend Stone…speaks in tongues. Not till one-thirty though, so as I said…I'm early. Thought I'd take the time to look around. Nice…ah…area…ah…campus the church has. Well landscaped."

"Two hours yet," Jimmy said flatly.

"Oh, I know…thought I would look over the facilities…never been here before. Very interesting. All this property belong to the church?"

Before Jimmy could answer, Fred rolled up on a golf cart that had been motoring at its top speed and then slid to a skidding stop in a silly way. It was an almost comedic entrance for a man who was always dead serious. He surveyed Ben Simmons quickly. The reporter was short, balding, and paunchy with pasty gray skin that appeared as if he were rarely outdoors. He looked somewhat effeminate, a might dull-witted, and ineffectual, but Fred knew full well Simmons was none of those things.

"You must be Ben Simmons," Fred greeted him with that phony smile he turned on when he thought he had to produce it.

"Yessir…"

"Welcome to New World."

Fred jumped from the cart with extended hand.

"Thanks," Simmons said lazily as he shook hands. "Like I told your man here…I'm way early…y'all weren't expecting me this morning, I know, but I gave myself lots of time for the drive down..."

"I know you've been here before, but I wasn't associated with New World then..."

"Yeah...a ceremony for the office building there...got more buildings since then...I heard a big house also..."

"We're just glad you're here...honored, in fact," Fred chirped, ignoring the comment about the house. "Come on...let's have some lunch. I'll fill you in on all the details before we meet later on with Reverend Kenny, Reverend Stone, and Del and Betty."

Thus began Fred Wallace's version of a razzle-dazzle play with a difficult member of the press. That is to say, his definition of difficult. Simmons was a reticent man who let his writing speak for him through his weekly religion column and numerous high-profile articles he produced for the *Charlotte Observer*. There was an underlying cynical edge to him when it came to the instigators of modern miracles, habitual and unverifiable faith healers, seers of iconic visions, and other self-proclaimed insiders to the only true word of God. Therefore, he approached the Reverend Stone–Del situation with practiced suspicion. Simmons understood and could succinctly articulate the mythology of religion and yet respected the multitude of tenets that guided all worshipers. He did not attend a church of his own, but was in church of some kind almost every Sunday. He was not involved with any organized church group, gave pan-theistic credence and acceptance to all of religion, and so, was about as unbiased and impartial a person to write about religion as could be found. Without being religious, Simmons was highly spiritual and had a deep sense of some kind of higher power.

Fred had read enough of the reporter's articles and columns to know that Stone's interpretation of Del's strange sounds would come under severe scrutiny. He would give close examination to the claim that Del was speaking in tongues. It could not be helped, Simmons had to interview Del and Stone, but maybe, Fred considered, just maybe he could make it easier for them.

The two men sipped iced tea in the comfortable dining room surroundings of Fred's private golf club; his membership, church-paid, a part of his secular life apart from New World. They had ordered and the quiet reporter listened to Fred describe Del, Stone, New World, and Kenny.

"...Reverend Kenny made a cautious and calculated decision to bring these folks from Ohio. One that we all don't regret. Reverend Stone is a fabulous preacher...gifted, one might say, to the level of Reverend Kenny...certainly well able to transform this man Del's strange language into coherent meaning for the Word of God. Something you must witness. Next Sunday, I would hope that you would be in attendance...at our service."

"I'll definitely watch it on television...that I assure you."

"We'd love to have you here, but...but that's good...good of you to watch."

"I suppose this all means big revenue for you?"

The question came out of blue and struck hard like a body blow. Fred figured the financial side of things might become an issue, but the suddenness surprised him. Simmons wrote about his distaste for what he called, "the insidious pandering to the ministering of true needs that are seemingly fulfilled only through donations." The Blessings of an Almighty should not have to be purchased. Certainly, he recognized the operating expenses of a church body had to be paid, but he objected to blatant hawking of materials and Forgiveness and Solace tied to dollars. Fred considered the question for a moment before he answered.

"That may well be the case, but I think that if you've seen any of our services on television or attended our worship, you would find that we do not push for money. At the end of the television program we show that donations are accepted and provide an address, e-mail, and phone number…none of which is shown during the service. We do not pass a plate at our services. We do, however, provide envelopes in the lobby for cash donations and a brochure that gives a detailed explanation for other forms of giving to New World. This has been very successful for us…a voluntary method of giving. It's supported us well for years."

"I commend you for the Church's restraint in that regard. Do you think that Reverend Stone and this farmer will produce a lot of revenue for New World?"

"All indications are that they will."

"How much?"

"That's hard to say."

"About…approximately?"

"It could be thousands of dollars…"

"Hundreds of thousands…?"

"There is no way of knowing that right now."

"Christian Gospel Broadcasting has to be quite excited about this. Any feedback from them?"

"Yes, there has been. They are very pleased. We have told them that Reverend Stone and Mr. Howe will be part of three successive services, and right now, frankly, they are…very pleased."

"I understand a dead body was found on the grounds yesterday morning…"

"Yes, it was…"

"Anyone you know?"

"Yes, a man we…New World…has done business with…a vendor."

"What was he…?"

"You know, Ben, I don't have any answers to that stuff. It's a police matter. They are investigating, they interviewed Reverend Kenny and myself and others on the staff and were told no one with New World is under suspicion. That's all I know about it right at this moment."

"Hmmmmm," Simmons grunted in a slow sustained way.

The grilling went back to church finances and lasted another twenty minutes or so before Simmons suggested they get back to New World for the interview.

"Thanks, for lunch, Fred. Most informative…appreciate it. Y'all were very hospitable…very…informative."

The interview with Del, Stone, and Kenny lasted almost an hour and a half. Betty sat quietly next to Del, holding his right hand in both of hers, letting go periodically to pat his shoulder, and smiling encouragement when he tried to respond. After several attempts with Del - Stone his interlocutor for meaning - Simmons directed his questions to Stone and Kenny. He never delved into the financial nature of New World again, confining his questions to the nature of speaking in tongues and their Biblical references, the spiritual mission of New World, background on Stone and Calvary Fundamentalist Christian Church, Stone and Kenny's philosophies of religion, their take on modern social problems, and their impression of society's current spiritual condition. He made few comments of his own mind and let them know he was finished by slowly closing his note book. He tapped the notebook several times with his pen and stood.

In the background, the somber audience of Fred, Tom, and Katherine Louise watched with fascination as Simmons conducted the interview. They passed notes back and forth that concurred the interview had gone well.

After the interview, Fred walked Simmons to his car.

"Most thankful for your time, Ben…glad you came down. Think you have a good story here?"

"Sure do...excellent story. Nice folks the Howes...and Reverend Stone...very sincere. Your Reverend Kenny is dedicated, that's for sure..."

"Thank you, thank you...God Bless..."

"But I have to tell you...I don't think Mr. Howe is speaking in tongues...something wrong with his brain. Probably should see a doctor. Take care, y'all."

Simmons was in his car before Fred could respond. The driver side window slid down and Simmons leaned toward the opening.

"I'll send you a fax of what I write...advance copy. Let me know if there is anything not accurate."

He was gone, without another word from Fred.

11.

Have mercy upon me, O God, according to Your loving kindness; according to the multitude of Your tender mercies, blot out my transgressions. Wash me thoroughly from my iniquity, and cleanse me from my sin.

-Psalm 51:1-2

The winds of the past can sweep into the present like an unholy plague. Memories best forgotten, circumstances dimmed by time, yet here they were, catching up with Tom at such an inopportune moment. This was a convergent pestilence of two dangerous locusts, one revengeful, the other just plain nasty, both ready to pounce on the unsuspecting victim.

She was tall, wisp thin, with light brown hair that got twice-weekly beauty salon treatment, brown eyes, and she would be considered pretty even if it were in an odd kind of way. Her expensive pantsuit tailored for the successful business woman and the European-made loafers gave her a commanding air of means and achievement. Just the right amount of unostentatious jewelry was a fitting touch to her ensemble. She tended to fidget with the lady Rolex on her left wrist.

He was a head taller than she, with blonde, long hair pulled back to a pony-tail, dull pale blue eyes, and a square tanned face that carried a perpetual scowl. With a well-muscled physique that showed through his tight fitting clothes, he liked to flex his body in several ways periodically just so no one would miss the muscles that were there. He appeared to be stupid and physically dangerous, and he was both – a very bad combination if you were a target of his flagrant meanness.

She used the phone in the New World lobby to reach Doris while he hulked about, ready for action. She told Doris her name and that she wanted to see Tom Fletcher. Doris asked her to hold and relayed the name to Tom. For a nano-second, the name did not click with him, but then when it did his neck stiffened.

"She's in the lobby?" Tom choked getting out the words.

"Yes, says she knows you…from awhile ago…in Alabama. Says she was in town on business and thought she would come by…say hello. Should I show her in?"

"Ah…ah…

"Do you know her, Mr. Fletcher?"

"Well…ah…yes, I do seem to remember a woman by that name, but…I don't know…"

His voice trailed off and Doris waited, not sure what to do. After a moment she asked again.

"Should I show her to Mr. Wallace's office?"

"I guess…yes, show her in."

As he waited in shocked agony, Tom wondered how she turned up here, how she knew he was here, how she had the connections with Calvary and New World, and what in the devil she would say. Obviously, she wanted her money back. Coming here would indicate she probably would use extortion. Threaten. What would he do? There wasn't much time to think and his brain felt as if it had turned to grits. He knew this might happen some day, but why now?

It took a long time for Marcia Dowling to get over the fact that Tom left her. The hundred thousand dollars was one thing, she had bundles of money, but dumping her to scoot with the money was another matter. The getting dumped part was what really steamed her. She cried and drank and went through several affairs and partied, and cried some more, but nothing helped. She was drunk and miserable for six months and then intermittently for another six months. Almost a year after Tom was gone, she left a friend's party in a drunken stupor and tried to drive home. She managed to get into a three-car pileup that put her and several others in the hospital. Fortunately, no one got killed. Her worst injury was a dislocated shoulder. She also received some cuts and bruises.

The accident and its aftermath of recovering from injuries helped her redirect her life. She reacted to her circumstances in recovery as an omen, a message from a God she had previously disregarded, a God she had rejected, and a God she now felt she desperately needed. Marcia had never been very religious, but she knew this was the time to get religion. She figured she had to quit drinking so much, lose some weight, get serious, and take control of her future. It amounted to all that wonderful positive stuff that straightened out peoples' lives. And she had to quit moping around about Tom Fletcher.

She refused to entertain any of her solicitous friends who came by the hospital to cheer her up and drop off little presents. Instead, she asked for visitation from the Baptist preacher who ministered to the patients there and instructed the presents be given to the nurses and other staff on her floor. The preacher came by twice a day to read verses from the Bible to her and to counsel the way of the Lord. She was enthused with this new found comfort and invoked the name of Jesus as her Lord and Savior. Amen, said the preacher, you shall be quickly healed.

Out of the hospital after three days and home to her fabulous condo, Marcia began the strategy of her comeback as a new woman. Stronger, capable, and with direction, and with the comfort of Jesus, she was ready to move ahead. First, she contacted her attorney to deal with the citation she received for the accident, and second, she made phone calls to line up a private detective who could go to work for her immediately to find where Tom Fletcher had landed. Her lawyer kept her out of jail, although she lost her drivers license for a year, and the detective easily located Tom.

Marcia ran a small blind classified ad in the Birmingham *Post Herald* to recruit a full-time driver and assistant. She avoided the Florence *Times Daily* because she did not want anyone from around town to be involved with her business. An out-of-town person would be better, she figured. She received a pile of letters in response, each included their photograph which she had requested, and then she spent several days sorting through them trying to decide how to narrow the field. Eventually she chose five – four men and one woman, actually a nineteen year old girl as it turned out - that she talked to on the phone. She selected a man from those conversations who agreed to come to the condo for a personal interview. She hired Jess Stokes on the spot. Besides, she had liked his looks right away. His photo had been blatantly beefcake and she loved it. Jess was her man for hire.

It took almost three weeks for Jess to graduate from driver and errand runner to sex partner in the bedroom. Not long after that, he moved in with Marcia bringing all of his worldly possessions, including his weights. Everything he owned could be jammed nicely into the trunk of his five year old previously-owned Lincoln. His clothes consisted mainly of tee shirts, sweat shirts, and two pair of denims. He only wore Nike cross trainers with white socks. It was a wardrobe Marcia detested so she outfitted him with new casual shirts and slacks, and one suit, white shirt, and tie for more formal occasions. She did not know what his background was and she cared less. She did know he was certainly rough around the edges, but he would do.

At first she felt self-conscious about having a driver and slouched down in the car as they moved through town. It did not matter, because although there were quite a few Mercedes automobiles in Florence, Alabama, no one else owned the big S600 sedan like Marcia's. Everyone knew when she was on the move or her errand boy was after something for her. The car was recognizable a block away.

Eventually, she got used to the arrangement and, head high, she went about her business.

Her business, a result of her new positive life, a life that meant being productive instead of sitting around getting drunk, was a small boutique that sold collectables and hand-crafted merchandise. She also had incorporated a small, sort of combination tea room and sandwich shop on one side of the store. She called the place *The Answer*. She told prospective customers she had the answer to what they wanted. To herself she said it was the answer to her need for purpose. She also had another purpose which had been quietly festered and motivated, and that was the determination to keep track of Tom Fletcher. She decided that since she had her day of reckoning and the coming to terms with things, then Tom should have his as well. It was just a matter of time.

So when she saw the Christian Gospel Broadcasting program Faith For Your Future coming from New World church in Columbia, South Carolina, featuring Reverend Randy Stone and Delwin Howe speaking in tongues, she surely took notice. Her detective had tracked Tom to Reverend Stone and Calvary Fundamentalist; this could not be a coincidence. If Reverend Stone were there, Tom had to be there, too. However, it was a coincidence to turn on the television in their suite at The Ritz-Carlton in the Buckhead section of Atlanta, do some channel flicking, and lo and behold reveal Reverend Stone. She knew all about Tom's tight connection to Stone and his church. What a clever cover for him, that bast... What? Stop! She almost said a bad word, but settled on scoundrel. Scoundrel was not a word she ordinarily used, but she thought it sounded sophisticated and she wanted dearly to be sophisticated. She emphasized her distain by adding conniving, two-timing rat to the word scoundrel. She said the words to herself as she stared at the TV. Jess stood close behind her, not quite comprehending until she told him the significance.

"Our boy's got to be there in Columbia...he's got to be..."

"So?" Jess mumbled.

"So...so when the convention ends I think we should drive over to Columbia and see what Mr. Fletcher has to say for himself. I believe he'd be real surprised to see us."

"Show's over Wednesday afternoon..."

"I know. We'll drive over, get a motel, and be ready to call on him Thursday morning. Tomorrow we'll call that... What is it? New World Church. Make sure he's around. I'd bet he is...he's there, believe me."

"Okay," Jess said in a dull way, as if he were only half listening to her, and he was only half listening to her.

They had come to Atlanta in order to attend the National Hand Crafted Arts Convention that opened the next day. It was a buying trip to order new items for *The Answer*, but they arrived on Saturday in order to entertain an old friend of Marcia's in The Dining Room of the Ritz-Carlton. This also gave Marcia two or three days to shop for new clothes. Florence was not much for high style and the kinds of things she wanted.

Even though she had known where Tom had landed she had not decided when and how she would get to him. The fact she would have to go to northwestern Ohio, on his turf, had stalled her from making plans for confronting him. Jess had wanted to drive right up to Ohio when he found out about Tom, but she kept him contained. Every so often he brought it up, but she resisted. Now, this blessing: Tom delivered to her in the South, nearby, accessible, and unsuspecting. And highly vulnerable, since more than ever he would not want anyone to know just why some woman was coming after him. A self-righteous woman and a lame-brained lummox who liked to hurt someone if he got the chance, merely for the fun of it.

Doris showed Marcia and Jess into Fred's office where Tom was standing stiffly behind the large solid cherry desk. His knees almost buckled when he saw Jess, because Jess was big, obviously well-muscled, and had a look that all but snarled. It was as if Marcia had brought along a giant pit bull that was pulling on her leash to attack. Fear was something Tom understood; large quantities of courage were not in his makeup unless his size, strength, and the odds were in his favor. Nothing was in his favor right now.

"Thank you, Doris," Marcia smiled, dismissing the secretary, and then turned her attention to Tom. "I bet you're surprised to see me…and of course, Jess."

Tom raised his eyebrows when he looked at Jess.

"Yes…well," she went on, "Jess helps me a lot these days…keeps me from being defenseless. He does all sorts of things for me, most of them quite well. Are you surprised to see me?"

"Hello, Marcia…Jess. Have a seat…"

Tom could be very cool under pressure, very cool indeed. He was groping for time, time to figure out how he was going to deal with them.

"Well?" she snapped.

"Yes…and no. I knew you were tenacious, perhaps you might look me up one day…just didn't expect it to be today…"

"Or this week or anytime soon…"

"You're looking very…very healthy…fit…vital…"

"You mean as opposed to that drunken party doll you took advantage of?"

"Ya want me to tear his heart out?" Jess snarled, spit flying every which way from his mouth.

"No, Jess, contain yourself…at least until we find out how cooperative Mr. Fletcher is going to be."

"Have a seat," Tom offered the second time.

Marcia sat, but Jess stood there with his arms folded waiting for the command to pounce. He was a well-trained pit bull.

"How can I help you?" Tom asked calmly, collected in his demeanor, and scared silly.

"How can I help you…wow, that is so like you, Tom. So cool…really cool. You can help me by telling me how you are going to pay back my one hundred thousand dollars…in a way that doesn't take a dollar a year for a hundred thousand years. Something much better than that…way better."

"Well, look…"

"Look, nothing…I can have Jess take you apart limb by limb, maybe put you in a coma, break your spine so you can't walk…or I can talk to these fine folks at New World. Reverend Kenny…he would be very interested in you, Tom…finding out how you scammed me, how you are probably planning to scam them. By the way, how are you going to get them, Tom?"

"This is all legitimate…we're doing the Lord's work and the Goodness of what we are doing is reward in and of itself."

"How much is your church getting out of this?" she demanded.

"I don't know yet…thousands of dollars, anyway."

"Quarter of a million?"

"Maybe…"

"Half million?"

"No way."

"Lots of money, though, for your church, isn't it?"

"Should be."

He was struggling to decide where to go with this conversation, struggling to figure out how to handle her and the big guy.

"Surprising as it may seem to you," Tom offered, "it's good to see you…hear your voice…see your…energy…"

She looked into his eyes intently, looked at her lap, and then fiddled with her Rolex.

"There was a time when that line would get it done for you. It doesn't work today. I'm way beyond that kind of stuff. It's a simple matter, easily remedied…I'm here to collect my money…a hundred thousand dollars. I want it, I intend to get it."

"How did you get to me here…and why haven't I heard from you before now?"

"Well, hon, we knew where y'all were for awhile. Had a private detective find you…that was easy. It was just a matter of time before we got to you. Made it happen sooner rather than later by accidentally seeing Reverend Stone on the TV while we were visiting Atlanta. Knew you were part of his church. Could not believe my eyes when I saw him preaching with that fellow talks in tongues…knew you had to be here, so we drove over. Just want my money, hon. That's all I want."

"I'd like to believe that…really would. Most women in your position would want revenge…"

"Who, me? Not me darlin', I just want my money."

"I thought the money was a gift…there was no note signed, no contract…just money you gave to me because you liked me…maybe even loved me. That's my memory of what happened. Never thought I had to pay it back…never thought of it any other way than as a gift to get me going in life. After all, you had tons of money…that someone gave to you…you never worked for it. I thought you were passing some on to me. That's how I took it to mean, anyway."

She was dumbfounded by his answer and he knew it right away. For the first time in several minutes, he did not feel afraid. He felt as if he were gaining control and he relaxed a notch.

"Look, I know how you might be upset about me, but it never would have worked out between us. It was right for me to move on…get out of your life…"

"I want my money or I tell my story to Reverend Kenny, to the newspapers, and to anyone else who will listen."

"Is this your lawyer?" Tom asked, trying to make a joke.

"He's my…," she caught herself from saying something nasty. "He's my insurance policy for getting back my money…he's my playing hardball kind of personal support."

"Look, we're in Columbia, South Carolina…all of my financial stuff is in Ohio…I can't even think right now…how I would get you that kind of money. I can write you a check as down payment, after that we could work it out. Why don't we have lunch later and we can discuss how I'm going to do this."

"What kind of check?"

"What do you mean?"

"How much?"

"Ten thousand…I can cover ten thousand today and we can talk about how I get the rest back to you. I…I…I can't let this interfere with the work Reverend Stone is doing…it's too important…"

"Oh, please…"

"No, it's true. What he does means a lot to me. I'm not the same person you knew once, you're not the same person…I've changed…this church work means a lot, it really does. Why else would I be sitting here at New World when I could be hustling for clients back in Ohio? Have lunch with me…we'll work it out, I'll give you a check."

"Well…," she hesitated, "okay. Where?"

"There's a diner down the road about a mile…called Ernie's. I'll meet you there at noon."

He came around the desk to get the door. Jess moved out into the hall first and Tom touched her arm to hold her back for moment."

"Come without the gorilla," he whispered.

"Maybe," she said as she brushed by him and out the door.

She arrived at Ernie's without Jess. She wheeled the Mercedes into a parking spot in a way that took up three slots and came inside. She had changed clothes and was now dressed in short skirt to show off her legs and a somewhat provocative low cut blouse that showed full cleavage. This was a far cry from the severe outfit she had on at the office in New World. She couldn't stand it, he figured, she still had to show off for him, entice him just a bit, make him wish he had not baled on her, make him regret leaving, and make him wonder what it would be like to have sex with her again. She was transparent and this would be easy.

"I see you changed…"

"Yeah, I had to after rolling around in bed with Jess…he's such an animal…I had to get changed. Something lighter for the hot afternoon.

"Looks nice."

"Could have been you with me on that bed awhile ago. I didn't shower or wear any perfume so you could still smell the sex on me."

"I can…and you're right."

"What is there to discuss?" she insisted.

"Well, I figured we needed to work out the terms of payback. I'm not interested in getting my neck broke by your goon. That's what you had in mind for me, wasn't it…if I didn't pay up right away?"

"I thought you might have to be persuaded. Plus, I'd tell all if I had to. You were so right back there at the office…nothing was in writing. But you know I'm right. This is a moral issue and God is on my side…you know He is."

"I suppose He might be at that…"

"Of course He is."

He smiled at her. She was unable to recognize that it was a knowing smile Tom gave when he was sure he had everything under control.

"You said ten thousand. Then what?"

"Then I arrange a loan through my business for ninety thousand and you get paid. I can't finalize that until I get back to Ohio, but I can get the ball rolling this afternoon with my banker. I can have her give you a call at your hotel…confirm what I'm doing. How's that?"

"Her…? My, my. You can get your hands on that kind of money that easily?"

"I think so…well, I know I can. I've got a great relationship with my banker."

"That's really nice, Tom, but your plan is not really very good…"

"What's wrong?"

Hon, it'd be much better to have your banker overnight the papers to you as soon as there's approval. You overnight them back, signed, and then your banker overnights a check. Let's see…overnight from tomorrow is two days, another day back is…"

"There's a Sunday involved…"

Right you are, darlin', right you are. Sooo…you send back on Monday, the check comes on Tuesday. For ninety thousand dollars Jess and I can hang around for a few days. Anyway, I would love to see your Reverend in person. We just might attend Sunday service at New World, Tom. I've rediscovered God, you know, a great service like your Reverend conducts might help my troubled soul."

He smiled again, but this time it was different; this time he wasn't relaxed or confident about anything and he could not let her suspect that.

"How about writing that check...make me feel better that we're on the right track."

"Oh, yeah...sure."

He pulled a leather case from the inside pocket of his sport coat and laid it on the table. It looked like a check book holder only slightly larger in size and somewhat thicker. He flipped it open to reveal a clear folder that contained several credit cards on the one side, and a check book on the other. He took a pen from the same pocket, tipped open the check book cover with his left thumb, and wrote the check for ten thousand dollars. He signed it with a flourish, tore it carefully away from its binding, and handed it to Marcia.

"Well, well, well...that's a start. Let's see...First Meridian Bank of Swanton, Ohio. Bet you're one of their best customers, Tom."

"I should be...they've asked me to be on their board of directors...term starts later this year. I guess I am one of their best...hard to say. Lots of rich farmers around Swanton...sort of like Del."

After they had ordered lunch, Tom pulled out his cell phone, touched a speed-dial number, and waited. He drummed his fingers on the table and smiled at Marcia.

"She's probably at lunch, but I'll leave her a message. Yeah...hi Jackie...Tom...I'm here in Columbia...South Carolina. Trying to get some business accomplished with an associate of mine and I need to borrow ninety thousand...need you to get the paperwork started and I need you to confirm with my associate that the wheels are in motion...this is really important...I want you to give my associate a call this afternoon..."

Marcia was curious about his banker since it was a woman. Jackie Olson would be giving her a call – the banker. How nice, Tom, another woman for you to dazzle. They went to the parking lot after lunch and parted with her notice that she would be in touch after she heard from Jackie. She had one more bit of advice for him.

"I just want you to remember, Tom...that old saying is true...cheaters never prosper."

He smiled again and nodded assent. He wished he could tell her what he was really thinking. It didn't matter, though, because soon this would all be behind him. He needed to talk with Stone.

The past had also rushed into the present for Reverend Stone. All of his errors, each of his sins, everything that would counsel St. Peter for Heavenly rejection came tumbling into his consciousness. A chilling wind of self-imposed judgment, the terrible taste of fatal unworthiness, and a brutalizing sadness gripped him as surely as if the hand of God's judgment were manifested as a clenched fist that had snatched him.

Keri had not been around since Monday and neither had Larry. Fred was upset because of the planning that needed to be done for Sunday's service. Larry had finally shown up that afternoon without Keri and had given Fred a detailed script for Sunday. He had arranged for which musicians would perform and when, and had scheduled practice for Friday evening. Since the Saturday service would be a simple prayer meeting nothing was required for that other than the usual organ work. Fred was satisfied with his script, but not happy with Larry's four-day disappearance. Larry was apologetic and said it would not happen again. Unusual circumstances, he explained. Fred had no notion about Keri.

Once Stone had known Larry was in the building he assumed Keri would also be around. She was not and he sulked to himself. Since Sunday, he had busied himself writing an e-mail newsletter to his Calvary parishioners, helped with the phones, answered e-mails and correspondence from viewers of Sunday's service, and assisted with the fulfillment of merchandise orders. None of this busy work could distract him enough to forget about Keri. Hard as he tried to convince himself that it was over, that it was best, and that he should move on, he still lingered with the void in his life. The void hurt, but it was good, he told himself. An immoral and potentially destructive situation was erased. For him the erasure left a smudge across his ego and a dirty blank space in his psyche.

Confronting the loss of his illicit lover was a challenge he felt up to, eventually succeeding…getting over it, they say. Confronting his evaluation for the rest of his life with Helen was a struggle yet to be endured, yet to be examined and analyzed, and both of these conditions yet to be reconciled with his Lord.

His wickedness on the one hand and Helen's sheer goodness on the other skewed the life-scale completely out of balance. In the deepest recesses of his soul were the answers for two critical questions that determined how he reconciled his life with himself. Did he really feel guilty about his affair with Keri, and, more importantly, did he truly love Helen? Those questions must be faced and the answers revealed before he could be released from the Lord's grasp, and that grasp was crushing his chest. The cold wind of reality that he had not faced made him shiver from its chill.

Perhaps Tom could help. Tom could often clearly sort out the issues for making a tough decision or take apart a challenge in such a way that it became more understandable. He would talk to Tom after dinner.

Dinner at the mansion was somber, contained, and with little, if any, conversation. The police had called several times since Monday, the media was relentless for additional interviews and comments, and the prosecutor's office called asking for an informal meeting with Fred and Reverend Kenny. The fact that money was flowing like water into the New World bank account and merchandise sales were the highest anyone had ever seen did not seem to relieve the tension. Reverend Kenny and Katherine Louise excused themselves as soon as they finished eating, Del and Betty headed out for a walk, and Tom and Stone were left at the table. Tom had seemed at ease during the brief meal, but acted nervously after the others left.

I need to talk to you Randy…let's go outside."

"Sure...and I need to talk to you. What's wrong, Tom?"

"Let's get outside."

They walked straight out from the mansion front porch, across the road, and onto the large open lawn that spread away in three directions. If either man had been in a better state of mind the soft radiant light of the warm evening might well have been a comfort. It was lost on them because neither took notice of the serenity and beauty that could have been their solace.

"I suppose you're muddling over the girl," Tom guessed with a tinge of sarcasm.

"Keri…"

"Yeah, Keri…"

"From the sound of your voice it seems as if you have little sympathy in there…for my muddling…"

"I'm always sympathetic about someone's muddling," Tom returned, emphasizing the word muddling. "Not always sympathetic to what it's about…"

"Judgment time?"

"Not really. I'm certainly not one to pass judgment on you…I have enough of my own sins to contend with let alone deal with yours. It's that…you're a grown man…consorting with a young, impressionable girl…"

"Was…"

"Yeah…was. What do you need?"

When Tom asked the question there was a softness about it, the tone of sympathy, the quality of caring.

"What do I do about Helen?"

"It's simple," Tom said quietly after a long pause. "Go home, admit nothing…and I mean nothing. Don't try to explain anything to her. Tell her Keri found a lover here in Columbia and she is not coming back to work…in fact, tell Helen you really don't want Keri back. She wasn't working out as well as you wanted…tell Helen that you want her to help you in the church office…a little bit at first, get the hang of things, then more down the line. Tell her you are not interested in trying to hire someone else. Then you, Reverend, you get used to having her around you a lot. It you're trying to figure out whether you love her, forget it…it doesn't matter. Suck it up and stick it out and learn to love her if you have doubts about it. You married her once for a reason. Rediscover the reason and make it work out. In the long run, when your hair is a lot grayer than it is now, you'll be glad you did. Take it from someone who has nobody…it will be worth it. Making the tough decisions are hard, I should know…that's the one I think you need to make. You asked…that's my take on it."

"Thank you…and God Bless."

"Don't mention it."

"You think Keri is not coming back with us?"

"I'll be surprised if you ever see her again. Lucky for you if you don't."

"I suppose you're right. Now, what did you want to talk to me about?"

"You feel any better?" Tom looked at him squarely, a steady gaze of concern.

"Yes...lots."

Stone waited, raised his eyebrows questioningly, stopped walking, and turned to face Tom.

"Everything has changed," Tom said slowly, giving his earlobe its usual tug, "whole new ballgame. I'm not even sure this was meant to last a long time, anyway..."

"What are you talking about?"

"Working with you...the church. I have to admit, I sure have enjoyed the ride. I went into it...got involved a few years back so it would help my business. It did, big time. But I got more and more into things and the next I knew I was sort of the kingpin of the trustees. I believed in the mission. I do believe in your mission, Randy. Your success is locked up..."

"You're not making any sense..."

"I've got to move on...tomorrow. I'll be gone tomorrow..."

"What? But why...what do you mean?"

"Long story, Randy, a very long story...too long to tell you right now...too complicated...too revealing about me, and too damning. I've not always been a model citizen and some folks are after me. They could ruin us...ruin you. With me out of the way, you and Calvary will be just fine..."

"Some people came to see you today...a woman and a man." Stone put his hand on Tom's shoulder. "Are they threatening you?"

"That they are...and their threat is real...even though their cause is unjust and not based on law. But that really doesn't matter right about now. I'm packed...got all my stuff together...I'll be gone in the morning before you get up..."

"What do they want? Can't we deal with them?"

"They want, Dear Reverend, one hundred thousand dollars that does not belong to them…they only think it belongs to them. It belongs to me because I earned it and that is a big part of the story. They want the money or they will destroy us with the so-called truth…their truth that is lies and misrepresentations. I can't tolerate it…I can't let you endure the mess they would make if I fought them about the whole thing. I made a down payment to the woman at lunch. A check for ten thousand dollars. It was a phony check on a phony bank…a way to stall. She'll find out soon enough that the thing is bogus and she'll come after you. You know nothing, you refer her to my office in Swanton. I'll be gone. She wants me, but she might try to pressure you. Get Fred after them. New World has a big stake in you, Dear Reverend, so Fred will keep them off your back. They'll move on…it's me they want. She wants more than the money from me…she wants a piece of me...she wants…I think she wants my life. She can't have it. If it were just the money I might pay it just to shut her up and get rid of her, but she wants more than that…so I…I've got to get…get away."

"Where are you going, what will you do?"

"I'll be fine…don't worry about me. I've made plans…prepared for this…in case it happened…that she came around. I figured she might some day. Today was the day. I can handle it. Do your thing next Sunday and the next and you'll be in clover. Good luck with Del; I'm not sure how long he can hold out. Del might need a doctor sooner rather than later. Anyway, good luck. It will be awhile before you hear from me, so don't be concerned if a lot of time goes by…"

"But you can't go like this…"

"Have to, Dear Reverend…have to. No matter what you might hear, I've only tried to help you and the church…that was my goal. Besides helping myself, of course. Never took any money that was church money, never needed to. Church gave me back all that I asked for."

"I'm stunned…"

I'm sure you are."

"I'll miss you…a lot."

Tom Fletcher smiled. It was a broad very real smile that made his face almost glow. This smile, this beaming glorious smile, he fashioned with deliberate concentration so that it hid the sadness that made his body ache.

12.

The wicked is ensnared by the transgression of his lips, but the righteous will come through trouble.

-Proverbs 12:13

There was a stale smell about the room that Tom could not place. He had only been gone a week, yet his office had taken on an odor of disquieting depression. He stood there for a long time, looking around, trying to decide what he wanted to pack and what did not matter. As he speculated about it, he put his laptop into his briefcase. He pulled a leather duffle bag from the storage closet, slowly opened it, and bit by bit, piece by piece, he carefully and systematically disassembled his business life in Swanton, Ohio, and placed the residue in the two bags.

He judged that running away isn't always the answer, but sometimes it's the only answer. It was the reason he made his move; his only alternative, what he had projected might result if Marcia ever came at him. Just after four that morning he had walked from the Kenny mansion to the main road. He carried one small softside suitcase of the three he brought with him and also his briefcase. He waited for several minutes until a taxi he had arranged picked him up for the drive to the Columbia airport. After stops and plane changes in Atlanta and Cincinnati, he was back in northwestern Ohio shortly after nine. A taxi took him to his condo.

He repacked the suitcase and left it lying open on his bed. From the second drawer of his dresser he retrieved a small lock box and opened it with a key from his key ring. He removed the lock box key from the ring and placed it on top of the dresser. Inside the box were six letter size manila envelopes that he removed and placed among the shirts he had packed in the suitcase. He closed the suitcase and set it on the floor. Still remaining in the box was a sheaf of hundred dollar bills, twenty-five in total, and his passport. He fanned five out from the others, put those in his wallet, and put the remaining bills in his leather breast pocket case. He slid the passport into the other breast pocket. He put the suitcase in the Town Car trunk, the briefcase on the seat next to him.

Next stop was the bank. His personal checking account contained a little over seven hundred dollars which he withdrew, although he did not close the account. From the business account he withdrew fifty-six thousand dollars that he received in a cashier's check. Slightly less than twenty thousand dollars remained. He folded the check and tucked it into his shirt pocket. He was nonchalant about these transactions and with a bright smile and a wave of his hand he exited the bank.

From the bank he headed the Lincoln over to Briner's Café on Main Street, ordered coffee and a substantial breakfast of eggs, sausage, home fries, and toast, and skimmed through the day's USAToday as he methodically ate. He knew what his timeline was and would not rush. There was plenty of time to get done what he had to get done.

When he entered his suite of offices, briefcase in hand, his secretary greeted him with a quizzical look of disbelief. She had not expected him back for another two weeks at least.

"Wow, I didn't…this…this is a surprise," she sputtered.

"I'll explain…give me a few minutes, Gina, let me get organized" he said grimly.

When he walked out of his office with the briefcase and leather duffle, she stared. He moved quickly right by her, out the door, and placed the two bags in the trunk. Then he came back to her desk. Her mouth was slightly open, her eyes wide with all the questions she wanted to ask.

"Sit down," he commanded, "and listen…carefully."

He explained it all to her in a superficial way that would show why he was not at fault and yet why he had to move on. There was money in the business account to pay all of the current commissions and bills, he would default on the business lease, and she should cancel the phone. His condo would be repossessed, but there was nothing he could do about that. Anyway, it didn't matter, he told her. She could write herself a check for whatever was left after the bills were paid. Should be about five grand, he figured.

"I appreciate your help since you've been with me, Gina…sorry this has happened."

He pulled open a file folder he carried and signed his name to one of the papers he pulled from it.

"Call Gloria in Ben's office and have her come over and notarize this…right away, if she can. Tell her what we want and bring her stamp."

Gina picked up the phone, punched in the number for Ben Howard's law office, and got to Gloria. A few minutes later Gloria was at Gina's desk notarizing his signature on the title to the Lincoln. She gave them both a look that said "I'd like to know what is going on," but returned to her office without asking any questions.

"The Lincoln is yours…but I want you to drive me to the Detroit airport. Okay?"

She shook her head in disbelief.

"This can't be happening…it's like a dream…a very bad dream…"

"Don't worry about it," he said as he played with his favorite lock of unruly hair. "Pay off the agents for the month as you usually would without explaining anything, pay the bills, get your money, get out of here, and don't look back…look for another job. You might hide the money for awhile…in a mattress…don't put it in the bank. I'd slowly deposit it or invest it over time. I don't want anyone coming after you for what is my doing. If that money shows up in one of your accounts, someone might think you were my accomplice."

Tears welled in her eyes and she came around her desk and reached for him. They embraced, an embrace not of passion, but of caring and friendship and the bitter sadness that comes from it all ending this way. She fought back the tears and kissed him on the cheek.

By late evening of that awful Friday, Tom was drinking a marguerita on the terrace of a condo in Guadalajara, Mexico. Beside him was his friend Gorge Quintaro, a business partner of some skill, a partner Tom had been sending money for several years. It was time for a new life and Tom knew that he was rid of Marcia. He had planned for this eventuality, it just came sooner that he wanted or expected. All was in place financially and for a comfortable living. He would not look back.

Friday had also been an awful day at New World Gospel Church. There was so much happening early that none of the others realized Tom was missing. Carlton was caught in the vortex of a whirlwind of activity at the parsonage, what with the phones ringing almost nonstop, Reverend Kenny up early and impatient, terse with his comments which he almost never was, and Katherine Louise flouncing around the house, first moaning and groaning upstairs, down to the dining room, into the kitchen, and back to the dining room where she threw herself in a chair and hung her head in her hands and moaned some more. Betty and Del heard her moaning and groaning, stayed away from the dining room, and instead, carefully went down the back stairs and out for a walk until they hoped the commotion would have ended.

Stone came downstairs, saw Katherine Louise in distress at the dining room table, and went straight to the kitchen. He ate a plate of scrambled eggs and sausage standing up as Carlton and Jessie nervously watched him, took a cup of coffee and a piece of toast, and went out the back door to the golf carts. He was at the desk in Fred's office in minutes, safely away from the tumult, he thought. He wanted some quiet to reconcile what he would say about Tom and time to make sure he was ready for Sunday. He wondered where Keri might be.

Cal Dobson appeared at the open door of Fred's office. He looked hung over. He raised his hand in salute as Stone looked up, then coughed involuntarily with a hacking, racking sound and corresponding reaction that made him bend forward from the waist.

"Morning, Rev."

"Good morning."

"Where is everybody?"

"Well...I just got here so I..."

"Never mind...I'll find someone."

For all his gregariousness and seemingly devil-may-care attitude, Cal was a tenacious investigator. Something about Fred did not sit right with him when he had been here before and, consequently, he dug deeply into who this man is. He had found out more than Fred would have wanted him to, of that he was sure. He wanted a face-to-face to put some tough questions into play. He wanted some answers. So did the police.

Not far behind Cal in the discovery zone were Detectives Mitchell and Ross. Although they were not as tenacious as he was, they managed to plod forward following the leads of everything that came to their attention. Cal made sure several items got their notice and he did so anonymously. As a result, they thought they were pretty sharp detectives. They did work hard, but there was nothing original about their thought processes.

Cal ducked in and out of empty offices until he came face-to-face with Doris.

"What are you doing in here?" she demanded. "You need to wait in the lobby until someone can see you. Who...who do y'all want to talk to?"

"Fred Wallace, ma'am...sorry if I overstepped my bounds, but no one answered the phone in the lobby...so I just came in..."

"Well you can step right back to the lobby until there is someone here that you can talk to."

She was adamant and he acquiesced accordingly.

Coming down the hall was Detective Mitchell trailed by Detective Ross and they would not be so agreeable to being deferred. Mitchell breezed right by Doris.

"Want to see Mr. Wallace," he threw at her and kept walking.

"Wait a minute," she snapped, "you can't just barge in here even if you are the police. Y'all have to follow some rules like everyone else...besides there's no one here to see you. Mr. Wallace is..."

"Wallace is here," Mitchell snapped back at her, "I know he is for a fact."

Cal leaned against the wall in the background. He had never made it to the lobby when the two detectives charged by him. He had waited to find out what was going on this morning at New World. Excitement for sure and he liked excitement. And he could create excitement.

The commotion, the words of anger, the violation of the usual morning quiet in the building added to the other distractions in preparing for Sunday. Tom's unexpected departure, the continuing anguish he had about Keri, and his concern for Del's health all contributed to Stone's frustration with getting his work completed. And why were they after Fred? What was going on? He got up and went to the doorway. He could see Doris confronting the two men. She was incensed and he applauded her grit.

"Well, I don't know he's here and I'm in charge when he and Reverend Kenny are not here, and they are…"

"They're both here," he sniffed, "believe me I know. The man I had posted to watch the building saw them both come in here some time ago…and the wife…she's here, too. They're all here. I want to talk to Wallace. I would appreciate it if you took me to him, although I imagine he's with Reverend Kenny in his office. I know where that is."

"I'll announce you," she said officiously.

Doris knocked on Reverend Kenny's office door, but Mitchell did not wait. He flipped the handle and brushed past her into the room. Startled, Kenny, Fred, and Katherine Louise stopped their animated conversation and stared.

"I'm sorry…," Doris started, but Mitchell cut off her words.

"Not her fault folks…I didn't want to wait so I came right in…"

"That's all right Doris, we'll be fine," Kenny assured her, his face quickly reddening with constrained anger.

She closed the door and went back to her own office.

"What is it Detective?" Kenny's strong tone belied his anger and his nervousness.

After all, what could they want? It was bad enough to have to deal with the news media let alone have these guys come back. Kenny was frustrated, but did not want them to know. For them, he must remain the calm, concerned minister who could counsel to and pray for his flock, a man who should not be filled with anxiety and surely not one who is near the point of exasperation. Marva Eckels had added to his morning's frustration. Among the morning phone calls bombarding New World was one from Marva Eckels. Marva, a fifty year-old parishioner with three teenage daughters, had been arrested. Disorderly conduct, resisting arrest, assaulting a police office, and trespassing were some of the charges against her. She wanted Reverend Kenny to come to the county jail to bail her out and speak to the press about the injustice of her arrest.

She had developed a mini-career of staging demonstrations for various causes she felt self-righteous about and about which she wanted to do something. Others with causes found it easy to get her help for their issues, also. These were solid Christian issues, fundamental to her thinking, things that were at odds with the Bible and all that is right and good and decent, and truly signals that the Devil was incarnate on this earth and in her world. Her latest target of sin, evil, and transgression was the Planned Parenthood office near Columbia Mall. Their guilt was for several violations of Marva's sensibilities, including polluting young minds with their teachings about sex, contraception, and abortion. She had already decided, with no doubt whatsoever, that with the Devil's help they would soon have another abortion clinic available.

This Planned Parenthood office had been open about six weeks, but had not come to Marva's attention until two weeks ago. She was on them like flies on rotten apples. She initially mustered a protest group of forty-seven that gradually diminished over succeeding days until she had her hard-core picketers. Marva and sixteen staunch fighters of evil. They carried signs decrying these agents of the Devil as they marched back and forth in front of the office. Each day, the stubborn protesters carried their signs, sang hymns, and talked to anyone who would listen to their rant. This morning it got out of hand and soon the police were there trying to restore order.

Planned Parenthood had been patient and had not called the police when Marva and her gang had begun their marching. But eventually they had enough of cat-calls, derisive yells, and the obvious negative publicity. Today, when a fight was on the verge of erupting, it was time to call for help. They called the police to put a stop to what they deemed abusive harassment.

Marva tangled with the obviously sympathetic police sergeant who showed up in response to the call. He tried to talk to her, but she was in no mood for dialog and the interchange became quickly heated. Unfortunately, Marva poked Officer Nelson with her sign to emphasize a point and he took exception to having the butt end of a stick jabbed into his chest. It got worse from there and Marva was eventually secured with handcuffs, stuffed into Nelson's patrol car, and taken away. She was booked, finger printed, photographed, and allowed to make a call before she was placed in a holding cell with several other women, mainly prostitutes. Her call was to Reverend Kenny.

The discussion at hand when Mitchell and Ross entered had been about who would go bail out Marva. It had almost been decided, although not affirmed, that the dubious chore should be carried out by Katherine Louise.

"Why does she have to pick today as the day she gets arrested?" Katherine Louise was asking the question rhetorically, she already knew there was no answer.

Marva had been arrested four times since she had become an activist. Her new-born Christianity was defining her, a shield against the ugliness she saw in the world around her. Katherine Louise had come to her rescue before; now was not the time to abandon Marva. It was, however, not the right day for it, inappropriate at best, terrible in terms of getting help from New World. Katherine Louise nodded agreement to her mission and was ready to walk out of the office as the two detectives barged into the process.

"We'd like to talk to Mr. Wallace, Reverend…alone, if you don't mind."

Mitchell made it sound like some kind of order although both men knew full well that it was not. Kenny nodded and moved toward the door with Katherine Louise.

"Let me know when you are finished," he said, "I'll find some place to work. Lots of reporters want interviews…"

"Thanks, Reverend." Mitchell gave a half salute to the departing minister then turned his attention to Fred. He didn't say anything, but rather lowered himself into a nearby chair and stared at Fred.

Fred watched, waited, and sat down in Kenny's chair. He could feel the eyes of both men bore in on him and he reacted by not reacting. He refused eye contact; instead, he looked out the window.

"We'd like to ask you a few questions," Ross opened. "Do you mind?"

"Not at all."

"What was your relationship with Turco?" Ross asked quickly.

Fred hesitated, looked at Ross, turned toward Mitchell, then picked up a pen and tapped it on the desk in front of him.

"What is it you want?" Fred asked.

"The true story," Mitchell said flatly, "we're always after the true story. Y'all can help us with that…I think."

"Meaning what…what is the true story?"

"About you and Turco," Ross said, "we know some things, Mr. Wallace, so I think you better fess up about Sam Turco."

"We did business with him, we…"

"Naw, come on…we're not stupid about this like you think. We know some things…"

"I don't know…"

"Save it, Fred," Mitchell fired, "Ross is trying to tell you we know about you and Turco…the sales kickbacks, the private deals on the side, the mutual businesses you had with Sam, the reason you'd have for wanting him dead…"

"Wait a minute…"

"No, you wait…you had the motive…you had…"

"I did not kill Sam Turco...and let me tell you...let me say...you know it. You're not satisfied with knowing I didn't kill him, you want to get after me because you found out about a few details you didn't personally like. Well, get over it...my dealings with Sam have nothing to do with his death, but they do have something to do with your intent to punish me for something else..."

"This is not my church, Fred...I attend New Providence Christian Church...in a less advantaged area of the city as New World...but we prosper, we expand, we do proper Christian ministries. I believe in certain principles...guidelines, if you will, about my behavior, about the behavior of people in this world. Deceit is decadence...reason for judgment by the Lord. You have been deceitful, Fred, and I think you should pay. You should not continue to prosper from your misguided partnership with Sam Turco that put you first and you church second. That was not a good thing, Fred. Now tell us what you know about Sam's murder."

"I don't know a thing...you know more than I do. All I know is that Sam was found dead...out there. I don't know who would kill him or why. That's it."

"Okay, if that's how you want it. Y'all better be prepared for trouble, that's all I've got to say.

"Let us know when you've caught the killer," Fred said boldly, "it will be a big relief."

Mitchell knew he had been dismissed and he hated it, but there wasn't much he could do about it. He slowly rose, tucked his notebook into his coat pocket, and turned toward the door.

"We'll interview Reverend Kenny before we leave," he said menacingly, "see what he has to say. He might appreciate knowing about your situation with Sam...maybe not."

Cal Dobson saw the two detectives leave Kenny's office and depart down the hall. He managed to hide from their view as he watched. He had flitted about the building ever since he had arrived, staying out of Doris' sight, ducking into this office and then another, talking to anyone who would chat with him, probing, questioning, digging to find out what might be known about Fred here at New World. After awhile, he became satisfied that Fred was operating on his own – his deal with Sam was special and separate from the church. Fred was a simple profiteer taking advantage of his situation in a position of power and authority. What a great story, he thought, what a wonderful article for *The State*. If only he could overhear something really juicy. More slinking around might make that possible. But the chance was now for the confrontation with Fred.

He boldly sprinted into Kenny's office as soon as he saw the detectives disappear around a corner. There was Fred looking out the window, a glazed look on his face, almost catatonic, stripped of the power he once held, stupefied into submission, and choice meat for Cal's questioning grinder. He jumped when Cal spoke.

"They're on to you, I guess. Y'all are in deep pucky if you ask me…"

Fred turned his head without moving his body, a snap reaction in response to the new voice, reacting to the insinuation. He knew right away that he was in trouble with Cal by the way the man swaggered, by the way he sneered, and by the manner in which he slid into the chair Mitchell had vacated and threw his leg over the arm. This was trouble far worse than the police.

"What would it take…," Fred started to pose.

"Lots…oh yeah, lots of money…if that's where you're going with that question. Yeah, lots of money."

"What's lots?"

"Try one hundred thousand…"

"Ridiculous…"

"How about seventy-five?"

"You're dreaming…"

"Fifty?"

Fred was silent.

"Never mind, you crud, there's no price. I keep at it until I know all, then the readers know all…or almost all that I know about you. You're done, Mr. Wallace, your position here at New World is over and you will be lucky to stay out of jail."

"Cal, it isn't like you think…"

"Isn't it? I think it is."

No, it's not…"

Cal waited, pen poised, his notebook in his lap.

"Sam threatened to…to…to tell Reverend Kenny about me…"

"How much did he know…besides what you two worked out?"

"He…we…ah…we were…"

"Yeah, right, I get the picture. You two got involved; Turco used that to control you. Right?"

"Something like that…"

"Good motive for a murder…"

"And put the body here, where it would bring the investigation to New World? I don't think so…that would be stupid. I'm not stupid…"

"Who killed him…a jealous other lover?"

"Perhaps…probably not…more likely someone of his connections from the Middle East…"

What makes you think so?"

He would not pay fast enough. They wanted their money right away. They needed that money…they were not…"

"What?" Cal put his pen to the end of his nose and squinted at Fred.

"They were not normal business types…they were something else."

"Using the money for…"

"Who knows? I don't know…it's just a feeling I had. Something was wrong about it all. I don't know…"

"Well, well, well…you've given me something else to get after. Thanks, Fred. I'll work on this. And I won't say anything to Reverend Kenny…yet. If you think of anything else y'all will call me, right?"

"Yes…I will…I assure you I will. And…thanks."

"Don't mention it, Fred. See ya."

By the time Cal left the building and Kenny finished with the last of the phone interviews with reporters, Katherine Louise had returned with the argumentative recalcitrant Marva Eckels. She could be heard once she entered the building. Katherine Louise tried valiantly to mute her, but that was near impossible. Marva would not be shushed and she wanted to talk to Reverend Kenny. This was war, she exclaimed, this was a battle for the hearts and minds in favor of Christian values. She was not to be deterred nor dissuaded, and not to be detoured from her fight against Planned Parenthood.

"This is a basic Christian issue," she screamed, "This is worth fighting for and I'm going to make the fight. I want my minister's backing…I want to know why my minister is not protesting down there in front of the Planned Parenthood office…I want to know why he hasn't taken a stand against what they are doing. Why, why, why?"

What made Marva Eckels' presence worse wherever she was in conflict was her dominant size. She stood over six feet tall and weighed slightly more than two hundred fifty pounds, quite like a National Football League linebacker. Marva was a linebacker for Christ and the avowed ministry of New World Church, or so she thought. Ready to tackle the sinners. She firmly grasped the idea that abortion was wrong and she riled against others stepping into the role of sexual educator of her children and the children of others, especially without parental consent. Marva knew she was doing the Lord's work and that justified protesting, yelling, confronting, picketing, and demonstrating as her rightly avowed Christian duty to uphold God's laws. She wanted to have affirmation from her minister. She demanded it.

Katherine Louise led Marva into Reverend Kenny's office, had her sit down and try to relax, and got her an iced tea. Marva seemed to ease up a bit, but when Fred and Reverend Kenny came into the room, she tensed, ready for conflict. She was a conflict person.

"Miz Eckels...I wish today hadn't happened for you, I wish you had not ended up in jail...but I am glad Katherine Louise could get you bailed out..."

"We were on the firing line, Reverend, we were seeing to God's work..."

"God's work does not mean getting arrested..."

"Police don't know nuthin'."

"Did you hit the officer in the chest?"

"Well, he..."

"Marva, Marva, Marva...did you hit the officer?"

"Yeah, but he deserved it and I..."

"Wait...wait...let's talk sensibly."

"What?"

"Rationally...calmly...so we can see how we can help."

"Okay, okay, calmly. As a black woman, I know the deck is usually stacked against me," Marva began, "I know that I am discounted, disregarded, and downgraded because of the color of my skin. Look at her, they say, she thinks she knows somethin'. Who is she? Some dumb black bitch...oh, yes, I'm sorry, that's what they say, that's what they call me, I know it...she don't know nothin'...and besides, she's uppity like some country club white woman when she's got no reason. I know the words, Reverend, I know the words. That's part of my story, but the real question is why aren't you helping us on the street?"

Kenny took a sip of the sweet iced tea that had been sitting on his desk. He didn't answer right away, but glanced out the window and slumped forward, arms on his desk, his head hung down. He looked dejected, which he was, and beaten, which he was not. His forlorn look was an affectation for the mood he wanted to project to deal with her. She bought it.

"So much has gone on around here that you aren't aware of, Miz Eckels. Your cause is just and right and we know that. But the issues I have to deal with here at New World are larger than that right now. We have had a near miracle take place here with our fellow Christians from Ohio, a near miracle that will benefit all of us both spiritually and materially. We are fortunate to have them here. And we are unfortunate to have had a dead body dumped on our doorstep...a symbol of the Devil in our midst and we have had to contend with that issue. For me...being a participant in a street demonstration...was not...was not where I believed I needed to be...as righteous as I believed in your cause, as strongly as I supported your efforts in spirit...I felt I needed to be here...in the best position for my flock and for our ministry."

"You're probably right," she said as she slumped in the chair, cold iced tea glass held against her right cheek. "Gotta cool down."

"Your brother is coming to pick you up," Katherine Louise whispered, "he'll take you home. I want you to come see me tomorrow...I know its Saturday, but I want to see how we can help with your protest. It's the right cause. We know the poison of Planned Parenthood; we'll help you all we can. We need to be in the background right now because of the other issues, but we'll support you. Now, go home and get a good night's sleep. Come on, I'll wait with you until Dixon arrives."

She led Marva from the office and Fred and Kenny breathed a sigh of relief. Fred flopped into a sofa off to the side of the office and Kenny fell back in the chair, hands behind his head, eyes riveted on the ceiling.

"If I were a drinking man, now is the time I would want one," Fred admitted. "Powerful lot of pressure on us."

Without saying a word, Kenny pulled open the bottom left hand drawer, reached to the back, and pulled out a shoe box that he unceremoniously placed in front of him. With an index finger he flipped off the lid. There lay an unopened bottle of Jack Daniels. He picked up the bottle, snapped out the blade of his pen knife, cut the plastic label, and unscrewed the cap. He sniffed at the opening.

"Get a couple of glasses from the kitchen," he ordered without looking at Fred.

Fred rose, went to the kitchenette that adjoined the office, and brought back two small glasses. He placed them on the desk in front of Kenny and waited as the Reverend poured. Two fingers, a generous amount for each of them.

"This is for your benefit, Fred, and my sanity."

Kenny clinked his glass against Fred's and took a sip.

"I always liked it neat," Fred said.

"Yes, I do too."

Fred went back to the sofa to relax and Kenny again settled back in his chair.

"Tell me about it, Fred."

Fred took a long drink before he answered. The words were almost contemplative, as if he were talking about another person instead of himself. He wished that were the case.

"Funny how these things happen to people, Reverend…getting involved…with things that should be left alone. But…and a big, important but, is that often they can't resist the temptation. If one comes from abject poverty…rotten, miserable, hard-scrabble dirt-poor poverty, then…then the temptation doesn't seem like temptation to them, it seems more like opportunity. Getting educated and citified and successful somehow doesn't erase what was there for those folks…they are always the wretch they once were only dressed up and talking better than when they were raised. Hard to pinpoint exactly how it happens other than that, but it happens…"

"I'm surprised," Kenny said softly, "that a man like I thought you were would be making excuses like that. Don't insult poor folk by tying lying, cheating, and stealing to being poor…that doesn't fly with me. I expected a straight answer from you…you who set himself up as a solid businessman for the Lord, willing to make less to be in service to God's work…"

"I was…I am…"

"Then why do your own deals with Turco behind my back?"

"What are you talking about?"

"What did the Detectives want? They wanted to know about you dealings with Turco. You were clever, but not too clever for Sol Weinstein…he figured something was going on…he put out some inquiries about you and Sam. Lo and behold, info came back to him. He told me about it right before the Ohioans got here. I didn't have time until now to ask you about it…"

"Listen, Reverend Kenny, I…"

We could have survived that maybe, but what was in the papers today…well, that we can't get past…"

"What are you talking about?"

"Our Mister Cal has dug up some things…some stuff he wrote about in today's *State*. Strange sexual stuff, Fred…the kind of thing we can't have around us. A little misunderstanding about commissions, certain money transactions…those can be explained. Sexual deviancy cannot be a part of New World, Fred, you know that…you have to know that. We can't abide in that. The Lord forgives you for your transgressions and we will forgive you…have Mercy on your soul, my brother, but you must move on…today. We will miss you…we appreciated your fine work, and we will truly miss you. But…I'm sure you understand. Go to Sol's office on Monday, sign the papers, get a check…and get away…as far away as the police will let you. Okay? You can leave your keys on my desk."

Fred sat stunned. He had not finished his Jack and Kenny took the glass from him and motioned to the desk. Fred pulled out his keys, slipped several off the ring, and dropped them on the desk.

"You can have the car for a few days, Fred, but Sol will want that on Monday, also. Make arrangements for a car."

Kenny held out his hand.

"Good luck, Fred, and God speed. Please don't ask us for a reference, however."

Fred looked like a boxer who had been in too many fights and had been knocked down and knocked out too many times. Punch drunk, weary to the point of despair, and hardly able to function, Fred staggered from the office and down the hall. Doris watched him lurch by her office and came to the doorway to see his exit.

"Doris, would you see if you can find Reverend Stone? See if he can come to my office. Thank you." It was a terse phone direction from Reverend Kenny.

Stone sat across from Kenny, steeled for questions about Tom. He didn't know about Marva or Fred, so had little sense that Kenny would not be that concerned about Tom being out of the picture.

"This has been one tough day…we really appreciate y'all pitching in and helping with the response to last Sunday. Been a big help. I did want to ask you about…"

The bottle had been put back in the shoe box and returned to its place in the bottom drawer, the glasses in the kitchenette sink. Stone thought he could smell whiskey, but the overwhelming anticipation for questions about Tom clouded that sense as he geared himself for the inquiry.

"…Sunday…I mean…I assume you're ready…Del's ready…?"

"Absolutely…"

"Good…good. You know…ah, Rev…"

"By now you should be calling me Randy…"

"Randy…sure enough. Randy, we've had some tough stuff to overcome today…things that will come to light in succeeding days and I didn't want you to worry about anything…just conduct your part of the service like last Sunday and we'll all be fine…"

"I…"

"No, I know you don't know what I'm talking about, but it will be out in the open in a few days and we'll have them under control and don't you worry about a thing."

"I won't…I have enough to worry about with Del."

"That's right. Say by the way, where is Tom…I haven't seen anything of him all day."

"Well, I didn't want to bother you with it since you seemed so busy today, but Tom got called back to Ohio…his business…something that couldn't wait, I guess. Anyway, he said it was something he just had to take care of."

That's no problem…not sure we need him here anyway. Do you?"

"No…no, I don't think so."

13.

Seek the Lord while he may be found, call upon Him while He is near. Let the wicked forsake his way, and the unrighteous man his thoughts; Let him return to the Lord, and He will have mercy on him; and to our God, for He will abundantly pardon.

-Isaiah 55:6-7

If the first service with Del had been a wonderful example of Christian ministry and presentation of God's word to the believers, the second Sunday was even more spectacular. The music program was geared specifically for Del and Stone, music that revered God's blessings, called for the acceptance of God's word, and promised the salvation for all God's creatures. This service could well have been the finest Gospel presentation ever devised, the most emotional delivery witnessed by Christians since the time of Christ. It was drama in a way that Hollywood could hardly copy, it was exhilarating in greater measure than a health club workout, and it was spiritually fulfilling beyond any witness of the emotion and offering that could be expected without ultimately dying and transcending to heaven.

Anticipation made it partly so, execution merely fulfilled expectations. Those in attendance were swept into the service with a musical presentation that overwhelmed the audience, captured the emotions of those who witnessed, and created a caldron of emotion for acceptance of God's enlightenment. Reverend Stone made the Word come alive for everyone, he entranced those before him and others watching on television, he brought forth a sacred manifestation of the Holy Spirit in Del's incantations and otherwise unrecognizable language from another world. Del was an image of sacrifice, a human who had ceased being human, a man possessed, a man charged with a message that needed transmission to sinners making their way. He was the voice of God in a strange and wonderful way that touched the hearts of all who saw him try to speak and who heard the translation through Reverend Stone.

Spittle flew from Del's mouth, spraying out across the front row of the congregation, onto Betty's lap, onto suits and dresses, in a way that paralyzed those affected, desensitizing them to its ordinary effects, creating a moment of acceptance that held them and the others in the church and the viewers on TV in absolute containment of belief and mutual excitement for this brush with the truth from God. Reverend Stone took Del's hand and pressed it to his chest and prayed for everyone, for the forgiveness of their sins, for the strength to overcome evil, to withstand the rigors of diseases, and for the understanding of and forgiveness for the hateful acts of others. He prayed thanks for Del the messenger, the conduit of God's word, and the contribution Del had made to all Christians throughout the world.

Del's voice reached a crescendo of what, in any other context, might otherwise be called the ravings of a mad man. Uncontrolled sounds came forth, his body shook vigorously, sweat poured from his face and neck, veins bulged, and the redness of his face made it seem that blood might eject right through his skin at any moment. He shook until his muscles reached near rigidity, one massive muscular Charlie-horse of constriction, as if he were having an epileptic fit, until he was so rigid he stopped moving. It was then that he stopped making any sound. Saliva dripped from his lips, mucous dangled from his nose, his eyes watered heavily, and his hands gripped the edge of his sport coat like he was holding on for dear life. Maybe he was. His eyes did not blink for several minutes.

It was a stunning performance. The spellbound congregation sat as if petrified when Stone finished, partly in awe of what they had seen in relation to their own connection with God and partly because there was a mass awareness that Del might disintegrate at any moment; not actually of course, but figuratively, as one who has a mental breakdown. Stone privately thought that Del might, in fact, die right there beside him.

"He has been God's Great Gift to each of us," Stone rejoiced as he pointed to Del. "The promise of Salvation through Jesus Christ our Lord came from God...through this man to each of us directly. We thank You, oh our God, for this wonderful Blessing. He is your gift so that our lives might be enriched, our faith bolstered, and that we may have reassurance of your promise of Mercy for us all."

In the control booth, Larry marveled at how well his production was proceeding, fascinated with Stone's ability to utilize this opportunity to take preaching to a new level, beyond anything he had seen before. Keri stood next to him, their bodies touching, with her hip tightly against his thigh.

"Man's got a gift," Larry whispered, "a real gift. Plays his cards right he'll be the next big star of Christian broadcasting. Only a matter of time...and if wants to, of course."

Keri nodded. She did not want to think about Stone. All she could think about was being in bed with Larry. My, how things had changed.

"Too bad about that Del...I think somethin's wrong with him. He's almost crazed...works on command just like a trained dog...all the sounds come out on cue nice as you please. See him around here and he's quiet as a lamb...course you can't understand him and he doesn't seem like much as a person. But you put him up there with Reverend Stone and he cuts loose. Stone's like his trainer...a dog trainer, getting his animal to go through his paces. It happens all in the way he wants it to. Scary...scary to think of what might happen to Del."

Keri looked at him questioningly.

"Yeah, you don't know...the way he goes at it, practically foaming at the mouth, look at him...his head might explode."

Near the back of the church Marcia and Jess sat watching Reverend Stone and Del with complete attention. Earlier on, before the service began, Marcia had scanned the congregation for Tom, but could not locate him. Her rubber-necking before the service allowed her to catch sight of the control booth and she assumed he would be in there overlooking his investment. She casually rose, moved to the back wall and across to the open door of the booth. She watched as a young man and woman exchanged tender kisses, little pecks at each other like birds grabbing at seed, but no Tom. Where would he be? He's here someplace, she figured, so eventually she knew she would spot him. She slipped back to her seat with Jess just as the choir began its first offering.

"He's not there," she hissed to Jess, "but he's got to be around."

"He split, I imagine."

"You're nuts…"

"Naw, he's outta here. You ain't gonna get him…"

"No way…I've got his check. If he were leaving he'd try to con it out of me before he left…"

Jess looked at her with a silly grin then turned back to look at the choir.

"Choir's good," he said, and he chuckled, mostly under his breath.

"The check…"

"Yeah, right…the check. Probably's no good. Like I told ya. You said you were to get a call about the money and ya didn't. You can find out tomorrow."

"We'll see…and we won't wait until tomorrow."

Reverend Kenny was both appreciative of and a bit envious about what he had just witnessed. Stone was a preacher of some magnitude whether he knew it or not. The power and glory of his message still hung over the congregation even as the last note of the choir faded away. The aftermath is what mattered, he figured, the results, the feedback, and the strengthening of New World's ties with Christian Gospel Broadcasting. No matter if he got the credit right now because he would make sure he received the credit eventually. He smiled at Katherine Louise as the hymn ended; a knowing smile of what this meant for them.

"There were several serious looking strangers in the congregation," she said through her smile, barely moving her lips.

"Serious like the law?"

"Yes…it's an instinct you never lose. Besides they dress and act like the law…"

"Government?"

"Probably. Like the FBI, maybe…"

"Sam Turco?"

"Probably."

"That's not good," Kenny sighed.

"Oh my…look." Katherine Louise nodded toward Stone.

A surge of joyous faces, some with tears streaming down, edged forward to the stage wanting to get near, to speak to Reverend Stone and Del, to say God Bless and Hallelujah and Amen up close and personal. Stone, with presence of mind, raised his hands as if in Benediction, the Bible still grasped in his left hand, and spoke to the closely packed group.

"Heavenly Father, bless these wonderful folks who have so graciously received Your message. Their response is a tribute to Your greatness and the tender and tragic sacrifice Your son Jesus Christ made for each and every one of us. Let us go in peace, the Grace of Your understanding our guiding light. Amen."

All said Amen and moved as one to the doors.

It was a stroke of genius in soothing the mass of people and made for an easy transition to get them to move on out of the church. The group flowed outside almost as one entity and did not disperse, but rather followed the golf carts up to the house. Marcia and Jess joined the entourage.

They stood at the rear of the crowd that had gathered around the front porch of the large parsonage. She looked around carefully at the beautiful landscaping, sniffed the scent of blooming flowers, and marveled at how gorgeous the setting was for this minister's home. The throng that pressed for a closer view of Reverend Kenny buzzed with excitement as he worked his way down the steps, into the mass of people, shaking every hand, giving personal word to each of those who wanted his attention. At his side was Reverend Stone, also giving special attention to each one who desired his notice. One by one, those who fancied something more than just the service were satisfied and moved off, lingering a bit then moving on to their own Sunday. One by one, they came until everyone had been attended to except Marcia and Jess. Reverend Kenny pressed Marcia's hand and placed his left in the hand Jess offered.

"I'd like to speak to you privately, Reverend Kenny…inside. And you, too, Reverend Stone. About Tom Fletcher. I know about him. I want to talk to you about him. I have some information you might want to hear."

Both men were exhausted from the service. In fact, Stone was so tired he could not even flinch when she spoke Tom's name. Nor could Kenny. They stood there looking at her trying to comprehend what she might want, adjusting their thought processes from receiving adulation to getting a gut check. Kenny sensed immediately that she meant nothing but trouble, Stone was right behind in his analysis of the situation. What now, Kenny wondered? How could things get worse with distractions from the outside? And such a fabulous service, the phones would be ringing for sure.

"May I...may we come in?" Marcia nagged, "I've got lots to say."

"Of course...yes, come right in. Have some tea, maybe some brunch..."

Carlton appeared as if by magic and held open the door for all of them to enter.

"Carlton, yes...I assume there is brunch ready..."

"Yes, sir."

"Let's get our guests settled in the dining room and see they are well fed. All right?"

"Of course, sir."

"Where is Katherine Louise?" Kenny asked quietly so only Carlton could hear.

"In the kitchen," Carlton whispered.

"Take our guests to the dining room, Carlton, I'll be right with you."

With that direction he ducked into the kitchen.

"We have another problem," he hissed at Katherine Louise who was tasting some morsel Jessie had given her.

"What?"

"A woman is here...upset...about Tom Fletcher. Who's gone, by the way...back to his business in Ohio...some kind of emergency, Stone said. I wonder...looks suspicious. Do you think she knows something...about Tom?"

"Hardly. Come on, let's deal with this gal and see what she wants. Probably money...which we are not about to give her, but let's see what she has to say. It'll be all right darlin', we shall overcome this bump in the road like everything else. Trust me."

Katherine Louise, the tired, but most gracious hostess swept into the dining room with a flourish, exuding Southern charm, taking command of the situation in her distinct way.

"My name is Katherine Louise Kenny, the Reverend's wife. We'd be pleased if you would have brunch with us. Please be seated, won't you? The Reverend didn't catch your names…"

"Marcia Dowling…this is my business associate Jess Stokes. We're here to collect an unpaid debt. We thought you might be able to help us…especially you Reverend Stone, and by the way, you were magnificent today, truly fabulous. We were privileged to see you up close. We saw you on TV last week…that's what got us over here…we were in Atlanta…at a convention. Came over to find Tom…"

"How can we help you? Katherine Louise interrupted as she turned to Carlton. "You may serve now…I'm sure our guests are hungry."

She turned to face Marcia, waiting for an answer.

"Where's Tom? That's how you can help me…tell me where he is. I know he's gone. He was here Friday. I talked to him…I had lunch with him. He gave me a check as a payment for what he owes me…"

"Owes you?" Katherine Louise wasn't sure she really wanted an answer, but she asked the question reflexively.

"He conned me out of a hundred thousand dollars. I want it back. That's why I want to know where he is.

"Well, we understand Mr. Fletcher went back to Ohio. The call of business and, of course, he wasn't needed here so it made perfect sense for him to attend to what he had to take care of, darlin', its that simple."

Katherine Louise sat down as she spoke, followed by Kenny and Stone, dutifully polite.

"He was running away," Marcia fumed.

"Where are Betty and Del, darlin'?" she said to Kenny, "I do hope they can join us. That Del is a miracle, I think. Don't you, Marcia? A wonder, an absolute wonder at best."

"Reverend Stone…?" Marcia glared at him, ignoring Katherine Louise. "Tell me; is there a First Meridian Bank in Swanton, Ohio?"

He looked at her without responding. He was having trouble following the confrontation, lost in his thoughts and feelings in the aftermath of the service. He was concerned about Del, concerned if there could possibly be another performance like today. And what could he say about Tom? He was gone.

"Reverend Stone is completely done in what with all he did in the Lord's service this morning…" Katherine Louise was now feeling protective to a higher degree. She could sense the intensity of Marcia's questioning of Stone.

"He knows," Marcia sneered, "he knows…"

"None of us know anything, Marcia, other than Tom has gone back to Ohio."

"Not that I know of," Stone said quietly.

Carlton came into the dining room with the first platter of food. He placed the tray on a serving buffet by the far wall and retreated to the kitchen for more.

I want my money." Marcia was almost yelling. "There is no bank, my check from Tom is no good, and I want my money. I want my money from him or from you. Someone is going to pay me what I'm owed or I go and spill the beans to the newspapers and TV and anyone else who will listen. You won't like it."

"Bring your plates," Katherine Louise said as she rose with her plate and went to the buffet, "let's have some of Jessie's outstanding fixin's."

Marcia knew what she was up against in Katherine Louise. She sniffed slightly, collected herself, then rose, and moved to the buffet with her plate. She would have their brunch. She would press the issue in a calmer way.

"You folks know that right is right," Marcia said as she filled her plate.

"We do," Katherine Louise concurred, still chewing a bit on a piece of bacon, "but what does that mean?"

The mound of food on Jess' plate caught everyone's attention, but, of course, no one said anything. He seemed to be totally removed from the dialog that was taking place, fully intent on filling his belly.

"It means y'all have some responsibility in this…"

"In what…?"

"In my getting my money back. Y'all became partners with Tom Fletcher when you got these folks here. There had to be a money deal for it to take place. Tom doesn't work any other way, I know that for sure. That means there was a payout to this minister's church, probably negotiated by Tom. Money, money, money…that's what it's all about. I want my money. These folks got to be making out quite nicely. You are too. I want my money. You folks can pay it."

Katherine Louise rose, walked around the table, snatched the plates from in front of Marcia and Jess, and handed them to Carlton who was by the buffet waiting to be of service

"Y'all are done eating, darlin's, we surely aren't going to have that kind of talk at our Sunday brunch. Good day. That means y'all can leave right now."

Marcia stared at her, stunned, some egg still clinging to the corner of her mouth.

"I don't know what kind of ideas you got in your head about this, but there is no big money deal like you think. This is the work of the Lord and Reverend Stone and Reverend Kenny have joined together to bring the Word of God to as many people as possible without any thought of money. That has been our way. We have lived that way for a long time…"

"This mansion ain't no shack," Marcia screamed.

"Move on, sister, your hundred thousand is not to be found here. This is the Work of the Lord taking place at New World. Move on or we get the police to move you on. Interesting, isn't it? I believe they describe your attempted touch on us as extortion. Better you take your complaint off to Mr. Tom, wherever he is."

Jess had risen when his plate had been summarily yanked from in front of him and now Marcia rose. They walked away without saying another word, out the front door, and to the big Mercedes parked in the lot across from the house. Marcia drove, taking a long look at the mansion as she pulled away, the view of Katherine Louise on the porch making sure they were going, the total opulence of the place and the setting, knowing full well Tom had eluded her grasp. She felt sick to her stomach.

"Y'all will hear from my lawyer," Marcia yelled from the car.

Katherine Louise simply waved, spun around, and went back inside.

As the last part of the confrontation had taken place in the dining room, Betty and Del stood listening in the back stairway. Instead of going into the dining room, Betty steered Del into the kitchen where Jessie helped Betty get Del seated at a small table in the corner. This was the table Jessie and Carlton used when they ate after the dining room service had been completed. Jessie could see Del was struggling and she patted his shoulder and talked soothingly to him in the nicest way. She brought each of them a plate of food and they quietly ate their brunch undisturbed and undistracted by the tension taking place in the next room. Sounds of the conflict filtered through to them, but were easily ignored.

"This is very good," Betty said politely, but truly meant what she said.

Jessie knew; Jessie could tell the woman's sincerity and appreciated the compliment. She felt badly about the man. His hand shook slightly as he fed himself, a palsy she assumed he suffered from the stress of the service she had watched on TV. She was taken with the fact that this was indeed the same man, had been living in the house for days, and could bring the Word of God to us with such power. The Reverend made it happen, of course, but still the power of it all came from this man even if it didn't make any sense. Jessie was very impressed that he was sitting in her kitchen. She knew God had to be close by, near enough to bless her, too.

When they finished eating, Betty ushered Del out the back door with the intention of taking a walk, but Del was too weak. A few yards from the back door, he shook his head and stopped walking. He pointed to the gazebo where there were two benches and he began staggering that direction. Betty held his arm trying to make sure he did not fall, trying to keep pace with him as he forced himself to move quickly, a rush of effort so he could sit down and make less effort to be upright. He lunged onto one of the benches in near collapse, breathing with difficulty, not making a sound other than the hard gasps he took. She was frightened, hardly knowing what to do for him, and very worried. For the last several days he had been sleeping more and more which she believed was not a very good sign.

She sat next to him and he slumped against her almost as if it were too difficult to sit up on his own. His head sagged to her shoulder. Here was this once proud, strong farmer, heartier than most, now with a rag-doll posture, barely able to walk or sit by himself. She patted his cheek and ran her fingers through his thinning hair. She wanted to soothe him in some way, she just did not know how. She kissed his forehead and realized in doing so that she wanted to cry. She held back the tears, because this was no time for her suffering, this was a time Del needed her strength.

Betty watched Marcia and Jess leave in their car without knowing who they were or caring much, only grateful they were gone and hopeful the stress and tension they brought had gone with them. She had heard the woman yelling in front of the house before seeing the car race away. Finally, there was peace and quiet; Del could go back inside and lie down.

"Feeling better?" She did not expect an answer, but part of the mothering instinct almost required that question. "Folks are gone that seemed to be causing the trouble. You can go inside if you like."

Del did not move. He gave no sound of any kind.

"Maybe in a little bit," she continued. "Fresh air is good…just relax, we'll go inside in a little bit…just relax."

She took hold of Del's shoulder to keep him against her and gently began to rock with a slow side-to-side motion, all the while repeating her request to relax. He did not move, accepting her rhythmic motion and sing-song comforting as a tired child might do. His eyes showed no emotion, a great emptiness in them, as though they did not see or as if there were no comprehension of what was being seen. Either way, Del seemed to be shut down from processing the world around him.

When Marcia and Jess left, Katherine Louise turned her attention to Stone. She did not sit down after coming back into the dining room from the porch, but rather stood by her chair, near the half-eaten plate of food before her, poised, expectant, and frustrated. She wanted to yell at Stone because she believed as Marcia believed that he knew the truth about Tom. Merely speculation, it could only be an accusation. She did not want that. She finally sat down as Stone continued with his brunch, fully aware of her stance across from him.

"Could you tell us what you know?" she said quietly, "it helps when we have all the angles covered. We don't want this to hurt us and that woman made a threat. I'm not sure she's through with us yet."

"Tom told me that he needed to go back to Ohio to take care of some things he had not anticipated. His business was in the hands of a young woman who, although fully capable, was not experienced enough to deal with whatever it was. I assume it was a complex real estate or insurance matter. Tom did both...mainly insurance, but at times, both. That's all I can say. His leaving surprised me a bit because he is so vital to our cause and wanted to be involved with our mission here, but on the other hand, I am not surprised that he responded to his feelings of responsibility to his own livelihood. Made sense to me. I never saw that woman before, never heard about her, and I know nothing about her. If Tom had a past with her...well, that was something he did not share with me...or anyone else I know of. We can call his office tomorrow if you like...see what the story is."

Mystified, Katherine Louise began eating again, ignoring the fact her food was cold, taking tiny little bites and chewing them rigorously. Stone was so convincing, yet her instinct told her that he knew, he had to be aware of the real reason for Tom's departure.

"I guess it doesn't matter much if she goes away and looks for Tom on her own. Let's hope so. She could make a mess for us. As if we needed another one."

"Excuse me," Stone said as he dabbed a napkin to his lips and pushed back from the table, "I want to find Betty and Del...got to see how he is doing."

"Certainly," Kenny said.

"You were awfully quiet through this whole thing," she said after Stone left the dining room. There was a tinge of anger in her voice.

"You did fine...there was no need for me to get into it...I could not have added a thing...except maybe some return anger at...at..."

"Marcia…"

"Yes…and the thug she brought along with her. You took care of it quite nicely and I appreciate that. I kept my mind in the clouds with our Lord as I think Reverend Stone did. He may know, in truth, it doesn't matter. He is part of our Blessing and for that I am grateful. That is my bottom line."

"Amen," she said without looking up and took the last bite on her plate, cold as it was.

Stone went into the kitchen seeking Carlton who he was sure would know where Betty and Del were. Carlton directed him to the gazebo.

"Betty…Del. Did you get something to eat?"

"Yes," Betty said, nodding, still continuing her rocking with Del.

"How's he doing?"

She shrugged slightly and looked down at Del, then put her cheek against his head.

"He's having a hard time getting around…thought we would rest here for awhile…get him up to bed for a good nap. I think he needs the rest. This morning was terribly strenuous for him, I think…maybe too much. He's not made a sound even to me since the service. Perhaps you can communicate with him. He seems so weak."

"Del, how are you doing?" Stone looked straight on into Del's face.

The eyes did not respond; glazed over as if the sign of a deep trance. The body motionless save movement from Betty's rocking; the body loose like a boxer knocked unconscious. Del did not look well and it worried him.

"Betty, I think he's really tired…let me help you get him upstairs so he can lie down, get proper rest. That will do him the most good, I think."

"Thank you, Reverend."

Together, they got Del to his feet and between them guided him to the bedroom on the second floor. It was a difficult chore, with much staggering, weaving, and near collapse several times. But they got him to the bed. He was a lump, like a mound of flesh nearly unable to direct his own movements. Betty eased him back on a pillow and Stone picked up his feet and got them situated.

Stone moved to the hall and motioned Betty to follow.

"Can we talk?"

"Yes, of course."

"Let's go downstairs."

"All right."

Stone moved away, but Betty went back to Del and covered him with a light blanket. He was sound asleep.

"I think he's just real tired," she said hopefully as she caught up with Stone on the stairs.

He did not answer.

Reverend Stone suspected the worst about Del. All along he wondered what would happen with him. Would he begin to get better or would his condition deteriorate. In either case, there would eventually be no speaking in tongues, no more mesmerizing services like this morning. He fought with his feelings about Del, knowing his own sense of responsibility for the man's health had been clouded by their success with God's message. The message was the most important factor for Stone, an exalted time in his ministry. He had ignored Del's struggle, the limitations the man exhibited, because when the time came for his contact with Stone, he delivered. The message came as nonsense sounds that brought some kind of word order in Stone's brain. Stone heard the nonsense and there were words to be formed, ideas to be given, and a full tableau of God's magnificence to come alive. He had a sense of his own charisma and the intensity that Del helped bring to that charisma.

On the one hand, he knew in his heart the importance of the Lord's work, on the other, he had chosen to deny the seriousness of Del's condition. Del might now be failing, he did not know, but he had the feeling that in some measure he had betrayed Del for his own benefit. He would have to live with that, he decided, however they probably could not continue with the mission here at New World. He had little grasp of what to say to Betty. He wished that Tom were here.

"Betty," he said, taking here arm, helping her down the staircase, "let's get some iced tea."

They sat down in the dining room which sparkled with light that bounced in from the patio and gave their request to Carlton. In a few moments, he was back with their drinks. The house was quiet for the most part although there was the background sound of Jessie singing some hymn in the kitchen. Without being asked, Carlton brought a plate with several pieces of coffee roll and placed that between them. This was a delicate and ponderous time for these two white folks, he realized, and disappeared into the kitchen without saying another word.

"I'm very worried about Del," she said after sipping from her tea.

"I am too."

"What do we do?"

The sadness in her voice dug at him, reinforced the anguish that he carried for the way he had ignored Del's condition. He was not sure what to answer.

"Maybe we should think about going back to Ohio, not trying to go on with…"

"Oh, no…"

"Betty…"

"We've made a commitment to do our work for the Lord…we'll have to stay. We said we would be here three Sundays…we have one more…"

"I know, I know, but…but…I don't think Del can make it. In fact, I think we should leave for home as soon as possible…tomorrow…"

"No…God is speaking to us through Del…this is important work…for you…for all of us…His work must be done…"

"Betty…Betty…I think Del is…not well…I think we have to get him back to Ohio…the sooner the better."

Let's see how he is tomorrow," she said, "then we can make a better decision."

"Call Dorothy, will you? See what she says."

"I will…tonight…and Don."

The thought of Don Howe getting back into things made Stone shudder and he hoped Betty did not see his reaction. That would be something if he came down here, Stone thought. Why couldn't Tom be here? He missed the comfort Tom gave him, his reassurance that everything would work out. Little did Stone know that Tom's reassurance of everything working out meant working out for Tom. It had always been that way.

14.

Do not be overly wicked, nor be foolish; why should you die before your time?

-Ecclesiastes 7:17

On Monday morning the long spell of stunning sunlit days was shattered with a light gray dawn. It was a gloomy sky that spawned the first showers, a precursor for the kind of nasty day it would be, a sorrowful reflection of the distressing mood gripping New World. The skies darkened as the morning progressed and by nine o'clock there was a steady, persistent downpour that saturated the ground, that ran away in ugly little rivers, and puddled unmercifully in the parking lot in front of the administration building. It was the kind of morning that made going to work hateful; battling traffic that was snail-paced and snarled from poor visibility and safety concerns, and the drenching plunge out of a car or bus into the workplace. It was a morning when riding on the golf carts at New World required umbrellas that jostled for position in order to cover the holders. Yet those umbrellas provided the brightest colors of the scenery. The relentless rain would go on all day giving a backdrop of dreariness to the already disheartened and disillusioned Reverend Stone and a fretful and discouraged Reverend Kenny. Both men tried to stay upbeat, which was their nature, but Mother Nature was against them.

The patter of rain that sprinkled against the parsonage had been reason enough to keep Reverend Stone from rising. He lay awake, tossing and turning, resisting the coming day, tense with the specter of growing doubt about Del's condition, caught in his own cold sweat of guilt. At this point, it was little consolation that yesterday's service had been a smashing success, that the response would be a tidal wave of kudos and donations. Perhaps there would be less pressure from the religious writers, but the pressure would certainly come from other areas. No doubt Betty had made her calls, no doubt that response would be negative, and no doubt this would be his main issue of the day. He would have to contend with and smooth out the situation in a fashion he could be comfortable with and accept.

Even without Del's children getting back into the picture, Stone would have had difficulty staying on even keel just dealing with Del. Suddenly, he saw Del as a stricken man, injured, struggling, fighting for some kind of physical normalcy that any stroke victim faces. He recognized that, now, he had a better sense of son Don's anger and frustration, and he connected emotionally with that fear and near rage. It was over: the services, the translation, and the use of Del as an instrument of God.

Looking back, he tried to protect himself, absolve himself from the self-imposed indictment of overstepping his ministerial duty. He knew that he truly believed that Del had been speaking in tongues. Of course, it was a logical assumption on his part, he had studied the phenomenon, he was attuned to the Bible notations of tongues, and he could reasonably conclude that Del was a prime example of that offering. It was God-based, it was spiritually centered, and it was important to bring to his flock. The extension of that initial appraisal was another matter, one he could not assess at this point. He pulled the bed sheet up to his chin and wished that he could wait out the rain. He knew he could not.

Reverend Kenny had learned long ago that you played with the hand you are dealt. Katherine Louise had taught him that and he well understood the significance. Wishing does not make it so, but that maxim deters few who want things to be different. He wanted things to be different. Fred a cheat and perhaps sexual deviant; police investigation for Sam's murder; possibility of government investigations, demand for settlement of someone else's debt; and worst of all, the likely end to a good thing with that man Howe's worsening condition. These were the overriding concerns for Kenny as he sat slumped in a chair in the master bedroom. He wore a blue warm up suit with the Nike logo emblazoned on the jacket. His bare feet were propped up on a leather hassock. He had not turned on a light or opened the curtains and the dingy morning cast weird shadows and ominous overtones to his already downcast disposition. He waited for Katherine Louise to awaken and he began to get impatient with that prospect.

Finally, she rolled over and sat up in bed.

"What's wrong," she asked as she tried to focus on his presence.

"Probably everything," he said, "maybe nothing. But the world has closed in what with this rain and I can't quite get revved up for the day. I think staying positive is all we can do. Despite the negatives, the rewards for yesterday have got to be tremendous."

She rolled out of bed and came and sat in his lap. She kissed his cheek and rubbed her hand on his chest. She combed his hair with her fingers. It was the tenderness he needed to face the day. She knew it and she could deliver.

"We did not kill anyone, cheat anyone, or cause the breakdown of anyone. We are blameless, we are innocent, we are well-meaning, and we are God's disciples. We will prevail, we will have greater awareness with this country's fundamental Christians as a result, and your contract with CGB will be extended. You will be their prime service from now on. Thank God for our blessings."

Betty wondered what God's blessings for her might be. A husband struck down in the prime of life, diminished before her eyes as he worked for the Glory of God. How could this be God's will? All of the questions about God's lack of benevolence came to her. What kind of test was this, what kind of sacrifice was required of her? Must she relinquish her husband in the name of God, or was that merely an idea that was not real? She had figured Del was needed, that he was called to do God's work with Divine intervention in his life, and that his fulfillment of that intervention meant something Sacred. She was not so sure and she hated her feelings of doubt.

The drab sky that she stared at did not help matters, the rattling sound of rain pelting everything compounded her feelings of misgiving, and she found it difficult to begin her day with the positive attitude she wanted to carry. She looked at Del sleeping so soundly, so quietly, he might well have died. There was almost no rise and fall of his chest that indicated breathing, no sound whatsoever, a totally inert being, and it was certain he was a lost cause for future services with Reverend Stone.

She harbored a secret about Del that she had revealed to no one. Since he had been afflicted by the lightening strike, he had not spoken to her in any coherent way. He merely produced sounds that were reinforced with gestures, vulgar sounds, sounds that made no sense. But after a few days, once they were home from the hospital, he had begun writing little notes. Not notes in some grand sense one might consider, but rather a few words, scribbled with difficulty, yet none-the-less able to convey meaning, to form miniscule communication between the two of them. This formed a continuation of their life connection, a very private bond they did not share with others. That was gone. Not only was he completely silent, he did not seem to even understand what a pen was when she handed it to him. She was cut off from him in a way that distressed her and let her know just how awful their situation was together.

His final note, day before last was: not rite – LUV U.

So she had been worried going into the Sunday service. Del was feeling something wrong, something he obviously could not explain, but in any case was bothering him more than usual. As she had watched him become more and more excited during the service, watched his body become rigid, his face inflamed, his voice rising to a demented pitch, she felt he might die right before her eyes. That he did not was her miracle from God, her blessing where she feared there would be no blessings. And now she suspected she was left with a shell of a man. His heart and soul, and finally his mind had been removed. His breathing was slow and shallow much like a contented baby or like the very sick or the terminally ill. He was a shell of a man with his character, his philosophy, his humor, generosity, caring, his innate humanity stripped away, discarded in some fashion, leaving this hulk that would have a difficult time to go on living.

Fred Wallace sat in his underwear watching the rain splatter across the well-appointed patio of his luxury condo. How wonderful it was to have this kind of day, swathed in gloominess, bathed by the hand of God. How beautiful it was and so appropriate, he figured. He was almost mesmerized by the sound, by the vision of wetness that overcame the plants and patio furniture, and strangely immune to the sight of his cat that was squeezing itself against the underpinnings of the grill as it unsuccessfully tried to stay dry. He ignored its cries to be rescued, to be saved from the deluge coming down. Instead, he turned his attention to his TV.

He punched up the sound with the remote as he watched the beginning of yesterday's New World service. He had recorded the service as he had initially watched it and now was watching it for the third time. He was fascinated by how remarkable it was in its power presenting the Christian message, as a television presentation, and in grabbing the attention of the viewer. It was unremarkable to him in its success because he had expected it to be so. He was watching for yet another time to catch the moments when the cameras focused on the crowd because he thought he saw in attendance the same men that Katherine Louise had seen. From their dark suits and their conspicuous conformity he had the sure-fire notion that these men were Federal agents of some kind.

Yes, there they were, three of them, in the middle, trying to be unobtrusive, but being so obvious to anyone experienced with law enforcement. Anyone who has had to smell the law, anyone who has had to look over his shoulder to make sure he is in the clear. Fred thought that the assignment at New World had put him in the clear, but when Sam turned up to do business that comfort slipped away. Those men wanted him, of that he was sure.

He pulled at the elastic of his boxer shorts as he watched the video, nervously appreciating the magnificent worship setting and well-honed production that he had created. Kenny could never have done it on his own without me, he said to himself, even with Katherine Louise pushing. No, this was his, it was primarily his, and he felt good about that, at least. He folded the note he had just written and tucked it into an envelope. He placed the envelope on the coffee table.

Fred clicked off the TV and turned on the CD player with something from Haydn already cued. He turned up the sound. As the music played, he went to his master bedroom suite, showered, shaved, and began to select what he would wear. He chose a gray, lightweight wool double-breasted suit, white shirt with narrow blue stripes, matching solid blue tie, blue knee-high socks, and black tassel loafers. He carefully dressed, obsessively tying and retying his tie until it conformed to the knot size and length to his belt that he wanted. He slipped his elongated folder-type wallet into the left inside breast pocket of his suit coat, slid his key chain into his right pants pocket, and took one last look at himself in the mirror. He was quite satisfied with his appearance.

He stood for a few moments listening to the Haydn piece before ejecting the disc and placing it in its jewel case. He carried it with him as he left the condo, carefully locking the door, and moving on to the parking garage. When he got in his car he slipped the disc out of its case and pushed it into the dash slot. He fired up the 760 BMW, pulled out of the garage into the discouraging rain, and headed north. The music was soothing, something to help him overcome the depressive aspects of the weather, help him maintain peace of mind.

Driving to the Bluff Road interchange at I-77, he turned abruptly onto the southbound exit ramp, dodged several cars, an SUV, and a pickup truck that were blinking their lights and honking at him for going the wrong way, then he accelerated northward on the southbound side of the freeway. In less than a mile he targeted a semi rig running southbound at a little over sixty miles an hour and drove straight into the truck just as the BMW's speedometer needle ticked the seventy mark.

The resulting accident was tragic because of the consequences to others beside Fred. He wanted to die and took deliberate action to make it happen. On the other hand, the driver of the semi, fifty-six year old Andy Moore of Youngstown, Ohio, was an innocent participant in Fred's suicide and was critically injured. Andy died the next day. There were three other cars that became tangled in the exploding wreckage that flew in all directions with bomb-like intensity sending five more to the hospital. They all survived although the lives of two were physically shattered forever.

A cell phone call brought the State Police to the accident first and they, in turn, called in the ambulances and backup help. The Trooper who tried to direct traffic, assess the situation, and still comfort some of the injured felt the harassment of circumstance. This would be labeled an accident, he figured, but it was not an accident, of that he was sure. As he looked at the mangled mess of car and truck fused together he wondered what kind of person it might have been who caused this to happen. Probably some demented crazy who could no longer cope, perhaps someone out of touch with reality, or maybe a drugged-out loser gone wild. Traffic backed up for miles behind the accident as the late going-to-work crowd got caught by the stoppage. It was a terrible situation made worse by the relentless rain that played mischief with the morning; rain that flooded low spots, ran pell-mell in the gutters, and danced on the carnage. The Trooper could feel his uniform become soggy and wondered why the hell he had not pulled on his rain jacket before he got out of the patrol car.

Breakfast had been a painful meeting of the household, one where Del had not participated, where the pall of the weather had quieted Jessie, made Carlton grim, and had limited conversation to few words and many gestures in the place of words. A facial tic here, a nod there, a grimace, a half-hearted smile, a frown, a tight-lipped grunt; these were some of the modes for communication that morning. They all worked surprisingly well because each of the communicators felt lousy and knew the others also were struggling with the oppressive atmosphere of the morning.

Betty had finally broken the spell. She had the greatest burden to bear, but perhaps had the greatest resilience for life and the strength to overcome some rain. As a farm wife, weather was omnipresent in the conditions of her life both as benefactor and enemy. After all, a thunder storm was how Del got into the mess he was now suffering.

"We've had such wonderful weather, a little rain shouldn't spoil our day. It's not what we want, but we don't always get what we want do we?"

"True, so true," Kenny mumbled, "very wise words, indeed, Betty, very wise."

Her question had meaning beyond the weather and the others knew it, including Carlton who was standing by waiting to be of service. However, appreciation for its irony had seemed to escape them, but had not gotten by him. He wanted to smile at the question, but was impassive. Wonder how these two men of God factor that, he thought?

Each of them carried a load of anxiety they did not want, each of them suffered from the oppression of facing unknown circumstances, and each of them would have done better without the awful dreariness that pervaded the room. Maybe Katherine Louise was least effected. She could be a bit more dispassionate about what might be faced, although she had no idea that Del might not be in any future equation. She assumed everything would blow over and they would go on as before. For her, there was no reason not to think that way.

This breakfast was perfunctory and quickly finished. There was no lingering over coffee and no second helping of Jessie's cinnamon buns. Kenny and Katherine Louise excused themselves first and headed for their offices.

"Got to face the rain," Kenny said as he slipped on a light raincoat.

Katherine Louise pulled a nylon poncho over her head and followed Kenny out the door. Their golf cart had a vinyl roof, but they still would suffer the slanted strokes of rain.

"Reverend Stone…," Betty started, caught herself when she noticed Carlton nearby and stopped.

Carlton sensed that she was not comfortable with him close as she spoke to Stone and he exited to the kitchen. Betty hesitated until he disappeared.

"I have to talk to you…"

"Yes, Betty…"

"Del is silent…he is really silent. He is done. There are no notes and he is mute. I've called Dorothy and Don. He's coming to get his dad. I'm sorry Reverend Stone, but Del has to go home…he has to have medical help…something. He can't go on. I'm not sure he can get out of bed. I'm so sorry, so sorry…"

"Notes? What notes?"

"I'm sorry…I should have told you. Del has been writing me little notes…since we got back home from the hospital. Private notes about how he was doing and how he felt. Nothing complex…very simple…just to stay connected to me. Nothing about what was going on around him. Except one…"

Stone cocked his head toward her waiting for the revelation.

"He said you were doing the right thing with him. That's how I knew to let you go on with him. It was all right with him. I knew it from Del. I'm sorry it's come out this way, but it…it was so private…those notes were all I had…"

"Please, Betty it's all right. We have to take care of Del. It is God's will. Del has fulfilled his mission, he has been an instrument of God, and now we move on. God understands these things better than do we…his plan…the plan for Del has obviously been completed. We must respect that and understand that God's will be done. What is important now is that we get Del back to Ohio, looked after by doctors, and a remedy found for what ails him. It will all work out, I'm sure. Don't you worry."

Stone worried. He knew that whatever was wrong with Del was serious. He was glad, relieved actually, that the mission with Del was over, that there would be no more services with him. The whole thing had been stressful, more stressful than he had even realized, and the relief he felt this morning made him actually feel better than he had in weeks. The challenge of interpreting Del's offerings of tongues had taken its toll on him. He had not even sensed that fact until now or perhaps he had denied that image of himself.

"Betty, I'm going up to the offices…keep Del quiet…let him rest. We'll get him back to Ohio as soon as possible."

When Stone got to the administration building the turmoil there was near pandemonium. FBI agents seemed to be everywhere and Detectives Mitchell and Ross were waiting impatiently to get with Kenny and Katherine Louise. He went right to the office of Rebecca Howland. When he walked in she and Doris Miller stopped talking, turned statue-like with his presence, their coffee cups held in rigid attention, lips ready to form words, in suspension, wondering what bad news he could be adding and not wanting to share the bad news they already knew. The good news had been relegated to afterthoughts, discarded in a sense to the panic mode that seemed to prevail.

Stone realized immediately the nature of their stricken poses and expressions. He was intent on putting calm in the place of terror.

"Relax," he soothed as he placed both hands in the air, palms toward them, fingers extended, "this is not the time to get unduly excited by anything happening here or by the fantastic news that will soon be coming our way in response to yesterday. If you thought last Monday was something special, wait for the tidal wave of calls today."

"They've started," Rebecca confirmed, "it will be overwhelming."

"The law is here, then they will leave, and we will continue. That is how it will work. Chattering about anything…gossiping, if you will, is not going to help us. I know that neither of you ladies works for me, but I am asking you to get back to your duties and keep a professional demeanor to the rest of the staff. We have lots of work to get done today."

"Yessir," they spoke in unison.

Once the FBI got through interviewing Kenny and Katherine Louise, Mitchell and Ross were shown into the big office suite. Mitchell carried a white envelope that he tapped against his chin periodically. This time he let Ross do most of the talking.

"I see the Feds are checking things out," Ross smiled, "they certainly get nosey when they are after something. Checking out Fred Wallace, no doubt. Of course, we know they won't find anything here because you folks were not in collusion with Wallace. Or will they?"

"What do you mean?" Katherine Louise was indignant and with good reason.

"Relax, Miz Kenny, we think you folks are clean. However, the Feds gotta find out for themselves."

Ross paused, mouth tightly closed, and pulled his head back as if he were working out a knot from a muscle in his neck.

"We're here on another matter…Feds don't know about it yet, but we'll tell them after we get through here."

Kenny sat at his desk, head in his hands, staring blindly at nothing in particular on his desk, seemingly not listening to Ross. On the other hand, Katherine Louise was intent, wrinkled brow, face pinched, eyes squinting at the Detective.

"Well?" she snapped.

"Fred Wallace is dead, ma'am…took his own life this morning. Ran his car head-on into a semi…over on I-77. Dead there at the scene. Word got to our office and we checked out his condo. Seems he left a note for you, Reverend Kenny. We thought you might want to read it."

Mitchell handed Kenny the envelope he had held against his cheek.

A visibly shocked Kenny opened the unsealed flap and pulled out the folded yellow note paper.

The note was scribbled, but still legible:

Rev K – My time with God was good. My time without God was not good in terms of conventional morality. Unfortunately more of my time was spent without God. The good time with you and God gave me great satisfaction and for that I thank you. My not morally good time without God also gave me much satisfaction that I can appreciate in memory as in truth I really enjoyed doing. Some of the doing benefited only me. I don't feel guilty about that, however I am sorry that it brought problems to you. I am not interested in being hounded by the authorities or listening to any self-righteous Christians condemning me for anything I have done. It is better I exit the scene quickly. I did not kill Sam and I don't know who did and I am very sorry he is dead. I cared about him very much. Forgive me.

He signed the note with a large F.

"It doesn't make any sense," Katherine Louise exclaimed.

She never had been as enthusiastic about Fred as her husband has been, but she wished him no ill and truly felt badly now that he was gone.

"It does," Mitchell said, "when you know what he was involved with. We think you know some of it, that's why you fired him. Man just couldn't stand defeat or humiliation. He had both coming to him, plus maybe jail time. Not much nice for Fred's future. He took care of that."

"Fred and Sam had lots of irons in the fire," Ross added. "Someone out there killed Sam because of their shenanigans and it could be that Fred thought he might also get whacked. Who knows? We'll stay on it, trying to find out who the killer is. But if it's a pro job we don't stand much chance. Fred made sure the hard way he wouldn't get hit. Too bad."

The crass, insensitive comments of the detectives disgusted Katherine Louise. She turned her back on the two men and walked away to the kitchenette where she poured herself a cup of coffee. She stood there waiting for them to leave.

"Are you through?" Kenny asked.

"Yes," Mitchell said as he picked up the note, replaced it in its envelope, and put it in his pocket.

"May I have that?" Kenny scowled.

"It's evidence, Reverend. Maybe at some point down the road you can get it, but right now it has to stay with our office. Coroner will want it, I imagine."

When the two men left, Katherine Louise came back into the office.

"Why?" she mouthed quietly to Kenny.

"He said why in his note..."

"I don't understand taking one's own life...I just don't get it..."

"When someone sees no other way then..."

"I know, I know...it's just the craziness of it that gets me, that's all."

"May the Lord Bless him and forgive his sins, which is our hope and prayer for Fred. But the Judgment of God is firm. Fred gave no words of repentance in his note and he will be committed to eternal damnation. The fires of Hell are his reward; of that we can be sure."

"He said "Forgive me."

"Yes, I know. He wanted me to forgive him, he did not ask for our Lord and Savior's forgiveness. It's clear what he wanted. No, my dear, his fate is set and he is now in the confines of Hell."

The phone buzzed. Doris asked if Reverend Stone could come into the office.

"Yes, of course," Kenny said, "send him in."

As Reverend Stone opened the door another man pushed by him and went directly in front of Kenny. Leaning forward against the desk, he balanced himself with two fingers pushing on its top while the other hand held a yellow notepad against his side. It was an aggressive, arrogant gesture, one calculated to intimidate Kenny; for what reason was far from clear, maybe just an habitual way of dealing with people.

"We're through here, Reverend...at least for now. Nothing showing in the files about Wallace that we need. We might have to come back and spend more time, though, depends on how our investigation goes."

"What's your name again?" Katherine Louise asked casually.

"Special Agent Ramsey, ma'am, Federal Bur..."

"Yes, yes, we know you're with the FBI. Let me tell you, Mr. Ramsey, the next time you come to New World for anything other than church services…bring a warrant. We won't allow this kind of invasion to happen again. Is that clear?"

He looked at her with disdain, slapped the notepad against his thigh, and backed to the door without responding. He stopped, stared at her, whirled, and exited.

Stone stood there, stunned by what he had witnessed.

"This has been ten tough days, hasn't it Reverend Stone?" Katherine Louise sipped her coffee. "Let's see…murder…wonderful services…police…"

"More than you know," Kenny sighed.

"What do you mean?" Stone asked.

"Fred killed himself this morning…ran his car head-on into a truck…"

"No…"

"Oh yes, oh yes…" Kenny affirmed.

"But why? I didn't see him yesterday, but didn't think much about it, plus I was preoccupied with Del and I…"

"Sit down, Reverend Stone," Katherine Louise said quietly, "you wanted to talk about something…let's not worry about Fred at this point. We'll all say a prayer for him later. Although we don't think it will retrieve him from Hell. At least we'll let our God know where we stand."

"You already have," Stone said soberly.

"What is it you wanted, Reverend Stone?" Kenny tried to smile when he asked the question, but it was an effort he accomplished only somewhat.

"I…I…I don't know how to say it other than I have very bad news."

Katherine Louise who had stood up to face off with the FBI agent now sank back into a chair. Kenny put his head in his hands and again stared at his desk top.

"Del is not making a sound…to anyone…not to Betty, to no one. And I learned that he had been writing little notes to her all this time and those have stopped. He is wound down, busted. He is mute and barely functioning. We will not be having any more services with Del. His son is coming…probably on his way as we speak. His son will take him home immediately…"

"This is…" Katherine Louise started.

"This is awful for everyone, I know…I know, I know…I feel terrible about it. I regret we cannot live up to our agreement, but I feel worse about Del. He's in bad shape…believe me, very bad shape."

"We can't…" Katherine Louise began, but Kenny raised his hand for silence and she stopped. He stood, hand still held towards her, and after a moment he let it drop to his side.

"We will go up to the house right now and pray for him. We will bring the power of prayer to him, we will direct all of our energy to bear so that God's energy is focused on him."

Kenny walked out of his office without waiting for the others, without putting on his rain jacket, and headed a golf cart to the parsonage alone, leaving Stone and Katherine Louise trying to catch up to him. All of them were soaked from the rain by the time they reached the mansion.

The ugliness of the rain seemed to be more evident now than before as it slashed across the grounds. The gray sky had turned to near darkness as if day had gone to night in an ominous and foreboding symbol of all their problems.

15.

All this has come upon us; but we have not forgotten You, nor have we dealt falsely with Your covenant.

-Psalm 44:17

Kenny had that "look what the cat dragged in" appearance as he stiffly climbed the stairs, disregarding Carlton's offer of help. Water dripped from him in a wet trail. He carried himself as if his body were racked with pain, as if each movement hurt, as if each step might be his last. His labored, deliberate movement was an exaggerated exposition of how he felt inside. Stoically, he would go about changing into dry clothes without giving in to his churning emotions. He would not reveal a thing and with single purpose he would keep his face frozen in blankness, with no sign of the anger burning in him.

Carlton was startled when he was ignored, then puzzled by the flurried entry of Katherine Louise and Reverend Stone, neither of whom paid any attention to him, either. He spoke to them, too, but it did not seem to matter. What was going on?

Clothes changed, hair toweled dry, Kenny relaxed a bit, steadfast in containing himself. Katherine Louise also quickly got into dry clothes and watched her husband as he pushed his feet into a pair of running shoes.

"Done at the office?" she asked, noting his casual outfit of chinos and polo shirt.

"For today. I've had all I wanted. Doris can call me with anything...Rebecca can give us a report later."

The sharp knock at the door jolted them. It was Carlton.

"Reverend Stone say to let you know he on the back porch."

"Thank you, Carlton."

Stone sat holding the iced tea Carlton had given him, shivering a bit, wondering when Don would arrive. He had not yet changed his clothes. He set the glass on the low table in front of him. Carlton caught his action and came to the doorway.

"Hot tea or coffee? Carlton asked. "Might be better than that cold stuff."

"Yes…it would. Coffee."

What a strange turn of events, what a cockeyed kick in the pants this venture had become. Caught in circumstances beyond his control, dealt bad cards from a lousy deck. His work for his God had brought him here and to some degree there had been success. Certainly monetary success, he assumed. At what price? That was the all-pervading issue for him right now. What was the cost of bringing Del here? His life, his future, what? Self-doubt is a debilitating waste of energy Stone knew, but he could not shake it off, could not release himself from its nagging preoccupation. He knew that was part of what was eating at Kenny. Doubt…and the consternation for all the other negatives that have collapsed in on him. Accepted responsibility for sending Fred off to his suicide. Being party to, even unwittingly, Sam Turco's dealings, whatever they might have been, and the loss of a sure-fire money maker in Del. What a terrible day this was for Kenny. Doubt conveys weakness and weakness removes the ability to lead, and without being able to lead Kenny cannot have the control he wants. God asks for strength. Doubt casts a shadow of uncertainty on everything, transforms faith into unsubstantiated myth, and turns the soul into Godlessness. Doubt marginalizes Christians, pries them loose from their God, and sacrifices them on the stone-cold doorstep of the Devil. Doubt tangles Christian minds, makes believers lose hope, and makes them lose commitment to meet Christ's challenge for life.

Courage is what was required and Stone knew it for sure. Courage removed doubt. Courage is what Tom had given him. Had Tom shown courage by walking away from all of this? Or was it cowardice that had always lurked in the background of his soul? He had played quite the role if it were the latter because Tom had given him a tremendous boost in confidence, the strength of belief in his conviction for his ministry, and the daring to lead that mission. Courage is no mere word, but for some it has to be acquired. Tom had helped him with that. Was Tom just faking all of that? It didn't matter now, because doubt had to be erased. What he had done with Del was right, with the Holiest of intentions, and with the best interests of his mission as the core issue. The results of that mission with Del overrode all else. Del made his contribution and Del could now rest.

Stone could see the vapors rising from the mug of coffee on the tray Carlton carried to him.

"Jessie say you should have a manly size mug for your coffee," Carlton chuckled, "stead of some tiny cup with a saucer. This is a big mug for you, Reverend. Would you like me to get you a blanket or something to wrap up in? You look chilled to the bone."

"Thanks, no, Carlton, I'll change my clothes in a minute. Just didn't want to go upstairs right away."

"I understand," Carlton said, even if he did not.

Katherine Louise came downstairs first, with Kenny several steps behind her. She called for Stone before she saw him and as she came into the living room she spotted him on the porch.

"There you are. Still soaking wet."

She came close to him and touched his shoulder.

"Penance?" she asked, not seriously posing it, but wondering all the same.

"Hadn't thought about it that way, but maybe yes…sackcloth, if you will…"

"Not necessary," Kenny boomed, "not at all. We know you are worried about Del. He'll be fine, I'm sure."

"I'm not…not at all sure he will be fine. That's only part of the feeling I have. I also feel as if I've let you down after stirring up a big to-do with Del…"

"Stone, we had a contract with CGB before you came with Del and we'll have one after you leave…don't you worry about that issue."

"Thank you…"

"Perhaps if you bring your coffee we can go upstairs and meet with Betty…Del…and pray."

"I think so," Stone said quietly.

They trudged upstairs and Katherine Louise knocked on the bedroom door.

"Betty…"

After a short pause Betty opened the door. She saw the three of them standing there, opened the door wider to ease out into the hall, and closed the door behind her.

"Del's sleeping…I don't want to wake him…"

"We don't want you to wake him, Betty…let him sleep." Kenny spoke softly. "We want to pray for him…with you."

"Oh," she said, but still looked confused.

"By his bedside…so he can hear…although he is asleep he can still hear, I believe. We want him to feel the positive energy of our spirit."

"All right." She opened the door and led them inside the room.

Betty had pulled the drapes closed so that the room was dimly lighted from the dull outside light that was partially able to sneak around the cloth. She pulled them apart, casting more light on the scene with a primary swath of illumination that fell across the bed to accent Del's pallid face. He was sleeping soundly with the barest hint of movement to his chest.

Kenny lifted a chair close to the foot of the bed while Stone pushed another near the side table by the headboard. Katherine Louise sat with Betty in a small sofa across the room.

Betty clutched at her throat, pulled at her nose, and bit at her lip in an effort to keep from weeping.

"Let us pray," Kenny began. "Dear Lord…"

His voice was soft, soothing, and with a well-practiced tone of urgency and sincerity. Command of Scriptures was his and he was able to bring forth Psalm 103 that evokes the blessing of the Lord, the One Who heals all diseases, plus other verses from Isaiah and Jeremiah that dealt with healing. He spoke from the heart with passion, his voice gathering in volume, asking God to Bless this fine man, and to thank God for the gift he had already given to the community of believers. Amen.

All said Amen.

Kenny nodded to Stone.

Reverend Stone struggled for Biblical reference for a few moments, gliding along on several standard phrases he usually used in situations such as this, until he recalled Psalm 84, verse eleven. He could not recite it exactly, but the essence came through.

"Our Lord God is our sun and shield," he said majestically, "He will give grace and glory to all of his flock."

Stone continued with a well-connected series of his favorite comforting phrases and ended with a call for God's mercy for this proud and heroic Christian. Amen.

All said Amen.

Near the end of Stone's prayer, a black stretch Cadillac limousine slowly found its way up the rain glistened road to the mansion, around the circular drive that ran by the porch, and stopped. Umbrella in hand, the driver hurriedly opened the door for Don Howe, another man, and a young woman. He tried valiantly to keep at least one of them covered from the rain, although they seemed to ignore his efforts. All were dressed casually; Don in slacks and sweater, the man in designer jeans and sport shirt, and the young woman in tan slacks with a blouse. Despite the casual appearance there was something stern and stiff about the other man. He carried himself in a certain way and his manner was officious and aloof. He was not happy about being with Don and did not care who knew it. For Don, it did not matter, he wanted the man with him and that was how it would be.

The man was John Lewis, a doctor, a neurological specialist who was an expert in dealing with conditions such as Del's. This cost Don plenty, but he wanted the man with him and he refused to accept a no answer when the request was made. Lewis had helped the recovery of at least three golfers zapped by lightening when they had ignored warnings to vacate the courses on which they were playing. He was well known in golfing circles and the neurological literature.

Don had chartered a jet for the day starting in Toledo. The young woman, a registered nurse with experience in neurological cases, flew with him to Atlanta where they picked up Dr. Lewis and then on to Columbia. On that leg of the flight Don filled in the doctor as best he could from the story his mother had given him the night before and from what he knew had initially occurred on the farm, plus what had been determined by Sid Fisher and Sarah White at the farm after Del had gotten out of the hospital. The plan was to return to Atlanta with Del so that he could undergo a series of tests at Piedmont Hospital where Dr. Lewis practiced.

Carlton was waiting at the front door. Rebecca had phoned to let him know she had directed Don to the house.

"I'm here to get my father," Don said brusquely as he barged past Carlton who held the door open for them.

"Yessir, he upstairs, sir."

Don was visibly angry, but understood the circumstances for what they were; the potentially critical condition of his father, and the probable limited ability of his mother to handle any further stress. Mindful of both of those factors, he held his temper and kept the volume of his voice well modulated when he spoke. He had promised his sister that he would not point fingers at Stone nor any of the others. This was difficult for him because he believed their religious fervor had brought his father to this terrible point. He was not, however, about to engage in niceties with any of these people. He was here on his own mission and that was to remove his father and get him medical treatment.

He followed Carlton up the stairs with Dr. Lewis and the nurse in his wake, nodded at Stone when he entered the room, ignored Kenny and Katherine Louise, and went straight to his mother. He embraced her warmly and held her tightly. It was at that moment when she no longer could hold back the tears. She wept until she shook, an agonizingly quiet release considering the emotion she had locked inside for days, and clung to him like a child who needed reassurance from a nightmare.

Dr. Lewis went immediately to Del's beside, took his hand and wrist, and checked his pulse. He pulled a stethoscope from his jacket pocket and listened to Del's heart. Del did not wake up from the poking and probing and pulling. The young nurse connected Del to a portable blood pressure apparatus. One ten over seventy. On the low side, but okay. At least it was not elevated. Del continued to be sound asleep.

"How long has he been like this? Lewis asked. "Asleep, I mean."

"Since yesterday afternoon," Betty answered as she wiped away the tears, "we barely could get him up here. He's been…well, I did help him during the night…he had to go to the bathroom…"

"Of course," Lewis nodded.

"Mother, we have an ambulance on the way." Don spoke with calm reassurance to his mother. "The plane we came on is waiting for us at the airport. We are going to fly you and Dad to Atlanta where Dr. Lewis has his office and take Dad to the hospital where he practices…called Piedmont. They'll run tests there…neurological tests…then we will know better what is wrong and what we can do."

"Atlanta?" Betty said quizzically, "why Atlanta?" It did not seem to make sense to her.

"Dr. Lewis is a very good specialist in these kinds of cases, Mother, lightening cases. He's treated golfers and forest rangers and lots of other people who have been hit by lightening and lived. I found out about him through a friend…one of my golfing buddies who heard about Dr. Lewis. He's an expert…he'll know what to do."

"But…Atlanta…"

Betty seemed to be in a mental fog at this point. Perhaps the stress that dogged her for weeks had finally taken its toll. She was so relieved Don was there with her, fully willing to let him be in charge. Maybe she could relax a bit. Her eyes rolled back and she collapsed against the young nurse who could not catch her in time. She sort of melted to the floor as if she were a modern dancer performing some ritualistic impression of dying. Dr. Lewis was at her side before the nurse could even bend over to help.

"Let's let her lie here for moment. She didn't hit her head…I think she'll be all right. I understand she has been under quite a strain for awhile. Not surprising she collapsed."

Betty's eyes snapped open and she quickly raised up on her elbows.

"I...I guess I fainted. I'm sorry..."

"It's okay Mother, its okay...here, sit over here...let me help you..."

"There's an ambulance here," Carlton called from the hallway.

"Excellent," Dr. Lewis confirmed.

"Mother," Don directed, "you ride in the ambulance with the nurse. Dr. Lewis and I will be following you in the limo."

Two EMS technicians carefully moved Del from the bed to their stretcher, carried him downstairs, and placed him in the ambulance. Betty and the nurse climbed aboard and they proceeded to the airport. Don walked back to the porch while Dr. Lewis went to the limo. He stood glaring at the two men and Katherine Louise. Carlton stayed in the background and knew what was coming probably was not going to be pleasant, but he wanted to hear.

"You two disgust me. You used up my Father like some disposable product...used him until there was nothing left...then you could throw him away. I hold you most responsible, Reverend Stone. You knew he needed further tests, but you got him out of town anyway and my stupid sister knew about it and allowed it. All in the name of God...God's good works, my sister claimed. God my foot. My Father was a means to an end...a way to generate money...'

"Not true," Stone yelled at Don, "That's simply not true..."

"Ridiculous," Kenny scoffed, "our motives relate to our Christian work. We had no idea your father would react this way. He seemed fine when he arrived here, he..."

"Could you talk to him?"

"Well..."

"Could you?"

"Ah...not really, he was having problems being understood when he tried to speak..."

"Yeah, right...he was a babbling fool just like he's been since he got hit by lightening. My guess is that Tom Fletcher masterminded this whole campaign with my Father as a way to bring money into your church, Reverend Stone...I hope you're satisfied. Just remember...any money you made off of my Father is going to my parents to pay for his care and to help support my Mother. You better make your mind up to that...both of you...all of you...your church included, Reverend."

Don pointed at Kenny.

"My guess is that the last two Sundays are going to bring a pot full of money into the coffers here. We'll find out. I'm going to have my attorneys working on it. They'll be contacting you. They'll be looking for a just settlement to take care of Mr. and Mrs. Howe. You can count on it...literally."

"There really isn't a lot of..." Katherine Louise started to say as she stepped forward.

"Tell it to my attorneys," Don said as he walked quickly through the pouring rain to the limo.

Once inside the limo, Don pulled his hands across his hair to squeeze out the water and looked at Dr. Lewis intently, his eyes asking the all-important question.

"We won't know anything for a couple of days," Dr. Lewis responded sharply, "but...but I don't like what I hear about his case and I don't like the little bit I have seen."

Katherine Louise's mouth was still hanging open when the limo pulled away, agape from the threat she had received from Don. It was the kind of threat that she particularly did not like, one that could jeopardize their finances, one that could diminish all of their work, and make them vulnerable.

She hated the idea of struggling again and slumped against the tall column at the head of the porch stairs. Splatters of rain hit her face and quickly matted her hair as she stood frozen with the thoughts of how hard she and Kenny had worked to build all of this. Thoughts of potential ruin depressed her as she descended into visions of a worst-case scenario for what was to come. The pounding rain made things worse for her, its volume such that she could barely see the administration building but as a faded shape in the gray distance. The storm seemed to have bleached the color out of everything and made a gray, gray world around her.

Stone could sense her sadness and depression and knew it was not just the rain water on her cheeks. He wanted to say something consoling, some words of encouragement, but decided against that. He was alone here, his mission uncompleted, his presence unnecessary.

"I guess I'll get packed," he said absently and went inside as Carlton held the door for him.

"No sense in leaving yet…in this nasty weather," Kenny called after him, "have dinner with us tonight and get started in the morning."

Stone stopped in the hallway without turning around.

"Thanks," he said.

He hesitated for moment as if there were something else he wanted to say. But he said nothing and went on upstairs.

"You know," Kenny said, turning his attention to Katherine Louise, "you always say, 'well darlin', everything is going to be fine.' And you're right. I know what you're thinking. When you get this down-in-the-mouth it means you've got a big worry on your mind and it's always one that can't and won't exist. It's that old paranoid part of you sneaking back into things. That Howe boy is a big talker…don't think about it. Besides Sol can make it mighty tough on him if he tried to collect anything."

He pulled her away from the column, wrapped his arms around her, and held her tightly, rubbing her back as he whispered in her ear.

"Nothing is going to happen, sweet thing, nothing to spoil what we have here. You can be sure of that."

Carlton followed Stone up the stairs to the bedroom. Stone noticed when he opened the door.

"Carlton?"

"I did not have a chance to tell you before now, Reverend. The young woman…Miss Keri, she come this morning to get the rest of her things. She completely moved out…gave me this note for you." Carlton handed him a small envelope. "She tell me she's not coming back with you to Ohio…says her life moving on."

"I knew that. Thanks anyway, Carlton, appreciate it. You've been very helpful…and kind to all of us. I know Mrs. Howe was thankful for all the help you gave her and Del, and I know she didn't have a chance to tell you. They whisked her husband away pretty fast."

"The son?"

"Yes…yes, it was their son. He's been very concerned from the start of this…perhaps we all should have paid more attention to him. Who knows?"

"Lord God know. Lord God used Mr. Howe in the right way. He coulda just wasted away in some hospital somewhere back there in Ohio not doing nuthin'. This way he was a messenger from above, sure enough. He was one glorious inspiration for awhile, Reverend, and that is important. Best Mr. Howe did what he did. Who knows how many lives his sounds reached…translated by you into the Word of God? The Word of the Almighty God's power made it all possible. The Almighty worked through you, Reverend, and the Word was revealed to us all. Jessie and I watched you on the set in the kitchen. We saw how magnificent you were,

Preacher...you were the Enlightenment for us all. You gave us the good and gracious Word. And the Word was Redemption for us all. Redemption...powerful stuff, Reverend, powerful stuff. I thank you for Jessie and me. You touched us hard and we heard the Word and we know how sincere you was. You are Blessed, Reverend."

"Thank you, Carlton, those are very kind words. This has been a very unkind day to all of us what with the heavy rain drowning our spirits. Sometimes it's difficult to overcome what should be so easy to surmount. It's just rain and cloudy skies. But the effect is devastating, I'm afraid."

"Can I help you pack, Reverend?"

"Thanks, Carlton, that would be very nice of you."

Stone sat on the edge of his bed and popped open the little envelope Carlton had handed him. He flicked his thumb over the flap as he delayed removing the note. There was that moment of debate as to whether or not he should read what she had to say, but the decision was forced by basic curiosity. He slipped the note free and unfolded it. It had been generated with a computer on a standard sheet of paper and obviously cut to size and folded once.

RANDY, THERE IS SO MUCH I WOULD LIKE TO SAY BUT DON'T KNOW HOW TO PUT IT IN WRITING. COULD YOU CALL ME? KERI

She included a phone number.

He was absolutely confused by such a message. His thoughts tumbled possibilities every which way, but no matter what scenario, whatever meaning or motivation or excuse, one thing was for certain. The message made little sense in the scheme of things and was not valid enough to warrant a phone call. Carlton had gotten his bags out, had folded some shirts, and was beginning to get socks from the dresser drawer.

"Thanks, Carlton, let me finish the packing...it will be good for my mental state."

"Yessir."

"And get rid of this if you would." Stone said as he tore the note to shreds and handed them to him.

"Yessir, I can do that. Anything else, Reverend?"

"Yes, please tell the Kennys I'll be glad to have dinner with them."

"I will, sir. And I'll let Jessie know...just the three of you folks tonight."

"Right."

As he slowly packed, Stone's thoughts were on Del. What a journey it had been since that first day he had gone to the farm to be of support. How unpredictable the circumstances have been. The relationship with Keri a thing of the past, Tom gone somewhere, and Del's condition worse. He was alone, would return to Ohio alone, and would face the future alone unless he re-determined his life with Helen. It would seem somewhat strange being in front of a congregation without Del.

When the ambulance carrying Del reached the Columbia airport, the driver was escorted directly to the jet Don had chartered. He was placed on board and transferred to a specially prepared berth that had been made ready for him. Betty and the young nurse carefully adjusted a safety belt that would hold him securely for take-off and landing. He was still asleep. Don and Dr. Lewis came aboard moments later and it was not long before they were airborne on the way to Atlanta. When the jet reached cruising altitude, the co-pilot came back to show where snacks and beverages were stowed, but only the young nurse indulged in a diet cola and pretzels.

During the hour plus flight to touch down, Dr. Lewis asked Betty a battery of questions most of which she could not answer. They were questions that would have best been answered by Del if he were able.

"Will he wake up?" Betty finally asked the doctor.

"I think so, Mrs. Howe, I think so. Once we get him to our facility, and after we have taken a better look at his condition, and after we assess that condition, we will then be able to treat him properly. He may be just severely weakened by the stress that the religious services put him under. We'll see. I'm very optimistic and we have excellent facilities at Piedmont."

His words were not consoling to Betty. They seemed too professional, too rote, too pat. Her instinct in reacting to the tone of his voice was that he did not care one way or the other about Del. Del was his job now because Don had paid for his services. She realized that might not be fair, but it was the way she felt. She relaxed a bit when the plane finally landed at Dekalb Peachtree Airport in northeast Atlanta and accepted the fact that she could let down some more once they got Del to the hospital. They were met by another ambulance and limo. It took less than fifteen minutes to get Del from the jet to the hospital, where he was quickly moved to a private room in the neurological section.

As Del was wheeled into his room Betty noticed that he was suddenly awake and she clasped his left hand. He smiled and winked at her as if to say that he was all right. She kissed his cheek and brushed his hair back from his eyes. He seemed alert, but he was silent. She wondered if he would ever speak again.

Being able to speak was Reverend Stone's great talent, his abiding asset as a Christian gospel minister. But he seriously questioned himself as to what he had achieved by himself so far with that talent. He wondered whether he was just the product of Tom Fletcher or if he were really the man he wanted to be and the man God wanted. The force of Tom's personality had built the church from its early beginnings beyond anyone's imagination. Tom had brought him to

Calvary, Tom had championed the work with Del, Tom came up with the idea of videotaping services to get Calvary on television, and Tom engineered the move here to New World. If he were merely the product of Tom's handiwork then the future held little for him. He felt weak and powerless and alone. It was time to talk straight on with his God.

Stone stopped packing, got his Bible, and sat down in the chair opposite his bed. He placed the Bible in his lap, folded his hands, placed them on the Bible, and turned his thoughts to Almighty God for inspiration, for strength, and hope. He closed his eyes and instantly a vision of Helen appeared as an eerie mental picture of her as an archangel floating over a field of lavender lilies, dressed in a creamy-white gown, and projecting a serenity and calm that overcame him even as he waited for words to come to him for praying to his God. Had God anticipated his intent and this was the concurrent answer? Inspiration, strength, and hope were what Helen had given him when first they met and mingled their lives. He had strayed from her support, he had assumed it was no longer needed, that he was self-sufficient in those regards, self-sufficient and independent of her. He had moved beyond her in his involvement with Keri and it had been a lie and he had deceived himself. All of this flashed through him as if a sword had been thrust into his body. He reacted viscerally and winced with the perceived pain. It was a ponderous revelation and it hurt, but he felt the connection to God and thanked God for His answer. Amen.

He went to the phone on the night stand and punched in the numbers to his home phone. Helen answered.

"It's been a few days, sorry…"

"Are you all right? I was just thinking about you, thinking something was wrong somehow, something…"

"Yes…yes, I was thinking about you too…something is wrong. A lot is wrong. Del has taken…"

"Is he all right?"

"No, he's not. His condition seems to have gotten worse and Don came here…with a doctor and a nurse and flew him and Betty to Atlanta for testing. And Tom has…"

I heard he is gone. What happened? What is going on? He left the country the police said."

"Police?"

"Yes, they thought at first there might be foul play, but he seems to have just left. They think Mexico."

"I don't know. But…"

"So it's just you and Keri?"

"No…no. Not at all. Seems Keri has taken up with a young man who handles production for the New World church services. We haven't seen her much since we got here and she isn't coming back to Ohio. I…I'm alone…except for Reverend and Mrs. Kenny. I'm going to start back tomorrow with the van. I'm almost packed. I…I miss you."

"I miss you, too, sweetheart…and the kids miss you terribly…"

"Couple days I'll be home."

"I love you. I wish I could be there to help you. A few minutes ago my thoughts of you were so strong, so real it was as if I were standing there watching you struggling with something. I'm glad you're okay.

"It is uncanny isn't it?"

"Yes."

"I love you, too. I'm eager to get back. There's a lot we have to talk about, a lot of work I have to do, and an apology to my congregation for making them watch me on television for the last couple of weeks."

"We'll take care of everything, dear."

"See you Wednesday night."

"Call me tomorrow while you're on the road."

"I will. Good night. I love you."

"I love you," she said. There was just a hint of sadness in her voice as it trailed off when she spoke.

He hung up the phone and flopped back on the bed. He should have felt comforted, but it was not so. He should not have still felt alone, but he did. Alone except for his connection with God and caught with his own judgment of himself, his evaluation and assessment of his motivation and actions. He fell asleep with those thoughts raging and with the blurred image of Helen jostled about in an awkward scenario of some kind that made him feel uneasy, made his face feel hot. He had some sense that he was dreaming, but it seemed so real.

Carlton's knock startled him awake. It was mid-afternoon and he could hear the rain continuing to pelt the house.

"Mr. Fletcher on the phone, sir" Carlton called through the slightly open door.

Stone grabbed at the phone.

"Randy?" Tom's voice sounded as clearly as if he were in the same room.

"Yes. Tom? Where are you?"

"In Mexico. How did it go yesterday? I assume you were terrific as usual."

"Mexico? Where?"

"I'd rather not say. Better that way. Tell me about yesterday. How is Del doing?"

"Del is…" Stone paused before he continued, "Del is struggling…Betty is struggling to hold up…and I'm struggling…with myself…"

"Go home…like I told you. Go home as soon as you finish there and get renewed…get your energy back…"

"I'm done here. Don came with a doctor this morning and got Del and Betty and took them to Atlanta. The doctor has a practice there. Del will go back to Ohio from there. At least I hope and pray that he will…"

"That bad?"

"That bad…very bad. He could not go on anymore. He's too worn out and he's gone silent…no more sounds of any kind."

"Not surprised. Figured we had a limited time with him. Never thought he…"

"You never said anything…" Stone was stunned.

"No…no point. His affliction was a chance for us to give your mission a boost. Del presented an opportunity that the good Lord wanted us to take. We did that."

"You…you didn't believe he was speaking in tongues…ever?"

"I don't know…maybe. It was not for me to say. After all, I'm no medical expert. But he might well have been…and if that was the way it was, then we…you…had an obligation to the Almighty to bring forth the meaning of his babbling. Didn't matter if it was tongues or not. Result was the same…for everyone concerned…"

"He may be near death…"

"Not because of what you did, that's for sure. If he was going to get better he would and if his condition was to deteriorate it would and nothing you did changed those circumstances. The Lord giveth and the Lord taketh away, Brother Randy, keep that in mind. Such decisions are made by God, the Great Controller, and not by our actions. It is part of the Master Plan, make no mistake about that. Now tell me how brilliant you were yesterday."

"It was the most animated and impressive Del has ever shown. I was inspired in a way I had never felt before. I was truly an instrument of God and Del through me and the results might be called astounding…"

"Electrifying, no doubt. That's what I thought."

"I was very gratified…"

"Sorry I had to run off on you like that, but it couldn't be helped. Anyway, you don't need me. You'll be just fine. What did the good Reverend Kenny and the lovely and talented Katherine Louise have to say about the way things have turned out?"

"They're fine…understanding about Del…not being able to continue. Kenny said there would be no problem with the CGB network…they have a contract…"

"What about the money?"

"Money?" Stone seemed puzzled.

Yes, dear Reverend, the money. Two blockbuster Sunday services mean a big take for them. Many thousands came in after the first service. Yesterday would be even better, believe me. Don't leave there without a nice check."

"What sort of arrangement did you make with them?"

"Nothing solid, but they said we would benefit financially. Let them know you think fifty thousand would be about right. That number shouldn't pinch them too much."

"Tom, I…"

"I have to go; I just wanted to see how you were doing…"

"Tom, was it Fred that told you that…about benefiting?"

"Yes, it was."

"He killed himself this morning…ran his car head-on into a semi."

Tom did not answer and Stone could envision him tugging at that special patch of hair.

Tom...Tom...you still there?"

"Yeah...I'm still here. Too bad about Fred...never can figure those things...suicide...doesn't make any sense to me. Listen, Randy, ask them for seventy-five. You were worth it. I'll stay in touch. Adios."

The line clicked dead.

Stormy Mondays can be brutal; this one had been. The usual brilliance of the New World grounds were now sodden and dull, colors muted, the sweeping view full of mist and fog, and the trees sagging with folded leaves and weeping branches. As dinner time approached, the rain lessened, although still delivering a steady shower. This was unrelenting, uncaring rain that contributed emotional suffering to a day that was already ruined at its start. Its demise would not be soon enough for the three dinner companions at the parsonage.

16.

I said, "Lord, be merciful to me; heal my soul, for I have sinned against You."

-Psalm 41:4

Reverend Stone was determined that he would be up and gone before the Kennys arose, although Carlton and Jessie were already at work in the kitchen when he came downstairs. They were busy preparing for breakfast, Jessie cooking, Carlton with the table already set for three. The delicious smells of sausage and coffee were just beginning to escape the kitchen into the rest of the house. Stone took a deep whiff as he strode into the kitchen.

"Good morning," he whispered and put down the larger of the bags he was carrying.

"Good..." Jessie started, but Stone tempered her response with a finger to his lips.

"...morning," she finished softly.

"Morning," Carlton said quietly, having seen the warning sign.

Stone motioned to them to come closer to him. It became almost a football huddle, ready for the play to be called.

"I wanted to get out of here without dealing with them," he said solemnly, finger pointing upward. "No offense to them, but last night was enough. I need to get going without extracting myself, if you know what I mean."

"Yessir," Carlton voiced acknowledgement of the understanding he had.

Jessie nodded.

"You load your van, Reverend, I fix you some food. We have bottled water...you take that, too."

By the time Stone had gotten his belongings into the van, Jessie had a large brown bag and two small plastic grocery store bags ready for him. Carlton placed those three bags in the van on the passenger seat. He and Jessie stood by the van to say good-bye to this man they recognized as essentially good and a mighty fine preacher.

"Glad to have a chance to meet you, sir, God be on your side...all the time...all the time, now." Carlton cocked his head to one side when he spoke, his way of giving the words emphasis.

"We know your soul," Jessie said tearfully, "we know your heart and soul. God bless, Reverend."

She kissed his cheek. He patted her shoulder, got into the van, and was gone.

Stone knew that the drive back to Ohio would be tedious and difficult. He had not had to do any of the driving on the way down to New World, Tom had seen to that, but here he was, by himself, making the effort to get home to comfort and security as quickly as he could. He wondered if it were comfort and security he deserved. Perhaps, perhaps not. Time, he hoped, would be on his side and sort things out favorably for him.

The dinner with the Kennys had been tolerable, not all that unpleasant, but in the end, unnervingly disappointing in many respects. Although he had not been motivated by the potential big dollars like Tom had been, the thoughts Tom had given him about being compensated changed his outlook considerably. There was polite conversation, the assurance that New World would move ahead just fine without Del and Stone, which most certainly Stone knew.

He had listened carefully as the two of them had openly bantered back and forth about Sam Turco's murder and their relief the investigation didn't center on them, speculation of who the killer might be, and the subsequent investigation of Sam and Fred's potential illegal activities.

"Who would kill Sam?" Katherine Louise asked, as if she were referring to some abstract persona, some unknown, remote victim seen on television news.

"Hard to say," Kenny responded with a similar disconnected, dispassionate tone of indifference.

"Someone who knew him well," Stone offered. "Aren't most murders committed by someone close to the victim? A lover, an enemy, perhaps one of his employees…you never know. But that's how it usually happens, I understand."

They looked at him blankly and turned the subject to how wonderful Jessie's cooking was and how truly lucky they were to have her in their service.

They avoided any further comment about Fred's death. There also was the avoidance of any discussion of how successful the last two weeks had been. It was as if the subject of that success were a non-topic because it could also mean the matter of money. Maybe their omission from the conversation was his imagination under the circumstances, but that was how it seemed to him.

Stone changed that.

"What did Rebecca have to say about the response to yesterday? She must have given you some kind of feedback."

"She told us it was very good," Kenny said through a mouthful of food, "good response, you bet."

"How do you like Jessie's chicken, Reverend Stone?" Katherine Louise questioned "Real Southern fried…the real thing."

He ignored her obvious attempt to change the subject.

"I thought we had a fabulous service, if I do say so myself. I would have thought the response would be more that just good."

"Well, we don't have the details, yet." Kenny was chewing when he spoke, trying to be nonchalant. "We didn't go back to the office…she called here with a report…wanted us to know everything was all right…going well and that we were getting good…very good response. Just a short phone call. We'll find out more tomorrow."

Stone pressed the issue.

"When we came down here as a result of your invitation it was our understanding that our success would be your success and the sum total of that would be a financial benefit to Calvary Fundamentalist Christian Church. Especially since my congregation has been deprived of their minister for two weeks…especially since New World would be the recipient of considerable donations, plus heightened recognition and attention which I believe you received…"

"What are you trying to say, Reverend?" Katherine Louise asked.

"We need to be compensated. That's blunt…maybe crude, but that's the way it is. You benefit, we benefit. I think that's how it works. I think that would be fair. Don't you?"

Kenny looked at Katherine Louise, made a little face as if to say "how do you like that," and laughed. She smiled broadly and then laughed almost as loudly as her husband.

"I'd like a check before we finish dinner," Stone said with a commanding tone, his manner and the words stifling their laughter.

"Of course you would, Reverend, of course you would. And you will…after dessert…it will sweeten the effect of Jessie's delicious pie a la mode, I'm sure." Kenny was very calm as he spoke.

"Thank you," Stone replied and finished eating.

"The office is closed, Reverend Stone, we couldn't possibly get you a check tonight…"

"No, no, Katherine Louise, we should take care of the good Reverend tonight as he wishes. We can do that."

Only until after dessert, after Carlton had cleared the dishes and brought coffee, and after Kenny had left the table and returned with a checkbook and pen, did the issue of money get addressed again. Kenny wrote vigorously in the checkbook and with a flourish tore out the check and handed it to Stone. It was for twenty-five thousand dollars. Stone glanced at it briefly, tore it in several pieces, and dropped them on the table behind his coffee cup.

"Tom told me what would be fair," he said, again using the commanding voice. "Seventy-five thousand would be about right."

Katherine Louise noisily sucked in a breath that was a half choked reflexive response and her jaw dropped open uncontrollably.

Kenny did not flinch. He wrote another check, tore it from the pad, and flipped it across the table to Stone. It was for fifty thousand dollars.

Stone looked at it for a few moments, folded it once and put it in his shirt pocked, and rose from the table.

"It's been a tough day. I need to get to bed. I thank you for all your hospitality. Good night."

"Good night," Kenny said almost jovially, "we'll see you in the morning for breakfast. Give you a proper send-off."

Stone hadn't replied and he had gotten away without further irritation and agony.

From upstairs, Stone had heard them talking, a mush of high intensity phrases, sharp words, and muted responses. Katherine Louise had become an uncoiled loop of bull whip that slashed at Kenny with hissed ferocity for his easy beneficence. She was for giving nothing to Stone and she made her position quite clear. He deserved a gift, a memento, a token of their appreciation, some artifact, some kind of trophy, at best a minor, less costly recognition for his efforts. But money, significant money? No way.

"We will have taken in over a million dollars because of him…and Del. What I gave him was not unreasonable…he was worth it. Rebecca gave me a full report before she went home this afternoon. It's pouring in…to match the day's rain. Donations beyond anything you might have imagined. Relax, trust me, we want Stone to go away satisfied. We don't want him on the side of the young Howe. He will be content with what I gave him and we, my darlin', will be well-endowed for our part in these last two Sundays."

"Over a million?" Katherine Louise asked. "Are you sure?"

"As sure as Rebecca's report. You can check it tomorrow. I think you're going to like the results."

Stone's morning was a labor of dull monotony from freeway driving. He had hardly noticed the world that had slid by as they made this trip almost two weeks ago. He had been intent on his mission with Del and how that would succeed on television. He had been deliriously enraptured with thoughts of being away with Keri. How all of that had changed in such a short period of time. Del was struggling for his life in an odd kind of way. And yes, time would tell, time would surely tell. Now, Keri was a notion of the past, a memory that would quickly fade. She was an extinct vision of infatuation, a fleeting lover, a forbidden romance erased in a way he did not understand, but now accepted. It was time for newness in life by reestablishing himself with Helen. That possibility now energized him, gave him strength for the journey home. It would be his home with her and the children and it would be his spiritual home with his congregation. None of them would know what had been his fumbling dilemma, his battle with doubt, his drift from his Lord and Savior, and his subsequent revival and rebirth. These were his private conditions, secretly held close, save for Tom's knowledge; no subject for revelation, and no matter, as far as he was concerned, in his relationship with his God and his ability to minister to his flock. Tom would be proud of him for his ability to compartmentalize the issues and move on with life. God bless Tom, wherever he was.

As Stone motored north, the Kenny's morning started with a quiet breakfast and the anticipation of record-setting donations. Katherine Louise was in the kitchen first to learn that Stone was long-gone and quite relieved she did not have to begin the day being polite to him with small talk and coffee. Kenny was not surprised Stone had left early.

In Atlanta, the reality of Del's condition was beginning to come into focus. Testing had begun the previous afternoon and with grim results for the professionals involved. Dr. Lewis had enlisted the assistance of Dr. Beverly Cramer, as he moved on with other patients. Dr. Cramer's initial physical examination of Del had already left her discouraged about his prognosis. The first test results did not help alleviate her concern for him. She agonized over the preliminary report that came from a Cerebral Angiogram which indicated damage to significant blood vessels. When the initial information from a CAT scan, EEG, and MRI were given to her, it was a piling on of negative data. The results pummeled her diagnostic efforts like the buffeting from a severe storm that blew an ill wind of prediction at her.

She caught a glimpse of Del's future from those reports. Not good, none of it was good. It was obvious his speech center was affected, but the data showed why this was so and why his speech would not be recovered. Dr. Cramer made the nasty decision that Del would have a difficult time recovering from the brain damage she could see and perhaps might not have long to live. She tried to determine what she would say to Betty and decided she would dump that ugly task back in the lap of Dr. Lewis. After all, this was his patient.

The hospital made a valiant attempt to bring a stilted sense of attractiveness to its décor as a countermeasure for the pain, suffering, and death that stalked it halls. Balanced against the necessary methods of sterility, this environment made Betty uneasy, a feeling of almost being sick herself. She sat across the desk from Dr. Lewis as he shuffled various papers back and forth in front of him, scowling first at one, then frowning at another, and back and forth again several times. Don sat next to her, ill at ease, hunched forward, expecting the worst. Dr. Cramer stood nearby, arms folded across her chest, eyes bouncing around the room, not focusing on anything, trying furtively to settle on some point, any point, that would help her gain composure. Betty was not hopeful about what Dr. Lewis would say and rubbed her hands together in anxiety. She studied Dr. Cramer who was awkwardly groping for some way to be calm and professional. Only Dr. Lewis seemed relaxed, oblivious to the discomfort of the two women, each for different reasons, caught in the pregnancy of his own deliberation.

After several more minutes of paper shuffling, he cleared his throat and sat back in his chair. It was then that he took full account of Betty and his associate. He could have asked Dr. Cramer to be seated which would have been polite, appropriate, and kind. He did not. Instead, he let her stand there, the dutiful pupil before the master, frozen with anger and frustration at him and at the medical situation that had been presented to them. She realized they might have helped Del early on, but now that was out of the question. Dr. Lewis must have had some contorted sense of amusement at seeing her standing there in rigid attention because the faintest glimmer of a smile flickered and went before he turned his attention to Betty.

"Mrs. Howe…Don…I can't be optimistic…based on what we have here." He limply pointed at the confusion of papers on the desk, a pallid gesture of his own fateful acceptance.

This was what Don feared. He took his head with both hands as if he were checking the ripeness of a melon, faced the floor to somehow find solace there, and sucked in an uncontrolled gasp of air that signaled his anguish and frustration. He was removed from any discussion temporarily by his deep reaction.

Betty did not react so visibly, with expression unchanged, no body movement, and a blank almost uncomprehending glaze to her eyes. She had expected the worse and she got it. She, before anyone else, knew that Del had been in a debilitating, desperate slide to a worsened condition. Dr. Lewis' lack of optimism was no surprise, his out-loud expression of that was not a shock to her. She wanted to take her husband home. She knew he could die in peace there.

"What can be done? More tests? What? What are we supposed to do?" Don's voice bordered on the hysterical.

"There's really no point in conducting more tests. You might as well take your father home…make him comfortable, keep him stable…"

"Until he dies?" Don glowered at Dr. Lewis.

"For as long as he lives." Dr. Lewis played with the papers in front of him when he spoke.

"Thanks a lot," Don sniped.

"There are no miracles in the real world, Don. We work with the facts as they are, with the conditions that present themselves, and the prognosis that is appropriate. We can accept the conditions and prognosis or we can deny. That's the way it is."

For Don, Dr. Lewis gave a brutal assessment of his father's condition, but for Betty, it was merely confirmation of what she feared, what she secretly expected, and what she had already accepted would be her husband's fate. It was time to move on and get back to the farm.

How Del was being treated and tested preoccupied Stone's thoughts as he neared the end of his ride across the Ohio Turnpike and reached the exit that would put him closest to church and home. He debated with himself as to his first destination. Church office or home? He opted to get to Helen and the children first. The office could wait. In fact, it could wait for several days if necessary.

His thoughts slipped to a vision of himself that was the exaltation of a triumphant return, the return of a hero, and he could see himself on some type of raised throne surveying thousands of wildly cheering parishioners clamoring to be close to him. He could hear himself speaking to them calmly, yet forcefully with words that easily flowed, that readily brought peace and harmony to their lives. He caught himself up short with the stabbing thought that his vision was terribly Christ-like and badly presumptuous. He was a long way from being their Savior and he considered that perhaps he was a long way from even being a man of God.

Reverend Randy Stone was now moving into the zone of repentance and the requirement of mediating with himself for redemption. Repentance is a difficult scheme when it's truly meaningful. In his case, the full value of such effort cannot be revealed to others. His mea culpa would be a private, distinct communication with his Lord and Savior and not a public, evaluated session of confession and apology. His private, internalized, directed conversation with the Almighty would be his first stride down the road of repentance, and his own internalized realization and acceptance of his sins would be a first step toward his redemption. Fully accepting that God is forgiveness and that God is willing to overlook that he succumbed to weakness will be the centerpiece of his renewed contract to fulfill God's mission. Receiving His blessing and all-abiding love is Stone's fundamental gathering of redemption. He and God have a new contract. His life as he wants it to be now depends on the formulation and fulfillment of that contract. Amen. And there is no one else to hear that lamentation to join in with the communal Amen. It is his Amen alone. He says it softly, out loud, fully understanding what it means in the singularity of the context, wishing mightily that there could be a chorus of Amens for support.

As he drove through the neighborhood, as he neared his house, he was stunned with the realization that he was seeing everything clearly for the first time. He did not consciously recognize houses or landmarks, but knew he was going the correct way. Previously, he drove home automatically, without seeing the surroundings, a programmed, rote exercise to reach his house. Turn here, turn there, and he was home. There had been little consideration for other houses, other neighbors, or the full context of where his family lived. He had been absorbed with his world, his lust, his expectations, his desires, and his work that hardly included this neighborhood and his own household. Today was a new experience and it exhilarated him. He was willing to be reborn to this new realization; he was willing to accept redemption. He was a new apostle for the Lord.

Helen held him tightly and that felt so good. It had felt good once a long time ago and he remembered that and knew that this felt better. The goodness of that feeling had been forgotten and revived, and he relished its effect. The children clung to him in acceptance of their own feelings and in response to their mother's reaction. This was a homecoming worthy of a hero; the secret cad, the deceitful cheater its glorious recipient. It was the beginning of how their lives were going to be put back together, yet Helen, least the children, had little inkling the near destruction of their world that had been faced, deflected, and revised. Shelby, the oldest, laughed and pulled at his arm, while Madison and Brent chased round and round in some primitive childish joy they felt and knew was appropriate.

Later, the hugs given, the kisses planted, the soothing words rendered, the children were abed and the adult time was in effect. The face-to-face dialog began as a restrained, tentative calling for connection and communion with each other. For Helen it was poignant, for Stone painful. It was necessary and it was right.

"Things have been out of whack...," he started. It was at best a tentative approach, but the beginning had to happen somehow.

"We've gotten..." he struggled for the right words, pulling at his substantial ability to say the right thing and the pause was heavy, powerful in the context of what he wanted to say to her.

"...almost alienated...pulled apart because of..." Here he stopped, distressed by what he wanted to say, caught in the imperative of what he thought he should say. Now was the time to reconcile that distinctive difference.

"...what I do...my work for the Lord, should not be a stress on our relationship..."

She nodded and pressed her head to his chest.

"I know," she murmured.

"I've let that happen out of my uncontrolled zeal, my step to the Glory for God, and I did not bring you along with me."

She clung tightly to him.

"That will not be the case anymore," he softly vowed.

Hallelujah! Again it was too bad there was no choir to give praise.

Repentance was at hand, could redemption be far behind?

They kissed, they fondled, and they made love in passion from the past, energetically, with connected mutual affection, and mutual satisfaction that resounded between them.

Helen, his children, and the surroundings took on new meaning the next morning with coffee in hand as he sat on the rear deck reflecting about the preceding weeks. He was lucky to survive and he believed Del would not have the benefit of such luck. Today he would meet with key trustees and his world would resume. He knew that Del did not have that chance. Del's world on the farm would never be the same.

Don's rented jet brought Del and Betty into the Toledo airport well after Stone had returned home. A waiting ambulance carried Del to the farm and this time Don rode with his mother. He was dejected and angry, always angry, believing fully that had Del not gone to South Carolina his condition would not have worsened and he could have been properly treated. However, he said little. His blame contained for the time being, he had turned his attention more fully to his mother. She would need help and he would provide what she needed.

Throughout all of the testing in Atlanta, all of the plane travel, and all of the commotion around him to determine his well-being, Del had remained impassive. He had been cooperative, docile, and compliant. He had made little resistance to those attempts to find out what was wrong with him. He had showed scant emotion, maybe a smile here or there, but in large measure he had been stoic and seemingly unaffected by what was happening. When, however, he realized he was back at his farm he became agitated and almost fretful. He recognized his home, he knew where he belonged.

Betty realized right away that he was reacting to being back on the farm and had him placed in a chair on the porch when they brought him from the ambulance. Del was able to rock himself. He smiled as he gazed out over the land. Nothing was much different since they had left, nor from this year to last, from the year before that, and forever as long as his memory could take him. Jack Jefferies and Red Crier had kept things going and harvest would be the same. It was the same wonderful, comforting farm he had left and that he remembered. He could relax a bit and he could drink iced tea and know all was well.

The easy going atmosphere of Ernie Bolger's coffee shop was a reflection of the contented farm community it served. There was no loud music, no rushed or raucous behavior, just the gentle murmur of conversation. These were the soft tones of simple language expressed quietly and with a certain air of gentility that comes from rural folks. Stone surveyed Ernie's as his coffee was being poured, noting the count of those church members he had spoken to before he was seated. Seven parishioners were present, all delighted with his return, excited about seeing his services on the big screen television, more than cordial and complimentary as they each shook his hand.

Stone sat down to join Burton Strong, Chester Overmeyer, Alan Trucor, and Walt Densmore at the large round table near the rear of Ernie's. This was a prime location that provided private conversation for a business meeting. A lowered voice was difficult to overhear from another table. The meeting had been called by Burton after Stone let him know of his return.

The men were in good spirits, eager to chat with Stone, ready to move ahead without Tom. None of these men would ever know of his anguish and feelings of guilt. He would never share those feelings with any of these men. As he surveyed their faces, smiling, jovial, he understood that he would not, could not have the kind of relationship with any of them that he had developed with Tom. For whatever Tom was, he had been leader, mentor, and confidant to Stone. Tom had been a man to turn to, when necessary, for advice and sage opinion. None of these men were like that: with vision, energy, and passion for his work. He realized right then, as the waitress plunked down the breakfast menus, how much he really missed Tom. There was the feeling that something was not right without him, there was an empty space, the lack of the gentle push to do his job well. Tom had surely been an agent of God whether or not he wanted that mantle. He had performed well in the role and his part would be vacant, unable to be filled by any of these men. Sadly, Tom had some kind of murky past, some negative trail that could not be reconciled. By him, at least. Stone knew that Tom's legacy for him was that he was stronger as a person, better at his job, and truer to God Almighty.

"Since we found out that Tom was gone, we've done a lot of talking...me and the rest of the board," Burton stated in a voice almost of pontification and some smugness, it seemed. "Board wants me to take the head job...replace Tom."

So sad, Stone thought, you cannot replace Tom, none of you can, but he smiled at Burton, nonetheless.

"We're mighty proud of what you've accomplished Reverend Stone, very proud indeed..."

What I have accomplished, Stone reckoned, was to put even greater stress on my marriage, make a lot of money for New World Gospel Church and Christian Gospel Broadcasting, expose Tom to his past, and endanger the life of Del Howe. But, of course, there was the check.

"Thank you, Burton, I appreciate your vote of confidence. I do have a surprise for you to start your tenure as head of our church board...and I want you to also know that I have a renewed vigor and...and...strength for my job and a closer, even more personal alliance with our God Almighty. I am reestablished in my commitment to our mission here in Swanton."

With that, he handed the check to Burton.

Burton took the check and was stunned.

"This...this is...fabulous..."

"What is it?" Chester asked.

Burton handed him the check.

"God Bless," Chester whispered, "God Bless."

He passed the check to the other two men. They each held an edge of it and stared.

"You can thank Tom for that," Stone said pointedly. "He made sure our trip to Columbia was worthwhile. We did not do as well as New World...after all, it was their services, their connections to CGB, their broadcasts that made this possible. Tom figured it would happen and put us in a position to reap the rewards…with God's help it became so."

They all nodded and voiced the appropriate words of concurrence about Tom, all the while feeling so good that he was gone and they were in charge.

"Something else…," Stone paused, took a sip of black coffee before he continued, "Keri did not return with me. She stayed in Columbia. Seems she found someone to share her life with…at least for now…and made the decision to remain there with him. I'd like your permission to let Helen fill that roll…work in the church office. It would not be full time, but we can work around that I think and the cost savings for the congregation would be very good. It would be good for her, for me…for all of us. Give it some thought. That's what I would like."

They each got their breakfast order out of the way and then questions came in profusion about New World, the Kennys, Tom, and Keri. The subject of Keri was danced around lightly because his relationship with her had been suspected to be more than minister to church secretary, but no one knew for sure. Not much is secret in a small town even if there is no concrete evidence. Her departure was a relief for them, now a non-issue. The conversation was animated and cordial, congratulatory and supportive, and Stone knew he would have little problem with these men. They all talked about and rejoiced in his return the coming Sunday when the congregation would welcome him back. There was much to be done before then, but Stone fully understood his assignment.

The emotion-filled greetings of his parishioners were an outpouring of admiration, respect, and of love. Yes, of love. Love for the man they determined worthy of God's blessings, the man they believed to be – "of higher caliber" – as one person put it, the man who brought sense and meaning to God's word, and they were lucky to have him as their preacher. Those that had a chance before the service crowded around him like sheep converging on a spot of prime pasture. Each wanted some kind of contact, a hand shake, a touch of his sleeve, or perhaps a pat on the shoulder; being close to him was exciting and gratifying for them, dynamically charismatic in a way it had never been before even though they had always admired him.

Stone realized – maybe for the first time – how much he loved the adulation. He was a star with his parishioners, magnificent in their eyes, and he basked in the radiance of their intense attention. He noticed, too, the broad grin on Helen's face as she stood nearby, some of the glow overflowing to her. There was satisfaction within him about that and a rush of excitement he could feel and yet not identify. Tom was right again. Everything was falling into place.

Stone had worked as if possessed since he returned, first preparing a detailed sermon about redemption, and then developing the lyrics for a new hymn. The idea for the words had come to him as he was making the solitary drive home and had been festering in his thoughts since. Once completed, he asked Helen to help him with the tune. She fashioned the melody of the hymn on their piano and she transcribed the notes so they could be duplicated and given to the musicians.

The choir and the musicians had one day to work on Stone's hymn, but they were talented enough and the hymn was musical enough, and with strong meaningful words that, simply stated, could best be remembered.

As the congregation came into Calvary that Sunday, they were handed a printed sheet with the words of the new hymn. This was how the service would begin, Stone announced, a new hymn for a new commitment of outreach for God and our thanks for His blessings upon us.

> "Deep in the love of my Lord,
>
> Great are his blessings for me.

> Once lost I have newly been found,
> Once blind to his Grace I can see.
> Deep in the love of my Lord,
> The joy in my soul is supreme.
> Once hopeless I now have a chance,
> Once desperate I now have a dream.
> No burden is brought from my past,
> No shadow of guilt can be cast,
> I've come to the Almighty at last."

There were several more verses, but the hymn ended with "I've come to the Almighty at last." Stone was home again, his wife and his congregation welcomed him with fond embrace, and he was right with himself. The burdens of his past were eased. In his heart, the burden of the present was the condition of Del Howe. He could not shake the dread of Del's fate. In his imagination he wanted something different for Del, something profound and miraculous, some distant calling that gave Del's voice and gibberish meaning in the eyes of the Lord, some magnificent transcending glory that truly staked his effort in the eyes of God. Stone created that image; he could see Del ascending a long, gradually rising staircase towards a huge stage of angels with hands upraised in praise. But he could not sustain the image, distracted as he was with the power of song from his own congregation and he moved slowly, assuredly to the lectern with gracious smile and heavy heart. None of them could know his frustration. He issued his own silent, private prayer for Del as the hymn's last notes faded.

There was a quick, convulsive hush that grasped the congregation as Stone readied himself to speak. He adjusted the notes in front of him, pulled at his nose a bit, and surveyed the frozen mass of parishioners before him. He had a power that had not been his before and he could feel the absolute control over them that he had achieved without wanting to or trying, and he had some inkling that there was a new world before him. One he did not have to imagine.

He was eloquent as he delivered his carefully crafted sermon. The words flowed in rhythm and sequence in a slow, deliberate cascade of ideas expressed in basic terms, in language for everyman, and vitally in tune with their lives. It was a lesson of morality without being moralistic, a lesson of proper behavior without finger shaking, and the message of God's love and His redemption. So much emotion swelled within him that he struggled to control its pressure. Ready to burst, contained, but pressured in a way that made him giddy, as if he had succumbed to the stroke of too much of Aunt Bernadette's home-made wine. Giddy in the contained sense that he was light-headed and could fall down without support, but still in command of what he was saying, fully aware of what was happening, and secure in the feeling he could deliver the words he wanted them to hear. The sort-of-swoon passed quickly, his head was clear, and he had an acceptance of his own charisma, a charm that emanated from his emotion, a striking, powerful voice that carried the guts of what he was feeling as well as the words and the significance of their Holy meaning. He was at that point, a conduit between the higher Power of Spirituality and his congregation, fully connected, palpable, and exciting. They were delivered and he was the ultimate facilitator.

Stone completely understood the hypocrisy of his life, but God, he believed, needed him for His work. And Stone felt redeemed.

17.

Let the rivers clap their hands; let the hills be joyful together before the Lord, for He is coming to judge the earth. With righteousness He shall judge the world, and the peoples with equity.

-Psalm 98:8-9

The deep, persistent buzz of nasty black flies filled the air around the yard of the Howe farm house. They added to the discomfort of heat and humidity that brought even more challenge to party goers who had spilled out of the house into the shaded areas provided by the large maple trees that had stood there diligently in solemn array for so many years. It was Labor Day, the well-accepted transition from Summer to early Autumn, the signal that the warm, lazy days would soon enough be over, and that the part of agrarian cycle for getting ready to bring in the crops was at hand. That holiday weekend was special for the Howes, one they had celebrated together for years.

Don was there with a young girl whose name no one could remember. Something like Kira or Kara or Kinla, but no one knew for sure. No one else cared. With Don, these young women came and went and no one bothered to remember their names. She was pleasant enough, but others knew she would not last. If any one spoke to her it had not been noticeable. Dorothy and husband Jerry with children Daisy Land, Tim, and Jocelyn came early so Dorothy could help her mother prepare. There were a variety of neighbors invited, including Jack Jeffries, each bringing some kind of prepared dish or dessert to add to the buffet. There was lots of good food to eat. There was plenty to drink, including beer and wine. Hard liquor was not in the open, but Jack and Jerry had their share from a bottle of gin Jack had with him. They mixed it with Betty's lemonade and sipped their drinks carefully. It was near ninety in the shade, so that anyone consuming alcohol was in danger of losing control either of temper or consciousness. Don had three beers already, before any food had been served and was the first victim of the heat-alcohol snake bite. He regaled anyone who would listen about the condition of his father and who was at fault. The blame, as he presented it, fell squarely on the shoulders of Reverend Stone. The good Reverend was called a man of God, but in Don's mind, he was a messenger from the Devil.

"It was too much for Dad...he should have stayed in the hospital. He needed better care, not going off doing church services all over the place with that Stone. I warned them...he needed professional care...someone looking after him..."

Don lost his balance, but caught himself on one of the chairs that had been set out for company and managed to stay upright. He seemed indifferent, or perhaps oblivious, to his own lack of stability.

"...not constant stress. He was...he was...he was being shown off like some freak or something, babbling nonsense sounds no one could understand. The man was injured...he had been injured...the lightening...the lightening did it to him. He needed to be treated for that. I knew that..."

"Honey, maybe you better take it easy until you get something to eat." It was the woman Kira or Kara or whatever that cajoled him. She made little affect.

"Yeah, we'll get to that. Mom's a damn fine cook. All these folks around here...the women...are fine cooks. It'll be a good meal, don't you worry."

His body twisted and he did not seem able to keep his feet moving in touch with the twist so that he twirled slightly and fell down in an inglorious heap on the grass. He rolled over and made himself spread-eagle, then he laughed. He did not try to get up, but stayed where he was to continue his criticism of Stone.

"This man Stone is an opportunist of the worst kind," he said to the drape of leaves above him, "and I'm not just saying that because I'm not religious. It's because I know an opportunist when I see one. This guy is one. Oh, sure, he had help from that Tom something or other. Tom...Tom...I can't remember his name..."

"Fletcher," one of the neighbors volunteered.

"Yeah, right, Fletcher. This Fletcher guy took advantage of everything, but it was Stone that came to the house and diagnosed my father as speaking in tongues. That was stupid. My father had brain damage, plain and simple, and he needed treatment."

Most of the party gatherers tried to ignore Tom as he ranted, still on his back on the lawn. The woman with the name no one yet knew stood over him, then bent down to help him to a sitting position, and eventually onto his feet again. She held on to him for his stability and he did not resist.

"Boy, this heat is fierce. Get me another beer, will you Kelly?"

Kelly. That was her name and not so strange. Maybe now they would remember it. The way he had first said her name it surely did not sound like that, but now it was clear to them. She looked around as if she did not know quite what to do. She finally decided the best plan was to go to the cooler on the porch and get Don a beer.

"We think your father did a wonderful thing with Reverend Stone." This was expressed by a neighbor woman who lived three farms west. "He brought the Word to people and uplifted our church. I believe we all benefited from his words...even if we could not understand them. Reverend Stone could and brought them to us."

"It was nonsense," Don yelled.

"It was the Word of God," the woman countered, "no disrespect, Mr. Howe..."

"Yeah, well…"

Just then a cloud of dust erupted as a car rushed up the drive toward the farm house. It was Reverend Stone's car with Helen, the three children, and the Reverend. A grand entrance, appropriate for one held in such high regard by all of these folk. Everyone except Don. Stone's had been invited by Betty, would be welcomed by all despite Don, but the circumstances of the afternoon would be interesting. Stone opened the door for his children and they ran to play. Helen nodded and waved to those outside and quickly went into the kitchen to find Betty.

"How about a beer?" Don said. He wanted to intimidate Stone if he could. He did not realize he was no match for the preacher.

"Lemonade would be real good." He shook hands all around and spoke just the right words of thanks and appreciation for the attention he was getting. "Del resting," he asked, not directly to anyone, but rather as a query to the group.

"Yeah, he's resting all right." Don growled. "Maybe it's time we got him out here to enjoy the day."

He snarled "enjoy the day" with all the invective he could muster, not wanting to let anyone mistake how he felt about the choice of words.

With Betty's approval and with the help of neighbors, Don maneuvered Del from the upstairs bedroom to a chair on the lawn in the shade. He was obviously very frail and Stone was shocked to see how much Del's condition had deteriorated since he last saw him. Del's eyes brightened when he recognized Stone and this affirmation of their bond was not lost on those assembled except Don. Don was at work on another beer, at rest on the ground, back against one of the maples, beads of perspiration covering his face, and with glazed eyes staring at nothing in particular.

"That was an effort," Don said as he finished a swig from the beer can, "but I think he'll appreciate being out here. I think…maybe not."

Stone took Del's right hand in both of his and spoke directly to his face. He was close up, intent, and direct in his words to Del.

"We know you love being out here…where you can see your farm. Smell its fragrances, hear the birds, feel God's earthly gift to us all."

Del smiled slightly and his head slumped to one side. His eyes were fixated on Stone and for several moments he did not even blink. There was a trifle of movement to the right side of his mouth and then his eyes closed and his head fell back against the chair. He appeared to have passed out or simply gone to sleep.

"There's your big time farmer. Right there. Can't move himself, can't talk, can't write anything down…just a lump…a pathetic lump. A pitiful semblance of who he had been. Tell me friends and neighbors, how does God take care of this man?"

The neighbors and friends did not shrink away from Don's challenge.

"Through us," Jack said solemnly, "God uses all the resources at his command. We will take care of him if you cannot find it in your heart to take care of your father."

It was a slap in the face, but Don was four beers away from being able to respond with anything sensible.

"Yeah, right," he muttered and fell back against the tree and eased himself to his side on the ground.

Stone had pulled a chair close to Del and others stood around.

"We are all thankful for your work, Del. I am especially. It changed my life."

The call came from the porch that the food was ready and they all moved toward the house. Stone stayed behind with Del and patted his hand. Del tried to smile and when he did his face twisted into a strange look. Stone knew that it should have been a smile.

The buffet that Betty and the neighbor women prepared was designed for and would feed a small army. There was choice, selection, and satisfaction. Get your fill. Come back to the buffet tables until the food is gone, except that the food would not be gone because there was so much. Bountiful as God wished, bountiful to express thanks, and bountiful because it was possible to provide this much food. Plates were filled with chicken and beef and rabbit and pork, salads and baked beans, deviled eggs and marinated herring, sausage and asparagus and broccoli and green beans, berry and peach pie and German chocolate cake and several kinds of pudding, and deep, rich black coffee that smelled delicious and yet tasted therapeutic. This was a harvest feast too early in the season for harvest, too sumptuous to be anything else. It was a spread of food to be savored, gluttony be damned, and relished in the pure harmony of nature that the day provided.

"I'd like Reverend Stone to say a blessing for this food," Betty chirped, "so please let's just pause right here."

There was the reflexive, mandatory hush that came over those who had already crowded into the large kitchen and family room, a reflection of their respect for Betty and Stone. This was no perfunctory commendation of prayer, some rote recitation of what should be said or ought to be said, no, this was a heartfelt exclamation of thanks.

Stone cleared his throat, clasped his hands for concentration, and brought the tips of his fingers to his forehead. He paused for a moment to collect his thoughts and then delivered an eloquent, poetic message of thanks for the blessing of food they had before them, a message that also was at once a fervent plea to keep Del whole and with his family, while in some measure holding God responsible for continuing to help Del. Contrition and contract. Stone believed it was a worthy equation. Stone begged God to listen and deliver.

All said Amen, and with that, Stone filled his plate, went outside, and looked for Don who had preceded him in the buffet line. He wanted to minimize Don's complaints if he could and shortstop any continuing complaints against him and the church. It was important for Betty and Dorothy and it was important for him.

Don was alone at a table in the center of the front lawn where the farthest reaches of the maple trees supplied fragmented shade. Stone joined him and, noticeably to him, others stayed away from them as if they sensed he had some sort of mission with Don. This was fortunate because he wanted to talk to Don privately, if that were possible on such a public occasion.

Don glanced at him as he sat, but did not say anything at first. He kept eating, ignoring Stone's presence, without lifting his head. He finally stopped his overzealous chewing and took a sip from the tumbler of red wine that sparkled in front of him, throwing sunlight-charged burgundy splotches on the white plastic covering. He wiped at his mouth with his bare hand, thought better of that, and used the large paper napkin he had stuck in his belt to finish cleaning his face. He did not look at Stone when he spoke.

"Whatever happened to the young girl you took south with you? The office girl. I don't remember her name."

Don's voice was accusative, snide in the way he said it, fully intended to make Stone ill at ease.

"Keri?" Stone answered as he ate without looking up at Don. It did not matter because Don would not have met his gaze. "Why do you ask?"

"Because I figure you were banging her, padre, or she never would have made the trip. She made the other road trips with you, made a nice built-in deal for sex, made it real easy to be away from home."

"Actually," Stone said slowly as he gnawed at a chicken leg, "Keri was very skilled, very efficient, and a hard, hard worker. She was a tremendous help with everything we were doing to develop the congregation, expand our capabilities…"

"And she was good in bed…"

"I think that you are…"

"How'd it start, Reverend? A little touch here, a little touch there…then a caress that moved to a kiss? A passionate kiss that moved to a rendezvous? How did you reconcile it with yourself?"

"I think you're jumping to conclusions. I think you want something to be that wasn't there."

"What happened in Columbia, because I figure you went down there with her with the idea you were going to be in sex heaven? Away from home, away from scrutiny, free to indulge your affair with Miss Keri."

Stone stopped eating and stared at him. Don stared back.

"She didn't come back and her job was taken over by your wife. Nice touch, in fact, a fabulous ploy. Congratulations, no one is the wiser…except me. I know you were nailing her on a regular basis."

"She decided to stay in Columbia," Stone muttered.

"Why? She get tired of you…too old for her, were you?"

"She felt her future was in Columbia with a man she met there. Simple as that."

"Terrible blow to your ego, but certainly convenient." Don turned sideways to the table and dabbed at his potato salad. "Made it easy for you, didn't she, even if it hurt?"

Stone sipped at his iced tea.

"The trip to Columbia...working with the folks at New World has given my life new meaning," Stone reflected, not looking at Don, but rather staring across the yard to where Helen and the children were eating with one of the farm families. "I am rededicated to God's work."

"Oh, good," Don sighed. "Hey, Kelly," he yelled to the young woman he had brought with him, "grab me another wine."

She had seated herself nearby, savvy enough not to intrude on the conversation he was having with Stone. She was, however, ready to attend to whatever he wanted. She quickly went to the house and brought back a bottle of already-opened red wine and placed it on the table between Don and Stone. She retreated to her seat without saying a word. It was as if a robot had carried out his command.

Stone was determined to change the subject.

"I understand how upset you've been" Stone said, "But what happened to your father was a natural accident...his condition was brought on by what happened in that field over there three months ago. Not by me...not by being part of our church services...not by New World Church, his condition was what it was...no more, no less."

"A blessing from God," Don snapped.

"That he didn't die on the spot," Stone countered. "We could have had his funeral back then. Perhaps that speaks to the mission God invested in him."

"Perhaps," Don slurred as he drank more wine.

Stone rose and moved away from Don. That was enough of Don for the time being. He moved, carrying his chair, to the table where Betty and Del were sitting. When he was seated, Del reached toward him. Everyone at the table stopped talking. Del touched his arm and then he rubbed it slowly and the strange look came to his face that Stone knew wanted to be a smile.

"You've done a wonderful thing, Del. You have touched thousands of lives for Christ and you shall be rewarded in the Kingdom of Heaven."

Stone took Del's hand and held it in both of his. As he watched Betty pat Del's shoulder he knew the man's time was limited. The wonderful bond of this courageous man and gallant woman would soon be broken and there was simply nothing he could do about it.

About two weeks after the Labor Day get-together at the Howe farm, Stone was in his church office making notes for his upcoming sermon. Helen was nearby in the office Keri once occupied, conducting a meeting with some of the women of the congregation planning a fund raising bake sale. He paused for a moment to hear her voice. She was in charge and it gave him a sense of pride. They had become a team again, certainly a different kind of team than he and Tom had made.

But the results had been dramatic. Membership had swelled to the point that required the creation of a second Sunday service, two new Sunday school classes were formed, and the offering plates' collections substantially fattened the church bank account. Volunteers clamored to be of service and there was a waiting list to be in the choir. All because of Del and New World and television. Calvary Fundamentalist Christian Church was blossoming in ways only Tom might have envisioned and his flock was enthralled with his work in the church and in the community. He had not had a vision about such results; they were real.

The phone spoiled Stone's reverie of success, redemption, and self-satisfaction. It was Tom. Tom, the man who escaped, again inserting himself, curious of what he left behind, wanting desperately to be there to revel in the joys of Stone's life, and sorry for himself in no small measure that this world moved on without him. He had figured such would be the case. He knew it all along. He had planned for it and he was sure of the outcome. He just missed being the maestro of the results.

"I assume by now you are doing very well…"

"Yes," Stone replied softly, "very well in all respects."

"Means the marriage is okay?"

"Marriage is great."

"That's what I meant."

There was a pause.

"I really am surprised to hear from you again."

I couldn't resist checking in. How you doing with Don? I figured he would be your big problem. Excuse me, I meant challenge"

"Not…not very well, I admit. He's working with a lawyer to sue New World…maybe us…me. Depends on how much he has been drinking to be sure of his target."

"The wrath of the son. Can I offer some advice?"

"Please."

"Get hold of Chris Boyce…I think you know who he is. Explain the situation. Have him write a lawyer letter to Harland Dewayne Kenny…he'll know what to say. Get the money for Don so that it can go to Betty and everyone can stay out of the courts. You don't need the negative publicity…neither does Harland. What's the word on a TV deal?"

"We're just about ready to sign a contract. It will…it'll help us a great deal…financially."

"Wish I could help you with it."

"Thanks, we'll manage."

How you doing with the trustees?"

"They love me...the congregation loves me...and the media loves me, too."

"I'm not surprised."

Stone knew that he should ask about Tom, what he was doing, how he was, and that sort of thing, and he sensed Tom wanted the questions. But he could not bring himself to probe. He did not want the answers, he did not want the persistence of memory. He wanted the past with Tom to be closed.

"Tom..."

"Yes?"

"Tom, I know you're interested, know you have my best interests at heart, but...but I would appreciate it if you would not call again...ever."

There was painfully dead silence after that request, silence that screamed for a reply. Stone wondered if they had been cut off or Tom had hung up.

"Tom?"

"Yeah, I heard you. Good luck, Reverend...and God Bless you."

And, then for sure, he was gone.

That afternoon Stone took Tom's advice and contacted Chris Boyce. The lawyer was cool at first, but when he explained Tom had suggested his help and after Stone gave a brief outline of the situation, Boyce said he would stop by before the end of the day, around five. Stone was usually gone from the office by then, but he didn't tell Boyce that and agreed.

Almost twenty minutes after five Boyce arrived. Helen was long gone home. The office area was quiet, tomb-like and Stone was going over his notes again when he heard the outer door and the man's steps approaching. Boyce stopped and spoke to the seeming emptiness, his voice echoing slightly in the hallway.

"Stone, you here?"

"Yes, come on into my office."

Chris Boyce was a tall, rod of a man, thin enough to cause concerns of anorexia, yet exuding an energy level that meant he probably was healthy. He tossed his old leather briefcase onto one of the chairs in front of Stone's desk and slid casually into the other. He had the relaxed demeanor of most country lawyers, but when he spoke he commanded attention.

"Tom Fletcher said to call me?"

"Yes…I talked to him this morning."

"How well did you know him?"

"He…he headed up our church trustees. I think I knew him fairly well. But then he just left and I…I guess I didn't know him very well at all. He surprised me with his decision to get out of here."

"No, I'm sure you didn't know him…didn't know what made him tick. Not sure anyone did."

"And you?"

Boyce flipped open his briefcase and pulled out a yellow legal pad before he answered.

"Probably knew him better than anyone else, but that's not saying much. Set up his finances for him. Made it possible for him to bail so easily…so quickly. Never even said goodbye before he left. Got one card from Mexico…having fun, wish you were here, that sort of thing. Then I got a letter with a check to pay what he owed me. Said we were all square and to have a nice day."

He tapped his pen on the pad before he continued.

"Fill me in."

Stone related the entire story of Del to Boyce and the man took careful notes. He asked Stone dozens of questions, listened carefully, and scribbled intently. Finally, he said that he had everything he needed and that he would go to work on it. The following week he sent a seven-page letter to Harland Dewayne Kenny and New World Church, with copies to Stone, Betty, Don, Dorothy, and Christian Gospel Broadcasting. The letter was on behalf of Calvary Fundamentalist Christian Church and Reverend Randy Stone stating in eloquent terms the position of responsibility Reverend Stone and his Church had for Delwin Howe, his wife Betty and their children. It was an effort of responsibility that surely included Kenny and New World. No specific amount of money was mentioned, but it was suggested there should be negotiations. Help is needed, the letter emphasized, and it is expected help will be received.

Betty didn't think she needed help, but she did. Help not only with the practical day-to-day functioning that was required to take care of Del, but help dealing with the emotional frustrations that now confronted her. Del was alive, unable to speak or communicate, so he might as well be dead. But he was there, in the house, every day, and every day a burden she refused to acknowledge. She was filled with their memories of sweeter times, happier times, even though those precious moments had been big islands in a stream of worries, hardships, and disappointments. Farming was a tough life and the glory limited. Del's true glory, she figured, was his recent contribution to his church, helping bring the Word of God to more people.

She had farm-wife resiliency and toughness of spirit that gave her the attitude she could deal with anything that came along. It was not easy for her to imagine that someone could or even should help her. She was disconnected from how she had helped her aging parents, did not remember how she gave her mother comfort and tended to her ailing father, and made no association with those emotions. She could not seem to grasp what Dorothy was trying to do for her. So steadfast was she in her own determination of caring for Del, so set on getting as much out of life with him as long as she could, and so stolid in her efforts that she steeled herself against suggestions of help.

Her reckoning that life was not perfect by any stretch of the imagination meant expectations should be assigned accordingly. This approach had made it easier to overcome the bumps in the road over the years, and certainly now able to face one more difficulty – her husband's condition – with ease and with grace. She could sense his life slipping away like a block of ice melting on a hot afternoon, unable to discern his diminished condition on a minute to minute basis, yet obvious to her day by day. She treated him as vibrant and able, she cushioned him from the process that lessened him, and she never stopped talking to him even though he gave no reply. She felt the humiliation she believed Del must be feeling and worked carefully to surmount what some would call a pitiable circumstance for him.

Betty had been a trooper dealing with all of the complexities of Del since the lightening strike. She read the pain of frustration in him as he realized he would not be able to harvest the crops that he had so carefully sowed in the spring and tended to until that terrible day when he had been stricken. She coped with his somewhat ability to silently function day-to-day, coped with the strange looks, the lack of clear communication, the loss of affection and endearment he had once shown to her. All gone now, obliterated by that searing sting of nature, God's nature, uncontrolled and uncontrollable, wild and indifferent to the feelings and emotions of those it touches. Eventually, she could not cope any longer and succumbed to the bitter reality of what it was to take care of Del. It had become too difficult.

She called Reverend Stone for his help. Stone suggested that he and she meet with Dorothy and Don and decide the best course of action. They got together at the farm the following Saturday. It was a cool day, full of sunshine. A hint of the coming Fall was in the air even though the trees were far from beginning their color change. When Stone arrived just before ten, Don and Dorothy were already there. Dorothy's husband Jerry was playing with the three children in the side yard. Don had come alone and stood on the front porch waiting.

"Any response to that guy Boyce's letter?" Don threw at Stone as he approached the porch.

"I don't think so…not yet. But I believe they will answer…answer appropriately."

"What makes you think so?"

"We took the action at Tom Fletcher's suggestion. Tom believes we'll get a positive reaction from Reverend Kenny."

"Our runaway former business manager thinks so…well, well."

"Yes. He called me to see how Del was doing. He pointed me to attorney Boyce. Said a letter from Boyce would get help for your mother."

"We'll see," Don huffed.

"We will indeed."

They went inside where Dorothy and her mother were intensely discussing Del. They were in the living room and Del was no where to be seen. Holding a meeting in the living room instead of the kitchen indicated just how important this was.

"Hi, Reverend Stone, thank you for getting us together. I think it's about time something is done to help Mom."

"Whatever we do it's going to cost a lot of money." Don was determined to make this a miserable situation.

"I think we should discuss some practical options," Stone began, "and chart a course of action before we worry about money. Besides, if money is an issue, I believe our Church would be willing to provide substantial help."

"That's not the point," Don spouted, "we don't need the help. We…I can pay for anything we need to do…"

"I think we should talk about an assisted living facility," Stone continued, "or perhaps professional help that comes here every day. Those are two viable alternatives for Betty, I believe."

"He can't feed himself any longer…" Tears welled in Betty's eyes.

"Mom," Dorothy choked in mid swallow of coffee, caught by surprise with this revelation. "Mom, why didn't you say something? I could have given you more help."

"It just started the other morning…I didn't want to upset you. That's why I called Reverend Stone."

Betty did not continue crying even though she had a perfect right to do so, but she did lapse into a kind of melancholia. She was preoccupied with her own thoughts as Dorothy and Don discussed what to do. They lost track of their mother as they talked of the pros and cons of how to proceed. Eventually, as Reverend Stone listened without comment, they decided it would be best if Del were placed in a full-time care facility.

"What do you think, Stone?" Don asked.

"I think you've made a wise choice. Your mother deserves the help…the relief."

It was as if an awful cloud of sadness had overcome Betty as the decision was reached to put Del in Valleywood Center. She was caught up in the regret that Del had no part in the decision, although Del had decided almost nothing since the accident. She had been the decision-maker and with this issue she did not want that responsibility on her own. But in the end Dorothy and a reluctant Don relieved her of that burden. By the following Wednesday, arrangements had been made and Del was moved into Valleywood. It was fifteen miles from the Howe farm.

With this change came the daily routine for Betty of driving to Valleywood to check on Del. She accepted this responsibility as she had with all the others in her life, with stoic perseverance, good nature, and the grace of the noble woman that she was. There was nothing she could do about it, Del was in the process of leaving her. She could not stop the process, merely accept the gradual loss of her husband's life. After three weeks Del was not aware of her presence for the most part and no longer recognized her. The spark in his eyes was gone, the attempt at a smile no longer there, the random twitch of his hand would not greet her. He was not yet gone, but he surely was not with her as she was with him.

18.

Surely goodness and mercy shall follow me all the days of my life; and I will dwell in the house of the Lord forever.

-Psalm 23:6

Harland flipped Boyce's letter at his desk with a snap of his arm that knocked over his half-filled coffee cup. He stood up, jaw clenched, as he watched the brown liquid search for the most important papers it could ruin. He silently cursed. The pages had landed on the spilled coffee. He ignored the spill and paced for awhile before calling Katherine Louise. She immediately came to his office.

"It's there on the desk...soaking up the coffee I spilled" he pointed, still walking back and forth, his hands clasped behind his head. It was if he were trying to wring some answer from within, some way to dodge the inevitable.

She retrieved the pages daintily with thumb and forefinger, holding them out away from her until they stopped dripping. She laid the letter on a file folder to dry, put on some reading glasses, and stared down at it.

"Well," she snapped, "this is a fine thing to come back on us..."

"Better than a lawsuit from his kid." Harland was still moving.

"Y'all have any ideas how to answer this?" She left off the Mr. Smartypants, but the tone was there.

He suddenly stopped and pointed both hands at her, palms together.

"Yes, it just came to me," he said with anger abated and that energy converted to constructive thoughts. "We're going to make some lemonade. I'll call this man Boyce right now."

"Lemonade?" she looked at him quizzically.

"Yes. The saying is that if y'all have lemons y'all make lemonade. You know what the meaning is...turn adversity to your advantage."

"How so?" Her tightly pinched face and the tone of her voice still indicated she wanted to call him Mr. Smartypants.

"We are going to conduct a month-long series of fund raising services in honor of Delwin Howe. Let our national audience and our own congregation get to know about his condition, the help he needs, his sorry state, the poor wife to be pitied and praised for her suffering, etcetera, etcetera...you get the idea. We'll pull in a bundle for him, get them the financial help they want, and not one penny will come out of our account. What do you think?"

"I think you're a genius." She came to him and kissed him lightly on the check, then full on the mouth for emphasis.

"Thank you, my dear, I appreciate your accolades...and your obvious change in attitude. And the...the...the expression of loving emotion that perhaps we can embellish upon later today...say this afternoon."

She smiled coquettishly at him.

"I'll leave you to make the call to that lawyer and the arrangements," she said as she left his office, "and I'll alert the staff to get planning on this right away. Oh, and I'll get someone to clean up your desk"

Harland's phone conversation with Boyce was brief and to the point as he quickly explained what he planned to do. He emphasized that the result would probably be in the hundreds of thousands of dollars. Boyce agreed to Harland's proposal knowing full well that this was better than he had hoped for based on his conversation with Stone. It was far better than threatening a lawsuit, and far better still than actually going to court to get help for the Howes.

Christian Gospel Broadcasting, Harland quickly found out, was reluctant to assume any financial responsibility for Del's condition. However, Harland was able to persuade their general manager that the ensuing bad publicity for not helping Del would not look good for the network. They might as well get on the bandwagon and take advantage of the situation that was about to present itself. CGB finally agreed to kick in half of whatever Harland was able to generate. Little did they know what that might mean in dollars.

The following Sunday began the month-long series of Delwin Howe memorial services, with special appeals to help the man who so sensationally brought the Word of God to us all in recent weeks as he spoke in Tongues for everyone to hear. He was not well, in fact, slowly dying, leaving us in a painfully terrible way to move on to his Maker, depriving us of his miracle of bringing the Word, and unaware of his own condition. Del was, as Harland described him, "a tragic figure of Shakespearean proportions, almost larger in life than one would imagine for a man of such humble circumstances." Harland was able to evoke just the right amount of sympathy necessary to bring many in the congregation to tears and probably so of those at home in the national television audience.

Each broadcast contained special messages for and about Del, special prayers, and songs by the choir specifically for honoring him. Letters were read by Harland and Katherine Louise that came from around the country to praise Del for what he had Delivered to them. Reverend Stone was also mentioned for his part interpreting Del's Voice of God. And suffering wife Betty was honored for her strength and compassion in caring for Del. Each service was a love and Glory fest of magnificent proportions.

And each week following, the money poured into New World with a rush that Harland and Katherine Louise had never before experienced. Several volunteers were added to the staff just to sort and open envelopes. One factor that

Boyce had not considered and not even thought about was accountability for the money. After all, he was dealing with the honesty and integrity of a church and religious folk. Why should he be concerned about their handling of the money? He thought about it later, but it was too late. The donations could have come to an independent account at a bank in Swanton or some system of auditing could have been set up in Columbia. Neither precaution was taken. The money all flowed in to Harland and Harland was the auditor. Although the money designated for Del was commingled with all of the New World donations, Harland keep close account of its running total. By the end of the month, the amount was just over seven hundred thousand dollars. Harland wrote a check for $335,765.00 which he sent to Boyce. He felt the odd number would keep Boyce from any suspicion that it was not the entire amount and he felt strongly that New World was entitled to the difference for their effort.

Betty was embarrassed by all of the attention that was given and was secretly glad Del did not know that these services were taking place. He would not have approved, she thought.

The season's change was apparent as Betty stared out the window of Del's room at Valleywood Center. Leaves that had turned golden and crimson hues clung with determination against a brisk wind randomly gusting, but eventually relented, silently carrying bits of color by the window before skipping across the yard. There was a noticeable calm within the room as Betty held Del's limp hand. His roommate had died during the night, his body carefully taken away. The bed had been remade and was now waiting for the next fateful soul. The calm was a result of Betty's demeanor as she steeled herself for the day, jaw slightly clenched, and also because of the peacefulness that comes with death. She had known without being told when she entered the room that Mr. Howard was dead. He too, had not been able to speak and no one had visited him. So she had spoken to him casually as she spoke to Del, knowing full well neither man would respond. Somehow they might hear me, she thought, and they both need to know that we still care about them.

It was the kind of calm that almost startles one with its incongruity and perplexity as it can just before an hellacious storm batters across the landscape. The kind of storm that started all of this. Betty found herself clutching Del's lifeless hand, reflecting as she had done at the hospital that first night after he had been struck. This wonderful man was leaving her. She remembered thinking that death was going to be the case that night in the hospital, but his time to go was only postponed. Postponed in an agonizing trip of service to the Lord. This wonderful, sweet man who was so courageous. He could be generous to a fault and loving and tender to me, Betty allowed, and she found herself entertaining a fleeting glimpse of their long-past lovemaking. She radiated warmth and she was embarrassed, cheeks red, and she looked around to make sure no one saw her or could even sense what mental images she had. They had never gotten to the passion that Del referred to the day he was struck.

Del was a man to be admired for the things he did and for those he did not do. He was quick to help his neighbors and friends and loathe to say anything critical when assistance was not reciprocated. He lived a life of charity and asked no thanks or recognition for his efforts.

Because of Harland's month of services memorializing Del, there was heavy media coverage. It went well beyond the local papers that kept up with his progress on a regular basis. Betty spent part of every day submitting to interviews, either by phone or in person. Helen and Reverend Stone helped her with those interviews, but mainly it was Helen. She was the coordinator who scheduled and made sure the sessions did not last too long, she was the person Betty turned to for help answering some questions, and she was the one who helped Betty cope with that stress.

Betty responded to each question as if it were the first time it had been posed to her even though it was the twentieth or fiftieth time. She spoke quietly, deliberately, each time making the answer seem measured and reflexive, yet spontaneous. This was all part of not disappointing any of the reporters, Helen had explained and coached.

The excruciatingly slow passage of time was now Betty's enemy. Waiting without being able to help Del in any way made time stand still. Everything seemed in slow motion, like walking through a vat of molasses. As the days passed, Betty eventually realized that the trees had almost no leaves and those that still resisted the wind were brown and withered. Winter was close at hand. She thought of all those seasons in the past when Del would harvest. There were the moist smells carried on cold air as she had watched Del pilot the big machine back and forth across the fields of dried up and haggard looking corn stalks. Well on into darkness he worked, machine lights eerily bobbing and darting as the equipment pushed its way forward. Swath after swath came down, the corn collected, the shattered stalks cast aside to be plowed under in the spring. This had been part of the consistent cycle of their life; a cycle of seeding, flourishing, and harvesting, and the cold quiet of winter. She faced the prospect of the cold quiet of winter by herself as she readied for the sober surety of Del's passing.

This harvest season, Jack Jeffries brought in the crops Del had so diligently watched after and tended. He stepped in with his men and equipment. Nothing would be lost and the results would be abundant. Betty was grateful and expected Jack to take a percentage of the sale which he strenuously refused.

"The money doesn't mean anything," she told Reverend Stone one day as he sat with her. "It's a cliché, but it doesn't bring my Del back to me."

He nodded.

"Oh, I am thankful…it has eased my burden…paying the bills…more than paying the bills, really."

"Will you stay on the farm?" he asked.

"Its funny, Reverend Stone, the morning Del got hit by the lightening the subject had come up of selling the farm, planning our escape from all of the work. We never got a chance to talk about it...what we would actually do. I just don't know without being able to talk to Del about it. Where would I go? It's been my home so long. So very long. I might as well die there...if I'm lucky and don't end up in a place like this."

"This is a very nice facility," Stone defended, "could take good care of you."

"I don't want to be cared for," she said firmly. "I do the caring."

Early in November, almost five months to the day from when Del was hit by lightening, Del died mid-morning quietly in front of Betty as she held his hand. The inevitable moment had come and she had not realized that he was gone. She had dozed a bit, eye lids flickering, sound and sight blurred, senses distorted, certainly not realizing at first that he had stopped breathing. But suddenly she became alert to his silence and sat upright as if some sharp sound had cracked her awake. In that instant, she knew he was gone.

Five months until this quiet, lonely death, she mused, tears welling in her eyes and she blinked quickly to force them back. He deserved better than this, but it is the way it is. She sat for awhile looking out the window at nothing, just staring, wishing something wonderful were in view, wishing the sun were shining, wishing the moment were more profound than it seemed to be. The inevitableness of it all had caught up with her and she was numb to the result. She walked, shoulders sagging, arms dangling helplessly at her sides, to the nurses' station to let them know Del was gone.

That afternoon Betty spoke with Reverend Stone for more than an hour determining her wishes to memorialize Del with appropriate ceremonies, but in the end she gave him control of what would happen. She had one specific request and that was that the choir would sing all of the refrains of "What a Friend We Have in Jesus." That was easy enough for Stone, however dealing with CGB, Reverend Kenny, and his own congregation was another matter.

Arrangements for the funeral were complicated because of the media attention that had been created when Reverend Kenny announced on national CGB television that he and Katherine Louise would be attending. Reverend Kenny was never one to miss the chance to find the full focus of the spotlight. But it created quite a furor for northwestern Ohio.

Stone had hoped for a quiet, respectable service that reflected Del's approach to life, but the outside pressure made that plan impossible. What developed would have made Tom proud, Stone believed, and there was no way to reign in the interests that wanted the service their way. It would end up being a production of epic proportions. All the right pomp and solemnity and religious fervor combined in a scrumptious stew of worship that the congregation and television audience could eat up with reverential relish. Yes, Tom would have loved those ingredients.

Of course, Reverend Kenny would speak as would Katherine Louise. It was their legacy in light of all they had done for Del, don't you know, and CGB cameras and equipment would duplicate Calvary's own video facilities that Bo Anders and Craig Stevens had ready for the occasion. A huge block of seats had to be set aside for the media, insistent on their right to be close at hand for the passing of Del to the care of God. Everyone who had any connection with Del, even the remotest contact, wanted in on this action. Almost a week before the service, CGB satellite trucks were in position to uplink their broadcast and provide coverage to other cable networks and even the big three broadcast networks which had taken some interest in this clamor over the death of a special man. For CGB this would be a tremendous payoff for their investment of matching by half the money Harland had raised for Del. They would end up selling video tape recordings of the funeral service for $14.95 plus shipping and handling with an initial commitment of orders for over fifty thousand. Everyone would benefit and the money would roll in for big time amounts with Harland, CGB, and Calvary posting substantial donations. Del's death and funeral were a bonanza.

Nasty looking, ominous steel gray clouds hung low over Calvary Fundamentalist Christian Church as mourners, attendees, and the curious pushed their way inside. The hordes of people kept arriving until the crowded church overflowed out onto the front steps and then to the surrounding parking lot. Loud speakers had been arranged for so the throng outside could hear the service. The ceremony was scheduled for two in the afternoon and the music began at one-thirty. The damp cold air clawed at those standing outside and this mass of folks seemed to huddle together in some unspoken, yet necessary agreement that their combined body heat would be worthwhile. Shoulder to shoulder they waited, shivering, teeth chattering, eager for the service to begin and end, hoping the inevitable rain would hold off until later.

Betty arrived at the church with Jack and Red. Jack eased his car through the crowd until he was near the front door and parked right there. He helped Betty from the car to her seat that was reserved in the first row directly in front of the lectern. He sat beside her with Red on the other side. Even before the music began, Red started to bawl. His shoulders shook as he tried to contain himself with quiet sobbing. Betty handed him a tissue, patted his back, and whispered something of comfort to him. It seemed to help ease the tears temporarily, but he continued to shake slightly.

Judy Darby Kent began the music with a soul wrenching version of "Amazing Grace." Then the choir took over, alternating with and supporting the Gittle brothers, Davie Young, and the band as they performed for almost forty minutes. After several moments of silence following the musical presentation Judy sang the first verse of "What a

Friend We Have in Jesus" as Stone, Harland, and Katherine Louise moved out onto the dais to begin the service. Harland and Katherine Louise sat on a special red leather two-person sofa just behind and to the left of the lectern. The sofa had been rented for this service at Katherine Louise's insistence and direction.

Reverend Stone stood at the lectern for several moments with head bowed, silently meditating, caught in his own particular vision of himself. The choir, under careful direction, continued humming the strains of "What a Friend We Have in Jesus," as Stone collected his thoughts for Del's eulogy. What transpired was a beautiful litany of Del's life and devotion to his faith, his family, and his friends, and to the work of farming that he loved so much. The words were exquisite and yet, for the careful observer, there was a detached quality to this eulogy, without the energy and vibrancy that Stone ordinarily brought to his preaching or even when he merely delivered a simple prayer. No, this was academic in both syntax and presentation, certainly an accurate and somewhat poignant portrait of a man, but lacking the vitality that he normally mustered.

Del had helped make him prominent not only in his own community, but with a nationwide audience and now Del was dead. Stone would, and his career would, transcend Del and all of the effort that had gone into working with Del. So although he was delivering a eulogy for Del, he was in affect determining the death of the old Reverend Stone and proclaiming the redeemed and remade person he would become: The new Reverend Stone. The words of praise for Del were the superficial expression of the deeply held praise he had for himself. He was the New Man of God, reborn, reconstituted, and resurrected from the ashes of self-drawn humiliation and limitation. The unlimited world of opportunity lay before him and he would fulfill the glorious vision he had always held for himself and had hoped that he could achieve.

No matter what mode he used to circumvent the truth in his own mind, Reverend Stone was caught by the fact that this was Del's funeral. No one would or even should recognize this as the day of his rebirth, this was Del's Funeral.

Stone knew that it was not a part of anyone's thinking concerning him, it was all about Del. All about Del except in his own mind. He considered this service as his move closer to the Holy Land of resurrection, bypassing any worldly judgment, eliminating the need to consult with anyone about his posture in life. He used Del as his entrée to the world of God that he wanted. Wanted, and now, in fact, demanded for himself. After all, Stone was a new Christian, recertified, reenergized to do the work of the Lord.

"All our sins and griefs to bear."

Stone looked at the lyrics and knew this too was true for him. The Lord would carry him through to what he wanted to achieve, there was no doubt of that.

"What a privilege to carry everything to God in prayer."

When he finished his eulogy for Del, Stone launched into a sermon that was a springboard from Del's memory into a visionary evaluation of his own connection with God, although no one, not Helen or Betty, the congregation, the television audience, and least of all Harland and Katherine Louise understood that he had made a transition, that he had now fully focused on himself. But when he was finished, most in the audience close at hand wept openly and loud sobbing was a part of the reaction. Red was not able to sit upright, so constricted was he with uncontrolled sobbing.

Stone had become a master at grabbing their emotions and rolling them back on the witnesses, and he was better at it than even the past master Harland Kenny. Near the wind up, Katherine Louise realized suddenly how good he was and she understood what he was doing and had done and she appreciated his technique and his success even if Stone himself had no full awareness of his own prowess.

Stone was so successful in making the mental transition from Del's funeral oration to his own celebration of redemption that he almost lost track of where he was and what he was really doing. When he finished the eulogy and the sermon he stood, held trance-like, solidified to salt or rock as if he were Lot's wife, without blinking, transfixed, and not willing to give up the lectern to Harland and Katherine Louise.

Davie Young began the second verse, *"Have we trials and temptations? Is there trouble anywhere?"* and Stone relaxed slightly. Harland and Katherine Louise rose and stood behind him and he sat down. Harland knew that there was little chance he could outdo the power of Stone's presentation and so he went for the kind of effect he wanted by using an affect that would be good production value on the video he would be selling. He had a wonderful voice and manner that he accentuated by way of how he handled the leather-bound Bible he grasped in his left hand. Each gesture was exaggerated; each important point was articulated and trilled with southern-accent mellifluence. For her part, Katherine Louise was much like a hand puppet what with her nodding agreement in the right places and mugging agony with deeply furrowed brow. When Harland finished with a flourish, her Amen was loud and clear.

"It all has been spoken now," Katherine Louise said in her most sanctimonious voice, "about our dear departed brother Delwin Howe…and our hearts are with all the family…Betty…Dorothy and her family…and Don and his family, and all the relatives and friends and neighbors who mourn Del's passing today…accepted into the Kingdom of God…a righteous man who will live in our memories. He brought something special to our lives and we are thankful for that. Thank you dear God, Amen."

All said Amen and the choir began the plaintive strains of "What a Friend We Have in Jesus." Judy sang the third verse to its completion and then the band and the humming choir carried through with the music as Stone rose again to give a quiet benediction to close the service.

Near the end of Harland's presentation it had begun to rain, a misting kind of drizzle at first, but then changing to a steady drum beat of drops falling straight down, coldly adding to the misery of the day.

Stone again prayed for Delwin Howe as he prayed for all God's children, all sinners, all who claim the Faith, and those who doubt and turn away from the light of God's blessings. He thanked and praised Harland and Katherine Louise, his congregation, and then pointedly spoke to the television audience about the responsibility of caring for others, tending to the sick Lambs of God's flock, and how important it was to care for the unfortunate as Del was, as Betty is, and to find a way to support that burden of caring with financial help.

Harland bowed his head when Stone said this and clasped his Bible firmly at his side. What a terrific way to end the service, he thought, ask for the order, because the time was right. So clever, so appropriate, and so powerful. Harland knew Stone's subtle request for money would yield a rich reward here on earth for all of them. Katherine Louise turned to him slightly and pushed her thigh against his. She too understood the full meaning of Stone's carefully worded plea and knew the bounty would be great as a result. She said a few silent words of prayer on behalf of Reverend Stone.

Eight men, neighbors of the Howes, were the designated pallbearers. They lifted the polished mahogany casket and carried it outside to the hearse through the dreary, icy rain. Nearly a dozen honorary pallbearers dutifully followed, including Red who continued his weeping and wiping at his nose with the back of his hand. The crowd was slow to break up as if they could not bear to give up this sacred and emotional moment, this time of reverence and honor for this man who brought them together on this day. When the hearse pulled away and the large entourage was gone the spell was broken and most went their own ways, back to their own lives.

Few attended the burial, but the CGB cameras were there dutifully recording this dreadful moment for the family. The cemetery was less than three miles from the church and those that did go proceeded carefully, easing their way through the few town streets and two-lane county roads necessary to get there. The nagging, cold rain continued in slanted sheets driven by a steady wind out of the northwest that often surged with biting gusts. Although mid-afternoon, it had grown darker as if the sun, wherever it was behind the layers of grimy gray skies, were ready to set. This was a backdrop that would have put a pall on a circus let alone a funeral and lowered the overall condition of everyone's spirits except Reverend Stone. And perhaps Harland. Katherine Louise could have done better overcoming the horrendously negative aspect of the weather, but the rain was ruining her eighty-dollar coif even though covered by one of the umbrellas provided by the funeral home. Her realization that eighty bucks was getting wasted made it difficult for her to have a positive outlook. Her grim look, however, matched the occasion.

For his part, Harland saw the practical, financial side of things. Let it rain, it did not matter; the Lord was on their side. Sunshine or rain, the Lord was always on their side.

On the other hand, Stone was enveloped in still another vision he had created for himself. This was the vision of martyr he had constructed, of sacrificing himself in these awful conditions on behalf of his parishioner Delwin Howe. He was carrying on for Del to praise the Glory of their God. In reality, he stood in a cold rain to bury the man. His sacrifice was forgoing comfort and ease to stand here as his duty; his martyrdom was a fictional posture of no consequence except now he was no longer having sex with the church secretary who was not his wife.

Stone stood graveside in the driving rain, hatless, his Bible pulled tightly to his chest as if he were afraid it would somehow escape. Helen dutifully held an umbrella over him, but her gesture of accommodation and affection in protecting went unheeded by him. His words again were for himself, not Del. He was fulfilling his vision. It did not matter what the rest of the circumstances were.

Betty hardly heard what Stone said. She was focused on the casket which was shielded by a green canvass awning that bucked and swayed as it resisted the wind. Little good it did. She was composed, with her own thoughts of despair, aware of her loss, and calm in her sadness. When she said Amen at the end of Stone's self-indulgent words it was perfunctory, without connection to what he said. She stepped forward, touched her finger tips to her lips and then to the casket, and smiled ever so slightly.

She turned away from the grave site, took Red's arm, walked with him to Jack's car, and rode with them back to the Howe farm. The true impact of Del's passing was yet to come and she knew that and figured she knew how to cope.

Betty stood on her porch looking out over the brown fields, inhaling the sweetness of the wet air, and alert to how quiet it was. The rain had turned back to a misty drizzle and it seemed colder than earlier.

"No more communication to the space commander," she sighed. "I'd love it if I heard him call back one more time."

Jack did not respond and she knew there was no point in explaining.

"Almost feels like snow comin'," Jack said absently, trying to ease his discomfort at being with the widow at this moment.

"Hmmm...a little," was her reply.

"Let me know if there is anything I can do...you just name it..."

"I will Jack, don't worry. I think Red and I can handle things. Crops are in, that's not a concern...Don says I should go to Florida for the winter. Can't picture myself in Florida, though. But I might think about some kind of trip...a getaway kind of thing. Who knows, might be good for me. Del knew I wanted to escape…he sensed it correctly. But I never wanted it without him. We'll see, Jack. For now I'm set. Thanks…thanks for all your nice help."

"I'm not sure if I really told ya how sorry I was about Del passin', but I am. Real sorry. Under the circumstances…" He paused for a moment, looked away, and turned back to her. "…Del's death is when sadness is somehow a blessing. We all die, it's just a matter of when."

She nodded and held her hand out to him as he turned to leave, but not in a manner that would have it shaken. The fingers were slightly apart and loosely held. It was an innocent gesture, quite like that of a queen to one of her subjects so that a bow or curtsy in return might be appropriate. Jack reached back with his left hand and lightly squeezed her finger tips. He got in his car and was gone.

Betty shivered as she watched his car head up the drive and she looked at Red, his eyes puffy and watery from all his released emotion. He was still her responsibility, ignored in the past months, and who now could be the focus of her care.

"Come on, Red, let's make some hot chocolate. You'll feel better…then you can do chores."

It had been a difficult season. Farmers know that some seasons can be bad, very bad.

Printed by Libri Plureos GmbH in Hamburg, Germany